"HELLO HAMMERSMITH!"

Tim O'Shaughnessy

This is a work of fiction, although there is reference to actual people and events. All other characters and incidents are products of the author's imagination and any resemblance to actual people or events is coincidental or fictionalised.

No part of this book can be stored on a retrieval system or transmitted in any form or by whatever means without the prior permission in writing from the person holding the copyright.

Copyright © TPW Levey 2023

The moral right of the author has been asserted.

All rights reserved.

ISBN: 979-8353-229315

Prologue - Here's Where The Story Ends (1 July 2003)

"OK! How about... 'Hello London'?"

Gerry Stanford's excited voice cut through the wind as he and his wife drove along a Kent country lane close to home. The summer day sun shone on their 1969 British Racing Green MGB roadster. The open-top car had been Gerry's pride and joy for many years. There wasn't a great deal of room for even the two of them, but as they were both 'much shorter than you look on TV', they were actually quite comfortable.

Bernie pulled a funny face. "Not very original, is it?" Her lilting Welsh accent disappeared in the breeze behind her.

"I suppose you're right," Gerry sighed. His voice immediately picked up as if a brilliant idea had just put its volume back on, "... which means it will have to be – 'HELLO HAMMERSMITH!'"

"I guess that's better," she screwed her nose up, "but there's no need to shout. I can still ruddy hear, you know."

The pair had experienced some hard years after their previous glory as founders of the 1980s synth-pop band Stanford had evaporated. The years of fame were crazy, without a chance to stop for breath and take stock. Recent times had brought it all back, but there was plenty more time to think about it now. A classic single by The Sundays was playing on the retro-fitted CD player as they pondered.

"I can't believe we only played Hammersmith the once. How did that happen?"

"Oh, that's an easy one," Bernie replied. "When we were on our way up, it fitted us nicely. And then suddenly we were too flipping big."

"And then we were too small again. It seems the bad times are in the past. Our time has finally come around again, old girl!"

"Don't 'old girl' me, pet; I'll always be 11 years younger than you…"

Bernie paused in the realisation that she had said these or similar words before. In fact, it was many years ago, as they stood outside what was then the Hammersmith Odeon.

They reflected as the countryside wafted by. Something else was on Bernie's mind as she swept strands of hair away from her face.

"Aren't you worried about Jackson at all?" she finally asked.

"Oh, a little. I know he's a quiet and thoughtful lad, but then I was at that age, and look what became of me." Gerry gave a toothy smile to his wife before turning his attention back to the road ahead. He changed down through the gears and slowed, ready for the next blind corner. Having lived in the area for much of his life, he knew the road well.

Bernie sighed. "You know I'm worried about him. I feel like the only way that we can stop the school from complaining about his lack of contribution and literacy skills is to have him properly tested, you know… just to make sure that everything is alright with him."

"Yes, but he's only five and he's the youngest in the class. He'll catch up in time and he'll be fine."

Her husband's eyes looked dead ahead and he paused as he shifted down two gears to prepare for the next left-hand bend.

"Look, they also say that he has a great imagination and that he's been creating stories and pictures well in advance of his years, so it can't be all that bad. Anyway, let's talk about this morning's offer – brilliant isn't it?"

Bernie looked at her husband. It wasn't that he didn't care. He just wasn't worried. Maybe he was right. He could always calm her worries down. Yes, Jackson was a creative child, so the other things would probably develop in time.

The thought snapped her out of her pondering and she realised Gerry had asked a question. As she worked out where his mind was, she could finally reply.

"Yes, I suppose it is. You know, I thought that the standing ovations were behind us but, apparently, left to their own devices, everything works its way back into a circle."

Gerry smiled. "Talking about things coming around again, it's a shame I gave away those flares. I'll just have to pop down to that Revivals shop in town to see if they have any second-hand ones."

Bernie grimaced. "There are some things that you hope the circle won't bring around again. Anyway, you looked ruddy terrible in flares. Come to think of it, most people looked terrible in flares. Is Harvey sure that there's going to be enough demand to sell out a UK tour after all these years?"

"Yes, he reckons so. It seems we've become quite the heritage act as people look back fondly on Thatcher's Britain. What with the Hammersmith date selling out so quickly and the new *Stanford's Greatest Hits* album looking like it will head back up the charts, the promoter took the option on offer. We'll have to see how we manage at Hammersmith though. No point in booking the full tour if we're rubbish and the press still hate us."

Bernie pulled a funny face. "I think it's best that nothing gets announced until Hammersmith is done. It could all fall flat on its arse, couldn't it?"

"Absolutely. Mustn't get carried away. I thought the rehearsals seemed to go OK though. It felt like half therapy and half school reunion and it was great to play the old songs. It was also great to see the guys again and Jim picked up the bass parts quickly, didn't he?"

"Yes, he did. I reckon he's practised a lot, which is good. We haven't quite made the connection that we had with Bruce, but then it will take time to achieve that. Hopefully, he'll be the most dependable bass guitarist that we've ever had?"

It was Gerry's turn to screw up his face. "That won't take much!"

"I had a bit of trouble hitting those high notes alright – need more practice. The in-ear monitors made a tremendous difference though. Oh, and this will make you laugh. I had a call from Angie asking if she could be on the flipping guest list!"

"What, old Angie Pogo?" Gerry laughed. "That's a bit of a cheek after the stunt she pulled. And surely she's got enough money to buy her own ticket?"

"You would have thought so. Funny how you don't hear from people for yonks and then they're in touch when there's a freebie going. I told her the guest list was full."

"Good move…," and as if he'd suddenly realised something else, "let's hope we can still fit in those old stage outfits we stored – they'd cost a fortune to replace."

"You're hoping that the moths haven't eaten them by now, I presume?" Bernie laughed. "It's been ages since we've been to the store. We'd better pop over there soon, just in case we need to go up to London and do some searching."

"You might not need to; those things can probably be found online these days. I read about a US company called eBay that is planning to start an online auction site in the UK before too long."

"Oh handy," Bernie opined. "Maybe we can use that to flog the moth-eaten clothes and my old stage hats to mad collectors!"

Bernie playfully slapped Gerry on the arm as they both laughed.

"That reminds me. Are you going to dye your hair blond again?"

Bernie scoffed as she ran her hands through her natural auburn hair. "Not ruddy likely! That dye did enough damage back in the day. I might dig out a blond wig for the encore, though."

Gerry chuckled. His pigeon laughter struggled to be heard above the tapping coming from the car's valve cover. It sounded as if humming bees were hovering over the steady pace and sound of a sewing machine. The tappets talking coupled with the car passengers' focused discussion as the car drove on. In their concentration, they couldn't see or hear the cars approaching around the next bend. The hedges were too high and Gerry's car was too low to the ground. Too late, Gerry suddenly heard an engine revving up as it went down a gear. There was no time to even register a hint of concern on his face before a white Range Rover appeared from the bend, side by side with a smaller Ford car. The driver of the overtaking Range Rover realised too late that there was no room to swerve back into safety and the hedge was preventing any evading action from either car. All three drivers hit their brakes and the passengers covered their faces with their hands. The anti-lock brakes on the Range Rover skipped and pulsed, but the older MGB had no such assistance. Leaving two trails of rubber, it skidded into the front of the Range Rover. The two metal frames collided with a sickening thud, which sent the birds in the nearby trees flying away.

On impact, the MGB was shoved to the right, so that the driver's door was then hit by the Ford, pushing it back around and into the hedge. The driver of the Ford was well past the point of impact before he came to a halt and could jump out and run back to the mangled MGB. The bonnet of the MGB had folded up. Both the driver and the passenger were slumped in their seats, their heads and shoulders covered in blood as they had been thrown forward to hit the steering wheel and dashboard, neither of which had the benefit of airbags.

The young driver of the Range Rover looked over the steering wheel where the airbag had now deflated – wide-eyed, breathing deeply and clearly in shock, as was the older passenger sitting next to her.

The driver of the Ford reached for his mobile phone and groaned as he realised that there was no signal this deep in the Kent countryside.

By the time the rescue services arrived, they had no choice but to certify that Gerry and Bernie Stanford had died at the scene of the crash.

Chapter 1 - Home (September 2013)

Jack Michaels was a loner and he didn't feel the need to talk much. Over 10 years after his parents had been killed in the car crash, the 16 year old lived quietly with his auntie and uncle in a sleepy Kent village.

On his own on the bus to town, he always went upstairs and selected the same seat. It was halfway up the aisle on the left-hand side of the bus as it moved forwards. That meant that he would not be distracted by the traffic coming the other way, but could look at the fields as the bus passed them. He could also see how many people were waiting to get on the bus at each stop and be able to steel himself for the prospect of a stranger coming to sit next to him. He dressed in his usual and preferred black attire, with a hoodie over his head no matter what the weather and matt black trainers on his feet. The music of the latest Radiohead album escaped from his earbuds. He either looked aimlessly out of the window, seemingly deep in thought, or drew on the A5 artist's pad that he carried with him. Sometimes the drawing stopped and he would scribble down other ideas in a different notebook before it was tucked into the front pocket of his black rucksack.

His Auntie Mabel was his dad's only sibling and they had been very close. Since his mum's family all lived miles away in Wales, it made sense for Mabel to take over his upbringing, especially as they lived near the converted chapel that his family had called 'Home'. Her husband Jim was a local builder of high spec homes and was always busy with a job. He and Mabel had no children of their own, but Mabel had been the number one babysitter for the Stanfords when the rare need had come up. For much of the time, Bernie had covered the primary duties of caring for her treasured son. It just so happened that Jack was staying with his auntie at the time of the fatal accident. He would use their spare room when needed. In the immediate aftermath, this provided him with the stability of being in familiar surroundings.

"HELLO HAMMERSMITH!"

Events of the days and months after the crash had become a blur. To nobody's surprise, Jack had disappeared further into the shell that his mother had been so worried about. Mabel was well aware of Bernie's concerns about Jack's slow development. She shared his mother's observations with the family doctor, which prompted a series of tests. The results confirmed her fears, as they put the boy on the autistic spectrum with Asperger's syndrome. When Mabel thought back to her youth, she wondered whether her brother had been undiagnosed with a similar condition. She received several recommendations to help the family with the situation. Among others, she particularly wanted to implement the suggestion that Jack receive social skills training. She knew he would never be the life and soul of a party, but it was an encouraging place to start. Try as they might to encourage him to do otherwise, Jack was content to stay and occupy himself in his room, fully immersed in his own space.

When they became Jack's guardians, Jim and Mabel Michaels made things easier all round by letting the boy adopt their surname. In addition, they shortened his first name to avoid the school bullying that the name "Jackson Michaels" might guarantee. Jack was too young to mind the name change and only shrugged his shoulders when it was gently suggested to him. Unfortunately, neither the name change nor the social skills training were enough to stop the bullies who found in Jack's quirky mannerisms a great excuse to pick on him, especially given that he was shorter than average. They tried hard to engage with him and encourage him to look them in the eye, but to no avail. All they would hear was a quiet "space please." Jack would take whatever treatment he was subjected to. Their frustration turned to anger and the anger to harsher treatment. But the boy seemed able to cut himself off from the world around him. After a while, his lack of response exhausted them. They grew bored and moved onto other targets from whom they could get a better reaction.

The Michaels had taken Jack out of the small rural primary school where his parents had placed him. The new, much larger, primary school in

Home (September 2013)

town was better suited to his needs, allowing him on occasions to disappear in its crowd. His mother had always been worried that he wasn't able to keep up with the others in his class. Being one of the youngest in the year with a birthday in late August didn't help. The trauma of losing his parents so early clearly made the situation worse. Jack would sit quietly in lessons. He seemed distracted and unable to concentrate on the task at hand. Direct questions were met with a shrug. Try as she might to help, Mabel was rarely allowed near Jack's homework.

"All under control" is all that he would say, but the work was often left to the last minute and handed in unfinished. Parents' evenings throughout the years would have a consistent message: "We are finding it impossible to communicate with Jack."

But in the new school, there was one subject in which Jack appeared to have some interest. Art became the silver lining of this behavioural cloud. Here he excelled with a clearly natural talent. The walls of his bedroom became plastered with intricate drawings whose details were absolutely intrinsic to their quality. He would superimpose elements of reality with surrealist patterns so that it was difficult to know which was alien to the picture.

He didn't have any real friends at his new primary school or his secondary school. With the wide catchment area of both, none of his classmates lived within easy distance of his new home and nobody could share the school run with his auntie. This didn't trouble him at all. He was happy with his own company and often blocked out the world with some indie music blasting through his headphones.

Jim and Mabel often tried to talk to Jack about his parents and offered to answer questions that he might have about them. The interactions were always short-lived, as he seemed to have no interest. It was as though he'd locked the door to the pain and distress in his past. Jim reckoned it wasn't worth the trouble to keep asking, but Mabel was more patient and gently persisted.

"HELLO HAMMERSMITH!"

Life became a predictable affair. Few words were exchanged at the breakfast table, where Jack would pour five different cereals into his bowl in a strict order, before adding slightly too much milk and munching through. He would then eat his lightly buttered toast and drink his mug of tea last. After school, the teenager would retreat to his room, which he kept scrupulously tidy, unlike most boys his age. In this sanctum, he would draw, listen to music, write, or play Final Fantasy on his Xbox 360. The game took him outside the confinement of his life into a world of new possibilities. There, he would become someone else, even further than when he had to change his name in real life. It allowed him to be lost in becoming something beyond his fate, something he felt he could control; somewhere he felt he had more choices.

On the new world's battlefield, he was a hero battling great evil. His purpose was clear and so was his connection to the world. The world was suffering from a few people's wrongdoings and his character empathised with those victims and was there to fight against this suffering. To help without having to subject himself to normal physical proximity was ideal. The hero role-playing was reflected in his pencil drawings, where the details of the suffering matched the complexity of the thoughts in his head. His writing also lyrically paralleled the indie rebellious pieces that blasted in his ears on his travels.

This alternatively playful and creative period would last until he was called for dinner.

Once Jim was home, he and Mabel would talk about their day and tried to tempt Jack into opening up. They rarely extracted more than a few words out of him. They were thankful that Jack had not gone to the worst extreme of falling in with a dangerous crowd and disappearing; they knew not where. They could always be sure that he was safe and sound under their roof.

As he grew up, Jack did at least spend time outside the house in the fresh air with their white Labrador, Macy. He would take the faithful pet on the paths in the nearby fields. Jim and Mabel found Macy specifically

Home (September 2013)

for Jack following the doctor's recommendation that puppies could help children like him develop closer emotional attachments. Jack and Macy would bump into various local people when out walking. Macy would almost systematically make a fuss about them, just in case there was a spare treat available. But the walkers had all given up on getting any acknowledgement or even some eye contact from Jack, who used his hood as a screen.

That meant that the trips outside in the fresh air didn't improve Jack's complexion, and his skin remained pasty. He would be overdressed whatever the conditions and would often return home perspiring from every pore.

Unbeknownst to his guardians, one other thing had caught Jack's imagination. By the time he was 14 years old, Jim and Mabel felt confident enough to leave Jack in the house on his own with Macy. Jack would often come out of his room and sit at the old Danemann piano in the living room. He had shown little interest in the Music lessons at secondary school, which he always found dull. But something about the old instrument drew him to it. He vaguely remembered his father showing him music basics on this old piano. Those precious moments could be re-enacted by lifting the lid when he was alone or had only Macy for company in the house. In that time, he would play fragments of music that were in his head or he would recreate songs he heard on the radio. This was usually frustrating as his lack of music knowledge turned finding the right keys to the tune in his head into an exercise in trial and error. But he persevered and would not give up easily. It would take the noise of tyres on the gravel outside or the clunk of a closing car door to bring him out of the zone. He would quietly shut the piano lid and his secret remained undiscovered.

His auntie would listen to BBC Radio 2 and songs from the past seemed to appeal most to both his guardians. Anything by Michael Bublé, especially *Home* was guaranteed to have Mabel singing along. She had a sweet voice. Jack realised that every so often his auntie would press a preset button and Classic FM would come on instead. After a while, Jack realised that sometimes his auntie would brush a tear from her eye, which meant that a Stanford song had been playing. It didn't happen often. He had been told that they were a successful band in the 1980s. At the beginning, this puzzled the teenager a little. While his guardians tried to engage him in conversations about his parents, their music was never used as a catalyst. His auntie's reaction convinced him that nothing could be gained by being too inquisitive on the subject.

Today Jack was on his way to start his second week at college, where he was studying Graphic Design. He hadn't enjoyed the one-sided interview with the school's Careers Officer. Art was the only subject in which he achieved an A grade, therefore he couldn't stay at his school for A Levels, and instead needed to go to college for a year until he could leave and do - he knew not what. His auntie was particularly worried about him and his uncle quietly accepted that the boy was unlikely to achieve anything on his own. Jim had tried taking him along to his building sites to help, but Jack clearly wasn't interested.

Jack was always early, religiously following a daily routine. Once he left the bus, he would visit the subterranean Music Department before the first Graphic Design lesson started. But for now, as the bus approached town on his way to college, more people were getting on. He would do his best to give off 'leave me alone and sit somewhere else' vibes and often this worked. If he was unlucky, someone would plonk themselves down next to him. If they did, then he shrunk further into his seat and tried to make himself invisible. Other school children chattered to each other but otherwise no words were spoken between the other passengers and Jack felt at once safe yet uncertain about the future.

Home (September 2013)

Chapter 2 - Out Of The Blue (3 January 2003)

Gerry was tinkering away on his old Danemann piano when the doorbell chimed. He was at the wrong end of the Chapel to answer, so left the task to Bernie, who heard the bell above the Christmas Number 1 by Girls Aloud that was playing on the radio.

Pulling on the handle of the sturdy door, she looked up as the smiling face of Oscar Good, their old friend and record label boss, towered above her.

"Hi Oscar, alright or what? How was your Christmas break?"

"Yes, it was great, thank you Bernie." He strolled in and Bernie made way as he continued. "Much the same as always in the Good household. It's the one time of year where we refuse to rush around everywhere. If people want to visit, then they know where to find us and luckily few can be bothered. So, we had a lovely time with just the four of us."

"That sounds like a good plan, Oscar. We're lucky that Gerry's relations all live quite close, but mine are all around South Wales and can't be doing with travelling all this way, so we have to go across there. They all seem to want to see Jackson as he's growing up, so we end up charging around between Christmas and New Year."

"Yes, of course. How is Jackson? I haven't seen the little lad in a few years now."

"Oh, he's fine. He's a little quiet and shy. Gerry sits him down at the piano every now and again and has been trying to teach him on and off. He's picking it up fairly quickly and he's making up his own stuff rather than whatever his dad gives him. He's probably drawing in his room at the moment. If he knows that there are other people in the Chapel, he's unlikely to come down. I worry sometimes…"

"I understand. My son was just the same. Trust me, he'll be fine. It's good that he's showing some musical inclination. With the two of you as parents, he could be a musical genius."

Gerry had prised himself away from the piano and had come out into the hall. "You must be joking, mate; I think we've drained the music gene pool dry between us. Great to see you again, Oscar. I was surprised to receive your call. It's all a bit 'out of the blue' to coin an ELO album title! Anyway, come through, you'll probably need a strong coffee after that drive."

"That would be great. The stronger the better for me. Milk and no sugar, please. It was a longish drive. Mind if I use the loo before I come through? "

"No problem. You know where it is." Gerry and Bernie both went into the kitchen to prepare the drinks. When he heard the flush followed by the sound of running water from the taps, Gerry came out to escort Oscar down to the lounge area.

As they walked past the drum booth on their right, Gerry kept the conversation going. "Well, tell me, what's going on in the record business at the moment? I've been fairly out of touch lately."

"There's nothing much to report. The big labels are still protecting their dying business model. Privately, my fear is that these reality music shows are going to take a hold. And you know my thoughts on manufactured music."

Gerry smiled, remembering the aversions of his old record company boss. "Sure. It will pass though, won't it? And The Monkees were good back in the day, weren't they?"

"Mmmm," Oscar noised, unconvinced. "We also had Stock Aitken Waterman."

Out Of The Blue (3 January 2003)

"I loved what they did with Donna Summer though... and I seem to remember that you did too?"

"I'd quite forgotten how cup half full and convincing you could be," Oscar smiled. "It would always take me all of my resolve to deny you what you wanted."

Gerry laughed. "Yes, I know, but let's not talk about *Album 5* now."

Oscar laughed as well. "Yes, that *was* painful at the time – it has had a long tail though. The sales still keep ticking away and you don't find many in bargain bins anymore. Anyway, no sign of Harvey yet, I suppose?"

Gerry laughed, thinking of their ever late mate. "Not a chance!" His gaze followed Bernie coming through to the main room. She held a tray balancing a full cafetière, milk jug, sugar and mugs. "He's rarely been on time in all the days that we've known him. I have to admit that letting him go all those years ago was a bit of a relief. He did a fine job for us when we were touring around the world, but otherwise I'm sure we frustrated him and I was never sure what he was up to. Anyway, he's probably driving round the lanes in decreasing circles if the past is anything to go by and there isn't much of a mobile signal out here."

There was a relaxed silence while they waited. Suddenly Gerry had another question.

"How is your charitable foundation going, by the way?"

"That's good of you to ask. It's picked up nicely in the last few years. We've seen more young bands coming to us for grants and some of the early successes were good enough to mention us in interviews when they were asked how they started up. I think it's going to become a retirement project for me and I could spend more time mentoring new bands."

"Which was always the end game, I seem to remember?"

Oscar nodded and looked around the living area in which they were standing. He appreciated how it benefitted from the full height of the original religious building. "I've always loved this room. I often thought about buying a chapel of my own at some point."

A rueful smile crossed Bernie's lips. "Careful, pet. Chapels hide lots of secrets waiting to pop out and cost you all your hard-earned money."

Just at that moment, the doorbell chimed again. Bernie headed off for the door. As she opened it, her voice travelled back down the hall.

"Harvey! Alright or what? It's been so long! So nice to see you... I can't say you've changed a bit."

"I'm ever so sorry, Bernie," Harvey spluttered in apology. "I was quite lost. Nothing changes, does it?" he smiled. Harvey then stood to the side and Bernie could see that a very young girl had been hidden behind Harvey.

"Ah, you must be Harvey's daughter, Harte?" Bernie suggested as the youngster came in before her father with a confident hand outstretched.

"Yes, that's right. My name is Harte D'Angelo," was the clear response.

"Well, welcome to the Chapel, Harte," said Bernie. She then invited Harvey in and gave him a hug. "Don't worry about getting lost, pet. It's your first time coming down and most people routinely get lost on their way here. There aren't many signposts. Anyway, you and Harte are here now. What would you like to drink, Harte?"

"I'll have a cup of English Breakfast tea please. No sugar and a drop of milk."

"Oh OK, I'm sure we have something like that in the kitchen. Harvey, if you want coffee there's plenty in the lounge already; otherwise, the kettle won't take long to boil."

Out Of The Blue (3 January 2003)

"Coffee is fine. I guess Oscar is here already? I hope he hasn't stolen my thunder."

"No, not at all. We've just been catching up. I think Gerry has been pulling his leg about Girls Aloud."

"Oh, good grief. We'd better hurry and save them both." As he uttered these words, Harvey and Harte followed Bernie towards the sound of the voices, down to the other end of the Chapel where the main living area was. As they passed through the corridor, the guests' eyes were drawn to the left-hand wall and its covering of silver, gold and platinum discs. At this time of the morning, with the winter sun low in the sky, the reflected light gave out a spectrum of colours in different parts of the room. As they entered the main room, their eyes didn't know quite where to look. Harvey quickly glanced up at the gallery before spotting the old church organ and the series of pipes next to it.

"Wow. Does that still work?"

"Of course," Gerry smiled. "Jump on and have a go if you like."

"Oh no, *no*! I'd only make a fool of myself."

"What about you, Harte?" asked Gerry politely.

"No, thank you. Piano lessons didn't go well for me."

"Yes, Harte knows her own mind," sighed a resigned Harvey.

Once everyone had a drink, Harvey cleared his voice, ready to talk about the point that brought them all together. A shuffling noise came from the stairs and a young boy came down them into the living room.

"Hey Jackson," Gerry said. "Come and meet some old friends, Oscar and Harvey. Harvey has brought his daughter Harte along as well."

"Hello," Jackson quietly said before turning towards his mum.

Bernie reassured the boy. "Why don't you sit down and listen in, love?"

Jackson sat down on the sofa between his parents, but looked at the floor.

"Well, he still doesn't look like either of you," Oscar commented.

"He has his mum's eyes and youthful good looks," Gerry smiled almost nostalgically. "But it looks like he's going to be as short as we are."

Harvey waited for them to complete that discussion and finally saw an opportunity to start the main conversation. "Well, thank you both for agreeing to see Oscar and me at such short notice. You released me as your manager a long time ago, but that hasn't stopped me from keeping you in mind in case anything relevant turned up. Plus, it seems as far as the music world is concerned, I'm still looking after your music interests. I receive calls every now and again for product endorsements and I have always referred them to the phone number you gave me for your new agent, Archie, right?"

"Yes, that's right. Thank you for that," Gerry confirmed, surreptitiously winking at Bernie, who frowned. "But unfortunately, it's usually easy to say 'no' when Archie passes the requests on."

"Strange... I've been in the business a long time and neither I nor anyone else seems to know him apart from you."

There was a slight pause as Harvey seemed to wait for an answer, but the Stanfords did not elaborate. He carried on.

"Anyway, I was approached by Monty, a new promoter that I know of, late last year. It turns out that he was quite a Stanford fan growing up in the '80s and he reckons that there's quite a following for you these days."

As Harvey paused, Oscar took over. "And as you might have seen from the recent artist statements that we have posted to you, there's been a

Out Of The Blue (3 January 2003)

steady run on your albums, particularly *Re-Recorded Hits Plus.* Things seem to have picked up in the last few years. It's as though people have forgotten about what happened and what Gerry said, or they've forgiven you. So, between Harvey, myself and Monty, who was keen to promote this, we've cooked up a plan. The idea is this. We announce a Stanford reunion concert to take place in around six months. To coincide with that, we release a new *Stanford's Greatest Hits* with a few new songs that I know you have tucked away in the Stanford vault. New packaging will link in with the concert and we'll place adverts in the Sunday papers that your old audience are likely to read. We can just see how it goes. If it works and there is a demand, then maybe a larger tour next year. What do you think?"

It took a while for either Gerry or Bernie to answer. They had both seen this day approaching.

Gerry spoke first. "*That Song* isn't going to be on the album, is it?"

Oscar immediately replied. "Of course not. That wouldn't be very sensible!"

But Gerry really wanted a response from his wife. "What do you think, dear? Stanford has to be the both of us up there on stage, otherwise it can't happen."

It was quiet for what seemed like ages before Bernie spoke. "Well, I suppose Jackson is in primary school now and is less dependent on me to be there all the time. He could stay with your sister if she's OK with it and she's used to picking him up from school. You'd be fine with that, wouldn't you, Jackson?" Jackson shrugged his shoulders, kept them up as he paused for a moment of reflection and then nodded.

"But then, there is my hearing," Bernie continued. "The hearing aid has helped, but I don't know how the volume on monitors affects them now."

"Pardon?" Gerry joked.

"HELLO HAMMERSMITH!"

"Ha bloody ha."

"Yes, we thought you would mention that," Harvey replied with a dead straight face. "Since you retired from live touring, the technology for in-ear monitors has improved no end. There's a company in North Kent that moulds the silicone to your individual ear. I hear they're a revelation."

"That would be good to try out," Bernie thought out loud. "The ringing has lessened over the years, but I don't want to make them worse again. Anyway, is a live concert what you want, Gerry?"

Bernie didn't really need to ask that question and Gerry was quick to answer.

"I think the time is right. Six months gives us plenty of time to put things in place. I can cut down on my college time, so that we can be fully involved as we always were and we'll have time to rehearse properly. Plus, we have this space to use, so we won't burn money hiring somewhere." He waved around him at the enormous room. "And I think it's right not to be too ambitious at this stage. One night will allow us to see if there's anything there. Is it just us, or will there be support?"

"Ah, now that's an interesting question," Oscar smiled. "I wanted to mention that as well. I was approached by the manager of Gillian Fox who is currently planning a comeback. She doesn't fit my strict criteria to sign her for the label, but I thought with your previous connection she would fit the bill nicely."

"Oh yes, I often wondered what had happened to Gillian," Gerry mused. "She was doing great before her breakdown. Yet another casualty of the industry. Is she saying anything about what caused it?"

"No, it seems not," Oscar replied. "Apparently she's kept tight-lipped about the entire experience... Point blank refuses to talk to anyone about it. She was delighted by the offer to open for you, though."

Out Of The Blue (3 January 2003)

"Yes, I tried to call her a few times but the calls were never answered. I felt quite responsible for having helped her to be offered the record deal in the first place. Anyway, having her as the support would work nicely. And did the promoter say where the concert might be?"

"Monty's looking at the Carling Apollo in July."

Gerry and Bernie exchanged knowing smiles at Harvey's reply and laughed out loud.

"What's so funny?" Jackson whispered in his mum's ear.

Bernie put her arm around him. "Well, love, the Carling Apollo is better known as the Hammersmith Odeon and it's a famous London concert venue. Your dad always promised me we'd return to play on the stage there again one day and it looks like his promise is coming true."

"Yes, we joked at the time that you play Hammersmith once on the way up and again on the way down. We're going to be playing it for a second time, but hopefully on the way up again."

"Some years ago, your dad told a music journalist that Stanford was finished as a band. He insisted we weren't going to join all the desperate 'has-beens' that kept coming back to 'cash in'."

"Yes, I said that at some point, didn't I?" Gerry thought for a little while. "Except we're not really cashing in, are we? There seems to be a demand out there and it just feels like the right time now. When I spoke those words, it didn't. Hopefully, time has healed the emotions and pain for everyone involved. It's time for everyone to fall in love with the songs again."

"I'll tell you what Jackson; maybe you can come up and watch us from the side of the stage. Maybe Harte can come as well. Would you like that?"

"HELLO HAMMERSMITH!"

"Yes, I'd like that," replied Harte before Jackson could process the explanation and the offer. He remained expressionless and reckoned that Harte was quite hostile to him.

Out Of The Blue (3 January 2003)

Chapter 3 - Get Lucky (October 2013)

Jack had been in college for just under a month and had fallen into a comfortable routine. He would wait for the bus at the same time every day, which had a stop just by the college. That meant he didn't need to deal with the crowds in town.

There would be lessons for half of the morning and the pupils on his Graphic Design course would then have an hour or two to work on their projects before lunch. This suited Jack, who could sit quietly on his own, hunched over the desk and taking notes during the lessons before disappearing away on his own. He had a nodding acquaintance with a couple of people who seemed to be of a similarly introverted disposition. He was also quickly able to spot and steer clear of the more colourful and gregarious individuals who did their best to dominate the lessons with the sound of their own voices. So far, so good.

Come lunchtime, Jack would grab the rucksack that contained his course work and the lunch that his auntie had packed for him and go down to the ERCO Music Department in the basement of the Arts Building. There were some small soundproofed rooms that were used during lessons. These were tucked away so that any noise that leaked out was unlikely to disturb others. At lunchtime, these were often empty and with the pick of the rooms, Jack always chose the one at the far end of the corridor. It kept him out of the way of anyone else, meaning that he was unlikely to be disturbed. An old upright piano sat against the wall. It had the feel of the old Danemann at his house and Jack would spend the hour continuing the practice that he would do quietly at home on his own.

He would check inside the lunchbox to ensure that the usual cheese and tomato sandwich, small packet of Cheese and Onion crisps and partially green banana were present. Then he would shuffle through his MP3 player until he found something with a strong piano or keyboard line and listen to it a few times before laboriously working out the individual notes that built up the chords, which he then wrote out in his notebook. Some of the easier pieces came naturally but this usually needed a lot of backtracking. He would also use the time to continue the work of trying to make some sense of the fragments of tunes in his head. Anyone listening would have been amused by both these processes.

As they spent most of their lesson time underground, the Music students were all encouraged to go up and breathe some fresh air during the lunch break. That's why the rooms were usually empty when Jack ventured down. However, there were people listening in. The soundproofing of the rehearsal rooms wasn't perfect and some new students on the Music Composition and Performance course had been using the next room. Hannah and Liam found there was little to do above ground and would come back down after a quick break. Over the weeks, they realised that there was always someone in the end room. As a result, they took up residence in the room next door and practised on their guitars.

Liam was clearly the more proficient guitarist and would take the lead parts. Hannah would be on rhythm guitar and vocals. They made an odd couple. Liam was a typical lanky teenage college student with a hoodie, dishevelled hair in need of a trim, an untucked shirt and ripped jeans that hung, exposing a fair bit of his underpants. Hannah was half-Iranian from her mother's side and could have passed for a model. This made her uncomfortable and she would dress down. Her loose-fitting clothes covered her short and slender frame so that she blended in with the other students. Her long black hair had grown down to her shoulders. She either tucked her hair behind her ears or allowed it to hang down over her face. There she could use it to cover her eyebrows and sometimes her large brown eyes as well. To the amazement of those that had heard her sing, she was reluctant to perform very often. When she gathered her nerves - well, that was something else.

Get Lucky (October 2013)

Jack was vaguely aware of there being something going on next door, but wrapped up in his own world, thought little of it and carried on with his dissections.

After a few weeks of this, to Liam's annoyance, Hannah's inquisitive nature got the better of her. She decided it was time to find out who was next door and what they were up to. With a loud knock on the door, she led Liam in. Jack was hunched over the piano keys, had his headphones on and his back to the door, so nearly jumped out of his skin when he saw movement out of the corner of his eye. He looked round and saw a teenage girl and boy, both with guitar gig bags, and freaked out. "So sorry," he blurted. "Thought the room wasn't being used. Lost track of time. Just going."

And with that, he started collecting up his notebook and pens and shoving them into the rucksack. Some pens spilled onto the floor. This flustered him, as each notebook and pen had a correct place in his bag.

"Heh, don't worry," Hannah quickly replied, seeking calm. "Nobody's due in here for another half hour. It's just that we've been listening in from next door and we were fascinated by how you're picking apart the piano and keys parts of all these songs. It seems unusual the way you do that. Also, you seem to work on some of your own stuff. We were just wondering if we could practise, maybe together."

"Don't know," Jack quickly said, keeping his eyes on the floor. "Only ever played on my own. Not sure how much use I'd be."

"Don't worry about that," Liam reassured him. "We only mess around with songs at lunchtime. It's a break from the tutored stuff that we have for the rest of the day. What are you looking at there?"

"Nothing really, just *Get Lucky*."

"Cool choice. And just four simple chords. We've done that one ourselves, right Hannah?"

"HELLO HAMMERSMITH!"

With a nod from Hannah, they both undid the gig bags and took out their acoustic guitars. Liam had a capo in his pocket and Hannah picked hers out of her own bag and they both fixed them just in front of the second fret before sitting down on the spare seats in the room. With a "1 – 2 – 3 – 4" they launched into the song's chord sequence of A minor, C, E minor and D. Liam copied Nile Rodgers' choppy style almost perfectly and Hannah played the same chords but with a simpler strum pattern. After a couple of rounds for the intro, Jack turned back to the piano and followed with the same chords but with some little flourishes on the original. After they had the pattern, Hannah started the first line, *"Like the legend of the phoenix..."*

Jack wasn't used to playing along with others and so was momentarily distracted and lost the rhythm; he hadn't expected Hannah to be such a powerful singer. He looked round briefly and then looked back at the keyboard. When they reached the vocoder part, Liam started the *"We're up all night to get lucky."* At which point, Liam corpsed into laughter and Jack followed. They had to stop.

Hannah glared at Liam. "C'mon, let's take this a bit more seriously, shall we?"

Liam and Jack carried on sniggering.

"Lighten up, Hannah!" Liam suggested after giggles had subsided. "We're just messing around!"

"I will not lighten up. This is important! You guys are pathetic!"

Suitably chastised by the scowling girl, Liam and Jack regained their composure and with a "1 – 2 – 3 – 4" they picked it back up again.

Once they had finished, Hannah interrupted the brief silence that followed it. "That was good, Jack. I don't remember seeing you during lessons. Are you in the older year?"

Get Lucky (October 2013)

"No. Doing Graphic Design for this year and then who knows...," he shrugged.

"Really?" said Hannah. "You must be jolly good at Graphic Design to be doing that instead of Music."

"Not sure. It's OK I guess."

"Hmm," Hannah looked at her watch and saw that the time was nearly up. "Look, what are you doing now?"

"Free hour for project work," Jack replied.

"Well, we have a Composition lesson coming up. Why don't you sit in and see what you think? Can't do any harm, can it? I just think you have a talent there that you're not using."

Jack wasn't at all sure about this, but at Hannah's insistence he went along to see.

♪ ♪ ♪ ♪ ♪ ♪ ♪ ♪ ♪ ♪ ♪ ♪ ♪ ♪

There were about 30 people in the Music Composition class. Jack sat at the back with Hannah and Liam. Partially hidden behind the students in front of him, this allowed him to observe without being disturbed or called upon to answer anything. In fact, the young tutor couldn't have cared less about the possibility of there being an interloper. He was clearly new to the role and had no control over the class at all. The proceedings were dominated by Harry Badger, the proud holder of a Music GCSE, who thought that enabled him to continually question whatever was said, egged on by his girlfriend Cynthia.

At the end of the hour, Hannah felt the need to reassure their new friend. "Look Jack, that wasn't representative of what we do. All the other teachers have been great, and we've learnt a lot. This is the first time that we've seen that guy. He's rubbish! He must be new."

"It's fine. Thanks for the invite, but don't think this is for me."

"That's a shame," Liam sighed. "Can we at least meet up again tomorrow? Lunchtime was cool."

"Um, maybe." Jack wasn't convinced at all. After what he had experienced, he was satisfied that the Graphic Design course was more suited to him just at the moment. He made his excuses and headed for the stairs up to his next lesson. Maybe he should just stick to what he knew?

"That's a bummer," Hannah mused. "He sounded quite talented. There's more to that guy than meets the eye."

"Except it's hard to get him to meet the eye." Liam purposely looked away from Hannah as he spoke. "Bit of an oddball… Seems to have a bit of trouble interacting."

Get Lucky (October 2013)

Chapter 4 - Happy Birthday (29 August 1998)

It was chaos in the Chapel on Jackson's first birthday with Bernie's 'Mother and Baby' group around for tea. The children themselves were too young to really appreciate what was going on. They could have been anywhere, but most of them loved the commotion and colour that went with these parties. The group had come together as part of a pre-natal class, with them all due to give birth at roughly the same time. So this was just one of a series of parties happening around this time. Conveniently, this year Jackson's birthday fell on a Saturday.

Various relations were there, including Auntie Mabel and Uncle Jim. Mabel helped with the food preparation. Jim poured the drinks, but it was obvious he'd rather be somewhere else.

To everyone's surprise, Gerry was missing when people started arriving. It was left to Bernie to explain that the college where he was teaching was moving into a new building during the holidays and the time allocated for the entire Music Department to move fell on this weekend. It was all hands on deck, with no excuses allowed. Gerry had negotiated to go in early so that his bits could be completed earlier. By 4 pm he was putting the large key in the big Chapel door and gently pushing it open. He was greeted with a cacophony of sounds.

The children were in a large circle in the lounge with a parent, generally the mother, kneeling behind them, but there were a few dads there as well. Children's music played on the expensive surround sound system as the parcel was passed from one group to the next. Jim was in charge of the music and tried his best to stop the music in such a way that everyone got the chance to tear open one piece of the wrapping paper. As the last layer was reached, he turned and closed his eyes before turning the music off for a last time and waited for the sign that he could now be released from his duty.

"HELLO HAMMERSMITH!"

"Thank *goodness* you're here," Bernie sighed at the sight of Gerry standing in the corridor. "Get that coat off, pet. It's cake time."

"Oh great – didn't want to miss that!" Gerry followed her into the kitchen and nodded at several spare parents congregated in there. Picking the matches from the drawer, he lit the single candle on top of the large Caterpillar Cake and carefully carried the plate into the middle of the lounge. Jackson was in the middle of the group with Mabel when Gerry carefully put the cake down on top of the Steinway piano and called everyone over. "Ok everyone. You know what to do. 1 – 2 – 3 HAPPY BIRTHDAY to youuuuu," he sang as he played along and everyone joined in.

As the singing subsided, he launched into Stevie Wonder's ubiquitous song as Bernie rolled her eyes.

♪ ♪ ♪ ♪ ♪ ♪ ♪ ♪ ♪ ♪ ♪ ♪ ♪ ♪

Once everyone except the close family had gone and the mammoth job of tidying up started, Bernie could finally catch up with Gerry. "Did you look at the other children? They all seem more advanced than poor little Jackson. Despite what the heath workers say, I'm convinced his difficult birth has had an effect on him."

Gerry shrugged. "My parents told me I was the same at that age. There's plenty of time for him to catch up."

Bernie briefly paused, then changed the subject. "You were back a bit earlier than you'd hoped. I guess the move went fine?"

"Yes, it all went fairly smoothly. I knew I had this to come back to, so I spent last week getting everything packed and prepared. That helped a lot."

"And did you make sure that they didn't junk your old college piano?" asked Bernie.

Happy Birthday (29 August 1998)

"Well, one of the first things that I did was to have that carried gently down to one of the rehearsal rooms. I chose the one at the end, as it's more likely to be out of the way there. They keep joking that they're going to put a blue plaque on it saying '*Gerry Stanford learnt to play piano on this*'. At least I hope they're joking. One bit of not-so-great news, though. I heard this morning that Gillian Fox has signed for ERCO. She was unveiled at their annual summer party last month."

"What?" Bernie exclaimed. "After everything you warned her about?"

"I'm afraid so. She's finished her exams now and has reached 18, so it was her choice. To make things worse, they've given her an enormous advance and set out a massive marketing campaign for her first single and album. None of her co-writes with me are going to see the light of day, of course."

"Of course. I really hope it doesn't end up in tears for her, but I'm afraid it will… Oh, and I had a phone call this morning. It was terrible timing with the party preparations in full swing, but it was Harvey so I thought I had better take it. He said that he'd had another promoter calling him, wondering if Stanford were ready to play live again. He didn't know that it was Jackson's birthday, so apologised. I said I'd talk it over with you, but you know how I feel at the moment. I'm enjoying being a full-time mum and Jackson's growing up so fast. Nobody seems to realise how much cleaning has to be done in a house with a small child! I don't want to be a part-time mum or rely on others, even though I know Mabel would love to do more. Anyway, my hearing is still not great and I don't need to damage it further. Mind you, you could always look for a new singer – maybe the promoter would be happy with that?"

"We've been over this before. If you're not part of the band with me, then it's not Stanford. Also, it's been 10 years since we've played live. We'll need a lot of rehearsing to get in shape and unless we want to go back in the studio afterwards, I just don't think it will be worth the hassle, even though the money would come in handy at the moment. Our PRS royalties aren't what they used to be."

"Yes, I know," Bernie frowned. "If Jackson wasn't around, it might have been an easier decision, but I just don't feel at all ready for this. Maybe in a few years?"

"Sure." Gerry smiled, putting an arm around Bernie and giving her a squeeze. "You're right. If you don't feel ready, then it's not going to work, is it? We're a team, aren't we?"

♪ ♪ ♪ ♪ ♪ ♪ ♪ ♪ ♪ ♪ ♪ ♪ ♪ ♪

By 7pm, the tidying up had been done and Jackson was up in bed. Only Jim and Mabel remained from the party. The doorbell chimed, and Gerry sprinted to the door to welcome their solicitor, Paul Eagle, to the Chapel.

"Paul, thank you for coming out of hours. It's much appreciated." Gerry stood back to let Paul pass. Everyone headed for the kitchen and sat around the large table that dominated the centre of the room. After introductions were complete, Paul took over.

"Well, Jim, Mabel, thank you for staying behind. It's good to finally meet you and have the chance to go through the details with you face to face. As you would have seen from the drafts of the wills that I sent you, you only come into the picture in the event anything happens to both Gerry and Bernie before Jackson is 18 years old. Of course, they want Jackson to be looked after as well as possible, so it's good of you both to agree to be named as guardians in those unlikely circumstances. Believe it or not, some families don't want to help like this."

"There's no question there," Mabel confirmed. "It's been great being around to help Bernie in a small way this last year. Bringing up Jackson wouldn't be easy, but we want everything clear, just in case."

"Splendid," Paul replied. "Should the worst happen, any assets that Gerry and Bernie have would be put into trust for Jackson, which he will have access to when he's 18 years old. In the meantime, you would be

Happy Birthday (29 August 1998)

trustees with me or someone else from the firm and you can access funds to support Jackson while he's living with you. I know from talking to you, Mabel, that you think you might need to give up your job to look after Jackson full-time, up to a certain age. We would also take that into account."

"There's not much money to worry about at the moment, but who knows?" Bernie said with a shrug.

"With any luck, it will never come to that," commented Jim hopefully.

With that, Gerry and Bernie signed their mirror wills, which left their estates to the survivor. They then signed a letter that Bernie had typed up and placed it in an envelope addressed to 'Jackson Stanford'. On the back, Bernie wrote the day's date, 29 August 1998. They all hoped and expected that the need to open the letter would never arise and that Paul could quietly throw it away on Jackson's 18th birthday.

Chapter 5 - The Leader Of The Pack (November 2013)

It was lunchtime; a fortnight after Jack first met Hannah and Liam in the rehearsal room. Colin Garrett was sitting quietly in one of the other rooms in the row. He had only been at the college for a few weeks, having responded to a panicked phone call from the Head of the Music Department.

"I hate asking you this, Colin, but can you step in and provide some temporary cover while we look for a permanent replacement, please? Our new guy hasn't worked out at all."

Colin had been planning to wind down and take life easy now that he was in his sixties, but here he was looking through the lesson plans that had been dumped on him. It wasn't that difficult. He had been a part-time tutor at the college before, so he remembered much of the curriculum and its requirements. While he flicked through the pages with his right hand, he held a fork in the other, which he used to spear the shreds of lettuce from the bottom of the salad box that he had prepared for himself that morning. This multi-tasking didn't come easy and every so often some food would spill onto either his blue check shirt or his jeans, which he absentmindedly brushed off onto the floor in the vague expectation that the cleaners would scoop it up later.

He was just about conscious that there was some movement along the corridor but continued his lunchtime work and finished eating. He ran his thin fingers through his greying hair and tucked some loose strands behind his ears. This helped to reveal muffled voices in one room and then the sound of two voices, two guitars and a piano fighting to cut through the soundproofed walls. Colin tuned out again and kept skimming the pages. As he reached the end, he became more aware of the sounds from down the corridor. "Not half bad," he thought. "I wonder who they are." He looked at his watch. It displayed 1.43pm.

He collected up his papers, placed his fork in the now empty salad box and then dropped the box into his plain white plastic bag. Taking his handkerchief from the right-hand pocket in his jeans, he wiped traces of salad dressing from his clean-shaven face. He then picked the glasses from his face and cleaned them on a separate part of the handkerchief. For a time, he sat quietly and concentrated on listening. He then stood up and left the room. He propped himself up against the wall outside the end rehearsal room, where he could hear a little clearer while he pulled his phone out to see if there were any messages. Finding none reminded him that, this far underground, there was no chance of getting a signal.

As the song ended, he quietly knocked on the door and entered, much to the surprise of the three people occupying the room. Liam and Hannah sat up straight with their guitars, while Jack remained hunched up over the piano.

"Hi guys!" Colin greeted. "That sounded interesting. Was that a new song?"

"Err, yes sir," Hannah answered. "We were working on that project that you gave us about taking two songs from the past and creating a new one from them. Sorry… were we disturbing you? We didn't mean to. We didn't think anyone else was down here."

"Not at all. And please call me Colin. I'm not comfortable being 'sir' to young adults such as yourselves. I was just doing a bit of prep before this afternoon's lesson and I know I'm going to be seeing the two of you later," he motioned to Hannah and Liam. Then he directed his gaze towards Jack, "but I'm not sure we've met…?"

Jack kept his head down and looked at the piano keyboard in front of him. "Sorry. Shouldn't really be here. Won't happen again."

"Don't worry," Colin reassured him, peering at Jack over the glasses which had slipped slightly down his nose. "There's no reason that

The Leader Of The Pack (November 2013)

someone on another course can't come and use the facilities down here. Which course are you on?"

"Graphic Design."

"I see. Anyway, I just thought your piano part was quite interesting. Incidentally, I've always thought of that as 'my piano'. That thing must be getting on for 50 years old now, so it's a bit of a relic. I played it as a student here back in the late '60s. I used to come in early to race another guy to it. We only had this piano in those days, not like the choice of keyboards that you have access to today. I'm amazed it's held together this long with the bashing that it has had over the years. I think it must have been reconditioned a few times since I left. One of the other tutors mentioned it hasn't needed tuning in the last 10 years, which is odd. Sorry, I haven't properly introduced myself. My name's Colin Garrett and I've recently started as one of the Music tutors here. And you are?"

"Jack Michaels, sir."

Colin paused for an instant then said: "Well, good to meet you, Jack. You're welcome down here anytime. And please call me Colin, rather than 'sir'."

♫ ♫ ♫ ♫ ♫ ♫ ♫ ♫ ♫ ♫ ♫ ♫ ♫ ♫

When Colin had taken his first lesson a week beforehand, he introduced himself to the students by saying that he had attended the college many years ago to study Music Composition and Performance. "This was way before ERCO became involved in sponsoring the department. Another guy, Gerry Stanford, was here at the same time. He later had some enormous hits with Stanford. Anyone heard of them?" There were blank faces all round. He then gave the students the edited highlights of his own music career in order to establish some credibility. He played them one of the shorter songs that he had written in 1971 when, as a graduate of the Royal Academy of Music, he had come back to Kent and formed a Canterbury Scene band called Disassociation, so named after a song on Caravan's third album. "I was at the Music Academy with someone that you might have heard of by the name of Rick Wakeman." His students again looked blankly at him. "You're too young, I guess. So, I see we have some catching up to do."

At the front of the class was a bored-looking Harry, who scoffed at the track that he played. Colin admitted, "Yes, that wasn't the best track I've ever written, but you start somewhere, and you progress."

"Well, I've never heard of you," Harry continued, sensing another kill. "So, you couldn't have progressed far and now you're reduced to teaching because you can't do anything worthwhile? All we seem to attract for tutors are youngsters straight out of teacher training or old has-beens."

Colin had been warned that Harry Badger had broken the last new tutor, so at this point he paused and gave his glasses a quick clean before reaching into the plain plastic bag that was next to him. He casually pulled out a statuette. "You're welcome to your point of view, Harry. Does anyone know what this is?" The room was silent until another student, Rick, ventured an answer. "Isn't that an Oscar?"

"You're close, Rick. Actually, it's an Ivor Novello award," Colin corrected. "This is the one that I was awarded for Best Original Film Score for *The Leader of the Pack*. It was one of the Top 10 grossing films that year and the soundtrack was in the charts for over 30 weeks. The musical that followed it is still doing the rounds, so the royalties keep rolling in and I don't really need to work at all."

The class held their collective breaths and looked at Harry, who had gone a shade of red and remained quiet for the first time that anyone could remember.

Colin continued. "I also have a couple of other awards for Best Television Soundtrack. But as you've never heard of Rick Wakeman, I wouldn't

The Leader Of The Pack (November 2013)

have expected you to have heard about me. What I can tell you, however, is that I've written three minute pop songs that have been in the charts, but I've also composed some lengthy bits of music which have clocked in at over 20 minutes. On this course, we're going to dig into all that experience. If you're interested in an 'old has-been', that is?"

Now that he had their attention, Colin then related how his major role in Disassociation was to use his music training to knit together the various abstract ideas that the rest of the band had and form them into a connected piece. He played snippets from one of the 20 minute opuses on their third album and pointed out the various key and time signature changes.

"We had five years on the album and tour cycle, with little time off. We toured the US and had about 50 different flights as we zigzagged around. You could even sit upfront with the pilot in those days! Anyway, the record label dropped us in 1977 as punk and new wave swept away anything remotely connected to progressive rock. I'll confess now that, as was common in those days, we all took illicit substances that we believed would enable us to be 'creative' and keep us going when we should have been sleeping. For me personally, it was a relief when the band broke up. It gave us all an opportunity to put our lives back together. Some were more successful than others," he said ruefully.

He then played a few extracts of work that he had been involved with in the 40 years since then.

"So my experience with composition of long instrumental pieces meant I was soon asked to do soundtracks for films and incidental music for TV programmes. I was happy with that – my name appeared in credits all over the place and there's a steady stream of royalties every time shows are repeated on digital channels. I can travel wherever I like without being recognised, except by a handful of people with excellent memories who had seen Disassociation live. A few times over the years, I've been invited back to the college to help with classes. Lately, I've

"HELLO HAMMERSMITH!"

been fed up with film producers who want me to copy a certain sound and interfere too much with what I was trying to create. After all these years, I need to do things my way, so I've scaled back on the work. Hence, when I took the call from the college this time, I agreed to step in as a tutor covering both Music Composition and Performance. If I can use this time to help a few stars of the future on their way, then so much the better. If not, let's enjoy our time together."

♪♫ ♪♫ ♪♫ ♪♫ ♪♫ ♪♫ ♪♫ ♪♫ ♪♫ ♪♫ ♪♫ ♪♫ ♪♫ ♪♫

Back in the rehearsal room a week later, Colin sat down against the wall. "Well, don't mind me if I just sit here. Keep on with the homework. Let's hear what you've got. I picked up that you had a feel of *Dreams* by Fleetwood Mac, which I mentioned when we were going through some two chord songs. I've met Christine McVie a few times. She lives around here, you know?" They shook their heads. "Yes, this is her escape to the country. She's become a bit of a recluse, sadly. Promised to introduce me to Stevie Nicks, but never did." His eyes suddenly took on a faraway look until he refocused. "What was the other song that you used as a base?"

"It's one that Jack suggested," Liam replied. "*Stealin' Time* by Gerry Rafferty."

"Interesting choice," Colin mused out loud. "Where does that come from, Jack?"

"It's one of my auntie's favourite songs. Mine as well."

"Fascinating! That takes me back. I bought the *City to City* album for my girlfriend when it came out. Rafferty was a genuine genius, you know. He did, in fact, compose the sax line on *Baker Street*, no matter what people say. The original demos have just been released after he died, so I've got myself a fresh copy. It's a shame that the sax player only received the £27 session fee though."

The Leader Of The Pack (November 2013)

The three of them looked quizzically at each other until Hannah suggested, "Let's go from the top then."

They played the song through while Colin listened. With an audience, there were more mistakes this time. When they had finished, Colin made some suggestions which they all agreed sounded better. He then encouraged them to play a few bits of it again, by which time it was just before 2pm.

Jack started packing up his notes, ready to leave.

"Well Jack, I'm sure that Music Composition and Performance's loss is Graphic Design's gain. Don't be afraid to come down here any time and practise with these two or on your own. And you'd be welcome to sit in on my next lesson if you wanted to sample it."

"Done a lesson already. Wasn't great."

"No, it didn't go very well," Hannah chipped in. "We keep telling Jack to have another go, but with you."

"Good. The offer's there. I'll leave it to you but if you don't take me up on it, then I hope we'll meet again soon. Right, let's clear the room."

Jack headed to his next lesson, but halfway up the stairs, he turned around and headed back to the Music Department. Seeing Hannah and Liam in their usual places at the back of the room, he put his head down and went to sit next to them.

Colin saw Jack appear and smiled, but waited until all the class were in place. "Great, thank you all for coming in today. Luckily, the snow that was forecast looks like it's going to dump itself elsewhere and the learning can continue.

"Last week, I set you an unusual task as coursework. I asked you to pick a decade, choose two songs from it, and then come up with a new one based on those two. These weren't supposed to be direct copies. We don't want you to end up in trouble with copyright, do we? Plagiarism is a terrible word, isn't it? What I asked was that your new song should have elements of both the originals.

"Now I know that some of you struggled with this and others found songs you wanted to work on that were a few years apart but in different decades. I agreed that this was fine. Now, who would like to start us off?"

Nobody spoke up, so, as usual, Harry broke the silence.

"I suppose the Rich Kids had better show the way then!" He strapped on his brand new red Fender Stratocaster and his band took their places. The Rich Kids' drummer, Rick, started a simple beat and as soon as the bass riff came in, it was clear the White Stripes' *Seven Nation Army* was going to feature heavily. When Cynthia's keys came in, the other song in the mix was obviously *Sweet Dreams are Made of This* by Eurythmics. Harry sang the White Stripes song and Cynthia the Eurythmics. Cynthia was enthusiastic but quite out of tune but they had everyone's attention as the two songs worked perfectly well together. Only Colin seemed distracted and halfway through, he opened up the browser on the PC in front of him and started quietly typing away before sitting back and waiting for them to finish.

Harry was full of smiles at the end of the song as all the students stood up and applauded. Only Hannah, Liam and Jack stayed seated.

"Very interesting," Colin, who had also remained seated, remarked. "So that was a clever mashup of the two songs. But can anyone tell me where the flaws were?"

Hannah broke the silence. "Well, I don't think they're from the same decade…"

"Didn't you listen?" Harry retorted. "Mr Garrett said that it would be fine if they were a few years out."

The Leader Of The Pack (November 2013)

"True. I said that, Harry. But Eurythmics were one of the biggest synth-pop duos of the 1980s and the White Stripes didn't appear until the late 1990s. Those songs must be nearly 20 years apart. Anyone else spot something?"

Liam cleared his voice. "Well, you set a task of coming up with something new for the two songs. Nothing was changed from the originals. They just worked well together."

"That's right." Colin looked squarely at Harry. "Just one other thing I can think of. Anyone? I'd be impressed if you knew this. Anything you'd like to tell us, Harry?"

"No sir. Me and Cyn worked quite hard on that one."

"Well, if you worked hard on that, it would have been wasted time. I've heard it before and I have the original version ready. Let me play it so we can all see how much you've copied." And with that, he played the song through the PC speakers pretty much as had just been performed.

Harry and Cynthia turned red while their Rich Kids' rhythm section glowered at them and each other. Harry stomped back to his seat and sat down with arms firmly folded.

Other groups took their turn. Most weren't brilliant, but they had followed the brief and Colin praised their honest efforts.

Hannah, Liam and Jack were the last to go, despite Harry's protest that 'the little guy' wasn't on the course.

Colin simply commented, "Depending on how this goes, he might soon be. Maybe he'll replace you, Harry?"

Jack programmed a simple drumbeat on a keyboard, paced at 110 beats per minute. He set the bass part to alternate between G and A minor chords, which were in Hannah's preferred key of G major. A few students in the class picked up that this was from Fleetwood Mac's

Dreams. Liam then picked up the guitar and played some simple chords, while Jack accompanied on the keyboard. Then Hannah started singing.

> In a life full of distractions, you can lose your mind
>
> You think you need to keep on runnin' – just to stay alive

Jack joined for the chorus:

> > But I'm stealin' time, and I'll be fine, Yes I'm stealin' time
>
> Who knows where the time goes to – it just disappears
>
> Days turn into weeks and then the months turn into years
>
> > But I'm stealin' time, and I'll be fine, Yes I'm stealin' time

Hannah then moved to the Middle Eight and Liam went to E minor:

> Don't try to find me, when I must be alone
>
> First thing I ever do is turn off my damned phone…
>
> The city life's all well and good if you can stand the noise
>
> But there's a time for peace and quiet, you can make the choice
>
> > And I'm stealin' time, and I'll be fine, Yes I'm stealin' time
> >
> > So I'm stealin' time, and I'll be fine, Yes I'm stealin' time

As they ended on the final chord of G, the students stood up again to applaud, except for Harry and Cynthia. Jack had had a few issues playing on a keyboard he hadn't used before and there were a few off-key notes.

Colin waited for the applause to subside. "Well done guys. I think that says it all. Simple but effective. The bass suggested *Dreams* with the feel of Gerry Rafferty's *Stealin' Time* in the lyrics. If Gerry were still around to hear it, he would have liked that. By the way, great singing again, Hannah," he commented and watched as Hannah blushed and covered her face with her hands.

The Leader Of The Pack (November 2013)

"Right! That's all for now. Don't forget next week's homework, and see you soon."

♫ ♫ ♫ ♫ ♫ ♫ ♫ ♫ ♫ ♫ ♫ ♫ ♫ ♫

Jack headed off upstairs back to his next scheduled class, but spent the whole lesson distracted and unable to concentrate properly. He was now properly torn between the two courses and unsure which way to turn. He was still deep in his thoughts as he approached the college gates as the day ended, only to find that Colin was there, waiting for him.

"Hey Jack. Glad I've caught you. Do you need to rush off?"

Jack's regular bus was going to arrive soon and he wanted to be near the front of the queue so that he had a better chance of getting his usual seat. But he still said, "No, not really."

"Good, come with me then. I have someone who wants to meet you and I have something for you to think about. It will be fine. Don't worry."

Colin headed for the nearest building by the gate, turned towards the stairs and started walking up. Jack had never been in this building. On the top floor, Colin knocked on the door and, after a pause, walked in. A smartly dressed lady was seated behind the desk. "Jack, this is Sue McLeod. She's the principal of the college."

"Hello again Colin, and welcome Jack. I'm glad that you found the time to pop up and see me." Sue carried the confident air of a lady in her mid-50s who had been the principal for many years.

"Am I in trouble?" Jack asked, looking at the floor for comfort.

"No, I've brought you here to see if we can help you, Jack." Colin tried to reassure the boy. "It seems to me you would be better suited to the Music Composition and Performance course than the Graphic Design one. I wanted to see how you felt about your current course."

"HELLO HAMMERSMITH!"

Jack shrugged his shoulders. "It's fine."

"Fine isn't a strong word," Sue commented. "Colin came up to see me after his lesson this afternoon and I've made some inquiries of your course head. I asked him for a quick assessment of how well you're doing. This is what he reckons. You don't seem that engaged with the coursework. You aren't one of the high-flyers, although you're not one of the worst either. We see some people here just making up time for the year. But Colin tells me you've quite some musical talent. So, if you'd rather transfer to the Music Composition and Performance course, then your course head isn't going to stop you – far from it. He agrees with me it's better to do something that you enjoy rather than struggle with something that you're not wholly committed to."

"I think that you have a raw talent that I've rarely seen," Colin added. "With some help, you could make it in the music business, but you'll need a band around you to start with. We should take this a step at a time though. First, you can complete the first year with everyone. At the end of that, you know you can leave and do something else. The other option is that you stay on, go deeper into the course in year two and have a crack at the A Level syllabus."

Sue took up the stance. "Yes, we have a proud tradition of people leaving here after two years on this course and going on to great things. Colin is just one example, but there have been others who went onto worldwide acclaim, including people like Ernie Conway who became a record label owner and now sponsors this college. There was also a girl called Gillian Fox, but that was rather tragic. And there was also a hero of mine called Gerry Stanford. I don't know if you've heard of them?"

Jack said nothing for a moment before saying, "Not heard of them."

"Well, let's leave it there then," Sue proposed. "There's no need to rush a decision, but term time is pressing on. I think you should go home and discuss it with whoever you need to. Why don't you let us know what you think next week? Would that be alright, Colin?"

Colin nodded in agreement.

Jack started scratching his head. "OK, thank you." He hadn't seen this coming and was really just relieved that he wasn't in trouble for using the Music Department facilities during the lunch break.

Once they had exited the room, Colin gave Jack an A5 sized white envelope. "Just in case you're interested," he specified, "here's a bit of extra homework to look through. I pulled it together after the lesson while you were in your Graphic Design class."

Jack looked at the envelope and thanked Colin before carefully and deliberately inserting it into his rucksack.

That evening Jack wasn't going to say anything, but Mabel informed him she had taken a call from the college mid-afternoon and had been updated by a tutor called Colin Garrett on his attendance in his class.

With nowhere to hide, Jack then opened up a little and discussed what had happened with his auntie and uncle. It was obvious they weren't terribly impressed. Their initial reaction was, "What a waste! Surely Graphic Design is what you want to do? What do you know about music, anyway?"

There was a long pause while Jack looked at the floor and considered the options. He quietly stood up and proceeded towards the Danemann piano and lifted the lid. It was the first time that they had seen him approach the piano. Macy then went and settled down next to the piano. Jack sat down on the green velvet-covered piano seat and found the right chord to start before singing the *Stealin' Time* song through again, but without Liam's guitar or Hannah's voice to guide him. Both Jim and Mabel sat open-mouthed as they listened.

"HELLO HAMMERSMITH!"

As the last notes of the song faded, it was Mabel who spoke first. "Jack, that's quite taken me by surprise. You've taken one of my favourite songs and turned it into something different. I didn't have a clue that you had that ability. How long have you been doing this?"

"Been using this piano a bit more recently," Jack confessed. "When you're both out. Play what's in my head."

Mabel still seemed very hesitant, and Jack guessed the reason. At least she was supportive, to some extent. It was clear Jim really wasn't comfortable with Jack changing courses at this stage. They agreed they would all give it some thought, which gave Jack the opportunity to retreat upstairs.

Mabel and Jim continued their discussion long into the night.

"You know very well what the music industry did to your brother and Bernie," Jim emphasised. "It nearly destroyed both of them. The course that he's thinking about transferring to is the same one that Gerry did back in the day, isn't it? I know that Graphic Design wasn't really a thing back then, but I think Gerry would have been better off doing that rather than Music."

"Yes, I know what you're saying," said Mabel. "But Jack's now showing just a hint of what Gerry had about him when he was that age. We should give him a chance and let him decide what's best for him."

"Look. I saw the state that you worked yourself into when Gerry and Bernie fell on hard times and I was there when you went to bits after they were killed. My thoughts are that it'll all end in tears and I'll be left to pick up the pieces – again."

"I know that, but there's something else that's going on here. You're not going to have realised this, but I haven't ever needed to dust that piano since it arrived. And I used to have it tuned every 6 months but stopped when the piano tuner said that it didn't need it. But clearly Jack has been practising on it while we're out and it still sounds in tune to me."

"What are you suggesting?"

"I don't know, really. It's just very odd, that's all."

This wasn't going to be resolved at the moment and they agreed to sit tight and see what happened. Perhaps things would sort themselves out.

Back in his room, Jack opened up the envelope that Colin gave him and looked through the notes. They had been photocopied from a piano tuition book and Colin had scribbled some extra notes in the margins. Jack read it through three times and thought about going downstairs to practise on the Danemann. Instead, he resolved to jump on an earlier bus in the morning in order to make it to the college piano before anyone else. That bus would probably be quieter, anyway.

Many conflicting voices in his head fought for his attention. It would soon be the end of term Christmas concert and maybe that experience would help him make his mind up.

Chapter 6 - New Born (28 - 31 August 1997)

Early one morning, a secretary from a record label that Gerry had never heard of left another message for 'Archie' to call back. Not wanting to appear too desperate, Gerry had left it until the end of the day to make the callback. When he made the call, he had his best Scottish accent at the ready. It turned out that an established artist was making an album of "Uncovered Covers," where nobody had successfully made a decent update of the original. A lot of them had complicated arrangements that alienated artists. Here, the song was *New Born,* which was a hit that Gerry had worked on as a session artist in the late 1960s. All that was needed was the music for his keyboard parts. That fundamental part of the song was unavailable as sheet music. 'Archie' promised to enquire from Mr Stanford and then come back to the caller.

"That could be good money, couldn't it pet?" observed Bernie, who was now heavily pregnant and worried about the future. "The timing would be appropriate as well," she added, as she massaged her stomach.

"They're only offering a few hundred quid for the music. It's not worth the time."

"Well, wouldn't you receive royalties from the new release?"

"No, it was back in the days when I was a hired hand. I'd turned up early to the studio and there was just me and the engineer around. We thought we might as well start, so I recorded my parts on the keyboards available in the studio and left before anyone else arrived. Next thing I knew, it was flying up the charts and everyone was commenting on the keyboards as making the difference. I wasn't even credited as I hadn't been involved in writing the song and when I questioned it, everything went quiet. All I ever received for it was the £10 session fee."

"Oh, I see. Well, why can't they work it out for themselves? Then they don't need to bother you?"

"HELLO HAMMERSMITH!"

"Because there were three different parts to the keyboard recording and the engineer insisted on bouncing them down onto a single track. That left him room to record the other parts. The separate bits no longer existed – to be honest, even I can't remember them! Serves me right for making things so complicated, I suppose."

Later that evening, Bernie went to have a relaxing bath upstairs. She left Gerry lying on the couch and laughing at the TV programme, 3rd Rock From The Sun. The main reception room of the Chapel was otherwise unusually bare as a new carpet was being laid the next day and all the other bulky furniture had been moved away to give the fitters a clear run at the job.

The pregnancy had gone with just a few complications. At around 7 months, they rushed to the hospital following signs that Bernie was going to go into labour. Luckily, they arrived at the Maternity Unit in time for medication to be applied, which stopped the process. More recently, Bernie had visited the hospital for a check-up and was told that the baby still hadn't turned around and so was in the breech position, which left her worried.

Gerry had been busy during the early summer getting the smallest bedroom decked out and ready. At all the scans, the baby had been unwilling to reveal its gender, so the decoration had needed to be neutral. They went for a purple tinted paint. As they both were fond of the stories of AA Milne, the theme of Winnie the Pooh was agreed upon. During that entire period, they had been the best customers of the local Mother and Baby store. Now everything was ready and organised.

Bernie called from the bathroom, "Gerry, can you hear me?"

"Yes dear, what is it?" Gerry didn't move.

"I'm pretty sure my waters just broke. Can you give the Maternity Unit a call to warn them?"

New Born (28 - 31 August 1997)

Gerry swore under his breath and raced to the phone. After a few minutes, he was connected to the unit and relayed the message. He listened carefully. "Yes, that's right. It's a couple of weeks early and a few days ago, the baby was still in breech position. You have our address, haven't you? I'm afraid we're right in the middle of nowhere." He listened again while they related the address that was on file. "Yes, she'll be ready."

"OK dear. Don't panic," he called as he put the phone down. "As there's a chance that you're still in breech, they're sending an ambulance to collect you. I'll follow along in the car."

Bernie appeared gingerly at the top of the stairs. "Right, I'm nearly there. Are you going to put the bag in the car?"

"Yes, plenty of time for that."

They sat quietly in the kitchen and waited. Around 15 minutes later, a knock resounded at the door. Bernie was slowly escorted by the paramedic into the back of the ambulance. "Really? I don't think I need all this fuss. You must have better things to do."

The paramedic was polite and looked to be in his mid-30s. Bernie was happy to talk to him on the way there but she was taken aback when he suddenly said, "I must say it's an honour to be getting Bernie Stanford to the hospital. I still listen to your albums. The Pogoes helped me through my tough teenage years. I had a poster of you all up on my bedroom wall and dreamt that I'd meet you someday, although I have to say that you looked much taller on the poster."

"Oh, really?" Bernie could feel the colour rush to her cheeks. "We were all quite short to be honest. Most of the photos shot us from waist height to make us look taller. The blokes in the business made the mistake of thinking that they could boss us around. We soon showed them," she grimaced.

"Yes, and it's a real shame that you didn't want to carry on with Stanford, but I read in an interview that your hearing had been affected. Still, I hope this all goes well for you." He pulled a scrap of paper from his top pocket. "Sorry to be cheeky, but could you sign this for me?"

"Oh, sure! Who should I make it out to?" At least the encounter had taken her mind off the worry of what was to be a long night.

"It's Dave. You know, if you ever think about doing some live shows again, I'll be sure to be there."

"How kind! Thank you." Bernie took the pen from his hand and scribbled as best she could as the ambulance negotiated the country lanes. She was still blushing as she handed the piece of paper and pen back. It read:

To Dave, the best paramedic ever. Love Bernie (Stanford) xx

It was Dave's turn to blush. "I'm going to treasure this."

By the time Gerry had both worked out the hospital car park machine so that it actually took his money and then found the Maternity Unit, it was around 11pm. Bernie was propped up in bed and wired to various machines that were monitoring her. "How are you then?" he asked.

"Well, the good news is that the baby's healthy and getting ready to arrive. The bad news is that it's still in breech position. They think it's an extended breech, which is worse. They're going to see how things go with a natural birth but if it gets a bit too dicey, they're going to give me a caesarean, so I've had an epidural just in case that happens. It must be working, as I can't feel a flipping thing down there. You're going to have to watch for the sign on the monitor that suggests that a contraction is happening and I'll try to push as best I can."

An extended breech was a fairly rare event, so various nurses in the unit popped in and out throughout the night.

New Born (28 - 31 August 1997)

"I feel like a museum exhibit," muttered Bernie as she braced herself for another contraction.

Early the next morning, Gerry remembered to call the carpet fitters to let them know what was happening and apologised for the likely delay.

Finally, at 1.29pm, a boy was born, and a nervous Gerry cut the umbilical cord. As he extended a finger and the new born baby clutched it for the briefest of moments, the image gave Gerry the idea for a song title, *The First Touch*. After months of planning and expectation, he suddenly started thinking of promises to make, many of which he would be unable to keep.

"Crumbs. What are we going to call him? There's been so much going on we haven't thought about names yet."

They went through some options and eventually settled on Jackson Thomas Stanford. "Can't go far wrong with the King of Pop," Gerry said as he left to call everyone from home to tell them what was happening.

♪ ♪ ♪ ♪ ♪ ♪ ♪ ♪ ♪ ♪ ♪ ♪ ♪ ♪

Bernie had a few restless nights in the hospital and was glad to return home a few days later. On the morning she was released, everyone heard the news that Princess Diana had been killed in a car crash in a Paris underpass.

As one life ended, another had begun.

Chapter 7 - She Loves You (November 2013)

Jake Bugg had just entered the album charts and many of the boys on the course were trying to emulate him in their cover versions.

Colin kept the pressure on with the projects that he set for his protégés. He continued to focus on Jack, who carried on developing his piano and lyrical skills. Colin had also remembered coming across a charitable foundation that was being run by an independent record label owner, Oscar Good, to help young bands buy equipment for practising and recording. He knew that although Hannah was from a well-off family of doctors, Jack and Liam weren't so lucky. This meant that they always used the same old second-hand instruments. He suggested Liam apply on the website. "Make sure you mention that you're at this college," he suggested. "I've heard that the guy behind it has had some links here over the years."

To their surprise, a cheque for £1,000 arrived at Liam's home within a week. While they waited for the cheque to clear, Jack and Liam visited the local music shop in town. Jack quickly reserved a decent portable keyboard, but then had to hang around while Liam spent hours testing a series of electric guitars before settling on a second-hand PRS Special Edition. It was a good brand and would mean that he wouldn't feel second rate next to Harry.

The band had yet to play in front of an audience of any kind outside of the college lessons. Hannah was very reluctant to go up on stage, fearing one of the panic attacks that she was prone to. Her affliction annoyed her but she found that getting uptight and angry about it made things worse. Thankfully for her, the boys were happy enough to stick to rehearsing to improve and get better connected with each other.

At one of Colin's Music Performance lessons, Vicky Tucker from the college sponsor ERCO sat in. This was unusual because she always concentrated on the final year students for the annual ERCO Music Prize. However, since she was in the building and there were no other Music lessons on, Colin had suggested that she check out some talented musicians in the lower year class.

She quickly introduced herself. Although she was short in stature, her North East accent and hard stare immediately put some of the class on edge.

Colin pulled up a streaming website and played *She Loves You* by The Beatles. Most of the students recognised the song. Colin then played the same song, this time interpreted by The Goon Show comedian Peter Sellers. The cover had also been a hit in the Sixties. The spoken vocal made the difference all the greater.

"Ok, into your groups," Colin said, handing out some sheet music with the lyrics and chords on it. "Your task for the next 90 minutes is to create a cover version of *She Loves You* but in a different music style, so not 1960s beat group and not using the spoken word. When you're all done, I want you to perform your version in front of everyone. Is that clear?"

And without waiting for a reply, he continued. "Good. Find a space where you won't be disturbed and try not to disturb anyone else."

Just to make sure that everyone was on track, Colin went round each group to see how they were getting on. If anyone was doing something similar to another group, then he would ease them to another style so that each of the 10 groups came up with something different. When he came around to Hannah, Liam and Jack in their usual rehearsal room at the end of the basement corridor, they were pretty much there with a reggae version. Liam had a gentle rhythm guitar going, while Jack stabbed the old piano in unison with the guitar chords. Hannah took the lead vocals alternately with Jack. The original was quite fast at 135bpm and they slowed it down to 110bpm. Colin nodded as he listened and only suggested a few changes.

She Loves You (November 2013)

When the class came together and played their songs, they displayed a brilliant range from bossa nova and jazz, through to '70s singer-songwriters. Harry and Cynthia still had their Rich Kids' band intact, although friction was clearly simmering. They blasted through a heavy metal version which had Colin turning down the master volume on the mixing desk to protect everyone's ears.

"That was bloody awful, Harry," Rick Sterling, their drummer, said as they went back to their seats. "We won't get a meal deal, let alone a record deal, with rubbish like that," he said as he threw his sticks into his bag. Even Vicky managed a smile at his comment.

Hannah, Liam and Jack were left to last as usual, partly by choice and partly as the others wanted to make an impression on their visitor Vicky, who was sitting quietly in the corner making notes. Neither Hannah nor Jack looked forward to these performances in front of the others. Hannah had purposely chosen a course with the Performance element to deal with her nerves. Jack's added problem was that the new keyboard in the main room had a different layout to the familiar pianos at home and in the rehearsal room. The keys were a little smaller and there were fewer of them than he was used to, nor were they weighted or touch sensitive. This frustrated him and meant that he couldn't recreate the sound and feel. This drew him further within himself as the song progressed and the group made it through their reggae version of the song to only muted applause.

"That was rubbish," Harry muttered under his breath but loud enough for others to hear. "I think your band should be called 'No Hope'."

Hannah felt on the point of exploding but went to the other extreme and lowered her head, embarrassed. Jack shrank further down into his chair and stared at the errant keyboard. Only Liam spoke. "I agree Harry. It wasn't *that* much better than yours." He then turned to whisper reassurance to Hannah, who brushed him away.

"HELLO HAMMERSMITH!"

"That's a shame," Colin commented thoughtfully. "You did a better job in the rehearsal room. No matter. Well done, everyone. That was good. The key lesson I wanted you to learn and remember here is that when you compose your own song, you don't need to stay in your usual comfortable style. Change things around a bit and try another musical style. That's pretty much what The Beatles did and maybe now you see that it's possible with most songs. What did you think, Vicky?"

Vicky wasn't one to chew her words. She put down the pen and pad with which she had been making notes, stood up and addressed the class in her tough North East accent. "Most of them were good, all things considered. I think that heavy metal one was a mistake though. Certainly not something that ERCO has any interest in. I'm not saying that we would be interested in releasing bossa nova or reggae albums, but a few songs that colour an album collection are always interesting."

"Clearly doesn't know what she's talking about," Harry shared with Cynthia under his breath.

"I can hear you, you know," Vicky interrupted with narrowed eyes, which focused on Harry.

"What a miserable cow," Rick the drummer added with his hand over his face. "She should lighten up a bit."

As the lesson ended, Colin quietly asked Vicky if she thought that there were any prospects in the group.

"You have a few decent performers," she said unenthusiastically. "But there's a lot of development that's going to need to happen next year."

Immediately after the Performance class, the students were joined by one of the guest presenters that regularly came to the college. Dave 'Solareye' Hook was a prominent Scottish hip hop artist who came to give them a Music Composition lesson in rap. It didn't take long for a less than impressed Vicky to gather up her notes and move out.

She Loves You (November 2013)

Most of the class had also been a little bemused to see a white rapper featuring as a guest, but they went along with it. The musician dissected one of his own tracks and showed the students the number of rhythms and rhymes that could be squeezed into a short space. His advice was simple.

"Think of something that you're passionate and angry about and let your imagination run away."

Some students struggled with this at first, but it didn't take long for Jack to focus on climate change and the damage humans did to sea creatures and the oceans. His first attempt started:

We kill the mammals in the sea, who need the krill to swim there free. They're choking on a plastic spree delivered there by you and me. Forgive us Lord when will we see; the errors implied in our ways; that fill the waves with rubbish tipped; from bins that we've put in the skip. The world we have can't be replaced; no chemicals can fix this place. The mix is set, the die is cast, if we don't change things pretty fast.

"Not a bad effort," Dave noted as he read over Jack's shoulder. "I hear the gist, but maybe shorter sections might work better." He picked up a pen and scribbled what he was thinking to illustrate:

Planet Earth, she screams in pain. A fragile world, by any name. It's still the truth, the ozone roof gets thinner. Guess what – blame the youth.

"See what I mean?"

Jack nodded. He'd always steered away from listening to rap, and he just didn't feel like he could be authentic with it. At the end of the lesson, he packed his notebook away safely, reckoning that maybe at some point the style might still come in handy.

Later on, Colin sat down with Jack to discuss the day. As always, he first gave his glasses their customary wipe. "Well, that was a shame about the performance. I can have that new keyboard replaced but I think you should practise more on it. As a performer, you need to be used to different instruments. That piano in the rehearsal room would probably fall to pieces if we tried to move it again."

Jack looked at the floor. "Keyboard just didn't feel right."

"It's something we can work on, anyway. And do you know what? I've been thinking about all the lyrics that you've been writing recently including what you did this afternoon with Dave. There's definitely an angry and disillusioned tone to a lot of your stuff. It's quite relatable, I think."

"Yeah... people are screwing up the world and most don't seem to care about the future. Not so sure it's relatable even for this generation who are in line to suffer the consequences. They complain more about the price of beer and the standard of some of the teaching... not by you of course, Colin!"

"Well, thank you for that. You know, I don't quite agree that your generation isn't relating to things like that. I think they do and I can see the temperature going up in step with the issues that are out there. Almost everyone else is writing songs about falling in love, or falling out of love. But it's all been done before and much better. What you could mine here is a different seam of content which is brewing inside you. I'd call it, for want of a better description, 'agenda rock'. I've spotted you fighting it a few times but I don't think you should. Let it all come out and see what you get. Does that make sense?"

It made sense. Jack didn't want to write the same songs as everyone else. He wanted to be authentic and say what felt right to him. He thought over his conversation with both Dave and Colin on the way back home. Once home, he spent the evening writing lists of things on which he wanted to do more research. He also pressed on with his idea of incorporating rap into a song which had the working title of *Planet Earth She Screams In Pain*.

She Loves You (November 2013)

As he was getting ready for bed, he looked around his room and twigged that he hadn't replaced any of his designs with new ones for weeks. He was now fully focused on a different path and realised more than ever what the day had taught him. He definitely was not interested in following the crowd.

Chapter 8 - Who's That Girl (December 1996)

Gerry drove his MGB to the college early that morning. A busy day loomed ahead. Wake Up to Wogan played on the car radio. There was a Christmas concert for which to rehearse.

But first, he took the lower year class. The week before, he had mixed things up and set everyone a task to write a song in the Motown style. He taught all the basics to the students to help them with this project work. He explained such concepts as the bass guitar sticking to the root and fifth; the guitar being bright and focusing on the 1st, 4th and 5th chords in the key, moving to the 2nd, 3rd and 6th for the chorus but sticking to the top 3 strings of the guitar. One by one, the groups performed the ideas that they had, with some using backing tracks they had pre-recorded. They all admitted that they had found it tough: for one, the sheer number of iconic Motown songs made creating a fresh one a near impossible task. The only one who pulled it off was Gillian Fox. In her research, she discovered that the Motown Revue, which featured The Supremes, Stevie Wonder and Smokey Robinson, had visited the UK in 1965. Her song was a prayer, wishing she had been alive to witness it.

In the afternoon, it was time to rehearse some acts for Thursday night's concert. One act was going to open some eyes and ears. Gerry kept it quiet and shared that knowledge with nobody at the college.

As the last rehearsal was ending, he saw Sue McLeod standing outside the room that they had been using. "Come in Sue. I'm just about finished here. How can I help you?"

"Well, I'm not sure that you can help me Gerry, except maybe by keeping calm and not resigning on the spot."

"That sounds serious. You'd better explain."

"Well, as you're probably aware, funding for further education is tight at the moment and there isn't much Government money available. The local education authority has advised us to look for sponsors if we want to put up new buildings and we've had plans in place for a new Music and Arts block for some time, but no funds available. As luck would have it, an old student got in touch. He was running a successful business in the music industry and wanted to invest."

Gerry paused. "So, Ernie Conway is going to be your magnanimous benefactor?"

"Yes, I'm afraid that's right." Sue scrunched her face. "I know there's some history between you two and ERCO have a reputation for being ruthless, but the governors have put me under a lot of pressure to go ahead with it and I don't think I can resist. They want a surprise announcement to be made on Thursday. I'm breaching the confidence out of respect for you. Ernie and his team are coming along for the Christmas concert and he wants to make a speech. Look, I won't blame you if you want to pull out of organising the concert."

Gerry thought for a moment. "Sue, thank you so much for warning me. It gives me time to prepare. I wouldn't dream of pulling out of the concert. I'm in too deep with its organisation and I don't want to let anyone down. Plus, as far as I'm concerned, it's in the past and there's nothing I can do to change it. Ernie is going to have more of a problem with me than I have with him. I wouldn't be surprised if he tries to cut my teaching contract as fast as possible… has he signed yet?"

"No, not yet, but the draft contract is with Paul Eagle of Barton & Co solicitors now."

"Well, you already know that you'll need to be careful. You have the best man on the job for sure. Paul will watch out for any ERCO games, of which there are many."

Who's That Girl (December 1996)

Sue was about to head back to her office when she had another thought. "Just one more thing. If you don't ask, you'll have no chance. How about Bernie comes along on Thursday and the two of you do a song, for old times' sake?"

"Hmm, I think that's a step too far. She has even less time for Ernie than I do. I'll ask her tonight and let you know but don't hold your breath."

"OK. I'll understand if it's a no-go." And with that, Sue headed upstairs.

Gerry mulled things over as he drove home afterwards. He pulled up outside the Chapel and removed his bag from the boot before carefully locking the car and entering through the huge front door. He found Bernie in her usual place in the kitchen, cooking the evening meal.

"Crumbs, what a day!" he sighed as he hugged Bernie.

"Tell me all about it. And then I have some news for you."

Gerry spoke about the Motown project and the results.

Bernie smiled. "You've got quite a soft spot for Gillian, haven't you?"

"Yes, that's true. She's certainly the most talented pupil in that class and they all know it. I think she could go all the way."

"Good. Can I tell you my news now?"

Despite Bernie's plea, Gerry was determined to complete his tale. "Just a sec. Let me finish before I forget... I then spent the rest of the day helping people rehearse for Thursday's Christmas concert. It's going to open a few eyes as I'm accompanying Gillian on her *Who's That Girl* mashup."

"Yes, I guess that will make people sit up and take notice." Her voice betrayed her growing impatience. And clearly desperate to reveal her own news. "Um, bit of a bombshell."

"Oh, just a couple of other things. Sue wonders if you could come along and do one of our old songs with me. Just an acoustic one, I guess."

"What? Are you kidding?"

"Well, I said that there wasn't much chance. We haven't much time to rehearse anything, anyway. But I think she could see the headlines and she clearly wants to make the most of me while I'm still here. It's not a runner, is it? Especially since ERCO are going to be unveiled as new sponsors who are funding the new Arts block... and Ernie will be there Thursday evening."

"NO WAY!" Bernie was clearly adamant.

"It's a bit of a turn up, isn't it? Just can't seem to shake them off."

"I'll shake them off if I ever have the chance. Now, for goodness' sake, sit down and be quiet while I tell you my news! You'll understand why going on stage on Thursday is a non-starter."

"Oh God, is there something wrong?"

"No, not really. I'm just going to be careful what I do for the next few months."

Gerry looked puzzled until Bernie presented him with a thin, white plastic object with a smile.

Gerry looked at it and saw a blue line in the middle of a small window. "Oh my God. OH. MY. GOD. I don't believe it."

"I didn't want to say anything and get your hopes up," she smiled. "But now you can see why there's no chance of me going up on stage. Sue McLeod is going to have to find her headline elsewhere. And you're going to have to be nice to ERCO for a bit. We'll need the money."

"Yes, of course. Absolutely. Quite right. Oh my God." It took the rest of the evening for some normality to be restored.

Who's That Girl (December 1996)

♪ ♪ ♪ ♪ ♪ ♪ ♪ ♪ ♪ ♪ ♪ ♪ ♪ ♪

A few nights later, the Christmas event was on. This was Gerry's first opportunity to organise the end of term concert at the college. He had made his excuses the previous year. He was left to do pretty much everything because of his extensive experience of putting on shows. Helping the various acts to rehearse had tired him but the adrenaline helped him carry on. The event was completely sold out for the first time in many years, as students heard he would be in charge of the night and on stage, supporting the students who hadn't been able to pair up.

What he didn't expect were the many parents, mainly male, who brought their 1980s Stanford albums with them for signing. Gerry spotted the square plastic bags as they were coming in and quickly guessed what was to come. He had kept a low profile in recent years and had been less recognised when out and about. Now this was happening.

The first brave parent took their chance and was successful. This led to more coming up and forming a neat line. They were all reverential and pleasant, apart from the usual 'you're shorter than I thought you'd be,' to which Gerry just smiled. Many of them were clearly in awe of him and had stories of buying the first single, which had a limited-edition picture disc (another expensive idea suggested by the ERCO label which the band ended up funding). Few were surprised when he refused to sign the CD of unearthed old songs that had been released earlier in the year. The culprit who had misread the situation skulked quietly back to his seat.

He spied Ernie Conway, the boss of ERCO, coming into the hall with a young man and a young girl. The latter caught the attention of people as she was wearing dark glasses, a black and white zebra-striped coat and a wide-brimmed hat that she eventually removed. They exchanged pleasantries and Ernie expressed his amazement that Gerry worked there. He introduced his son Eric as being ERCO's New Business Manager and his young daughter Erica, who said little and looked bored. Gerry tackled him about the old album release, but Ernie was unrepentant. "We found the old tapes and it was Eric's idea to package up some of them and release it. After all, the public always decides what they want to hear."

"Well, I know that ERCO have been good at getting some rubbish in the charts over the years, Ernie, but this one was quite the turkey. Anyway, it would be nice to look forward to a royalty cheque in time for Christmas," Gerry replied in a mildly sarcastic tone.

Before Ernie could disagree, Sue McLeod came in. Her last-minute arrival followed her working in her office into the evening. She took the Conway party to the front row only to find that the party's seats hadn't been reserved as requested. She looked at Gerry, who shrugged. Nobody had told him, or maybe they had and he had forgotten?

"It's ok, Father," Erica piped up. "We can go back there, where there is space."

"Don't be stupid, Erica," said her brother. "We need seats at the front to see what's going on. These people are going to have to move. I knew we should have brought security to this crappy event."

Sue immediately turned to the people in the front row and gently asked them to move back from the reserved seats. With order re-established, Sue and Ernie went up on stage to welcome everyone and Sue made the 'surprise' announcement.

"I'm delighted to say that the famous ERCO music label has given a large donation to the college to help with the costs of building the new Arts Department." And with pride, she added, "In their honour, we are going to call it the ERCO Arts and Music Building."

Ernie then announced that there would be a competition starting the following year. As part of its sponsorship agreement, ERCO would attend the college Music lessons and would assess project work. The best student or band would be awarded a recording contract at the end of

Who's That Girl (December 1996)

the college year. Not only that, but they will be the opening act at the famous ERCO Summer Ball that year!

"Many years ago, when ERCO was just getting started, we ran a similar competition as a trial at this college and I was always amazed by the talent you have here. The first year we ran the competition, the winner was a band called Splatt, featuring one Gerald Stanford, who later became one of the biggest pop names on the planet – before ending up here again." He paused for effect and looked around at Gerry with a smile – to be greeted by an embarrassing silence. "And now we're looking for another act to take on the world. Someone who is going to be even bigger than Stanford!" This was greeted with some applause as Ernie made his way down from the stage and back to his seat.

Most of the evening's acts had some performance experience in their secondary school, so Gerry didn't have to deal with too many nerves, except for the ones who have been informed by their parents that they are being accompanied by a genuine former pop superstar.

The last act was the one that Gerry believed was the most promising. Gillian Fox was quieter than most but always came up with fresh ideas. Earlier in the term, Gerry had introduced the idea of taking two songs from the same decade and creating a new song with elements of both. Gillian had come to him a little later and said that she wanted to bend the rules a little by taking two songs from different artists in the same decade and with the same title. She would then merge them together. When Gerry heard the songs that she was planning to merge, he was sceptical. He still gave permission, as much because he was curious and fascinated to hear whether she could smoothly manage the transitions.

Now, a few months later, Gillian stood at the front of the stage with only Gerry next to her behind his famous bank of keyboards. He had the drums and bass synth preloaded and set off at 105 beats per minute. As the song developed, the crowd recognised *Who's That Girl* by Madonna and Gillian pitched beautifully so that it would be hard to hear the difference from the original. After a couple of minutes, Gerry set another drum loop going as the first one fell away. The new backing was much sparser and Gillian then started singing the song of the same title by Eurythmics. There was an audible gasp from the crowd. Was Gerry Stanford really playing a song by his arch-rivals? It seemed so. After a brief interlude, they moved back to the Madonna song. The Conways and Sue McLeod, who all sat in the front row, stood up. Everyone followed and were on their feet, either gawping or dancing. The end was greeted with an eruption of applause. In the front row, a suddenly animated Erica was also whispering to her father, who passed on a message to Sue.

Gillian hugged Gerry while the applause continued but they decided it was better not to heed the calls for an encore. "Always leave them wanting more," Gerry whispered.

Sue went onto the stage to signal that the applause could end. As she went up, the Conway party disappeared from their seats and moved towards the door.

"Well! Wasn't that an amazing show, everyone? Definitely the best reaction that I can remember and I'm sure that you would like to give one more round of applause to our resident pop superstar Mr Gerry Stanford."

A visibly moved Gerry stepped forward to take a full bow before moving to the microphone himself. "Thank you so much. As you probably know, Bernie and I have been through some tough times in the last few years, but I've a huge amount of satisfaction from helping these students this past term. Long may that continue. I'm afraid that those of you hoping to witness a Stanford reunion tonight will have to be patient. As you know, Bernie has had some health issues and we found out today that there have been some complications that we need to deal with over the next year." There was a mixture of disappointed 'aahs' and sighs at this announcement. "But don't give up hope. Stanford might return in the future." Gerry knew Ernie was backstage, so could not comment. With that, after Sue's closing words of thanks, the clearing up began.

Who's That Girl (December 1996)

Sue took Gillian's arm and guided her backstage while Gerry started the job of powering down his rig and then the other equipment on stage. The Conway party were waiting backstage. Ernie did the talking while his children stood quietly next to their father.

"Well done, young lady. That was an excellent bit of work. I haven't seen my daughter so excited for a long time and she has a good ear for things that will work for youngsters today. Do you write your own songs as well?"

"Yes, I do. I've had a lot of help from Mr Stanford and we have quite a few rough recordings done."

"That's great! I would like to invite you to our office and studios in Central London, just as soon as you can, to record some demos that we can work with. I can see a bright future for you, young lady."

Gillian blushed. As the party was leaving, Gerry came backstage, and an excited Gillian related the events to him. Gerry's face turned serious.

"That's wonderful news, Gillian! I think that you have a brilliant future in this shark-infested business, but I've already shared some of my ERCO experience with you." She nodded. "Please be careful about ERCO and the Conways."

♪ ♪ ♪ ♪ ♪ ♪ ♪ ♪ ♪ ♪ ♪ ♪ ♪ ♪

When Gerry reached home, he told Bernie all about the evening. "I don't know if I can continue working there. There's no evidence that ERCO have changed for the better since we left."

"I understand that, but don't we need the money? What about the baby on the way?"

"Suppose you're right. I'll have to grin and bear it and just keep out of the way when they're around. The rent from letting out next door doesn't go far, does it? Oh, it's a good job you weren't there, love! There would have been a riot if we'd been there together! Gillian Fox's *Who's That Girl* mashup went down a storm. I had to stop people from suggesting that I was going to re-form Stanford with her instead of you on vocals."

"You could risk everything on a younger model," Bernie teased jokingly.

"The problem for Gillian is that Ernie took quite a shine to her. I've seen that look in his eyes before. Almost as if the pound signs were rotating. Oh, and that reminds me. They are restarting the ERCO Music Prize that I won with Splatt all those years ago. I wouldn't be surprised if Gillian's name is engraved on next year's award already."

"Well, I hope you can convince her to find another record label. ERCO could easily be the ruin of her."

"Of course I'll try, but I'm not sure I have that much influence. It's a shame that you're not in a place where you could manage her. Let's hope it's not a disaster. Remember that many of the female singer-songwriters that ERCO take on do very well."

"Yes, but ERCO's greediness has destroyed lives before and will do so again."

Who's That Girl (December 1996)

Chapter 9 - Who's That Lady? (December 2013)

As had been the custom for many years, the Music Department was hosting a Christmas concert in the college hall. The history of the event had been passed down over the years and the 1996 concert that launched the ill-fated career of Gillian Fox was routinely mentioned. More people claimed to have been there than could have possibly fitted in the hall.

Nobody had warned Colin that organising the event was a poisoned chalice, so his efforts to point out that his experience of putting on performances was in the 'dim and distant past' were swiftly dismissed. He didn't actually mind at all and resolved to help the various groups prepare, filling in where he felt he was needed, on guitar, keyboards or drums.

He was at the same time surprised and amused when some attendees brought forward their dog-eared Disassociation albums. He had been certain that the parents were too young to have been aware of his prog rock past. It didn't take long to realise that these were grandparents, mainly grandfathers, who had never thinned out their vinyl collections. He joked with a few of them about the possibility of vinyl making a comeback. A few quietly asked whether a reunion was at all possible. Colin politely shook his head and explained that it was all such a long time ago that he couldn't see that ever happening. A few commented on his blue check shirt, jeans and blue jumper uniform and asked whether this shouldn't have been an occasion to dress up a bit more.

Just before the 7.30pm start time, a commotion arose as a large black car pulled right up to the hall door and three people disembarked. They looked out of place as they swept to the front, with a bulky bodyguard on one side and a tiny Vicky Tucker on the other side of a moderately built Erica Conway. Shielded in the middle, Erica was dressed to draw attention to herself. She was now in sole charge of ERCO following the sudden resignation and disappearance of her brother, whose indelicate comments about the record shop owners who had contributed to the family fortune as being 'imbeciles who can't tie up their own shoelaces' had been the beginning of his undoing. Soon other recorded comments, including one where he called his artists 'halfwits who can't write hit songs to save their lives' also surfaced from an undisclosed source. He had refused to apologise, saying 'I don't regret anything and I've done nothing legally wrong.' Within weeks, he had quietly disappeared out of the UK and could no longer be traced.

Erica perched her designer sunglasses securely on top of her immaculately presented hair. She wore an expensive designer suit covered with a bright red shawl. Her perfume threatened to overpower the musty latent smell in the hall. She spoke quietly on her phone and could be heard saying, "Yes, we've just arrived," while she waited impatiently for the reserved seating to be sorted out.

Vicky was there to ensure that everything went smoothly and this was not a good start. The short and dark-haired woman who referred to herself as "Ms Tucker to you" had become well known to the Music students, as she sat in on many classes in the first term. "Don't you know who we are, laddie?" she asked. She didn't cut any ice with the offending parents in the reserved seats who shrugged and argued there were no signs on the chairs, so they would stay where they were. In the background, the bodyguard reached for whatever was in the holster under his coat, until he saw Erica glaring and shaking her head.

It took Sue McLeod to diffuse the situation. She politely apologised for the absence of the usual signs on the seats and offered a glass of wine to each of the offended parents and the ERCO party. The tumult had the attention of Colin, who looked down from the stage and shrugged helplessly – how was he to know that some seats needed to be reserved? Erica put the glass of wine to her lips and sniffed the contents, then passed it to her bodyguard instead, leaving more than a trace of deep red lipstick on the rim.

Who's That Lady? (December 2013)

Colin eyed the group and remembered what he had been told. ERCO would review the progress of all students in the Music Department during their final year and would have first refusal on signing contracts with any of them once they were ready to leave the college. It was later rumoured that Simon Fuller had heard about this arrangement and incorporated the first refusal idea into the contracts of anyone who wanted to appear on his Pop Idol show, which started in 2001. ERCO now had a fierce reputation for taking young talent from colleges that they sponsored and pitting them against each other at their annual Summer Ball, with the winners getting a prized record contract.

First up was the Rich Kids band. During their original song, written with a small amount of help from Cynthia, Harry hammed it up for Erica and looked directly at her throughout his performance, ignoring everyone else in the room. At the end of the song, it was clear Erica wasn't impressed as she sat impassively with her arms folded and a disinterested expression on her face, evading all eye contact with Harry.

Some of the other performances were cover versions but Hannah, Liam and Jack decided that trying out a song they had written over a few lunchtimes was worth the risk. *I Don't Understand It* came from one of Colin's class projects. He had asked the students to write a song based on their own recorded loops. The trio had come up with two loops: first, a guitar riff that could be repeated over the alternating chords of C major and E minor. They then layered an ascending deep male voice choir. Listening to the two loops they recorded in the college recording studio gave Jack some lyrical ideas. He particularly wondered how people weren't getting angry at things like poverty and climate change.

While others were performing, they hung around backstage and waited their turn. Jack was especially nervous as he knew that Mabel and Jim were going to be in the audience. His mind was taken from this while he and Liam tried their best to distract Hannah from her own nerves. A live performance in front of a real audience was her biggest fear.

"HELLO HAMMERSMITH!"

"Please welcome Hannah, Liam and Jack," announced Colin, to uncertain applause.

As the room hushed, Liam recorded his first guitar loop and set it running, before overlaying it with chords. Jack had his head down and raised it for an instant to realise that the stage lights and the low level of lighting in the hall meant that there was no way that he could see anyone past the front row and relaxed just a little.

With Colin on the drums, Jack started the ascending choir motif on the keyboard before he and Hannah alternated vocals. Jack started:

> *I don't understand it, why aren't you angry?*
>
> *The world spins in turmoil and people go hungry*
>
> *Your life looks perfect but open your eyes*

They both sang the chorus and an audible gasp escaped from the crowd when Hannah, positioned as far back on the stage as she could, eyes firmly shut, harmonised.

> *Your future's uncertain, how you gonna survive*
>
> *And keep yourself alive. The truth can't be denied*

There was then silence as Hannah's voice echoed away, leaving Colin on the bass drum beat before the riff started up again.

> *I don't understand it. Why aren't you angry?*
>
> *You know global warming destroys whole countries*
>
> *You're not even marching when will you get wise*
>
> *Your future's uncertain, how you gonna survive*
>
> *And keep yourself alive. The truth can't be denied.*

Liam stamped on his small pedal board and took his guitar solo under a spotlight. It was short and economical but effective, ending in controlled feedback as the bass drum took over again. The final chorus followed, ending with all bowing their heads in silence to signify the end. It was

Who's That Lady? (December 2013)

atmospheric and widely different from anything else in the show. Erica could be seen quietly whispering down to Vicky, who nodded energetically in agreement with her boss.

At the end of the show, the hall lights came up and Sue stood up to give her customary few words and thanked Colin and his team. Colin then introduced the last song in line with the upcoming season. A special Christmas song had been written by students especially for the concert. There was applause as Hannah, Liam and Jack again stepped forward, with Hannah now smiling for the first time. Jack looked out and saw a smiling Mabel sitting next to a glum-looking Jim.

Colin mentioned that the words of the chorus to this new song would be on the screen behind the stage and quickly ran through the melody with the audience. Jack and Hannah again swapped the vocals on the verses while Liam and Hannah both played acoustic guitars. It was much more upbeat that their previous song.

December's come around again, the last month of the year

It's time to buy some presents for the ones that you hold dear

The shops are full of people and the towns are filled with light

We make our preparations for that very special night

They encouraged everyone to join in with the chorus as Colin picked up the sleigh bells:

We wish you Merry Christmas and a – Happy New Year

So fill your glass and raise a toast, we wish you all good cheer

We hope you get the presents that you put upon your list

We wish you Merry Christmas and hope none of you get - missed

At the end of this verse, a laughter rose from the parts of the audience who saw the joke and ended with the shift to the second verse.

"HELLO HAMMERSMITH!"

> *Santa's sleigh is full of presents; he's all set to go*
>
> *The reindeer wait impatiently and now it starts to snow*

On Colin's signal, white ticker tape drifted down

> *The elves wave him goodbye and go to bed. They've earned a rest.*
>
> *The same goes for the children of the world, for bed they're dressed*
>
>> *We wish you Merry Christmas and a – Happy New Year*
>>
>> *So fill your glass and raise a toast, we wish you all good cheer*
>>
>> *We hope you get the presents that you put upon your list*
>>
>> *We wish you Merry Christmas and hope none of you get - missed*

By this time, even Erica can be seen quietly mouthing the words before the song changes direction following Colin's suggestion to add a bridge:

> *Spare a thought for those that're not as fortunate as you*
>
> *Help them any way you can; just think what they go through*

And onto the third verse:

> *The day itself arrives and finally everyone can smile*
>
> *The presents sit under the tree, and they make quite a pile*
>
> *The children rip the wrapping paper; they no longer wait*
>
> *The Queen is on the tele and the turkey's on its plate*

All the music students came on stage for the last chorus, with an awkward-looking Harry and Cynthia in the back row.

>> *We wish you Merry Christmas and a – Happy New Year*
>>
>> *So fill your glass and raise a toast, we wish you all good cheer*
>>
>> *We hope you get the presents that you put upon your list*
>>
>> *We wish you Merry Christmas and hope none of you get - missed*

Who's That Lady? (December 2013)

With a twist at the end by Jack and Hannah.

We wish you Merry Christmas – and now let's all get……

There was a mixture of laughter and applause as they finished, with hugs all around. Sue, Erica, Vicky and the bodyguard had quietly disappeared and were waiting backstage for the trio. "Miss Conway and Vicky would like a few words with you," Sue shared as she went back to congratulate more students.

Erica forced a smile for the first time in the evening. "That was a very impressive performance, all of you…" And looking squarely at Hannah, who could hardly contain her blushing cheeks. "Especially you, young lady. Definitely some promise there. As you know, Vicky and others from my team will sit in on more of your lessons next year to see how you're developing. We're serious about finding the music stars of the future."

The trio shrugged their shoulders. "That's cool," Liam said. There was then a bit of an awkward silence. Erica gave them a business card each and suggested that they send some more of their songs on a CD to her office in London.

Erica's phone was vibrating away while she was talking. She answered it brusquely. "Yes, it's finished. I do have one interesting possibility here for next year," before walking away to continue the conversation. She thought she was out of everyone's earshot, without realising that she was standing next to the curtain that backdropped the stage. Colin was on the other side, packing equipment away. "Actually, there's something of a mixed bag from what I can see. Some raw talent and some rubbish in there. We need to think about whether we're really getting value from this sponsorship. My father was keen on it, probably because he attended this wretched college but in the last few years the quality just hasn't been there. I think next year could be their last chance. There's more talent at the London College, for sure."

In the background, Harry and Cynthia glowered, while Rick and Dan, their rhythm section, were in a deep discussion with each other. Rick, in particular, was agitated and pointed at Harry as he muttered under his breath.

With Colin having been tied up with closing down the event, the trio related their experience with Erica to him later. He agreed it was great news but brought them down to earth a little by relating what he had heard of Erica's phone call from behind the curtain. They were aware of the rumours about what happened to Gillian Fox many years earlier. Nobody really knew what went on, but the unsavoury comments had unveiled some clues.

Mabel gave Jack an enormous hug when they met up at the end, which embarrassed him no end. In the back of Jim's car on the way home, Jack thought about what had happened. Right there and then, he decided songwriting was something that he had in him. He knew he had some catching up to do with the rest of the class, so resolved to find Colin as soon as he could and ask for more extra sessions.

With that, he put his earbuds in and pressed 'play' on the latest Arctic Monkeys' album.

♫ ♫ ♫ ♫ ♫ ♫ ♫ ♫ ♫ ♫ ♫ ♫ ♫ ♫

Erica was thoughtful in the back of the car on the way back to London. It had all been low-key but it had been good to get her first event as the new head of ERCO out of the way. She knew the Board had taken a gamble when they appointed her, given she was only 28 years old, but she had been shadowing her father since she left university with a 1st in Business Studies. Father would fully support her. She could always wrap him around her finger. She also had the support of the company owner, who she had known for many years.

It had been a shame that her brother had been forced out under a cloud but he had brought it on himself. It had been her duty to access the recordings of the internal meetings and leak them. She knew that she

Who's That Lady? (December 2013)

would have to be careful about loose words at ERCO HQ in the future, although her position wasn't under threat.

Anyway, there were going to be bigger events to attend over the next few months as the awards' season got underway and she reckoned that she might have to work on her public persona to ensure that people realised they were dealing with an important person in the industry now. She had to be seen as a player and not someone who could be messed with.

Chapter 10 - It Don't Come Easy (January 1996)

It was a new term and Gerry had the bright idea of getting his students to come up with a two-chord song. He had played them *A Horse With No Name* by America to show them that this simple structure could be an enormous hit. Only a few of them had heard it before. They were more familiar with *Jane Says* by Jane's Addiction, which went between A and G with added steel drums. A few more got interested when Gerry showed them that Led Zeppelin's *Whole Lotta Love* also alternated between D and E.

The students had complained that, even given those examples, they were unlikely to come up with anything too interesting. So Gerry relented a little by allowing them to use different voicings of the same chords to add some variety. The students still complained, so Gerry further promised to do the homework himself and come up with his own two-chord song, although he promptly forgot this.

Fortunately, an opportunity presented itself that enabled him to keep his promise after all. One of their neighbours, John, had recently come around to ask a favour. It was his 30th wedding anniversary and he wanted to sing an original song to his wife. He had some lyrics scribbled on a piece of paper, which he handed over with a look of embarrassment. Gerry didn't promise anything, but agreed to give it a go. The song was titled *You're My Pearl*. John then made things even more difficult by saying that he could play the guitar and wanted to do this live for an anniversary party of friends and neighbours, but he always struggled with certain chords given the short length of his fingers; Gerry now had to take that into account as well.

Gerry was tempted to hand the paper back and pretend that he wasn't going to have the time to do this before the party. However, not only did he have time, he also remembered his two-chord song promise to the students. The added constraint would convince his students that a song composition was indeed possible under those conditions.

Later that week, Gerry looked at the handwritten lyrics:

I may not always show it, but I'm still in love with you

You stand right here beside me, taking care and guiding too

There's never been another, and looking back it's clear to me

I was so lucky to find you – seems we were simply meant to be

    Cos you're my pearl, yes you're my pearl

Men go diving for pearls, but I have one in my arms

We've been lucky with the bad times, never really came to harm

Didn't know in the beginning if we'd make or break our hearts

Seems to me that we're still winning and we should never drift apart

    Cos you're my pearl, yes you're my pearl

As we look out to the ocean, who knows how many pearls lie there

The one I need is always with me. No one else could compare

We may not know the future, but I think that you'd agree

That we should stay together, face the world, you and me

    Cos you're my pearl, yes you're my pearl

The words were simple but heartfelt. Gerry picked up his old battered Hofner acoustic guitar and tried various chords that he thought would be simple to play. He remembered having previously used a C minor 7, which only involved two fingers, and E minor 7, which could also be done with two but sounded more complete with three. Each line in the verse seemed to contain a natural split that broke up the line into two parts. With the two chords, he worked on a fitting melody, adding some movement to generate more interest.

It Don't Come Easy (January 1996)

This guitar was the first one that Gerry had ever owned. His parents had bought it for him in the early 1960s when he first became interested in music. That The Beatles used Hofner guitars had been a major factor in his choice of that brand. The guitar's battered appearance was not surprising, considering its age. There were remnants of an old silver label inside which read "Hofner Guitarre. Seit 1887 Instrumente von vollendeter Qualitat" over which the importer had glued a 'Made in Germany' sticker. There was no scratch plate on it, which meant that there were obvious gouges just below the sound hole where Gerry's plectrum had marked it over the years. The Hofner name was not displayed on the headstock, as became standard later on, but a stencil showed the name at the bottom of the front of the guitar. In anyone else's hands, the instrument was worth less than £50 but the fact that the only owner had been Gerry Stanford made it a collector's item, at least it had been 10 years ago.

Bernie came in to see what her husband was working on. "See what you think?" he asked as he played through the first verse and she peered at the lyrics over his shoulder.

"Nice… but what about the chorus, you know, the 'you're my pearl' bit? You could repeat that and go up the scale to make it sound more 'up'. Go through the first verse again and keep those chords going afterwards."

Gerry did as she suggested and at the end of the first verse Bernie took over. She did two repeats of 'you're my pearl' and then took it up even higher for another two. The last one lengthened out and ended on the high.

Gerry smiled. "That's better. You see? I still can't do this without you, dear. Oh, hang on, I have an idea." He took out a piece of paper and wrote out the notes in the basic C minor 7 and E minor 7 chords before going up the fretboard to see where they could land. "Oh, here we go." He found that up at the 9th fret he could use the top four strings to reach both chords just by moving three closely placed fingers up one string.

"Let's run it through again." He played the chords through, and Bernie took all the vocals. Halfway through the chorus, they both moved up an octave: it all fitted perfectly.

"Boom!" he exclaimed, smiling. "Verse two." Before long, they were happy with it and went into the recording booths to record it quickly. Once it was down, they called John over with his guitar and played it to him.

"That sounds perfect," John said. "Hmm… Those chords sound difficult though."

"Not at all," Gerry replied before showing John where they came on the fretboard.

John looked pleased and reassured. "Oh, genius! I think even I can handle those chords. You'll have to come to the party now!"

"Well, I don't know. We'll see."

♫ ♫ ♫ ♫ ♫ ♫ ♫ ♫ ♫ ♫ ♫ ♫ ♫ ♫

A few weeks later, Gerry and Bernie resolved to go to John's party after all. They could give him some moral support but also quench their curiosity about how he managed. It was a reasonable day for January and most of the guests sat outside. They all gathered there, waiting for the cake to be cut. Once that was done, John prepared to speak.

"Now then," he started. "Most of you were here five years ago for our Silver Anniversary and you may not remember much about it, but I do. Back then, I had been working so hard that I hadn't prepared anything to say so I stood back and left it to Jane, who also hadn't prepared anything. I don't think she's forgiven me yet."

"No, I haven't," his wife concurred.

It Don't Come Easy (January 1996)

"So, this time I thought I'd do some preparation and fulfil an ambition at the same time. As you know, the Stanfords have been living in the village for some time now. We all know of the rollercoaster that they've been on. A few weeks ago, I took some lyrics around to Gerry and he kindly put them to music. I then found out that Bernie had contributed to the work as well. So, what I'm proud to share with you is an anniversary song that Stanford and I have co-written!" On that cue, Gerry brought John's guitar out to him. John strapped it on and launched into the first verse. As he was starting the second verse, the English weather reminded the audience of its whims and it started raining heavily, so everyone had to seek cover inside.

Gerry watched to see whether John would give it up as a bad idea but could see that he was undeterred. "Right, I think we need to start again," John said once everyone had settled down.

"Hang on, I think we can do better," Gerry said supportively. He sat at the piano and waited for John to restart. As John played the intro, Gerry joined with some complementary chords, which lifted the whole song and took it in another direction altogether. John could scarcely believe what was happening and fluffed through the first verse. Seeing him struggling, Bernie stood next to him and harmonised on the chorus, belting out the second part which she had helped with. By the end, the entire room was singing the chorus to an embarrassed Jane and the song ended with rapturous applause.

"I like these people," Gerry later said on the way home. "They're honest and hardworking."

"Just like we used to be, pet." Bernie smiled and looped her arm inside Gerry's.

Later that day, a guest at the party sent photos of the indoor performance with the three of them to the local paper. This was printed and then picked up by some nationals. Stanford fans expressed delight at the fact that their idols were writing and performing again, but critics joked about how far they had fallen, to be writing and performing two-chord songs at a neighbour's party.

In a darkened, smoke-filled room in London, Ernie Conway discussed the news report with a man dressed in a grey suit. "Do you think they're serious about planning a comeback?"

"No chance. The Stanford name is still mud in the industry. We've seen to that. I think I know how we can keep a better eye on Gerry though. ERCO should offer to sponsor our old college. I hear the buildings are all still there. They must be in a shocking state by now."

"Really? I can't believe that Gerry is going to stand by while that happens. He knows that ERCO will want to control things at the college."

"Sure, but what choice does he have? He was probably lucky to secure that tutoring place. They must have been desperate, with his reputation still in tatters. I hear that the principal has a soft spot for him. In fact, I've had an even better idea. You could restart the annual competition with a recording contract as the prize. That's how ERCO discovered Gerry and the Splatt boys. We could scoop up some new talent before the other vultures gather. Maybe a cute girl group. That would suit me nicely. You know how much I like fresh blood."

It Don't Come Easy (January 1996)

Chapter 11 - Let's Stick Together (May 2014)

It was some months after the triumph of the Christmas concert. Hannah was unwell and off sick, so Jack and Liam were on their own in their usual rehearsal room. They could vaguely hear sounds outside the door, an unusual occurrence at lunchtime, so they quietened down. There was a knock on the door. Before they could answer, the Rich Kids' rhythm section of Rick and Dan walked in.

"Hi guys, how is it going?" Rick started with a thumb up in expectation. "You're sounding good in here, if I may say. Look, we wanted to run something past you guys, if you have a few minutes." He rested against the wall and ran a hand through his blond mop of hair.

"Sure," acquiesced Liam, to encourage him to spill the beans. He unconsciously folded his arms in front of him. He feared that they might have been sent by Harry to spy on their progress.

The two incomers looked at each other, uncertain how to start, until Rick pitched in. "Well, me and Dan have been thinking about things. We're going to be honest and say that we only came to this college knowing that ERCO were sponsors of the Music Department and that we could escape this dead-end town and get up to London with a recording contract in our back pockets."

He looked at Dan, who took up the flow. "We know we're not the greatest songwriters in here. Performance is more our bag and we reckoned that there would be some talented songwriters here who needed a drummer and a bass player to help them out. We thought we had found the solution early on when Harry and Cynthia approached us, but it's clear now that neither of them have any idea what they are doing. Harry's all mouth and no trousers. Actually, even his mouth isn't up to much."

"HELLO HAMMERSMITH!"

Dan paused, so Rick took over again. "In the meantime, we've been mighty impressed with what you guys have been doing musically. Let's be honest, your image is terrible, but you have the musical ability and we just wanted to say that if you're serious about a career in music, then we'd be happy to move across from the Rich Kids and back you guys instead. You know, make a proper band and all that. We think we could really give you the solid backbone that you're missing. You guys can be the songwriters and we won't interfere. We'd just help with the rhythm arrangements. We'll also attract more of the girls on board as fans. Let's face it. The two of you aren't that great in the looks department. What do you think?"

"Well," Liam exhaled, barely holding back an expression of surprise. "I didn't see that coming. Jack?"

"No. Wasn't expecting that. Worth thinking about."

Liam agreed. "Look, why don't you both give us some time to think about it? We'll need to run it past Hannah at least."

"Sure guys!" Rick replied. "Take all the time you need and let us know what you think. If it's a 'yes', then we'll break it to Harry. He won't be happy but…" He shrugged his shoulders. "All we know is that we want a chance of getting a recording contract and we reckon that you guys are writing the best songs in the class. The rest we can sort out for you. Let us know what you decide." And with that, they left the room.

The room was silent for some time afterwards as Jack and Liam were making sure that they had actually gone.

Liam started. "That was unexpected! Anyone could see they're not happy with Harry in charge but I thought they were just going to take more control and not be bullied by him. I guess they are just trying to be honest about their own abilities and up their odds. I think we should see what Hannah thinks and have a word with Colin as well."

"Sure… Think they were quite rude though…"

Let's Stick Together (May 2014)

"That's because Rick doesn't seem to have much of a filter. To be honest, I didn't really think about the contract thing myself when I came here. I just wanted to spend a couple of years learning more about music and practising. It would be handy to have a strong backline. It means that we can do some gigs if we want to."

"Yeah! Gigs would be handy to test songs out." Jack paused. "Anyway, what was this song that you wanted me to listen to?"

"Oh, it's not brill. It's just what came to me for Colin's two-chord song brief." Liam pulled some notes from his rucksack and freed his guitar from its bag.

"It goes from E major to A minor or A minor 7 and back again. You'll have to excuse my singing – I don't do much and I don't really write lyrics. It's called *No Disguise*."

With that, Liam played through the chords before launching in.

> *You don't say that much my dear; you're quiet most of the time*
>
> *People barely notice you. It seems to suit you fine*
>
> *I know you better than most. We get along real well*
>
> *There's not a lot that we don't share so this I have to tell*

He strained his voice for the chorus to reach the higher melody, but the chords remained the same.

> *Girl! You let your hair hang down like a curtain tryin' to cover your face.*
>
> *Babe! I know you're shy but I think you're the prettiest girl in this place*
>
> *Girl! Just show the world those baby brown eyes and you'll get a surprise*
>
> *Guys! Well they'll look twice and say that you don't need...*
>
> *No disguise*

Jack nodded as Liam moved into the second verse.

> *You don't need no makeup on your face – that is so wrong*
> *To cover up that beauty that has been there all along*
> *It should help your confidence if I say what I feel*
> *There's no need for telling lies 'cos what I feel is real*

The chorus was followed by a middle eight:

> *You are like a flower that is just about to bloom*
> *That is why you're the best girl - in this room*
> *Those guys should open their eyes to see your charms*
> *They would be so lucky to be in your arms...*
>
> > *Girl! You let your hair hang down but you don't need...*
> > *No disguise, no disguise.*

Jack approved. "Cool! Funny that it's just a two-chord song. The melody moves around quite a lot. Could do with a picking pattern on the verse and then strumming the chorus to lift it. It's nearly finished."

Before long, they had pulled a last verse together:

> *There's still time for you to change and come out from that shell*
> *Nothing here could upset you as far as I can tell*
> *Please don't hide yourself away, the rainbow's over you*
> *Just one smile from you can make the sun come shining through*

When they played it to the group a couple of days later, Jack took the lead and Liam added a bass vocal to the choruses. As they played, it was hard to see whether Hannah, who was back at college, was blushing as her hair was swiftly unhooked from behind her ears and allowed to cover as much of her face as possible. Jack knew full well that the song had been for Hannah and was a touch disappointed, as he quite fancied her himself. However, he would never have had the courage to say anything, given his fear of rejection.

Harry was his usual dismissive self. "Ugh. I feel sick."

"It has the same lame message as One Direction's *What Makes You Beautiful*," scoffed Cynthia. "I hate that song."

"There's a point there," agreed Colin. "That One Direction song uses just three notes in the chorus, so is very simple. But it was a number 1 hit in the UK and a huge song all over the world. It's hard to knock it when it was so successful?"

The smile fell from Cynthia's face.

"Jeez, I hate One Direction," said Liam, looking at the floor. "I can't say that I've listened to it that closely."

"Looks like it's been sitting in your subconscious though," commented Colin. "Does anyone remember the word that defines this?" There was silence. "I'm not surprised. I probably only told you guys in passing. It's called cryptomnesia, where someone mistakes a buried memory for an original idea. It would be alright in this case, as it's only the sentiment that is common to both. The words and music differ. You can't copyright an idea or...," Colin paused and raised his hand to ear as he waited for the answer.

"... a song title," said some students who had been taking notes.

"Quite right," said Colin before moving on. "Cryptomnesia had been blamed for a few unjust plagiarism decisions over the years and it's hard to guard against it."

After class, Liam and Jack stayed behind so that they could discuss the possibility of Dan and Rick joining them with Hannah and Colin.

"Well, I understand what you say. It does indeed make it possible for you to do some live practice," Colin observed. "There's nothing better than rehearsing and playing live to test the song ideas that you have and hone them into shape. And, to be fair, the two of them are pretty good at what they do. There aren't many drummers in your year and Rick is easily the best of them. He's developing too."

"Bass guitarists aren't so crucial for recording," Liam added. "I could have a go at that myself. We need someone if we want to play live though."

Hannah was hesitant. "I've a funny feeling about both of them." She paused. "Rick seems to be a bit of an open book as he can't stop speaking about anything that's in his crazy head, but that could be an act and he's hiding stuff. There's definitely something about Dan though."

"Mmm, I know what you mean," Liam said. "He's quiet and can be rather creepy…"

"Could say that about any of us," Jack remarked, and they all laughed.

"I'm sorry to say this, Jack, and I really don't mean to offend you," Hannah suddenly let out, "but you're different from everyone else I know."

"What do you mean?" Jack asked, knowing full well to what she was alluding.

"Well, you're just more focused on stuff. It's almost as if you were on the spectrum somewhere."

"I am." Jack's words were uttered calmly and simply.

"Oh… ok. That was a good guess I suppose. Sorry if I've offended you."

"Not at all. Gets dealt with."

"Anyway, are you all going to give Rick and Dan a try out then?" asked Colin, who was keen to move on.

Let's Stick Together (May 2014)

Liam shrugged. "What do we have to lose?"

"Some teeth when Harry finds out and punches our lights out?" Hannah asked.

"Harry's all talk," Liam affirmed. "I think we go for it. The end of the year is coming, and we have the holiday to rehearse with them. That is, if you're going to carry on until next year, Jack?"

Caught a little off guard, Jack resorted to a little lie. "Haven't really thought about it much. I'm not really sure about all this."

Hannah, probably feeling the poor guy had been put on the spot enough these past few minutes, swiftly changed the subject. "What shall we call the band?" The question was important and they started brainstorming.

Jack kept quiet while Hannah and Liam considered and dismissed many possibilities, as they conducted a little research for each suggested name and found there was already a band with a record deal using an identical or similar name. Black Mountain? No, that was a prog band. Black Stone? No – there was Black Stone Cherry. This last proposition prompted Liam to pull a large paperback out of his bag, Light Stone by David Zindall.

"We could try this," he ventured. "The book is heavy going but as a name it's good. I think it suggests something that is weighty and solid but it's a contradiction by being not as heavy as you might think."

A quick search suggested that there weren't any bands using that name so for want of something better, this stuck for now. And so Light Stone was born and the search for local gigs started.

The newly named band sat around that afternoon and kicked around some basic song ideas and also side-tracked into verbalising some crazy goals.

"At least one Top 40 single," Hannah started with a laugh.

"HELLO HAMMERSMITH!"

"Maybe a Top 10 single," added Liam to more laughter. "Or the cover of MOJO Magazine."

"A platinum album," Hannah added, feeling more determined.

"Headlining a London show at Hammersmith?" Jack suggested.

They all laughed at what felt like an unattainable goal. But Jack remained quiet as he wondered where his idea had sprung from. A closed part of his brain opened as he recalled the mention of the Hammersmith Odeon and the Carling Apollo from many years ago.

♪ ♪ ♪ ♪ ♪ ♪ ♪ ♪ ♪ ♪ ♪ ♪ ♪ ♪

The end of term drew near. Exams were being marked. As they had feared, Harry royally kicked off when Rick and Dan announced they were leaving the Rich Kids for Light Stone. He had tried to seek the 'thieves' out individually to threaten them, but as the threesome would stay quite close to each other, he had given up and instead cornered them in the rehearsal room one lunchtime. They all looked fearful as Harry slammed the door behind him and put his weight against it. "What are you doing nicking my band members?" he leered as he moved in and peered down at Jack, who looked away and requested, "Space please."

Hannah stood up and attempted to look him straight in the eye, but had to settle for looking at his chin. "I wasn't aware that you owned them, Harry!" she started. "I kind of thought that they were adults, or at least closer to being adults than you are and could make their own mind up. Maybe they were fed up with being pushed around."

"I didn't push them around! I don't push anyone around!" Harry defended himself, moving closer to Hannah, which prompted Liam to move forward to protect her.

Let's Stick Together (May 2014)

Harry pointed a finger at each of them individually. "You've stolen my rhythm section guys and I won't forget this. You'd better watch your backs."

"Are you threatening us?" quizzed a defiant Hannah.

A heavy silence fell as he glared at the three of them. Hannah and Liam glared back, but Jack kept looking at the floor.

"You're all freaks! And he's a shrimp!" Harry pointed at Jack and shouted as he dramatically turned and flounced out, banging the door wide open as he left.

"Phew. Looks like that's done," Hannah sighed as she closed the door and their heart pulses returned to normal. "But Liam, you didn't need to move in and protect me. I can look after myself."

"Just making sure," Liam shrugged. "We have to look after each other."

"Don't think it's over," Jack warned. "Better watch our backs. Let's stick together."

"Come on, come on, let's stick together," vocalised Hannah.

♪ ♪ ♪ ♪ ♪ ♪ ♪ ♪ ♪ ♪ ♪ ♪ ♪ ♪

For higher-year students, lessons were now over and the summer had begun. But lower-year students still had to take lessons. It had become traditional during this period for the details of the ERCO annual competition to be revealed. Every year introduced some new tweaks to the programme, so it was rarely exactly the same each time. This year, Colin invited ERCO to send a representative to the college to introduce the competition to students. This would give them some background in what it was like to be signed in the music industry. He had suggested that his own experience of being in a record contract back in the early 1970s would give additional perspective. Vicky Tucker had come along from ERCO and sat at the back to listen to his story before bringing things more up to date with ERCO's plans.

Colin took his story up from when he was at the Royal Academy of Music. "There was lots of session work available in London. You turned up with your gear, which was tough for me as keyboards back in those days were a lot bulkier than they are now. If you were lucky and they only wanted some piano from you, often there would be a serviceable piano there. Sometimes, I was booked into Studio 2 at Abbey Road and played the 'Lady Madonna piano' which is still there after Paul McCartney used it in 1967.

"Sometimes the song was written out, but more often than not, there was just a cheap demo, which you listened through a few times and then had to be ready to rehearse. We would have a few run throughs, agree to some changes and then go straight into recording. Often, this was live with all the instruments in the same space and microphones picking up sounds from different areas of the room. It could sometimes be all over in a few hours and you had to clear out ready for the next session."

"What were you paid for that?" Rick asked.

"Oh, about £10."

"£10! I wouldn't get out of bed for that!" Rick joked.

"That was a reasonable sum in those days. There's a story that Herbie Flowers, who created the iconic bass line on Lou Reed's *Walk on the Wild Side*, received £17 for his trouble, but that was it – no ongoing royalty at all. So, it was hard work, but I learnt a lot and when I then left the college, I knew that I'd never earn much of a living doing sessions and would definitely do my back in from the heavy lifting.

"I returned to Canterbury, which in those days was a hotbed for music. You just had to go out to a few pubs. You'd meet up with loads of local musicians who had been offered record contracts or were looking to form a band. I tried out with different bands in the area. A lot of them already had songwriters who didn't want to share.

"So, I started a group of my own which ended up as Disassociation We did some rehearsals in my dad's garage. I remember he was a bit upset as in those days it was usual to keep your car in the garage and he couldn't when a drum kit was set up there for weeks on end. One of the band had a tape machine and recorded some demos. We never knew how to copy each tape, so ended up recording each one afresh, then sending them off to different record labels. Maybe 20 different tapes got sent and they still turn up in people's attics and appear at auctions every now and again. We were amazed when the second one we sent received some interest before going quiet again.

"One evening, unbeknownst to us, a label came down to see us at a local gig. They came forward and introduced themselves at the end of the night and said that contracts would be in the post by the end of the next week. There was one for recording and one for publishing. Although I was the principal writer, we all felt everyone contributed so we agreed to split everything equally. We were so excited about having been heard and getting signed that we didn't look at the contracts at all. Just signed them and sent them back. Didn't even keep a copy. I hope I don't have to tell you this, but I will anyway. Don't ever do that, kids!

"Anyway, this is when the fun started. We went up to London to record enough for two albums that came out six months apart. We only had a few weeks. Studio time was scarce in those days, and you had to be disciplined and ready to be in and out as soon as possible to keep the costs down. The label then started booking gigs for us all over the country. There was no attempt to line things up at all. They made phone calls all over the place and booked us support slots first. I remember being in Glasgow and going down to Cardiff with Soft Machine and then back to Edinburgh with Caravan, with no rest. We had to take turns driving the van and lugged our own equipment on and off the stage. A lot of bands would meet up at Watford Gap services on the M1 motorway and swap stories."

"HELLO HAMMERSMITH!"

"Were there many drugs around?" someone asked.

"Oh sure," Colin admitted. "With the lack of sleep and being constantly on the move, we took lots of different of pills to keep us going. They were all fairly cheap back then. It was 'take a handful' or 'keel over'. We all had to deal with the consequences later." He paused and looked faraway, remembering fallen comrades.

"After we had built a following with the first two albums, we started headlining and for six years we were in the 'record/release/tour' cycle with only brief breaks. This meant that the royalties that came in from the old albums went straight to the record label to pay for recording costs and promotion. So we were borrowing more money to keep recording and pay ourselves a meagre wage.

"It wasn't until 1976/77, when our last album sold little and we were dropped, that things caught up and finally the royalties came through without huge deductions. The contract hadn't been great and we thought about challenging it, but it didn't seem worth it. We'd been naïve and signed something without checking it, so it was our own fault. Anyway, I think that's enough of the old stories from me. Let's bring this up to date with Vicky, who you all know."

Vicky stepped to the front and explained what happened with a modern recording contract. "Recording is still an expensive process," she explained. "We spend a lot more time in post-production now, mixing all the tracks and mastering them to achieve the best sound. Promotion is still expensive as well. What a record label brings is the organisation and logistics experience. This allows you, the artists, to concentrate on writing and recording the hits while we take care of everything else. It's a win-win situation."

She paused as if to let it all sink in and then moved on to keep the audience's attention. "Let's explain next year's competition. You might have heard some stories from previous years. We've taken all that experience on board and we're sure that this year is going to be the best run yet. You're all able to enter, either individually or in a band. You will be assessed over the next 12 months and there can and will only be one winner from this group of students. That winner will get to play at the ERCO Summer Ball against the winners from other ERCO-sponsored colleges around the country, with a record contract as the major prize. To be in with a chance of winning, all you need to do is sign up by coming to talk to me before I leave." And with that, she held up a piece of paper with 10 boxes. "One individual or band will be selected based on your project work in the year and the exam performances that we come to see. The overall winner gets a record contract, starting with a single and then we have the option to extend it from there. It's a once in a lifetime opportunity. Are there any questions?"

And with that, the students put either themselves or their bands forward. To nobody's surprise, Harry and Cynthia put their new Rich Kids band forward with a promise that they would 'wipe the floor' with any competition. Vicky encouraged Hannah to enter as an individual, but Hannah said no. Jack committed to staying the extra year to study for the A Level by signing up as part of Light Stone. To say that he wasn't 100% convinced would be an understatement.

Chapter 12 - I Did It My Way (7 September 1995)

A singer-songwriter from the 1980s would never be as exciting as a battle of modern bands. Mainstream news media was enthralled with the epic Britpop battle. The race to number 1 in the singles charts saw Blur coming out on top of Oasis with their song *Country House*, a song about a record company owner who needed a quieter life.

Today would be Gerry's first day of formal teaching on the Music Composition and Performance course. He had been contacted directly about the possibility, given the Music Department policy of maintaining contact with their alumni. He had come in as a guest lecturer from time to time to tell the students about life in an Eighties pop band. One half of the students found this riveting and the other half were bored; after all, he was 45 years old, that's even older than their parents! Yet when the chance of doing some part-time tutoring was mentioned, Gerry thought it worth a try. There wasn't much else going on, anyway.

A few weeks before his first day, Bernie knew exactly where to find her husband, since he had spent a lot of the summer experimenting at the Chapel's studio. She opened the soundproofed door and was greeted by a cacophony of sounds.

"Ugh. Come on, pet, what's on with all the dissonant chords? That will just jar on the ear and turn people off?"

"Hmm, you could be right. It's good to try things out though. You never know where experiments may lead. I've done some stuff with some simple chords, so it's time to go to the other end of the scale."

"Sure, but we haven't a great record in terms of your grand experiments, have we? If I recall, they've mostly ended up in disaster for us?"

"HELLO HAMMERSMITH!"

"That's not quite true. Who would have guessed that a punk rocker and boy band songwriter could combine as an electronic duo and take on the world? That was a grand experiment. Also, I used to do a thing with Splatt where I start with a basic piano figure and then improvised. It was different every night and gave the other guys a chance to have a break. Also, it helped to keep the audience guessing what you might do next. It's just a shame that things are down at the moment, but if a few experiments come off, we'll be up again."

"Which doesn't explain why you're so against our songs being used in adverts? I've heard that some artists from the 1960s are now making a good living from their old songs being placed in TV and radio adverts and forming a fresh stream of income for them. They're then invited to tour on the back of it."

"There are principles involved."

"What happened to Van Gogh and Blake?"

"That's different."

Bernie realised she wasn't going to win this argument, so changed the subject. "Anyway, are you sure that you're prepared for your first day? You'll need to make a good impression on the new students. Maybe they'll be so terrified that they'll give you an easy ride."

"Yes, I'm all set. I have my prop ready." He pointed towards the plastic bag by the door. "Also, I've spoken to Oscar and we agreed who is doing what. If we have some spare time, I have a project for them to think about as well."

There hadn't been much of an interview process. In mid-August, Gerry had been shown around the college properly for the first time by the Head of the Music Department. The buildings hadn't changed much since his days there and the signs of wear and tear showed everywhere. The entire building should have been pulled down by now. His eyes lit up when he spotted a piano tucked in the corner. "Could it be...? Yes, it is.

I Did It My Way (7 September 1995)

My old piano!" he exclaimed as he walked over. He lifted the lid and touched the familiar keys. Before he knew it, his fingers were playing an old tune that he would have played on it as a 16 year old. "Ah, that same old sound and feel. I'd know this piano anywhere. I can't believe she's still here. This used to be the only piano in the department and I had to race in every morning to beat another guy to it." He smiled at the memory. "We ended up compromising and doing these strange duets, which mixed up different styles of music."

Gerry was later introduced to Sue McLeod, who was around the same age as him. She was in her second year as the college's principal. She was clearly star-struck. "Oh, Mr Stanford," she gushed. "It's so good to see you at our college."

"Please, call me Gerry." He was almost apologetic.

"Sorry, Gerry. I feel so honoured to meet you. I was a huge Stanford fan in the 1980s and I was so sorry to hear what happened to you. When they mentioned you may join the teaching team here, I had no hesitation in approving the hire. I still have my copy of *Album 5*," she winked. "And when I play *Blindside*, I always skip *That* song as well."

Gerry smiled. "Goodness, you're one of a select band of fans, then. There are few who admit to liking *Album 5*. I hear it's tough to sell them in car boot sales at the moment. I think a lot of them have been thrown away."

"I never got to see you live, but it's been on my bucket list to actually meet you. If I had my way, you and Bernie would get the band back together and record again. But from what I understand, that's not going to happen soon, so this is the next best thing for me. Anyway, it's not very professional of me to be gushing like a fangirl, so I'll let you look around and make your mind up whether to join us, but it would be great to have you teaching here."

"HELLO HAMMERSMITH!"

Gerry continued his tour, even though he had already pretty much decided in his mind. The college had given him a lot of support in the early days, and he felt it was right to give something back. His contribution might help some students avoid the mistakes he had made.

♪ ♪ ♪ ♪ ♪ ♪ ♪ ♪ ♪ ♪ ♪ ♪ ♪

The day before his first day of tutoring, Gerry gave Oscar Good a call to finalise the arrangements. "Hi Oscar. Thank you for agreeing to come along and present with me. Are you ready to be greeted by some unruly students?"

"Sure, what could go wrong?" Oscar laughed. "By the way, how honest do you want me to be about the business?"

"I want you to be as truthful as possible. There's no point in sugar-coating the whole thing or leaving a false impression. The serious swimmers need to think hard before entering the piranha pool."

"And are you happy for me to flag up my foundation just in case they're serious about going for a dip? I've spotted some serious talent out there and have pushed at least some of them in the right direction to start with."

"Oh, that would be great, Oscar. It's nice to know that you're still guiding people."

♪ ♪ ♪ ♪ ♪ ♪ ♪ ♪ ♪ ♪ ♪ ♪ ♪

The next morning, Oscar arrived early. He sat patiently at the back of the class while Gerry introduced himself.

"Good morning. My name is Gerry Stanford. Like you, this is my first day at the college. Except that it isn't really my first day here. It is my first day here as a tutor. Many years ago, I sat exactly where you are on my

I Did It My Way (7 September 1995)

first day as a student here, waiting to learn more about Music Composition and Performance. I'm going to take a risk here and ask for starters: how many of you already know about me and my history?"

About half the students raised their hand, which was more than Gerry expected.

"Ok, that's interesting. So, for those of you who don't know me at all, let me give you a brief history of myself. And for those of you who know something about me; please forgive me if I skip a few parts that are still rather too painful to share. Is that ok?" There were a lot of puzzled looks but mainly nods from the students. He could see one boy whispering to his neighbour though.

"Great, I needed to make sure that was understood before we go too far. So, I was born in 1950 and I grew up in a musical family. My parents met while they were both in a big band in the 1940s and if you go back further, I'm directly related to Charles Villiers Stanford, an Irish composer of the late 1800s. His father, John, was partly responsible for setting up the Royal Irish Academy of Music in Dublin. His portrait still hangs there, I think.

"So, the radio or record player was always on in the house. With an old piano in the front room, my parents spent money that they could ill afford on lessons for me. I came to this college from school in 1965. While I only had a few exam passes, I wanted to take this specific Music course, so it made sense for me to come here.

"I left here in 1967, a time when music was pretty exciting. I had joined a band called Splatt in college and we had a rubbishy recording and publishing contract that I won't say too much about for the moment. The Beatles were at the height of their fame and British music led the world in terms of music innovation. I used what I had learnt in this college to land a job as a songwriter in London. There were music publishers and studios everywhere and it was a great place to mix with people in the business. We used to go to this café where you could bump into Elton John, David Bowie and other pop stars regularly. Nothing quite like it now, of course. I earned a decent living for about 10 years, writing hits for other people, and we earned some sort of living with Splatt. All that time, I kept thinking about how I could make it big.

"By the early 1980s the supply of artists who needed songwriters was tailing off. I took some time out and looked at what was happening in the industry. After a bit of research, I reckoned that the swing towards electronic music using keyboards and drums was worth exploring. I auditioned some singers and found Bernie. Bernie was previously known as Bernie Pogo from the punk band The Pogoes, who had some hits in the late 1970s. Like me, she was interested in the electronic scene and had some songwriting experience. We actually wrote a song called *Today's the Day* at that audition and it became one of our early hits. Stanford had a few false starts, but then we were lucky enough to meet this guy." Gerry pointed at Oscar, who was still listening at the back of the room.

"The rest is history. Gold and platinum albums, world tours and a couple of these…." He reached into the plastic bag beside him and pulled out a gold statuette, placing it carefully on the table next to him. There were mainly quizzical looks from the students. "This," he paused, "is the Ivor Novello Award for Best Song that Bernie and I were presented with for writing *I'd Sing Along*. We received another award later, but I can't and won't talk about that because of the still very painful memories that I mentioned earlier. Whether you know or don't know about it, please respect my one rule which is to please not talk about it within my earshot. So I'll leave this story, for now, with the industry award. Whilst bad things have happened, I'm happy to be back and looking forward to working at the college where I learnt so much about the craft. I'm grateful for that and for a lot of things.

"Let me make something clear. My experience is mainly around writing three minute pop songs and that's the bit that I'm going to concentrate on. There are other tutors who are going to cover more of the long-form composition side of the course.

I Did It My Way (7 September 1995)

"So with that, I'd now like to hand over to Oscar Good. I've known Oscar for many years and it was his Good Record Co label that released Stanford's biggest albums. I've asked Oscar to speak to you about what you might need to do to land a record deal with him these days and about some pitfalls to look out for when trying to get a deal. Over to you Oscar."

"Thank you, Gerry." Oscar moved towards the front of the room. "Hi everyone. First, I'd like to be clear that I deal with only a handful of acts. Those that I do work with will have a certain mix of ingredients. So tell me – who would like to sign a recording contract?"

Many hands went up.

"Well, the bad news is: if you are lucky enough to land a record deal, it's almost guaranteed to be one that you'll be delighted to sign and later wish you didn't. The industry feeds on young talent and the playing field is tipped against you. What they are looking for is a few stars of the future who are kept locked in through the original contract. You might know about George Michael, who took Sony to court in 1992 complaining that the company treated him as 'no more than a piece of software'. He wasn't even fighting against his original contract. The original contract had been renegotiated a few times, so he hadn't exactly been forced into what he'd signed. It therefore made sense that he lost his case last year. The judge considered that his contract was both fair and reasonable. Incidentally, he claimed that over the previous five years, Sony had earned more than $52 million from him, while he had received less than $7.5 million. Doesn't sound too bad does it?"

A lot of heads nodded in agreement.

"In plenty of other cases though, the record company isn't so blameless, and I think that Stanford's fight with their first label was a case in point. Incidentally, I was working for their record label at the time so I know all the background. The moral of this story is, don't 'sign in haste and repent at leisure'. Look at whatever you are being asked to sign and don't just settle for any old solicitor to have a look at it. You need a specialist lawyer, one who knows the industry and understands what they are looking at. There are some good music business lawyers around. I never allow an artist to sign a contract until I'm sure that an excellent lawyer has confirmed that they are happy with it. It just saves so much grief later for both of us. Any questions so far?"

There weren't. He carried on. "Most new artist contracts will say that they will receive a royalty which might be 5% to 10% of the retail price of a CD. In very rare cases for mega successful artists, that figure can go to 25%. Traditionally, music publishing royalties are then split 70:30, with 30% going to the publisher as payment for their services and the rest going to the songwriter – or songwriters. As you can see, already your cake is getting smaller. Then from that, the record company expects to be reimbursed for recording and promotion costs it paid on your behalf and you'll be expected to pay for your own management. Since all the costs come upfront in the process and the royalties only come at the end, it doesn't take a genius to work out that the record company is going to be funding the upfront costs and all your initial royalties are going into paying that loan back. Everyone gets excited about the size of an advance from a record company, but actually it's a loan that has to be repaid from royalties. And that's how you hear horror stories of young artists who end up with enormous debts. If you aren't successful enough as an artist, the record label is more likely to drop you earlier than in the past. Plus, if the debt isn't written off, then it follows you. If you are successful, then the label will try to keep you on that old contract for as long as they can, as it will always have been drafted in their favour. So, who still wants to sign a recording contract now?"

Fewer hands went up.

"I'm not surprised. As a new artist, you negotiate from a position of weakness and there are more musicians looking for deals than labels are looking for signings. Do remember that you can hold out for a better deal or walk away if it doesn't look right. Earlier I said I worked for the

I Did It My Way (7 September 1995)

record label that Stanford was on. I saw the games that were being played on them and I thought, 'there must be a better way of doing this'. So, I made some plans, and as the song goes, *I Did It My Way*. Stanford were the first band who looked like they could make my model work. First, I liked what they were doing. That's a key ingredient for me. They weren't planning to spend a great deal on recording costs in the beginning." He paused and winked at Gerry. "That meant that when the royalties rolled in, they only had to pay back my company's promotion costs and actually we hadn't spent a huge amount. I always insist that the artist pays all the recording costs upfront and I account to them for marketing costs. Those seemed to be the biggest bones of contention with contracts – the costs incurred are opaque and random extras can be inserted. I know many bands who took years to realise that the magazines that flew journalists out to interview them in far-flung places on tour weren't paying for the flights, the hotels and the drinks – the label was! Which meant that actually the band was. So I'm transparent about anything like that and artists can decide who they want to fly out and where.

"The result of that is that rather than giving 5% to 10% to the artist and hold back the rest for the company, I split all income from sales 50:50. In reality, few artists have the funds upfront, as they were probably hugely in debt already. Although my way is popular and is held up as best practice, in the real world, only a few artists can come down that path with me. And maybe that's the way I like it. If any of you reach the position where you think you can make the model work, then do contact me. But remember, I have to like what you do first.

"In the meantime, if you are in a band, starting a band, or even doing this solo, then please reach out now. I set up a charitable foundation on the back of the money that the business earned from sales of CDs for Stanford and other artists. It makes grants for youngsters to use in buying equipment and recording some demos in a studio. We, of course, would love to keep in touch to see how you're getting along. Gerry has the details, if you're at all interested."

"HELLO HAMMERSMITH!"

Gerry was right. Oscar's views gave a lot of context and perspective to his students. At lunchtime, the two of them sat and reminisced about the old days.

"Thanks for doing that," Gerry said. "I really wanted to make sure that they heard a balanced view of recording contracts today and you were the only person I could trust to do that."

"That was no trouble. It's always a pleasure to help you out, Gerry. Any plans to return to the business again? You must be missing it by now, surely?"

"No, I don't think so. The memories are still too raw."

I Did It My Way (7 September 1995)

Chapter 13 - Judgement Day (June 2015)

The next year flew by for the second year Music students. Formal lessons ended and everyone at the college was preparing for the end of term exams. For those wanting to go onto Higher Music Colleges, the pressure was on. With only a few spaces available at the rate of only one for every five applicants, good grades were a must. A few colleges had made offers to a handful of really talented individuals based on their auditions. Vicky's visits became noticeably more frequent and her note-taking more furious.

James Bay was high in the charts, which prompted everyone who was copying George Ezra to try out Bay's hit *Hold Back the River* instead.

Jack and the rest of the band had been preparing for their final exams with some guidance from Colin. A lot was going to depend on the live exam performance, but other projects needed to be prepared in advance.

Harry had been winding up the five members of Light Stone at every opportunity. Rick and Dan confided he had attempted to lure them back to the Rich Kids with the promise of money and better gear. Unfortunately for him, the two were reasonably well off, so they just laughed at him and walked away. The threats to the other three were more sinister. "I have it on good authority that you're all going to fail and I'm getting an A star," he hissed.

One of the exam tasks was to present an original composition in four parts. Jack experimented with some dissonant chords in an instrumental piece called *Judgement Day*. He had been reading about the increase in artificial intelligence. His uncle and auntie had been amused at the Terminator 2 film's end of the world predictions. One of the main characters, Sarah Connor, announced that 29 August 1997 would be the day that disaster struck, with the mythical Skynet launching a nuclear holocaust. By coincidence, doomsday was the day that Jack was born! This had played heavily on Jack's mind. The holocaust obviously didn't happen on his birthday, but wasn't there a possibility it would happen in the future? The problem was that he didn't know how to go about composing a piece with *Judgement Day* as the theme and he asked Colin for help. A few days later, they were talking in the rehearsal room with the old piano.

"I've got an idea that you could have a go at for your exam composition. Want to try it out?"

"Sure."

"Okay," he paused. "How about you just play me what's in your head now?"

Jack thought about it for a moment. "Not sure you'd like that."

"Go on. Try me."

Jack placed his hands on the keys, shut his eyes and allowed his mind to guide his fingers. He started slowly at first as he got used to the different way of composing through improvisation and speeded up until he reached a point where his fingers were flying as fast as his brain would allow and dissonance crept in. At that point, he slowed down again until in the middle of a bar, when he stopped.

"How was that?" asked a smiling Colin, who knew the answer.

"Different," Jack agreed.

"Let's work on that. If you start each of the four sections in different styles, then you could conceivably improvise each. You can still call it *Judgement Day*, but change the styles and tempos as your brain dictates. Then you'll do the challenging piece that the judges are looking for."

"Interesting."

Judgement Day (June 2015)

The A Level performance exam raced up on everyone. They all had to do a live piece individually. Then they could do another one on their own or team up. Obviously, Light Stone would do a group song. Rick and Dan knew they were fairly weak on their own and therefore depended on a good group performance to achieve a decent grade. Rick could do a decent drum solo, but Dan was going to struggle with just the bass.

Parents and guardians could come and watch the performances to give more atmosphere to the recording for the examiners. Jack's uncle was at work and couldn't take the time off, but Mabel was going to be in the audience. Erica Conway and Vicky were expected to come and announce who had won this year's competition. That meant that Sue McLeod was also there, as were the local press.

With characteristic timing, minutes before the scheduled start time, a limousine pulled up at the doors and the ERCO party emerged. The car pulled away towards the car park to await the pickup call. Erica was on her phone as usual. It took a questioning look from Sue to force her to cut the call off with a grimace, as though her intrusion was unwarranted.

Colin was called on to manage the changeovers between performances and wasn't allowed to assist anyone on stage as he had done in the shows. Jack thought he saw Colin look out into the audience, smile and wink at someone. He was going to brush it off until he noticed his auntie blushing.

Liam was up first and started his performance with the short guitar tune *Horizons* from the Genesis album *Foxtrot*. The guitarist Steve Hackett had originally taken it from a Bach cello suite. He then moved seamlessly onto a more improvised piece which had the same feel. This led to him turning his acoustic guitar across his legs and 'tapping' the strings. He ended to great applause.

"HELLO HAMMERSMITH!"

Hannah had seen that Sia's *Chandelier* was on the list of singers' choices and gave it a go. Others had bravely tried it before her and had come up a long way short. It was an incredibly hard song that required a great range. It didn't help that, as expected, she had an anxiety attack just as she was about to be called on stage. An unscheduled break was introduced to allow her to calm down and breathe. After a period of meditation backstage, while the audience politely talked to each other, she moved up to the microphone, still visibly shaking, which affected the start of the song. But by the end, she had Vicky and Erica whispering to each other in an animated fashion.

Jack's piano performance could only be described as a disaster. The piano in the hall was a fairly new one and he had little opportunity to practise on it. He had asked whether the old one in the rehearsal room could be brought up but that wasn't possible. The new one was touch sensitive and Colin had done his best to find one as close as possible to the specification that he thought would suit Jack. But when he'd practised, it hadn't felt 'right', which neither he nor Colin could understand. This showed in the *Judgement Day* performance itself, with him being unable to play what came into in his head as he had practised.

For the Light Stone performance, they agreed to do an original song called *It's Time To Take Action*. Lyrics had been worked up mainly by Jack before the General Election in May and the others had contributed to the music. The performance started well enough:

Generation rent, you can't afford to own

A place to lay your head or even your own phone

The wealth's protected by a small minority

Who'll keep things the way they are with no equality

    It's time to take action and use your vote wisely

    We've got to work within this democracy

    We'll never win if we let them…

Judgement Day (June 2015)

But right as they were completing the first chorus, the fire alarm sounded. The crowd moved about in confusion before the building was evacuated in a hurry. Colin came out after half an hour; it was a false alarm.

Light Stone started again, but by then nerves had set in and they weren't together. Hannah was nervously looking around at the others, while for once, Rick had trouble keeping time and started slowing down for the others to catch up. Even Liam, who could normally be depended upon to keep his cool, fluffed both of his solos. Colin asked them if they wanted to have another run through as he thought the examiner would understand, but it was getting late and they didn't feel ready for it.

"We've blown it," Dan disappointedly let out afterwards and thumped the wall in desperation. "I think I saw Harry leave the hall a few minutes before the alarm went off. Maybe I'll follow him and have a word or two."

"I wouldn't bother," Rick advised. "You saw him go but he's only going to deny it. We have no proof, just a feeling. He'll deny that he threatened us beforehand. It's Liam who's come out worse here. I doubt he's going to achieve a good grade now."

"It's ok," Liam assured him. "I think we should keep rehearsing for our upcoming gigs. I won't need to go to the Music academy, anyway."

Colin called everyone back into the hall. He had half a smile on his face. Erica was having her make up fixed by her assistant, while Vicky stood on the stage and unfolded her arms as she moved towards the microphone, which she had to adjust down to her height.

"Right. This is the moment you've all been waiting for. For the last three terms, we have been reviewing your work and have now decided to whom we would like to award a spot at the famous ERCO Summer Ball, with a chance of winning a coveted ERCO recording contract. That winner is…

"HELLO HAMMERSMITH!"

"HANNAH ROSS!"

There was rapturous applause from everyone in Light Stone and their parents, and polite applause elsewhere. It was agreed that with that voice, Hannah would go far. She stood on stage between Erica and Vicky and tried to smile for the photos as best she could, but her face suggested disappointment. She was swept away for a private meeting with Erica and Vicky.

Colin approached the rest of Light Stone while their lead singer was escorted away. "I hear it was close and they nearly took you all as a band. But Vicky thought that you could have trouble breaking through at the moment, as your style is more singer-songwriter than contemporary. It's a shame for all of you, but they have a good recent track record with female singers and Hannah's just great, isn't she?"

"Yes, she deserves it," Liam agreed, a little ruefully. "But I thought we entered as a band and Hannah didn't want to go into this on her own?"

"Apparently it's not the first time that ERCO have made the rules up as they go along," Colin noted.

But the real question in everyone's mind was: 'Is this the end of Light Stone?'

♫ ♫ ♫ ♫ ♫ ♫ ♫ ♫ ♫ ♫ ♫ ♫ ♫ ♫ ♫

On the way back to London, tucked in the back of the limousine, Erica Conway could hardly hide the smug look on her face.

She was on the phone as usual. "Yes, we found the right winner. We pulled a few strings but nobody's going to complain. She's going to be an enormous asset to the research project. Oh, and *you* are going to like Hannah a lot! Just your type of girl." She disconnected.

"Well, that all worked out incredibly well. Congratulations Vicky."

Judgement Day (June 2015)

Vicky gave a thin smile. "Yes, Hannah has come on a long way since we first saw her at that Christmas concert. I told you then that she was the one. Her band of misfits have done a great job helping with her confidence issues and she's holding the stage better on her own now."

"They've served their purpose," observed Erica. "Let's speed up the process. We'll need to tidy her up ready for the Summer Ball and tie her up under contract ASAP so we can start recording her. We need some results, you know. If we manage this correctly, I can see ERCO making a ton of money out of this girl."

"I'll draw the standard contract up," Vicky replied brusquely. Erica reverted to her satisfied look out of the blackened window as the countryside swept past.

Chapter 14 - Love of My Life (August 1995)

Gerry collected the post from the front door mat. One package looked like it contained a CD, so instinctively that was the first one that he opened. To his amazement, the package was from ERCO and contained an album of their old demos called *Lost and Found*. There was a compliments slip with a handwritten note from Ernie Conway that read 'Found these tapes while we were having a clear out. I thought we'd lost them for good. Hope you're bearing up and like the new mixes!' A look of thunder crossed Gerry's face.

He had also received his subscription copy of Music Week and the discovery under new releases that ERCO had officially released these lost recordings did nothing to improve his mood.

Gerry shouted up the stairs. "Hey Bernie, come and look at this. ERCO are having a little dance on our graves."

Bernie came downstairs, looking a little the worst for wear. She saw the CD and screwed her face up, then read the article that Gerry offered her. "Crumbs. They must be desperate."

"If I remember correctly, these were some of the rough recordings that we worked up before we scrapped everything and started again with what became the *Separate Rooms* album. I can remember tossing the tapes away in a bin and later hoping they were buried somewhere they would never be found. I can't imagine that they're going to sell that many. We didn't even put titles to some of these and they were mostly just random snippets of ideas. We only came away with the rights to the songs that had been recorded for the albums. Better put it on and see what they've done to them, I suppose."

Gerry popped the CD into the surround sound cinema system in the lounge. The two of them sat down on the sofa and listened to the first few tracks. They were both speechless, opening their mouths in horror, looking at each other but not actually saying anything.

Finally, Bernie broke the silence. "They've made you a backing vocalist and just left me upfront."

"Plus, they've added a load of bloody horns and strings," Gerry added, turning the volume down from the remote. "This is awful. If we had any of our reputation left, then this will kill it. I knew Ernie could stoop low. I can't believe they can do this without our permission!"

"Probably nothing we can do. We didn't think these recordings would be of any value. They're still not but we'll see. I guess music has some value to those who don't create it."

Gerry went quiet for a moment. "Let's see how it sells. If it sells well, then maybe we should re-record all those songs, but here at the Chapel. We could do them much better and cut their revenue off."

Bernie smiled. "Just like the old days then. You definitely will need to re-record them to extract any money out of them. I'm sure ERCO will wriggle out of paying any royalties. Anyway, now that we've moved that out of the way, I have some more bad news for you. You'd better sit down. I'm afraid I've just miscarried again."

Gerry's face collapsed. He rushed to put his arms round Bernie and hugged her quietly.

Thoughts of re-recording some old demos were swiftly forgotten.

♪ ♪ ♪ ♪ ♪ ♪ ♪ ♪ ♪ ♪ ♪ ♪ ♪ ♪ ♪

The distress had partially dissolved itself later that afternoon. Bernie had gone upstairs to lie down while Gerry remained downstairs. Something had crossed his mind and he searched out his pile of old Music Week papers he was meaning to throw out. After a time, he found the feature on ERCO that he was looking for. It included an interview with Ernie

Love of My Life (August 1995)

Conway, which set out his impending retirement plans and the announcement of the handover of some of the management of ERCO to his young son Eric. 'He still has things to learn,' Ernie said, 'but he's a chip off the old block and has a good ear for the up-and-coming trends I would probably miss. His particular interest is in pushing the careers of female musicians and I've told him to look for the next Madonna or Kylie. There's definitely a great team behind him.'

Gerry vaguely remembered that prior to this, Eric had secured a job with a bigger record company but had left under a cloud. Why that happened? He couldn't remember. He phoned Oscar Good.

"Hey Oscar. It's Gerry. Sorry to trouble you, but have you seen that ERCO have released some of our rubbish old recordings?" He stopped to listen. "You did? Well, don't waste your money on it. I've a copy here that you can have; otherwise it's going in the bin. I can assure you it's awful. Anyway Oscar, tell me what you know about Ernie's son Eric. Oh… Really? Did he now?… Crumbs. No wonder they kicked him out. That's just confirming what was at the back of my mind. Thanks very much, Oscar." Gerry put the phone down with a pensive look on his face.

Going into the recording room, he was careful to shut the door so as not to disturb his wife. He picked up the Hofner acoustic and started looking for simple chords that sounded good together. Before long, he had come up with four chords, all of which needed only two fingers and could be moved smoothly from one to the next. Starting with E minor 7, onto C minor 7, which left one finger where it was, then A minor 7 and finally one that sounded good, but wasn't an obvious one. He pulled out his chord encyclopaedia to work out that it was a D9. The chords worked well together and the D9 could easily go back to the E minor 7 to start the loop again. "Oh well, at least it's not a standard I-V-IV-vi progression," he muttered. He recorded the four chords onto his Minidisc recorder for about 4 minutes and then listened back to it, thinking and jotting down notes on his pad. He played it through again, quietly singing along to the backing track before making a few more notes. On the third run through, he added a simple instrumental break

"HELLO HAMMERSMITH!"

and then, satisfied, recorded both the vocals and instrumental break onto the second track.

Bernie came down and entered the studio, rubbing her eyes. "What have you been up to, pet?"

"Oh, not a great deal, just wrote something simple and sweet for you. Take a seat." Bernie sat down on the spare chair in the studio while Gerry set the tape going and then sang over it.

> *I know when I open my eyes, you'll be there by my side*
>
> *You can sleep while I arise and know that I love you deep inside*
>
> > *Love of my life – love of my life*
>
> *We met so long ago, we've barely been apart*
>
> *If there's one thing that I know, it's that I love you with all my heart*
>
> > *Love of my life – love of my life*

He played the instrumental break before the last verse:

> *There's no doubt you are the one. You know where I came from.*
>
> *You must be second to none. You helped me be what I've become.*
>
> > *Love of my life – love of my life*

As he turned off the machine, Bernie brushed some tears from her eyes. "Oh Gerry, pet. That was beautiful. I knew things could only get better."

"I meant every word, old girl. We'll pull through, just wait and see."

"Less of the 'old girl'. I'm still worried about the money you know. We've cleared the old debts I guess and the royalties are still trickling in, but if things don't improve, we're going to have to sell this place and downsize again."

Love of My Life (August 1995)

"I hope not. This Chapel is the only place where I want to live. In fact, I talked about ERCO dancing on our graves earlier, didn't I? I think I'd like to be buried here. Just over there under the tree, I think."

"Crumbs. I think it's a bit early to be thinking about that, pet. We have plenty of songs to write. We've plenty of life to live yet."

"Now there's a song title! I think I should make a start on that."

"Two songs in a day?" Bernie mocked. "You'd better take it easy you old boyo. You'll strain yourself."

"Oh, there's plenty of energy in this boyo yet!" Gerry exclaimed as he gently put his arm around his wife.

"Oi! There'll be none of that just at the moment thank you. If you're not careful, you're going to feel a knee right where it hurts. I told you I gave Sid Vicious one of those, remember?"

Chapter 15 - Rock The Cuban (July/August 2015)

Since the end of term, Light Stone had kept to their schedule. They decided they would carry on without Hannah and rehearse as much as possible. Local concerts were arranged on at least one night every weekend. Colin continued to feed more and more advanced material to Jack and Liam. Also, Sue McLeod approved Colin's special request, enabling the band to rehearse at the college. This meant, to their relief, that Rick's drum kit didn't need to be taken apart and moved at the end of every day. Liam, Dan and Jack used the practice amps and only needed to bring their guitars along and in Jack's case, his keyboard. That sped up the setup time and meant they got started faster. As the rehearsal space was underground, they didn't disturb anyone except the building maintenance workers. The principal's only proviso was that Colin had to be present while they were using any of the facilities.

Both Jack and Liam had taken jobs in a local supermarket in town while they waited for the exam results to come through. They came to work from different directions and would pass notes of song ideas to each other while they were stacking the shelves in the evening. They practised on their own when it wasn't possible to get together with Rick and Dan.

Jack noticed Liam was more subdued without Hannah around.

"Really miss her, don't you?"

Liam shrugged. "It's OK. It isn't meant to be is it?"

"Who knows? No point in giving up on something you want. What d'you like about her?"

Liam shrugged again. "Well, she's better than me. We fight a bit but there's spirit in her. If she sets her mind to something, then it gets done, which is something that I've always struggled with."

"HELLO HAMMERSMITH!"

"Doesn't always help things, does it?"

"I know what you mean. Suppose not."

Jack was quite content to be stacking shelves late at night when there were few other people around. When they didn't have an evening shift, they looked for any local bands in concert. They would arrive as early as possible and watch as much of the setting up as they could. They would talk to the sound and lighting engineers and then stay until the last bus was due to see the dismantling process as well. Jack took detailed notes of everything that seemed important.

In the meantime, Colin had mentioned to his fellow tutors that there was an interesting band doing some rehearsals in the basement during the holidays. Before they knew it, a group of students from the Film course would come, film and edit rehearsals for upload on the college's YouTube channel. Other Art Department students would design posters for the local gigs for which the band were getting booked.

The band guessed Liam had quietly been keeping Hannah in touch with what they were up to. Every now and again, Hannah would turn up unannounced for band practice. Everyone realised they sounded a lot better with her in the band. They had expected that she would disappear up to London as soon as the ERCO announcement had been made. But it seemed her parents weren't in the least bit happy about her winning the chance of a contract.

When pressed during a drinks break in rehearsals, she explained. "Well, my parents obviously hoped that I'd follow a professional path similar to them as doctors and they'd always struggled to accept my interest in a career as uncertain as the performing arts. They're being over-protective about my confidence issues and they're trying as much as they can to counter this."

"Don't suppose that winning the ERCO competition really helped, then?" Rick commented.

Rock The Cuban (July/August 2015)

"You're right there. The spotlight has been on me way too much. Anyway, although I'm 18 and can legally sign a contract without my parents' permission, I'm sitting tight. I can afford to wait until A Level results are out before thinking seriously about what I want to do."

"Didn't they want you to sing at the ERCO Summer Ball competition?" Rick questioned. "I was hoping you needed a drummer!"

"Oh, that's been and gone. I had a load of pressure from them to take part and benefit from the exposure, but the worry that it was exactly the type of event that would raise my anxiety issues to the surface meant that I just didn't respond. Vicky ended up coming round to the house, at which point I told her firmly that I could only do it if Light Stone were my backing band. This royally angered Vicky who thundered something like there being absolutely *no way* that bunch of losers will be involved. She even tried banning me from seeing you. They reckon that every previous winner has been delighted to secure the chance of a spot at the famous ERCO Summer Ball and an ERCO contract. Nobody had questioned any of that before. Well, I'm not going to become their latest victim, no matter how bad it looks for me."

"But weren't they only going to award the contract to the winner at the Summer Ball?" Rick persisted.

"That was all hot air. Nobody who played at the ball was good enough to be a winner. They just wanted to get me under contract."

While Hannah and her family made a stand and refused to compromise, the downsized Light Stone carried on. Jack reluctantly took on all the lead vocals when Hannah wasn't available. With Liam's singing voice non-existent, Rick and Dan filled in on backing vocals as best they could.

Colin could also use the college van to transport them around. "It's not going to be doing anything else for the holidays. Just fuel it up and it's yours," had been Sue McLeod's verdict. Colin had also done a lot of work with the band on planning and pacing set lists, which included original songs and some suitable covers. He took care of the stage setup, sound and lighting systems. With all that in place, the band took the plunge and started looking for local low-key gigs for some proper stage practice. At their first show they had stuck to covers, which didn't work at all. They agreed afterwards that it had been dreadful but were determined not to give up. Things seemed to improve once they tried their own original songs. After all, as Liam reckoned, "Nobody knows what they're supposed to sound like, so they don't know when it's gone wrong."

As she still wasn't under contract, Hannah would quietly turn up at the gigs and creep onto the back of the stage where her microphone had been set up and there was no lighting. No matter how quiet and unobtrusive she was, as soon as her voice was heard, tremendous applause and cheering followed. This eventually coaxed her out from the wings, but Colin kept any spotlight away from her.

That prompted Vicky Tucker to come down from London with a bodyguard to see them at local gigs and begrudgingly agree that the practice had made them tighter. She soon realised that she was not alone. The publicity surrounding Hannah's contract issues had alerted other record labels to her talent and often at least a couple were represented in the audience. Some of them were quiet about it, but others didn't mind everyone knowing why they were there. Rick and Dan were happy about all of this, as they still harboured hopes of using this as a lever to move up to London. They didn't much mind whether it was with Hannah, Light Stone or anyone else. The band did notice, however, that Vicky's bodyguard was quietly going over to address some of the more vocal scouts, who either quietened down or left altogether.

The best gigs were when they were on the bill for local festivals. Even though they would be on stage in the early afternoon, the audience would have had enough time to have a few drinks and be determined to enjoy themselves. While the band would take the stage to little or no applause, they would usually leave to standing ovations and calls for an encore. In the middle of each performance, the others would leave the stage while Jack sat at his keyboard, shut his eyes, and played the opening bars of the *Judgement Day* improvisation that he had continued to practise since the ill-fated exam. It was different every time.

With Sue McLeod also allowing them to access the recording facilities at the college, they recorded some rough demos for the original songs that they had been rehearsing. By this time, rehearsals and recording sessions had been posted to the band's new YouTube account after a bit of editing. Some of the finished recordings were then posted to their SoundCloud account. From there, videos and recordings were shared on Light Stone's other social network accounts. Hannah was an uncredited vocalist given her delicate negotiations with ERCO. Before long, they had 2,000 followers on Facebook, which helped the publicity for their local gigs. It's fair to say that a good number of the audience had been attracted by Hannah's presence in the group.

Their most successful song at the summer festivals had been *Rock the Cuban*. The Cuban was a night-time venue in the middle of town that was popular with students. Jack was the only member of Light Stone not yet 18 years old, so he was limited to drinking soft drinks while Rick treated everyone else to cocktails. He seemed to produce cash from any of his pockets with a smile, especially if girls were around.

Colin had tasked Jack and Liam with coming up with a rockabilly song. Jack had an idea for the song's main lyrics while watching the others get drunk one Friday night. Liam helped him with the music over a fast beat. It was simple, quite rough, but captured the mood.

> *Well listen here – don't tell me what to do*
>
> *We've had enough of school and all the rules*
>
> *It's Friday night. The city's hot.*
>
> *It's time to pass around the shots*
>
> *Do what we can to make the Cuban rock*

"HELLO HAMMERSMITH!"

> *We're gonna – rock the Cuban – rock the Cuban – rock the Cuban – rock the Cuban*
>
> *Do what we can to make the Cuban rock*

The Jägarbombs have only lit the fuse

The Kamikaze takes away your blues

We've started now and we can't stop

Let's try a Flaming Lemondrop

Do what we can to make the Cuban rock

> *We're gonna – rock the Cuban – rock the Cuban – rock the Cuban – rock the Cuban*
>
> *Do what we can to make the Cuban rock*

It's 3am and later than you think

The barman says this is our final drink

He says there's rules that he can't bend

Or there could be a sticky end

Do what we can to make the Cuban rock

> *We're gonna – rock the Cuban – rock the Cuban – rock the Cuban – rock the Cuban*
>
> *Do what we can to make the Cuban rock*

This became the song with which they would finish their festival sets.

In the background, the wait had carried on for A Level results to come out in the third week of August. The results were finally pinned up on a noticeboard in a hall in the college. The staff witnessed the chaotic crush of students coming in to look at the sheet and relieve the suspense. There weren't many smiles from the Music students.

Liam and Hannah surprised nobody by topping the list with As, even after the fire alarm interruption. Rick and Dan were happy to achieve Ds and Jack scraped an E.

"Uh oh, I can't see Harry's name on the list," Rick whispered.

"Yes, I think we were all expecting better grades than we got," Liam suggested.

Later that day, a rumour did the rounds, undenied by Cynthia, that Harry's parents had bribed the Head of Music to increase his suggested grade, but this had been spotted by the Examination Board. There were repercussions on the entire class as everyone's grades were reduced by one in case others had been involved. All they knew was that Colin hadn't been in a good mood for the few days before the results were published and the Head of Department was nowhere to be seen at the start of the next term.

When Colin caught up with Jack later that day, they had a long conversation. Jack had learnt that taking risks, such as improvising on a strange piano in an A Level exam, wasn't always a great idea, but what good were qualifications anyway?

♫ ♫ ♫ ♫ ♫ ♫ ♫ ♫ ♫ ♫ ♫ ♫ ♫ ♫ ♫

Meanwhile, at ERCO HQ, discussions continued.

"Come on, Vicky, it's not like you to be defeated by some stroppy teenager," goaded Erica.

"Ah, I know, but little Hannah is a tough nut to crack. She knows her own mind and her parents are equally stubborn. I do have an idea, but you might not like it."

"What's that? I'm open to any thoughts at the moment."

"HELLO HAMMERSMITH!"

"Well, we could do what she asks and take Hannah with her crap band on a contract. Record some songs for the research project and present Hannah as the major talent, which she is. Dump the backing band, by which time we have her under a tight contract, with no way out. She can definitely be a troublemaker, so we sell on her contract to the highest bidder and recoup the investment."

"OK, I like it. You've got the makings of an evil record company owner yourself there, Vicky. Have that conversation with Hannah and her parents."

Rock The Cuban (July/August 2015)

Chapter 16 - This Love Story (June/July 1995)

Things were looking up again for Gerry and Bernie. Gerry's recovery was still going well but they knew that producing anything under the Stanford name was likely to be greeted with derision in the pop press. They had written a song in a different style which lent itself to a different audience. Bernie had been listening to a lot of Donna Summer since the New Year and wrote what felt like a disco song. As she ran the idea past Gerry, he quickly heard Donna in his head, singing it. He vaguely thought about asking if Donna's management would be happy for her to add some vocals to it, but saw that she was preparing for an *Endless Summer* tour, so dismissed the crazy idea.

"Hey, Bernie. Do you remember that disco song that you started?"

"Sure. Have you done something with it?"

"Yes, it's ready to be recorded."

"Oh good. Who's going to do the vocals on it?"

"You are, dear."

"WHAT? Have you gone stark staring mad again? You agreed with me it had a Donna Summer vibe. We have totally different vocal styles and I'm not in her league."

"Exactly. Nobody will ever guess that it's you."

"Well, you've lost me and you might have to go back to the doctor again. And that's without dealing with my hearing issues. It can't work."

"Look, I can treat your vocals so you sound more like a disco diva and we can fiddle with the headphone levels so that you can hear the backing track. Come on, let's give it a go. See what happens?"

"HELLO HAMMERSMITH!"

It was the first time in a while that Bernie had gone into the vocal booth and put on the headphones. Prior to the session, she had to warm up her voice over many days. It took a while for her to become used to hearing the backing track. She didn't want to do further damage to her delicate ears. She had listened to Gerry's rough guide track to hear the melody. As the backing track played through her ears, she shut her eyes to concentrate on the lyrics in the first verse:

Heaven knows – and everything around us shows

That we get stronger as it grows – with messages of love

You and me – together we'll make history

We'll take those opportunities – with help from God above

PRE-CHORUS:

One day they'll write the story – the stars are you and me

And that is when the world will come to see

And they'll say….

CHORUS:

    This love story tells it just the way it's s'posed to be

    Two people come together and share their history

    We don't know all the answers – but everyone agrees

    That we will stay as one – richer or poorer

    And turn the hurricane into a breeze

Verse 2:

Down inside – don't get caught with foolish pride

Blow the other things aside – it's only you and me

Believe in us – we were always meant to be

Me for you and you for me – 'til eternity

This Love Story (June/July 1995)

Gerry had various versions of the song. One was of a shorter single length which would work on the radio and another was a much longer extended mix, which featured a lengthy instrumental break in the middle. It was this latter version that unlocked the audience in the various London clubs after Bernie had the bright idea of privately getting some white label 12-inch vinyl copies made. She then sent them out to clubs with only Archie's phone number as a contact.

When some DJs took a chance on it and it was clearly popular, word spread quickly to other clubs who then contacted 'Archie' asking for a copy. By March, there was enough demand for a commercial release of both versions on a minor dance label.

The single was released under the mysterious 'Pigott' name. There was a connection to the Stanford name, but Gerry was pretty sure that nobody would work it out. The shorter version briefly brushed the lower reaches of the official charts after some limited airplay and then slowly disappeared. It was many years before word spread that disgraced pop singer-songwriters Gerry and Bernie Stanford were behind it, with plaudits for having foiled people for a long time.

♫ ♫ ♫ ♫ ♫ ♫ ♫ ♫ ♫ ♫ ♫ ♫ ♫ ♫ ♫

In the meantime, Bernie had been thinking about other ways to make a living from music and wondered whether they could move into creating film and TV scores from the Chapel studio. They had worked on a few ideas by taking some films and putting their own scores over the pictures, which seemed to work well, but it didn't feel right. Gerry knew a few people in that sector, but there was one in particular who would help them and be honest. Right on cue, the doorbell of the Chapel sounded. Standing on the porch dressed in his uniform of a blue check shirt and blue jeans was the smiling face of Colin Garrett.

"Colin, thank you so much for coming. It's great to see you."

"HELLO HAMMERSMITH!"

"Hey, it's great to see you out and about again mate. And thank you for letting me inside this cool place." Colin walked into the living area. "Oh wow, this is fantastic." His eye was immediately drawn to the pipe organ on the left-hand side of the room.

"Wow! Does that old girl work?"

"Absolutely. Why don't you jump on and give it a blast?"

"I don't mind if I do. Are you sure you're not going to race and beat me to it like the old times?"

"Certainly not. You're my guest this time."

Colin stopped, took off his glasses and gave them a wipe with the loose tail of his shirt. Popping the glasses back on, he settled down and had a quick look at the various knobs. He expertly selected a few to pull out before playing the first few minutes of Bach's *Toccata and Fugue* in D minor.

At a natural break, he smiled and turned around to take in the full effect of the rest of the room with its vaulted ceiling and the enormous windows around him. "This place is fabulous. Did you do all this?"

"Kind of. It had the original features when we bought it; pews and everything. Even had the altar and a font for baptisms. The font went outside for the birds to drink from and I needed room for the Steinway, so the altar was recycled. We kept the organ though; it needs some more work but as you can hear, it still makes quite a noise."

"It sure does. I bet it adds some atmosphere to your recordings, mate," Colin uttered pensively as he continued to look around in wonder. "Can I have a look in the studio?"

Gerry proudly showed Colin the control room with the mixing desk and a multitude of leads going in all directions. "It's all fairly up-to-date stuff, should last me a few years," he grinned, knowing full well that

This Love Story (June/July 1995)

technology was marching on and the equipment risked being obsolete sooner than he would like. "After what happened, we wanted to invest much of what we had left in this."

"I don't blame you, mate. What happened to you was a disgrace; could have happened to any songwriter though. There but for the grace of God and all that…" He tailed off as he realised what he had said. "Anyway, you didn't just invite me here so that I could dribble and drool over your cool home. Tell me your plans."

Bernie came and joined them as they sat down. Colin was curious about what they expected to achieve out of moving into TV and soundtrack work.

Gerry started the explanation. "Well, we think we could do with a total change of direction and spread our wings. We've been doing pop and rock songs for so long that we were inevitably repeating ourselves a lot towards the end. I wrote a new song last week and played it to Bernie. It sounded familiar so I wondered if she might recognise it."

"And, of course, I had heard it before and swiftly told him which one of our own ruddy songs he had copied. It was almost identical to one of the album tracks on the *Blindside* album!"

They all laughed.

"We could do with keeping a low profile for a few more years until people forget what happened."

"I understand all of that," confessed Colin. "First, I'd warn that it took me about five years before I secured a meaningful bit of film soundtrack work and 10 years before it became a full-time job for me. It's a hell of an investment. Also, I think you manoeuvred yourselves into a position with Stanford where you called the shots and could record pretty much what you wanted without the outside interference of record companies. I'm afraid you'll go back to square one on this. You'd be dealing with directors who have a certain style of music in their head and will want you to recreate it to their strict brief. The most annoying ones will say that what you've been spending weeks on 'isn't what we had in mind at all' and 'can you do something like X?' You can put up with the interference for a while, but I don't know for how long. With what you've been through, is that somewhere you think you would like to go?"

Gerry was thoughtful. "Hmm, I understand what you mean. That wouldn't be a risk that we would need to take at the moment. Are there any positives at all?"

"Oh sure. The royalty cheques keep rolling in from repeats if you negotiate the contract right and I'm now getting to the stage where I can be choosy about who I work with and what I work on. Also, I can walk the streets without being recognised at all. That suits me just fine."

"That sounds appealing. I was never that keen on the fame thing and being recognised. Bit late to change that though," Gerry smiled ruefully.

It was Bernie who drew the meeting to a close. "Look, Colin, we appreciate you taking the time to visit and help us cross that idea off the list."

"Oh, that was my pleasure. To tell you the truth, I'd never considered wanting to live in a church or chapel until now." He paused and looked around him. "You've done a great job here. If you ever find yourselves fed up with it and want to sell, would you give me first refusal? I don't need to live in London anymore and I often think we should move back now that my parents are getting frailer."

"It would be cruel to raise your hopes, Colin. I think we're settled here now and want to put down some roots. Anyway, it cost us so much to do the place up, we wouldn't get our money back. We'll bear you in mind if that changes."

"I'll tell you what though. Here's an idea to think about. There's a need for recording studios out in the country. They're stupidly expensive in

This Love Story (June/July 1995)

London and a lot of bands want to move out of the city and back to nature. You could make an interesting living offering your services as a producer. After all, you have all the gear here."

"Hmm… Thanks Colin. That's not a bad idea," mused Bernie. "I'll give that some thought."

♪ ♪ ♪ ♪ ♪ ♪ ♪ ♪ ♪ ♪ ♪ ♪ ♪ ♪ ♪

Over the summer, Gerry and Bernie started experimenting. They took Colin's advice and opened the doors of the Chapel as a recording venue. Bernie drew up an advert offering a chance to work with an award-winning musician and producer, without mentioning names. That generated a lot of interest. Some of it evaporated when their identity was revealed as 'just a pair of '80s has-beens in their home studio'. Eventually, it was the bargain prices that persuaded a few bands to take the chance and the venture made it off the ground.

Gerry and Bernie's previous experience recording in converted churches clued them up about the ideal recording acoustics of such buildings. Locating the instruments in the soundproofed recording room was fine, but sometimes being out in the vaulted lounge produced a fuller, echoey sound. In search of what The Beatles termed 'bog echo', even the downstairs toilet could generate certain of the more acoustic arrangements that were needed. All it needed was some air freshener, a microphone and the door shut as far as it could to allow access for the lead.

Every so often, Bernie found her kitchen invaded by a team of musicians looking for the 'right sound'. Since she hadn't seen Gerry this happy and focused on music for a long time, she took it all in good spirits. Her husband had been rarely inspired to write new songs recently, but now she could see ideas sparking in his brain.

The owners of the village pub were not keen when the first group turned up. Bernie herself was initially perturbed when the Demons of Death arrived to stay in the Old School House next door to the Chapel. All of their clothes were black, leather, or both. They had been drawn to the Chapel's recording studio by the prospect of recording some dark organ sounds. Bernie soon found that the band were the tidiest and best-mannered guests they had encountered in a long time. They became huge favourites in the pub, charming the old regulars. In the evening, after they completed their recording sessions for the day, they would play acoustic ballads such as *Whiskey in the Jar* for this audience. They would then ask their listeners to reveal their favourite songs. The regulars tried to catch them out by requesting recent popular songs such as Robson and Jerome's *Unchained Melody* or Take That's *Back for Good*. Luckily Gerry would be on hand to lead the proceedings on the pub piano and heavy treatments of these songs were soon dispatched with unnerving accuracy. Word soon spread and before long, the pub was full mid-week every time a band was recording in the Chapel.

The Demons of Death had only one issue. "I'm not being funny, Gerry," their lead guitarist pleaded one day, "but we're going to be mocked if the name Gerry Stanford appears on the liner notes as the engineer and producer of the record. Especially with you two having been a Prince and Princess of Pop and all that. Could we just dream up another name for you?"

"Sure," Gerry reassured him. They'd already issued *This Love Story* under the 'Pigott' moniker and got away with it, so the pseudonym of Sam Pigott appeared in the credits of a wide range of recordings.

Bernie was busy making tea, cakes and lunch. She was treated like Pop Royalty and they always referred to her as 'Princess Bernie', without a hint of irony. They kept asking her stories about her days in The Pogoes. She would blush, but still act up with the attention and reel off another tale about the revolving cast of characters in London in the late seventies and her life in the second wave of punk bands from the era.

Some bands who used the Old School House were a good deal untidier than the Demons of Death. As a result, they were on the receiving end

This Love Story (June/July 1995)

of stern words from Bernie, who would draw herself up to her full height and sternly point out that their clothes would need to go in the basket provided and not be left on bedroom floors if they wanted washing done.

If Gerry found he was fed up, it was with the lack of depth in the lyrics of most bands that passed through. "If I hear *Baby, I Love You* one more time I'm going to throw up," he confessed to his partner one evening after everyone had gone. "The Ronettes and the Ramones are the only versions you need. Incidentally, you said that you'd met the Ramones. I don't suppose you asked them why on earth they covered that song?"

"No, that didn't come up. They were too busy pulling our leg about copying their idea of making the band's name our stage names."

This thought took Bernie back to 1976 in a Welsh mining town. Hearing the Ramones for the first time inspired her for an alternative to marrying a miner who wouldn't have a job for long. Her dad often brought home likely lads hoping that she would be keen on one of them, but her rebellious nature always meant that they were given short shrift.

Although they didn't need to, the Stanfords also offered to use the space to help young local artists who were trying to establish themselves. Gerry had put a card on the noticeboard of his old college with the headline 'Free recording studio available for college students'. There wasn't any proper recording facilities at the college, so calls started coming in from students either at the end of their first year or awaiting their A Level results. This put Gerry on the radar of the college again.

One day the household received an unusual call. "Is that Gerry Stanford?" a girl's voice asked at the other end of the phone.

"Yes, it is," Gerry answered, a little warily.

"Hello Mr Stanford. My name is Gillian Fox. I hope you don't mind, but I saw your note on the noticeboard at the college today. I'm going to be on the Music Composition and Performance course next year and I'd like some experience of recording before I start there. Would that be possible?"

The relief that Gerry felt relaxed him immediately. It wasn't the crank caller that he feared. "Well, I don't see why not. Hang on while I have a look at the diary. Let's see…. Yes, I have a few days in mid-August and there's nobody else there. How does that suit you?"

"Oh, I'll take anything that you can offer, Mr Stanford. By the way, my dad has all your albums… even *Album 5*."

"Yikes, then he needs his head examined, Gillian. You should keep a close eye on him," Gerry laughed.

It only took a first visit for Gerry to realise that Gillian had a rare talent. Even Bernie was tempted out of the kitchen by the songs that Gillian had and the arrangements that Gerry could construct around them.

"I've got a feeling about this one," her husband said to her after the first night.

"As do I," Bernie confirmed.

There was only one thing that could have spoilt the summer for them, and it was good that they were too busy to contemplate it. *That Song* was covered by one of ERCO's new female artists and was the surprise hit of the summer. As it had steadily climbed up the charts, it had a chance of going all the way to number 1, so Gerry and Bernie were actually relieved that The Outhere Brothers monopolised that spot throughout July and fought off all incomers. Ordinarily, they would have hated hearing that style of song, but they cheered whenever it came on the radio.

Following on from that, Stanford's ex manager, Harvey, took some calls from people interested in discussing a Stanford reunion. As agreed, he had passed on 'Archie's' number for them to call instead. 'Archie' was

This Love Story (June/July 1995)

never available when the London number was called, but there was always a promise that he would call them back.

"Good afternoon, this is Archie," Gerry would say in a vaguely Scottish accent. "Tell me what you're interested in……"

On this occasion, he listened as the proposition was explained. "Oh, you want to use a song in the catalogue for an advert? Are you going to use the original or re-record it? You want to re-record it? Oh, that's a shame. The Stanfords don't approve any re-recording of their songs for adverts. I'm sorry I can't help you. Goodbye."

"Another TV advert request?" Bernie would enquire.

"I'm afraid so," Gerry would sigh as he'd put the phone gently down.

"And I thought this 'Archie' promised to discuss every offer with me before you made your mind up and called people back? There are times you make my blood boil. Some easy money would be useful you know!"

"Maybe."

"You could at least have told them they could have paid to use the original recording that we made!"

"They weren't interested."

"I didn't hear that mentioned."

"I could hear between the lines."

"You really are bloody useless sometimes," said an indignant Bernie as she stomped up the stairs and slammed the bedroom door.

Chapter 17 - The Letter (29/30 August 2015)

It was Jack's 18th birthday and he had returned late the previous night from Light Stone's gig at a pub in West Kent. This was the first time the band had ventured over that side of the county and the reaction hadn't been great. It was good that some of their local fans, including regulars Angie and Sarah, had followed them to give support. That had helped a lot. They both took a lot of photos as usual and had sent the best ones over to Hannah for posting on the band's various social media accounts. The set was a complete mixture of covers, party songs and what were becoming the Light Stone signature songs of agenda rock for disaffected youth. Bizarrely, any mistakes seemed to endear them to a core of fans. They secured a decent number of new email addresses on the list at the merchandise desk and the journey back in the van had left them in reasonable spirits. A video team of film students who were between years came along and filmed the concert as well. Colin dropped them all off reasonably close to their respective homes so they did not have to contend with long walks down dark country lanes.

Jack came downstairs at around 10am to find his auntie and uncle waiting for him in the kitchen. There was a pile of envelopes and presents on the table.

"Good morning, birthday boy. How are you feeling?" asked his aunt.

"Ok, I suppose. Bit tired."

"I'll do your favourite — a sausage sandwich with brown sauce. Is that ok?"

Jack answered, "Sure", but actually would have preferred his usual selection of assorted cereals. He opened the cards first.

"Good gig last night?" his Uncle Jim asked, trying his best to sound interested.

"Not bad. Bit worried that the stage monitors were too loud. Now got ringing ears."

"You should be careful about that," his auntie warned. "Your mum had terrible hearing by the end of the touring."

"If we ever make enough money, we'll buy in-ear monitors," Jack agreed. "There were a few tech issues that we sorted out and a few more names for the email list. There were also a few record company A&R people there."

"Did Hannah make it?" Jim asked.

"Yes. Apparently, she's stopped talking to ERCO and they're pretty angry. Contract isn't great and she's just not confident being on her own in the spotlight. Didn't like the way they seemed to want to package her either."

Before long, the birthday boy had been through nearly everything and left separate neat piles of envelopes, cards, wrapping paper, cheques and other presents. Only one envelope remained at the bottom. Addressed to 'Jackson Stanford' rather than 'Jack Michaels' it was dated 29 August 1998. Jack sensed who had written the contents and opened it with care, unfolding the thick paper and beginning to read the typed print.

Dear Jackson,

Happy 18th birthday, son. As we write this, we wish with all our heart that we could have been there to tell you this in person, but we hope these words can still convey our pride and our love for you. Please be assured that, if at all possible, we'll be watching over you, keeping you from harm and guiding you through life.

We have today signed wills which, in the event of our passing, will trigger a guardianship instruction to enable Mabel and Jim to care for you until you are 18 years old, using funds that are being held in trust for

The Letter (29/30 August 2015)

you. It won't have been a straightforward task for them, but we know they will have done their best for you.

Apart from the Danemann piano, which Mabel has agreed should be in the house, all of our belongings have been stored in an industrial unit just outside town. This now all belongs to you, along with whatever money is left in the trust after your expenses have been paid.

We hope that the trickle of royalties will be enough to cover costs of storage and your upbringing.

Always be assured that we love you dearly and would have done anything to have been with you on this day.

Love

Mum and Dad XXX

Jack read the letter a few times and showed it to Mabel, who had tears in her eyes. She handed it back and could only quickly utter the words. "Eat your breakfast. It's getting cold."

A long silence ensued. Mabel was the first to speak.

"Jack, we've been planning this day for some time. We've booked an appointment for you with Paul Eagle. He's the other trustee looking after your trust fund besides us. But before that, we've arranged for access to the unit where most of your mum and dad's belongings are stored. You can have a look through and see what you would like to keep. If you want anything thrown away, we can arrange that."

"There's a lot of old rubbish in there if you ask me," added Jim.

Jack nodded without speaking and made his way up to his room to wash and be ready. Jim and Mabel watched him leave and looked at each other.

"HELLO HAMMERSMITH!"

"I thought it would be a bit much for him. He seems dazed," Mabel remarked.

"Come on Mabel. He's always dazed. I don't think we'll ever work out what's going on in that head of his. I shudder to think."

In reality, Jack was keen to find out more about his parents and was dressed and ready to go within 15 minutes.

At the industrial unit, the site storeman unlocked the doors and swung them open. There was room to walk inside even though the space was packed. What looked like stage sets, lighting rigs and PA systems took up the most space. Down one side, there were flight cases which had been stencilled with the Stanford logo. Jack opened up a case and found some bulky vintage keyboards, far larger than the one that he carried from one gig to another. Inside an unlabelled box, he found a pile of MiniDiscs and one caught his eye. A handwritten note on it read 'Love of My Life'. He had never seen a Minidisc before, but he took that one and replaced the lid on the box.

Another heavy wooden crate was full of award discs; silver, gold and platinum. He could remember the colours that they reflected in the main room of the Chapel. In the corner was a guitar case that had seen better days and Jack felt drawn to it. He unclipped the catches, one of which was broken, and opened the case. There rested an old acoustic guitar. It had huge gouges below the sound hole and a stencilled name of Hofner at the bottom. For the first time that day, Jack smiled as he remembered his dad playing this guitar to help him drift off to sleep. He shut the case and picked up the guitar case by its worn handle and a suitcase that was nearby. The suitcase was heavier than he expected, and he briefly considered leaving it behind. Thankfully, Jim was on hand to give him a hand and the case was loaded into the car boot.

"Well done, Jack," Mabel praised him, putting an arm around the teenager. "That must have been tough. You've handled it well. There is just Paul Eagle to see now and then the day is yours."

The Letter (29/30 August 2015)

"Had enough for today," Jack almost whispered. "Need to go home. Take a break from this." Mabel looked at Jim, who shrugged.

"Perhaps you're right," she sighed. "It's a lot to take in. Let's go home and phone Paul from there. I'm sure he can see us another day."

When they arrived home, Jim carried the suitcase and Jack took the guitar case up to his bedroom. Once alone upstairs, Jack closed the door and opened up the guitar case again. He picked up the battered Hofner gently, holding it by its neck, and gave it a closer look. The strings still seemed tight, despite being stored all those years. Also, there was no sign of rust on the strings. That was odd, as there were no silica gel packs in the case. He ran his finger over the strings and it sounded much the same as the sound that he heard when Liam did the same. It shouldn't be in perfect tune after all that time so, puzzled, he took the guitar downstairs with him.

Mabel and Jim were sitting in the kitchen. Mabel followed him into the lounge and watched him lift the lid on the Danemann. He played the low E before checking the sound with the tuning on the guitar. Then he did as he had seen Liam do many times. He played the 5th fret on the E string and then the next string up which was A. And so on until the top G string was also checked as being in tune.

Mabel was as puzzled as Jack was. She had expected the guitar to need some tuning. Why wasn't some turn of the pegs needed? "Have you tuned that yourself upstairs?" she asked.

"No. That's how it came out of the case."

Mabel then remembered that she had seen someone else perform this operation many times in the past and, probably for the first time, saw her brother in Jack's posture and mannerisms as he leaned over the guitar. She went over to hug Jack and was surprised to hear his response.

"HELLO HAMMERSMITH!"

"Thank you Mabel. Appreciate everything you and Jim have done for me. Think I'm ready for you to tell me more about my parents."

Mabel was taken by surprise and didn't know where to start. She spent the next couple of hours telling stories about her time growing up with Gerry and what she knew about his life with Bernie. Jack listened, mostly in silence, taking it all in.

After this trip down memory lane, Jack prepared to join the rest of the band as scheduled. As he was about to leave, he received a call from Colin.

"Hi Jack. Happy birthday and welcome to adulthood! It's not all it's cracked up to be I'm afraid, but you'll find that out for yourself soon enough. I bet you've had some surprises this morning?"

"I have…. but how did you know that?"

"That's a good question. And tomorrow I'll answer it honestly. I'm guessing that you're going into town to get smashed tonight. So how about I pop around at midday tomorrow and bring you round to mine for a natter?"

"Sure, why not?"

"Good, see you then."

Jack celebrated his 18th birthday at the Cuban, proudly showing his college student card with his date of birth marked in order to buy his first legal drinks. He didn't overindulge and spent most of the evening deep in thought. In particular, he wondered why Colin wanted to see him.

He smiled as he watched Liam and Hannah talking earnestly with each other and they furtively held hands when they thought that nobody was looking. For a long time he had suspected that something was going on and as much as he was fond of Hannah, he'd realised that these two

The Letter (29/30 August 2015)

were probably made for each other. Every so often, there were some sharp words from Hannah, but any conflict was swiftly resolved. Hannah was outspoken, and possibly for the first time, Liam was opening up about his feelings.

♪ ♪ ♪ ♪ ♪ ♪ ♪ ♪ ♪ ♪ ♪ ♪ ♪ ♪ ♪

The next morning, Jack slept in. When he eventually came downstairs, the house was empty. This wasn't unusual, as Jim would be at work and Mabel would often take Macy for a walk in the fields. Before he thought about breakfast, Jack sat down at the piano to note down a part of a tune that had been going around his head as he awoke. If he could still remember it by the time he made it downstairs, then there was probably something worth exploring there. He then made his usual bowl of cereals and ate them on his way up the stairs. As he did so, Jack realised he didn't know where Colin lived. None of Light Stone did. When they had a gig and were using the college van, Colin would drive to college to pick it up and then collect them at various meeting points before reversing the process on the way home. Nobody thought to ask him how local he was.

The doorbell rang exactly at midday. Jack wasn't quite ready and quickly brushed his teeth before bounding downstairs to open the door, then pulled it shut behind him.

Once they had fastened their seatbelts in the car, Colin turned to him. "Good night last night?"

"Not bad. Went to the Cuban. Left before closing time."

Colin laughed, remembering the song. He then looked seriously at Jack and dropped the first bombshell. "Ok Jack, now that you're 18, it's time for confession number one. I know that you're the only son of Gerry and Bernie Stanford. I realised it the first time I saw you in the college rehearsal room."

"HELLO HAMMERSMITH!"

Following that, they didn't speak much on the journey, partly because Jack was apprehensive about what else he was about to find out and partly because the journey only lasted five minutes. He knew all the country roads that they travelled along but was dumbfounded when Colin pulled into the drive of the Chapel. Didn't this used to be his home?

"Confession number two. I visited your dad at this place soon after they moved in and loved it to bits. He told me they would never sell as they had too much invested in it. But after they died, I found out that it was on the market and bought it from the estate."

Colin opened the big front door, which was unlocked and stood back to allow Jack to walk in first. Jack stood on the threshold for a second and then felt something draw him through the door. He sauntered in and didn't progress far before Macy bounced up to greet him. "Macy? What are you doing here?" Jack walked down to the hall to where he knew the living area was and found his auntie sitting on the sofa. "Confession number three?" asked Jack, getting the hang of things.

"Yes. As soon as you told me you were Jack Michaels, I realised who you were. Remember, I told you I'd bought Gerry Rafferty's *City to City* album for my girlfriend when it came out? It was actually Mabel Stanford that I'd bought it for. We were an item when I was at college with your dad. Gerry wasn't keen on me seeing his sister, of course, especially when it looked like I was heading for the drug-riddled zone of progressive rock, so our relationship didn't last long, and we drifted apart.

"When I moved back to the area, I kept bumping into Mabel out in the fields at the back and caught up with what had been going on. She admitted that she still had the *City to City* album and played it a lot at home. Then she told me she was doing some local cleaning jobs and I needed a cleaner, so she's been coming and tidying up for me for a few years. She also told me about you and your diagnosis along the way. After I bumped into you that first time in the rehearsal room, I did some research on it and worked out that if you had some proper stimulation, you would probably respond well and develop your music skills quickly. Also, remember that I suggested you do some improvisation for your exam? Well, that was something that I'd seen your father do when he was on stage with Splatt. I was curious to know whether you'd picked up his musical ability unconsciously and it's clear that you have. I checked everything through with Mabel and Jim and assured them I would keep a good eye on you if you transferred courses. They trusted me and were happy to let me give you some extra stuff to get stuck into."

"That's all true, Jack," his auntie quickly reassured him. "I would come round to do a spot of cleaning here while you were at school or college and didn't want to risk upsetting you by telling you I was popping into your old home regularly. I called Colin yesterday afternoon and told him about your visit to the store. It's nothing more sinister than that.

"There were too many memories here for us and your parents didn't have much money when they passed away," she continued. "It took a few years for the *Stanford's Greatest Hits* money to flow in, by which time we had been forced to sell the Chapel to Colin. When you read the letter from your parents this morning, I'd forgotten about them putting in the bit about trying to watch over you from wherever they are. Maybe this has all been their doing."

"Jesus, this is getting too weird," Colin confirmed with a rueful smile. "I'm not at all religious myself, but I'm now wondering about things. Maybe this was all meant to be or your parents are keeping watch from up there. If it helps, you can have a look around and let's see how much you remember."

Jack remembered most of it. The Steinway still had pride of place on the raised area where the original altar had been. Colin smiled. "I did a deal on it as part of the furnishings. And they threw the organ in as well. I've spent a bit of money on it and it's as good as it will ever be. Jump on and have a go if you'd like."

"Thanks, not now." Jack walked past the studio, which was pretty much as he remembered it. The kitchen also looked much the same and still had the large farmhouse table in the middle.

They went through the connecting door to the Old School House. "This is usually empty," Colin explained. "Mabel keeps it tidy though."

Upstairs in the Chapel, Jack went straight to his old room. It had been repainted to lighten the original purple that his parents chose before they knew their baby would be a boy. His small bed had been replaced with a full-size one, but otherwise it looked just the same. A sudden warmth in his stomach caught him by surprise. His parents' room, which he used to go to when he woke up at night to climb between them on the bed, was just the same.

Colin had been following him. "This will amuse you," he said as he opened up the wardrobe to show that it was mainly full of blue check shirts and jeans. "I think you've seen nearly everything. There's just one more thing." He went downstairs and Jack followed him outside.

Mabel and Macy were there already. Of the number of old headstones in the graveyard next to the Chapel, they were standing by one under a tree that simply read:

In Loving Memory

Here lies Gerald Stanford and Bernadette Stanford

Devoted parents taken too soon on 1 July 2003

"Forever Together"

"*Forever Together* was an early Stanford song," Mabel explained.

"Remember being here," Jack muttered, realising that he had blocked out this and many other images from all those years ago and they were now flooding back.

The Letter (29/30 August 2015)

Next to his parents' headstone lay another fairly new one, which read:

Here lies Georgina Garrett – loving wife

25 July 1956 – 17 July 2011

"What happened?" Jack asked.

Colin seemed to drift for a few seconds. "She was in a cycling accident. Knocked over on a country lane in France. We were trying to improve our fitness after years of excess. It took me a bit of time to put it behind me."

After a period of silence while Jack took in the scene, they went back inside.

"There's one more thing that I need to show you." Colin led them into the small room where the mixing desk was and pulled back the rug that covered most of the floor. Underneath was a small safe that had been inserted into the floor. "In the old days, they would have put the collection money in here. There's no key that I could find, probably lost." Colin turned the handle and pulled open the metal door. Inside were hundreds of little tapes and discs. Jack pulled a few out and recognised his father's handwriting. "I think the removal firm missed them. I played a few of them on the Minidisc player that I found and they seem to be old demos and bits of songs that weren't properly recorded." He closed the door and replaced the rug. "Let's keep it our secret for now?" Jack nodded in agreement.

"Well, I think that I've confessed nearly everything that I can think of at the moment. Just to say that although I look at you and can't see a bias between your father and mother in your face, there is definitely something that you've picked up from your mother."

"Really? What's that?"

"Well, when you have tired of looking through the Stanford back catalogue you should have a look at The Pogoes, the punk band that

"HELLO HAMMERSMITH!"

Bernie joined in the late 1970s. She wrote the lyrics to a lot of the songs. They were quite political and anti-establishment. I saw you leaning that way in your own thinking and songwriting, so I hope you don't mind that I gave you a little nudge in that direction. Anyway, I'm relieved that everything is now in the open and I've nothing to hide now. I know that this has been a lot to take in and there's a lot of stuff for you to process, but you can come around here any time. By the way, if you haven't anything else on, you can start now. Mabel told me you'd taken your dad's old guitar from the store. If you like, I can run you all back home to bring it back and start some lessons on it. It will help you fill in on gigs when Hannah can't make it."

"No rush. Auntie says that dad used to write lots of songs on that guitar. Wonder if I can too."

"I think you've been doing fine without it up to now. If you've time, we can work on that blues project that I set you. It should be easier on a guitar. You can use a spare today."

"Have you got a spare gig bag too?"

"Sure, there's a couple in the spare room. You can take one with you."

By the end of the day, Colin had helped Jack with a new song *I Woke Up This Morning*. It was simple but effective. As a 'proper' blues song, it had depressing lyrics which didn't at all capture Jack's present feelings. He was happier than he had been for a long time.

They had just about finished when Jack had another call on his mobile. It was Hannah.

"Hi Jack, sorry to call you so late."

"It's no problem. I've been round at Colin's today."

The Letter (29/30 August 2015)

"Oh, really? I often wondered where he lived. Is it nice?"

"You could say that. What's up?"

"I think we need a band meeting. Can you collect everyone together as soon as possible?"

Chapter 18 - I'm Goin' Back (September 1993 to September 1994)

Gerry and Bernie had tried to lift their spirits by going to see the opening night of Madonna's *Girlie Show* at Wembley Stadium. They felt the need to go disguised under hats and dark glasses, so as not to be recognised on the Underground and in the stadium. There was a time, not so long ago, when they would have received a backstage invite from the lady herself, who they had met at a few awards' ceremonies. If not, then they would have been happy to receive VIP tickets and be recognised in the crowd. This wasn't the time for either.

They were content to buy seated tickets like anyone else and mingle unnoticed in the crowds. Even at the peak of Stanford's fame, they would buy tickets to the big stadium shows even though a backstage invite would have been easy to ask for. Bernie believed it was important to experience the big shows as their fans would. They could then see first-hand how others bridged the enormous divide between the band and a faraway audience. Some bands did this better than others. This time it was just for the fun of it. Given Gerry's fragile condition, the couple had no expectation of Stanford reaching those lofty heights again. They were relieved to reach home safely with only a few people showing signs of vague recognition.

It was their second recent visit to England's biggest stadium. A few weeks beforehand, they had been invited to watch Blind Race, this time from backstage as the band brought their epic show back to the UK after a year-long world tour. Their paths had crossed some years previously, when a young Marshall Charles had signed to their record label. Gerry and Marshall developed a bit of a father and son relationship and they stayed in touch. Now, Blind Race were one of the biggest bands in the world and Stanford were nowhere.

The day after the Madonna concert, they had a lie-in at their comfortable Islington home. It wasn't just Bernie's ears that were ringing the next morning from the late night show. At exactly 10am, the doorbell sounded. Bernie opened the front door and was greeted by the smiling face of Oscar Good. "Oscar! Alright or what? Come in, so good to see you."

"Oh, not so bad at all. How was the current Queen of Pop? I'm going to see her tonight."

"Well, she put on a big show as you'd expect, but I can't help thinking that this *Erotica* album is going to be seen as a mis-step in the future. Time will tell. Coffee?"

"Absolutely! Hello Gerry, how are you?"

"Ah, quite good, all things considered. I heard you talking about Madonna. You know, having seen her, I'm glad that we don't need to worry about those big shows anymore. Bernie noticed some hiccups. Far too many things can go wrong and the sound is always an issue in somewhere like Wembley. It's about time they knocked the whole thing down and started again!"

"Well, I hope they leave it up at least for tonight," Oscar joked as he went into the lounge. "No sign of Harvey of course?"

"Oh, he'll be here as soon as he remembers where we are," Gerry grimaced. "Some things never change."

It was another half an hour before Harvey D'Angelo eventually turned up, by which time Gerry had gone upstairs to lie down.

Harvey apologised profusely. "So sorry I'm late Bernie. Would you believe I was lost? The streets around here all look the same to me. Have I missed anything?"

"No, we haven't started yet. No point in getting going until you arrive to represent and advise us, Harvey. Anyway, I understand that home is

I'm Goin' Back (September 1993 to September 1994)

chaotic at the moment, what with your new daughter being born a few weeks ago?"

"Well, chaos is certainly the right word," agreed Harvey. "Everyone says that a new baby turns your life upside down but nothing actually prepares you for the reality."

"And you're decided on a name?"

"Yes, we agreed on Harte. Whether she turns out to have the 'heart of an angel' remains to be seen."

By now, Gerry was back in the room, so with everyone assembled, Bernie started. "Right, let me tell you where we are, Oscar. I know that you'll help us if you can. As you know, guys, we're in a bit of a fix at the moment. The last tour left us with some spare cash which we used to start on *Album 6*. But when Multiplier went bust and the trouble started, it made sense to stop what we were doing and put all our efforts into defending ourselves. When it all went against us, we were left with some enormous bills. In the past, there were a few ways that we could generate some quick cash to straighten us out again, but there seemed to be problems with each one. Normally it would have made sense to press on with finishing the album and releasing it to bring in some royalties, but following Gerry's outburst, sales of the entire back catalogue fell off a cliff and haven't recovered as yet. I knew Oscar wouldn't break the rule of a lifetime and give us an advance against the recording costs." She paused and Oscar shook his head as he had done when the suggestion was first made.

"When Oscar said 'no', I went to the bank to ask for a short-term loan. I was expecting to be offered something, albeit with a hideous rate of interest. After all, they had been happy to offer loans when we didn't need them. To my surprise, they weren't interested one bit. They had heard about Gerry's fragile state and brought up the uncertain prospects of repayment. I played them some demo tapes we had recorded. Before, the bank manager had said that he was one of our original fans. This time, he said that it didn't sound like Stanford at all, which is actually what we were going for. He said he wouldn't be buying it, should it ever come out. Then he said, 'I'm more into rap and hip hop these days, which I think will wipe away UK electronic bands like Stanford in the same way that punk wiped out prog rock in the 1970s.' I don't think he realised that was an ironic thing to say to me. It's funny how you can lose fans as you try to change and progress. So, I think the new album has to stay unfinished for now. That's about where we are."

Harvey chipped in. "I've been keeping in touch with promoters to see if there was a possibility of a brief tour to bring in some money, which would enable the album to be finished. I'm sorry to say that I can't tempt any interest at the moment. They just see it as too much of a risk given the negative publicity surrounding the band. That avenue seems closed at the moment. I also put some feelers out to see whether any of the ad agencies wanted to use some of your songs."

Gerry put his head in his hands. "I do hope the answer was 'no'. I couldn't live with myself if we had to allow someone to ruin the songs."

"Well, I'm afraid the answer was indeed 'no'. As the band has a reputation for saying 'no' to any opportunity that has come along, all the doors are now well and truly closed."

"I told you we should have sold rights to some advertisers while the going was good," scolded Bernie. "I wish you'd leave the business decisions to me as we agreed."

There was a frosty silence before Oscar concluded. "So you're stuck where you are for now. I had an offer from another record label to buy my back catalogue, but it was so low that it didn't make sense. I suspected that ERCO were somewhere behind it and sure enough I then got some veiled threats over the phone from an untraceable number. They could always sniff a bargain and sit on it until things improved and then make a killing. This is just to let you both know where we are and

I'm Goin' Back (September 1993 to September 1994)

we're just checking in to see if either of you have any bright ideas at this point."

Bernie looked at Gerry, who shrugged and shook his head. "Then I don't think we should take up any more of your time, Oscar."

"I'm sorry that I can't help the two of you more."

"We understand and appreciate that, Oscar," Bernie reassured, looking first at her husband and then at the label owner, while Gerry nodded in agreement.

Oscar stood up to leave, but before Harvey moved to follow, Bernie interrupted. "Actually, Harvey, can you hang on for a few minutes?"

Once Oscar had gone, Bernie could deliver the news to their curious manager. "Harvey, we appreciate all that you've done for us over the years, but we both think that just at the moment, there isn't much point in us having a manager to look after the business side of things when there isn't much business going on. We're sorry but we're going to have to let you go. I think we can deal with the bits that we have."

Harvey dropped his head. "I've been half-expecting that. I've been trying hard to come up with something but sometimes the market just isn't on your side, and I have to accept that."

"In the meantime, a friend of ours has just started a music management business. He won't be nearly as good as you, Harvey, but he offered to look after things as a favour until they pick up. If anyone contacts you, please pass on this number and request that they ask for 'Archie'," Bernie added, handing over a piece of paper with a London phone number on it.

Shortly after Harvey left, Gerry and Bernie sat alone, feeling all at once uncomfortable and relieved.

Bernie sighed. "Well, that went as well as we could expect."

"Yes, that's it really. I just can't see how we function in the music business anymore, especially in my current condition, so that was painful but necessary. Look, I know we agreed that you're in charge of the business things, but it wouldn't be believable if we came up with an alias for you as the new manager."

"I understand that," Bernie agreed. "But you must discuss any offers that come in with me. We have an agreement. Is that clear?"

"Sure. The question now is, what is the next bandage that needs to be ripped off?"

Bernie was pensive for a few seconds and as if she needed to justify what was coming next, she let her words out carefully. She raised her head to look at her husband. "I think we should downsize... you know... sell this place."

"Maybe move to the country and recuperate? Maybe we should see what it's like down in Kent these days. There's plenty of countryside to hide in and you and Mabel like each other. I have fond memories of the freedom of growing up there while being in touch with the local town and being able to get the train up to London if needed. What about it?"

"No harm in looking. We've not much else to do, have we?"

♫ ♫ ♫ ♫ ♫ ♫ ♫ ♫ ♫ ♫ ♫ ♫ ♫ ♫ ♫

The couple spent the next few weeks in Kent and stayed in small hotels while visiting local estate agents. Gerry was more cheerful than he had been in some time, as activity seemed to improve his mood and gave him something to focus on outside their problems. There wasn't much available on the market that interested them, as Gerry was adamant that they needed to live somewhere unusual. They focused their attention on the small villages close to where Mabel lived. Nothing looked right until Gerry saw an article in the local paper saying that the Church Commissioners were selling some property in areas of

I'm Goin' Back (September 1993 to September 1994)

decreasing attendances. "Hmm..," he thought. "I've always wanted to live in a church." He made some enquiries without telling Bernie and reckoned that he had found just what they were looking for.

The next day, he took Bernie out for a drive in the Kent countryside in the MGB roadster.

"Where are we going?" she asked.

"You'll see," was the enigmatic reply.

They pulled up outside a dilapidated chapel, with its 'For Sale' sign. Bernie looked at Gerry as though he had lost his mind all over again. "You can't be serious, pet!" she spluttered.

"Well, I know it's going to need a lot of work to make it habitable, but this is the chapel where mum and dad brought me and Mabel when we were younger. I used to be an altar server here, you know? And our first school, which was next door, is also up for sale." He smiled. "This takes me back to happier times. Let's at least have a look inside."

A little while later, another car turned up. An agent, complete with large keys for the front door, arrived to let them in. The interior was musty and showcased that the property hadn't been aired for some time. Yet, it was pretty much as Gerry remembered it. The altar, baptism font and pews were all in place, as was the pipe organ. Gerry tried to play it but could only draw a few windy gasps from it. Bernie pulled a face. She could sense the high costs of refurbishing this place to return it to working order. At the side of the altar was a piano. Gerry lifted the lid and saw the name as a signature font on the right-hand side, 'Danemann'. He played a few chords on the expected out of tune keys. He checked inside at the mechanics and the pads looked in reasonable condition. "I remember this – it has a pleasant tone and a nice feel."

"It's like the whole place, Gerry. Not used for years and waiting for some mug to spend more than they can afford to make it halfway decent."

"You're right," he seemed to admit. But still utterly delighted with the find, he whispered, "That's just what the agent needs to hear so that we can beat him down."

Bernie groaned. She knew what was coming.

♪ ♪ ♪ ♪ ♪ ♪ ♪ ♪ ♪ ♪ ♪ ♪ ♪ ♪ ♪

When they visited again a few days later, a van was waiting for them. The signwriting on the side proudly stated 'Jim Michaels Specialist Builders'. Inside, they found Jim looking at Gerry's rough plans and filling his pad with a multitude of notes and calculations.

"How are you doing, Jim?" Gerry asked cheerfully.

Jim ran his fingers through what was left of his hair. "I'm OK, Gerry. It's you I'm worried about though. I've barely scratched the surface. To be fair, it's quite solid and there's no water ingress, which can be a problem, but they're the only good things that I can see. Everything else needs building up from scratch. Total rewiring and given that you want to put in a recording studio you'll need the electricity board to increase the power coming in. That will mean digging up the road outside, which won't please the neighbours. There's no plumbing at all so you're starting from scratch, including new drainage. Extending out that upper floor will be a structural nightmare. It will cost you a fortune and could cost me my sanity. You're crazy, but I think you know that. Give me a laugh and tell me what your budget is."

Bernie was listening in from the other side of the room. "We've got about £100,000 to play with, Jim."

Jim thought for a minute. "In that case, it'll cost you £225,000 – could you afford that?"

"Not really," Bernie replied. "How did you calculate that?"

I'm Goin' Back (September 1993 to September 1994)

"Experience," said Jim, tapping the side of his head. "I always warn the client in cases like this that it's best to double your budget and add a bit."

"I think we could stretch to that," Gerry smiled while Bernie looked on helplessly. "And do you reckon that the old school next door could be converted into something like a B&B? The connecting door is still there."

"Yes, that would be easier. At least there is plumbing and power in there already."

♫ ♫ ♫ ♫ ♫ ♫ ♫ ♫ ♫ ♫ ♫ ♫ ♫ ♫ ♫

When the locals realised that some pop stars were interested in buying the Chapel and Old School House, they started a petition. However, once Jim had presented the enormous quote, Gerry told the agent that they were no longer interested, given the costs involved. Word spread and the petition quietly disappeared.

A couple of weeks later, with nobody else showing any interest, Paul Eagle put in a low bid for both properties. This reflected Jim's budget, the remaining funds from selling the London house and clearing their loans. All he said was that it was for one of his clients who wanted to make it their home, which was true. In the absence of any better offer, it was theirs and Jim quietly applied for planning permission, which was successful.

The Islington house was put on the market and sold quickly. So while Jim worked on the Chapel, Gerry and Bernie rented a cottage in the village. They took care to mix with the locals as much as possible, eventually convincing them that there weren't going to be any wild pop stars' parties keeping them up all night.

Twelve months after they first saw the Chapel for sale, Gerry opened the big front door and stood back to let Bernie go in first. Externally, the Church was little changed, although the stone had been cleaned up.

"HELLO HAMMERSMITH!"

Inside, the newly finished interior was a wonder to behold. The wood from the pews had been recycled into a set of stairs and a galleried landing which looked over the sitting room. This led to the three upstairs bedrooms. The pipe organ had been refurbished at great expense so that it could be played, with the sound echoing through the Chapel.

Downstairs in the studio, Gerry pulled back the rug and revealed a safe in the floor. "This might come in handy. It looks like a great place to put some of the old demo tapes... I think that I'll call this the 'Stanford Vault'."

Over the following months, Gerry slowly built the studio facility in the soundproofed area. He called in a favour from Les Evenson who had engineered the two Stanford albums on ERCO. He had prepared everything so that the desk captured the best and clearest sounds possible. Their tight budget forced them to source a second-hand mixing desk from another studio that had just closed. There were a multitude of problems that needed to be dealt with. First, it had to be on the quiet, as Les still did a bit of work for ERCO. They would have cut all links with him if they knew he was working for the Stanfords. Second, the desk was far too big for what Gerry needed. Finally, they were warned that it was cheap because it was far from perfect and not all of its channels worked.

With limited choices available, they took the gamble that it would be OK, and it was. It just fitted in the room available and the scuffs down the side would stay hidden for years until it was finally pulled out of the room. They had a good laugh about some labels on the desk, including one which read 'Please don't lose your coke in the faders'.

Les had a hard time fitting it in the space available. One day he took the knife that he had been using to strip wires and gouged 'Les Evenson Woz Ere' underneath where he thought nobody would notice it. While he was there, Les asked Gerry and Bernie if they would sign the albums that he had worked on.

I'm Goin' Back (September 1993 to September 1994)

"Are you sure, Les?" Gerry checked. "My signature could devalue some of these rare ones you have. There won't be many signed in permanent marker like these."

"That will be fine," Les assured him. "It's just for my personal collection, you understand?"

"If I had a pound for every time people said that!" Bernie muttered as she signed them with a flourish.

Chapter 19 - I Know We'll Meet Again Someday (1 September 2015)

As Hannah had requested, Jack called a band meeting at the Chapel for midday on the first day they could all make. Colin wasn't at college that day so he agreed Jack could arrive earlier than the meeting start time. He walked the mile or so from his home in about 20 minutes. His dad's guitar was in Colin's spare gig bag on his back and Macy bounded happily by his side. His heartbeat quickened the nearer he got. He reached the Chapel just before 10am.

Colin had been working on a soundtrack commission and showed Jack what he was doing to build up the musical textures from the old mixing desk. They then went through some songs that Jack had been working on to translate them into a guitar format. When Jack took the old guitar out of his bag, Colin recognised it immediately.

"Do you know there are just a handful of people who would recognise that guitar? Your dad was famous for standing behind a bank of keyboards and it wasn't well known that he found it easier to write songs on that old Hofner. He always said that if they sounded good on that, they would sound good on anything. Rick Wakeman told a similar story, that he was listening to David Bowie playing songs on an old 12-string that would end up on *Hunky Dory*. I'm not aware that the two of them ever met to swap that story but you never know; it was pretty crazy back then. I also heard Paul Weller talking about songwriting on an old splintered Ovation guitar. Come to think of it, there was a clip on Top of the Pops where your dad played that guitar instead of his keyboards. He did it as a joke I think. You should keep that guitar close – there's probably some of his spirit in there."

"Sure. Actually, there is something weird about this guitar. When I took it out of the store, it was still in tune and has been ever since."

"HELLO HAMMERSMITH!"

"Really? That's just not possible. Metal strings will always stretch and contract with changes in temperature. Show me."

Jack pulled the guitar from the gig bag and strummed the open strings. To his surprise, it sounded terrible. Macy whined. None of the strings were in the standard tuning anymore. A puzzled look spread across his face, unable to understand how things had suddenly changed.

"Well, that's no surprise," Colin commented as Jack tuned the strings again. "Anyway, let's have a look at something you've done recently. We've some time before the others arrive."

"Those basic chords you showed me yesterday… I wrote something at home… hmm… about… mum and dad… It's called *I Know We'll Meet Again Someday.*"

"Ok, that's an interesting title. Play it for me."

The chords were quite simple; G, A minor, G and E minor for the verses.

> *When I was young, you were my heroes*
>
> *Looked up to you - everyday*
>
> *There was no time – you let me down*
>
> *You loved me more than you could say*

The chorus was C, E minor, C, A minor, repeated with A minor and G on the end.

> *I know you're with me when I wake up*
>
> *You're watching over me all day*
>
> *At night you're there and you protect me*
>
> *I know we'll meet again someday*
>
> *I know we'll meet again someday*

I Know We'll Meet Again Someday (1 September 2015)

Colin stopped him after the chorus. "Right. So I think you can lift this up by adding a few 7ths at the end of the verse and the chorus." He showed Jack on the guitar. "Ok, let's hear verse 2 like that."

> *I know you're next to me right now*
> *Givin' me the words to this song*
> *Guiding me, as you always would*
> *With you so close, I can't go wrong*

The middle 8 had similar chords to the chorus but shifted up:

> *It's great, you gave me the gift of music*
> *A love we shared all the time*
> *It gave us comfort when times were bad*
> *With you close to me, I'm just fine*

Then a last verse:

> *There's many a time that I miss you*
> *Taken so young, it makes me sad*
> *No one else could ever replace you*
> *Cos you were always mum and dad*

Then the final chorus:

> *I know you're with me when I wake up*
> *You're watching over me all day*
> *At night you're there and you protect me*
> *I know we'll meet again someday*
> *I know we'll meet again someday*

"That's nice," Colin started. He followed hesitantly with, "Very personal though – probably not a band song?"

"HELLO HAMMERSMITH!"

"That's right. Don't think so."

"Might be interesting to rock it up though. Incidentally, that reminds me. There's something that I've been meaning to play you." Colin asked Jack to shuffle back and peeled back the old rug on the studio floor. Underneath was the safe that he had shown Jack on his first visit back to the Chapel. He picked out one disc and loaded it into the Minidisc machine. "Have a listen to this."

The song that he played was called *The Fun Has Only Just Begun* and Jack recognised the voices of his parents straight away and bathed himself in the sound until the song completed.

"Does anything strike you about that song?"

Jack smiled. "The lyrics have some similarity to *Rock the Cuban*. Both songs are set in a club as well."

"That's right. And this was the first time that you've heard this song?"

Jack nodded.

"Spooky really, how you've happened upon something that's so similar to a song your parents wrote. They didn't release this one as far as I know. According to the date on the disc, they did this in 1996; a bit before you were born. You'll be fine with this one since you can't copyright the idea of basing a song around a club, plus the chord progression and melody are quite different, but we might need to be careful about this. It will be tough but you'll have to guard against unconsciously copying songs that your parents might have already released. I guess that as you now own the right to Stanford songs, you'd have to sue yourself!" They both laughed at the idiocy of the situation.

Around midday, the band started turning up. At least one of them was going to find themselves hopelessly lost and it was Liam, who had to be talked in by phone. Hannah was the last to join. The rest of the band looked around the Chapel in wonder. None of them could be tempted to

I Know We'll Meet Again Someday (1 September 2015)

have a go at the pipe organ but Liam tempted some tasty chords out of the Steinway piano.

Hannah was uncharacteristically quiet as she explained what had been happening that they didn't already know about.

"They could see that I was reluctant to sign the contract that they offered me as a solo artist, so they invited me up to London to record some demos to convince me to sign. They put me in the hands of one of their stylists, who dressed me up in some designer clothes. It looked great, but it just wasn't 'me' and I felt really uncomfortable. Then someone else came in with some scissors and tried to cut my hair. Things just kicked off. Then they tried to impress me with a PowerPoint presentation explaining how they wanted to change my image and reposition me in the market, not as Hannah Ross, but as PERPETUATE."

"What?" exclaimed Liam.

"You're kidding," added Rick.

"Yeah, I know. I had a terrible panic attack and I ended up throwing a jug of water against the studio wall in frustration. The spray shorted out a mixing desk. I think at that point, they realised I couldn't do this on my own. They suggested having a band around me to give me confidence. I suggested you guys but they just laughed. The next thing I know, they introduced me to some other girls who won similar contests in other music colleges around the country. FRCO were trying to put us together, saying that we could be the next Little Mix! You can imagine what I said about that! To make things worse, they introduced us all to this creepy guy who I'd never seen before. I've no idea where he came from.

"After some shouting matches when we stood eye to eye, I finally convinced Vicky that they would achieve nothing by forcing me to sign. In the end, she agreed for ERCO to extend the offer to you guys, but only on the same terms. I've talked it through with my parents and they know they can't stop me now that I'm 18. We would all move up to London to one of ERCO's accommodations. What do you guys think?"

Obviously, Rick and Dan were delighted at this prospect. This is all they had wished for and they immediately said, "Yes." But Jack and Liam were clearly not so sure.

Colin came, it seemed, to the rescue. "Look, to succeed in the music business these days, you need connections. You need to find where the power lies and then pay homage to the mogul at its centre, the person who can open the right doors and make the right introductions to the media outlets. Now, there are only three major companies at the moment: Universal, Sony and Warners. A new band with no track record isn't going to get close to any of them. But look at Blind Race and what they have done. They started with a small label but had big dreams and soon ended up with one of the big three." The band were all aware of Blind Race and what they had achieved as one of the biggest bands in the world.

"You've had other A&R people come and see your gigs but when I put them on the spot and asked them what they were offering, they turned flaky and tried to bullshit me. I think they were just running up expenses out of town, but it could have been something to do with Vicky and her bodyguard being in hearing distance, come to think of it. So I think at the moment the only actual offer you have is from ERCO, although I'm not comfortable that this is the right move for you guys. Your best songs are musically throwbacks to the past but your lyrics are current. It's an odd mix. You could carry on building slowly on YouTube and doing local gigs but ERCO would cut through to the mainstream quicker and give you the distribution. They're known for playing dirty, but they break new artists all the time. It's up to you, but you're taking a risk whatever you do."

"I think we should all talk to our parents and guardians at home and decide in the next few days," Liam suggested. "My offer from the Music College has come in."

I Know We'll Meet Again Someday (1 September 2015)

"Accept that offer and the band is dead," Rick voiced.

"Rick's right," offered Hannah. "We can't take the ERCO contract if you're not around."

Dan grudgingly agreed.

In the meantime, they took advantage of being together as a great opportunity to do some rehearsal practice for some new songs. Colin let Rick use the Chapel drum kit and there were guitar and keyboard amps that had been left at the property by the executors when Colin bought it, some of which still worked. Liam later brought some of his guitars over so that he wouldn't need to carry them on the bus, but as time went on the rest of the band noticed he kept bringing new guitars to use and they never returned home.

♫ ♫ ♫ ♫ ♫ ♫ ♫ ♫ ♫ ♫ ♫ ♫ ♫ ♫

At home later that day, Jack tentatively raised the topic with his guardians. At first, they were unequivocally against it.

Mabel was apprehensive. "This is like history repeating itself. I distinctly remember your dad saying that the ERCO contract was the worst that Paul Eagle had ever seen and that they were lucky to extract themselves from it as swiftly and cleanly as they did. There were plenty of other artists who fell foul of ERCO and had their careers ruined. Light Stone could be the next one on the list!"

"Yes, heard some stuff about Gillian Fox," Jack noted. "Think there's a logical choice of going with ERCO and moving swiftly or going down the slow route we're on now and risk getting nowhere slowly."

"That's fine," Jim said, "but you're not signing anything until Paul Eagle has had a look at this contract. We don't want you to sign your life away. And remember you still need to see him about what will happen to your parents' trust fund now that you're 18."

"Ok, but not sure there's anything to talk about." Jack had made his mind up that if the others were keen to sign, then he would go along with them.

"And another thing," Jim felt the need to add. "You know that with your diagnosis you don't react well to change – this might well mess with your head."

"Can't stay working in a supermarket stacking shelves forever."

Mabel resigned herself to the obvious. "No, of course not, but there are plenty of other good jobs out there for talented lads like you."

"Nothing out there interests me..."

♪ ♪ ♪ ♪ ♪ ♪ ♪ ♪ ♪ ♪ ♪ ♪ ♪ ♪

Once he was back upstairs, Jack phoned Liam first. "What do you think, Liam? You going to the Music College or to London with the band? It hinges on you."

"You're putting me under pressure, man! Believe me, I've thought of nothing else since Hannah put us in the picture. Look Jack, I've a lot of confidence in you guys and in our songs. If you're willing to take a chance on this, I'm in too."

"Cool. Calling Hannah now. Speak later."

Jack phoned Hannah straight away. He was quite clear to her.

"Think we should do it. Moving too slowly here."

"That's great Jack. I must warn you though - no way are my parents 100% for it at all. You know how protective my dad is and he's been worse at the thought of me diving into the murky business of being in an indie rock band surrounded by a lot of guys, even if he knows you all.

I Know We'll Meet Again Someday (1 September 2015)

But I'm 18 now and I just feel I've a better chance of making it with the band. Your solicitor is going to look at the contract?"

"Not sure what the point is. We can all have a look at it before we sign it. It must be fairly standard and I'm sure we can duck out of it if we become successful."

"Oh, that won't work, Jack! Don't you remember Colin warning us not to sign anything without getting it checked out? He said 'don't ever do this kids'. They explained to me in some detail that when we sign there's a clause in there that agrees that we've had independent legal advice beforehand. If you don't have access to a solicitor, then they'll sort one out for you."

"Let's go for that option then. Don't have the money to pay someone to look at it."

Chapter 20 - I Fought The Law (2 July 1993)

It was the second scheduled day in court. Even though Gerry and Bernie were there early, press reporters were already gathering outside the building. Once in the building, they spent some preparation time with their barrister and Paul Eagle who briefed them about what to expect on the day.

The plaintiff, Joe Johnson, was the first to appear in the witness box. It might have been put on but he looked like he had not washed for many days and none of his clothes matched. His beard was unkempt and his hair needed a good cut.

The clerk of the court asked him to read out the time-honoured witness affirmation. "I do solemnly, sincerely and truly declare and affirm that the evidence I shall give shall be the truth the whole truth and nothing but the truth."

"Thank you Mr Johnson," said his barrister. "Please, could you explain to the court why you are bringing this civil case against Gerry and Bernie Stanford?"

"I've been writing songs and done lots of small gigs all of my life but I've never had the lucky breaks that others have had. My luck appeared to have changed when I saw an advert in Melody Maker from an unnamed 'established star' looking for co-writers to see if they could come up with some songs for worldwide release. I answered the advert and went to a studio in North London where I was surprised to find Gerry Stanford. I thought that he should have been alright writing stuff on his own or with his missus, but he told me he had a temporary writer's block and needed some outside impetus to help him. He told me he had tried a few people, mainly other artists with recording contracts, but hadn't found much common ground, so he was experimenting with some unknown writers."

"HELLO HAMMERSMITH!"

"Please tell the court what happened at your session with Mr Stanford."

"We kicked a few fresh ideas around for about an hour but none of them were doing it for him. So, he asked me if I had any songs nearly completed that we could finish together. I tried a few of those on him but that wasn't working either until I told him I had this great one that I was holding back, called *Let's Do It*. He said he'd like to hear it if it was that good. His face lit up when he heard it and I showed him the lyrics and chords that I was working from."

"Is that all on the pages that you have submitted as evidence?"

"Yes, that's right. We ran it through a few times, and he said it was the best new song that he'd heard for some time. There were a few things that we tidied up, that much I'll give him. Then he said that it didn't really sound like a Stanford song, but he promised to look for a record label for me to pitch the song to and keep in touch. To be honest, I didn't expect to hear anything on that side of things."

"And did you hear anything back? And may I remind you that you are still under oath?"

"I understand the oath. No, of course I didn't hear anything back. Most of the successful songwriters that I've met have a touch of arrogance about them, to be honest. Next thing I knew, this similar song called *Let's Do It Now* had appeared on Stanford's album *Blindside* and when it was released as a single it suddenly took off everywhere. I was sick of hearing it on the radio as it was almost identical to what I had played him, but it had been professionally produced, of course. I bought a copy to see if my name was on the credits but all it said was 'G Stanford & B Stanford'."

"And what are you expecting from bringing this case to court?"

"I'm expecting my name to at least appear first in the credits. Plus, I think I'm owed a share of the royalties, if not all of them. That was my song and it was stolen."

I Fought The Law (2 July 1993)

"No further questions, Your Honour."

Stanford's barrister stood up. "Now first things first, Mr Johnson. That *Blindside* album with *Let's Do It Now* on it was released over five years ago. Why has it taken you so long to come forward to make your claims?"

"I talked to a few solicitors but they all told me it would cost me big money to bring a case and I'd be better off forgetting it, so I did until I was contacted by someone anonymously who said he'd heard about the situation and wanted to see my notes. He put me in touch with a big law firm who took me on. They agreed to charge me nothing if I lost."

"And can you identify the person who is backing you, please?"

"Objection, Your Honour!" Johnson's barrister exclaimed. "The identity of the individual who wishes to put this wrong to right is of no consequence to the question at hand."

"Objection sustained!" acquiesced the judge. "Please keep your questions to the point."

"Yes, of course, Your Honour. Now Mr Johnson. Did you play this song to anyone else before it was released?"

"No. I write so many songs that it went into a file with the others for a long time until I heard it on the radio and then pulled it out to check it."

"So, there is actually no evidence that you wrote this song before it was released apart from a handwritten date on the paper which forensic experts have said could have been added afterwards. In fact, they have said that the notes could have been written at any time in the last seven to eight years. That's not a very convincing argument Mr Johnson, is it?"

"I wrote it before I saw Gerry Stanford!" Johnson said firmly.

"HELLO HAMMERSMITH!"

"And can you expect the court to believe that after all your time as a songwriter, you suddenly write a massive hit when none of your other songs have tempted a record company to take a chance on you?"

Johnson shrugged. "This one came to me in a flash. It wrote itself."

"Thank you, Mr Johnson. No further questions."

The judge looked at the witness. "You may stand down, Mr Johnson."

Gerry and Bernie looked at each other and smiled. That had gone as well as they might have expected. Joe Johnson had not been a credible witness. But they knew the next witness would be a tougher one.

The clerk announced the witness for the plaintiff. "Calling Bruce Dean to the box." Both Gerry and Bernie held their breaths as their former bass guitarist made his way to the stand and took the oath.

"Thank you, Mr Dean. Can you please reiterate your witness statement for the benefit of the court?"

"Yes, I can do that. On this date in 1987, I was getting ready for a gig with a local band in the evening when I realised I didn't have the leads to connect the bass up to the amp. I knew I had last seen them in the studio so I popped along to retrieve them. Gerry had been using the studio to try out some different writers, so I tried to be as quiet as possible and not disturb him. I came in just as Joe Johnson was playing through this song called *Let's Do It*. My ears pricked up as soon as I heard it. I knew it was special and had 'hit' written all over it."

"And did anyone see you?"

"No, I wasn't there for long. I found the cable and left while they were playing it through together."

"And what happened next?"

I Fought The Law (2 July 1993)

"I saw Joe playing in a North London pub a few weeks later and recognised him. I told him I liked the song that he had played to Gerry and advised him to do something with it, but he said that nobody was interested in it apart from Gerry. "

"And didn't you say something when Mr Stanford brought the song in and started recording it?"

"Yes, I recognised it and told Gerry so, but he didn't listen."

"No further questions."

Gerry's barrister stood. "Mr Dean, can you explain to the court the reasons for your departure from the Stanford band?"

"Yes sir. After the *Blindside* album took off, we ended up touring the world and, to be honest, I just couldn't cope. I resorted to taking drugs to keep me going and Gerry and Bernie found out about it. They had a zero-tolerance policy on it, so that was me out the door."

"And can you explain why the record of visitors in reception at the studio shows no evidence that you were there that day?"

"Sure. I knew the receptionist well and she was happy that I wasn't going to be long enough to warrant me signing in."

"So, how do you explain the fact that the receptionist herself cannot remember the event?"

"I can't explain that. I guess she forgot that I'd been there."

"But you must harbour some hard feelings about how you left the band just before they became really famous. Enough to consider lying to this court about the evidence that you have just given?"

"Absolutely not sir, I swear it happened like that."

"No further questions."

"HELLO HAMMERSMITH!"

"Excellent," the judge cut in, as if to avoid any unexpected lengthening. "It's 12.30pm so we will reconvene after lunch."

After lunch, Gerry was called to the witness box and took his oath. His barrister asked him to talk through the statement that he had provided.

"Well, after the second album with Multiplier Records had done fairly well and our following was building, I knew that for our third album for them, we needed to pull out all the stops. We decided not to rush things and spent a lot of time songwriting so that we could do the best album possible. We had completed a lot of songs before writer's block hit for the first time in my career. I guess we were facing a lot of pressure. The label said that we didn't have enough singles so we tried to write again. Bernie had no trouble coming up with song ideas, but I wasn't able to develop them. I tried calling some friends in the business to unblock things but that didn't progress me far. Out of desperation, I put the advert in Melody Maker. There was a history of people doing that and it had worked before. For example, Bernie answered an advert that I had placed.

"Neither the professional nor the amateur songwriters were much help. I distinctly remember Joe Johnson coming along and us getting nowhere. I asked him if he had any half-written songs, but that was it. He didn't have anything much with him. Our time together lasted about 30 minutes, if that, and he went off. Didn't hear from him again until a few months ago when the writ was issued out of the blue. I didn't take it seriously at first, as we have had a few over the years, all of which have been groundless. Early on I learned that 'where there's a hit, there's a writ'."

"And tell us what happened next."

"I gave up on those sessions. We had been messing about for too long. We had enough for an entire album and we had some excellent songs that were ready to be released. I wanted to wait for a bit until inspiration hit, but Bernie didn't agree. Her exact words were 'Let's stop

I Fought The Law (2 July 1993)

messing around, let's do it now'. Right then, something clicked in my head and I remembered we had this song called *Let's Do It Now* filed away. We experimented with it and recorded it over the next few days."

"So, you deny that Joe Johnson played a version of the song to you that day you met at the studio?"

"Absolutely. And I never promised to put him in touch with a record label, because he didn't play me anything good that day. That was never discussed."

"And were you aware that Bruce Dean had visited the studio while Johnson was there?"

"I've no idea how he can say that. If somebody had come into the studio, I would have seen them come through the door."

"But why would Bruce Dean lie about that?"

"All I know is that he had a great job in the band and when we found out about his drug taking on tour, we made it clear he had to go. It took him some time to find another job."

"And did Bruce Dean say anything to you once you started recording the song?"

"No, he did not."

"You are absolutely clear that Joe Johnson did not play his song to you?"

"He did not."

"And Bruce Dean did not visit the studio that day and so could not have been a witness to the scene?"

"He did not."

"HELLO HAMMERSMITH!"

"And you had already written *Let's Do It Now* yourself with no input from anyone except Bernie Stanford who gave you the title and helped with the song?"

"That's absolutely right."

"And nobody talked to you about the possibility of you copying this song while you were recording it?"

"Absolutely not!"

"And did you keep any voice notes, lyric doodles or any other records of the creative process?"

"No, not this time. It all happened quickly. We recorded it soon after we found the original piece of paper, but that was in a bit of a state so I rewrote it all out again. It's the rewritten paper that I submitted as evidence."

"No further questions, Your Honour."

It was the turn of Johnson's barrister to cross-examine Gerry. "Mr Stanford, can you tell the court how much you have earned out of this song in royalties?"

"It's difficult to be sure, but it will run into millions of pounds. It was our most successful song by some distance."

"And would you agree that you have to defend a case like this otherwise you face ruin?"

"Well, that's true, but I also need to defend the truth and the correct version of events."

"Can you please stick to answering the questions asked?" the barrister said sternly. "Now can you tell the court where the original piece of paper that you say was in a file for some years is now?"

I Fought The Law (2 July 1993)

"I binned it, I'm afraid. It wasn't in good shape."

"So actually you have no evidence that the song wasn't written the day after it is alleged that Joe Johnson played his version to you?"

"I'm afraid not," Gerry uttered quietly.

"I put it to you, Mr Stanford, that you have lied to the court to save your reputation and your career. Joe Johnson did indeed play this song to you and you stole it and credited it as your own. You took advantage of his position as a struggling songwriter and granted him no credit. And when Bruce Dean said that he recognised the song while you were recording it, you ignored him."

"Absolutely not," Gerry said again slowly and clearly.

"No further questions."

The last witness to be called was Bernie. The plaintiff's barrister addressed her on the stand.

"Mrs Stanford, can you confirm that Mr Stanford brought the idea of this song to you and that you worked on it together after that?"

"Well, that's not quite what happened. As Gerry has said, I came up with the song title without realising and we both took it from there while we were still signed to ERCO. We filed it away until later. It was mainly Gerry's song, to be fair."

"Were you only credited because you inadvertently came up with the title then?"

"Well, kind of, like. We always took joint credit no matter how much input we each had. A bit like Lennon and McCartney, I suppose."

"And you were not in the studio when Joe Johnson visited and cannot give any evidence about what happened during his visit?"

"HELLO HAMMERSMITH!"

"No. I'm afraid not."

"No further questions."

The judge stepped in. "Thank you, Mrs Stanford. I believe that all witnesses have now been called so you may now stand down while I consider my judgement. This court is adjourned."

♫ ♫ ♫ ♫ ♫ ♫ ♫ ♫ ♫ ♫ ♫ ♫ ♫ ♫

It did not take long for the judge to call everyone back to court for judgement.

"First, let's look at the parts of this case that are not disputed and that provide parts of the foundation for a claim. We have two songs which sound similar but two different people claim to have written them. Thanks to the evidence heard, there is no argument one has been copied by the other. The key decision lies in which one was written first.

"Mr Joe Johnson has given his version of events and his witness has corroborated his story. Mr Stanford has no witnesses to his version of events, apart from his spouse, whose testimony I must discount, as she is a co-defendant. He has submitted one page of lyrics which are undated and could have been prepared at any time, but he admits he wrote out this piece of paper the day after he met Joe Johnson. If I were undecided about receiving no credible evidence, this case would have been dismissed. However, as Joe Johnson has a witness, I have little choice but to side with his version of events."

Gerry and Bernie both put their heads in hands.

"I believe that there is some evidence that Joe Johnson did indeed play his song to Mr Stanford on the day that they met in the studio and Mr Stanford has then intentionally copied it and recorded it as his own for his record. I have no alternative but to award 100% of the royalties of

I Fought The Law (2 July 1993)

this song to Joe Johnson and order that past and future royalties be paid to him with costs. Future pressings should credit Mr Johnson only."

♪ ♪ ♪ ♪ ♪ ♪ ♪ ♪ ♪ ♪ ♪ ♪ ♪ ♪

The couple had to deal with a barrage of reporters that swelled their numbers outside the court as soon as the verdict was announced. They had prepared a statement in what they considered to be the likely event with the case being dismissed, but hadn't prepared anything in case the verdict went against them. When the cameras snapped away in their faces, they both had faces like thunder. Bernie started expressing their disappointment calmly when asked about the verdict but was stopped mid-track by Gerry.

"Let's stop this nonsense and tell them the truth, shall we, Bernie? We both know that this verdict is a travesty and at some point, that will become clear to everyone concerned. I've had decades of avoiding copyright issues in our music and the industry should today hang its head in shame."

"Yes, but what do you want to do about it?" asked a journalist who had a microphone close to Gerry's face.

"I think we need to go away and consider our next move," responded a calm Bernie. But Gerry had a markedly different answer.

"That's a brilliant question," he blasted. "Frankly, the only solution is for us to retire from this godforsaken business. I'm asking *all* radio stations to stop playing *all* our songs, not just the one at issue here. And I'm asking the public who have been so good to us over the years to stop buying our records, especially the ones that feature *Let's Do It Now*. If they are kind enough to do that, then we'll stop further damage being done."

After fighting their way to a waiting taxi, they made it home in silence.

When they made it through the front door, Bernie finally let her feelings out. "I don't believe it. How could this happen? I can't see that we have enough to move through this. We're ruined now, for sure. Especially now that you've asked everyone to stop buying the records."

Gerry knew she was right but said nothing. Their barrister had warned them that an appeal had little chance of success without fresh evidence. Another fear was the likely queue of other chancers trying to take a pop at the couple after one had succeeded.

Bernie was incandescent with rage. "One thing was for sure. We will never perform the song again. In fact, it will be in the future referred to exactly as '*That Song*', never to be named again."

Unusually, there was little talk that night as a depression hung over the house and more realisations burdened their mood. Particularly, they would probably be asked to return the Ivor Novello award they received for the song. This truly felt like a case of 'I fought the law and the law won.'

Gerry's descent into a full mental breakdown was swift and would scar him for many years to come. With his confidence gone, there seemed no way back.

As Bernie had feared, the success of Joe Johnson did then lead to further cases coming out of the woodwork. The law firm that had been successful on their 'no win-no fee' basis found themselves the first port of call in these fresh cases. However, on the first one that Bernie contested in court, they were on more solid ground. The case was defended away without a broken Gerry needing to give evidence. In his final summary, the judge was quite withering in his assessment and warned other potential opportunistic plaintiffs not to entertain such a case if they were not convinced of the outcome. His decision that the plaintiff should pay the Stanfords' costs and their own was enough to make all the other cases disappear. Having decided that another loss

I Fought The Law (2 July 1993)

would have meant that they would have needed to declare themselves bankrupt, the Stanfords counted themselves lucky.

Chapter 21 - Get You Into My Heart (January 2016)

It was all great fun. ERCO lodged Light Stone just off Covent Garden, near their Central London offices and studios. The flat accommodated the five of them in three bedrooms. Hannah ended up with a room on her own. The boys paired up, with Dan obviously agreeing to share with Rick. Jack travelled up by train with Liam and was glad to be sharing with him.

Hannah's dad drove her up to town and had a quiet word with each of the boys. He was clear that if they did not look after Hannah, they would be in trouble with him. Liam assured him that his daughter would come to no harm while he was around, which gave the doctor some comfort, as he knew they would stick together. Hannah joked about the situation, almost to ease any tension.

"Eh! None of your parents wanted to have a word with me about looking out for you all. Not fair!"

On the first morning, the band sat down with the solicitors introduced by ERCO. The meeting looked innocent enough. The five were talked through the contract in front of them. It was mainly Rick who asked the questions and most of these were answered fairly clearly, but some of them were answered with a shrug and the interjection, "Look, this is the standard contract. There's not much that ERCO will change."

Hannah called a 'time-out' for them all to discuss and make sure that they were happy with what was being put in front of them. After going around the houses one more time, they decided they had come this far and might as well go ahead. They looked nervously at each other, but when Dan moved forward to sign it, the rest all followed.

They all had to write out their full names under their signature. Rick caused much mirth when he printed his name as Timothy Rickard Sterling. Dan was the first to notice and felt a bit irked he wasn't aware of his best friend's full name. "Timothy! So uncool. No wonder you changed it to Rick."

"Yeah. I know. Not happy with my parents for that legacy."

They were given a modest cash allowance for the first week and quickly realised that it wasn't going to last them long if they ate out every night. The excitement of living away from home without the family rules to abide by disappeared once they realised that meal prices around the Covent Garden area of the city were insane.

The band soon split into two groups. Rick and Dan were clearly better off, and their parents seemed happy to subsidise them. They took full advantage of the situation and became nocturnal party animals. The others came to accept that their shared room would disgorge more than just the two of them in the morning, with Rick making a joke about everything and keeping spirits up.

Hannah, Liam and Jack opted to stick together and cook for themselves before kicking some song ideas around late into the night until the party animals returned.

At first, the band was given a large rehearsal room in the basement of the ERCO offices and could practise whatever and whenever they wished. They ran through all the songs that they planned would go on a first album in a live format, so they could then go straight out on tour. This would prepare them and allow them to go into the studio with a clear idea of their sound and reduce their recording costs.

After a few weeks, Vicky sat them down. She had batted away Rick's comment about her looking "gorgeous this morning," and she started. "Right, you've had some time to become used to the studio and the area. Now it's time to write your first single."

Liam looked confused. "Hang on. We've been practising and we're ready to record 15 songs that we've rehearsed. Surely one of them can be a single? I'm not sure why we would need to write another one."

"Well, I've been listening to what you've been practising, and I couldn't hear a single in there."

Rick interjected. "What? You've been listening? You must have big ears, darling. Wait, isn't this supposed to be a soundproofed room? How could you have heard it?"

"Have you been recording us as well?" Liam questioned.

Vicky snapped. "Never mind that! It's my business to know what you're up to. Remember that you've all signed a contract. We decide what's going to be your first single and what you're going to record. It's the ERCO Way. Now follow me. It's time to meet your producer. This guy is going to set you all on the path to the top of the singles chart, believe me." And with that, she marched out of the rehearsal room and up the stairs.

They looked uncertainly at each other before following Vicky. Up on the first floor, she opened a door off the landing and the unmistakable whiff of weed floated out.

"Ben, it's time to take a break from the research project and produce a hit," she shouted above the loud house music that accompanied the predominant scent. A dishevelled guy with short hair and a neatly trimmed beard eventually came out and rubbed his sleepy eyes before he peered at the five.

"Ah, Light Stone, great to meet you. I've been looking forward to this. Hannah Ross is in your band, isn't she? Quite a talent there. Follow me."

"Do you need to bring that doobie up with you mate?" Rick, who was first to follow, asked.

Ben ignored the comment and headed up the next set of stairs. They dutifully followed him. Behind them, Vicky made her way back downstairs and disappeared back into her office, closing the door firmly behind her.

"HELLO HAMMERSMITH!"

Up on the second floor Ben opened a door that seemed of a similar proportion to the party room that they had just stood outside, but to their surprise the room was quiet. It was an office that hosted a meeting table topped with an open laptop.

"OK guys. There's an open file on there with some things I've been working on for you. It's part of the ERCO research project. Have a listen through the tracks and choose something you like. Come up with some initial lyrics to it, but keep them simple. The team will pull them apart and improve them for you. Then we'll go into the studio and record it. After the magic is done, the first hit single will be yours!"

Hannah was the first to express frustration. "Hang on a minute, Ben. Why don't you at least listen to the songs that we've written already and choose one of them to record? They don't need pulling apart; we've some great ones just waiting."

Ben laughed. "Oh, those songs? None of *those* are any good for us. Your style is too dated for the current market. They all have old style verses and bridges and choruses. That stuff doesn't work anymore. You'll never cut through. Look, you want a hit? Well, I've written lots of hits for new ERCO artists. How many hits have you guys had? None? I thought so. And you're not likely to make it with your current style either. Save yourselves a load of grief and let's do this our way. I'm missing a party to do this." And with a wink and a smile, he left the room.

The five of them sat in stunned silence. Unusually, Jack spoke first. "Wasn't expecting that."

"I don't think any of us were," Rick replied. "Bit of a bolt from the blue that."

Hannah felt slightly guilty. Should she have warned the others that she thought this might happen? "You know, maybe I was expecting this. They behaved strangely all the time I was up here. All I did was spend time with the team who were trying to create some new image for me.

They were definitely trying to turn me into something that I'm not. I didn't receive that treatment about the first single though, because I never made it this far." Getting some courage from being in a team, she looked at everyone in turn. "What are we going to do? We could just walk and go back to the flat?"

Liam's tone was beaming with resolve. "Only one thing we can do. Let's stop wasting time and go to the top." The other four looked puzzled. "We haven't seen much of her, but Erica Conway must have an office here somewhere, probably on the top floor. Let's confront her. Tell her we're unhappy."

"Yes, that's right!" Hannah agreed. "I was taken up there a few times."

"Can't say I'm too worried," Rick added with a shrug. "But let's go and I'll charm her into getting this sorted out."

The door creaked on its hinges as they opened it and peered out onto the landing. There was nobody about. Keeping as quiet as they could, they headed for the stairs and made their way up. There was just one more floor in the building. Hannah went first and firmly knocked twice on the door with her knuckle before opening it. Jack made sure that he was at the back of the group. The layout differed from the floors below. She walked into a much smaller room with just a little light coming in from the window and a smart lady behind a desk.

"Ah, hello Hannah. Good to see you back here. Can I help you?" the woman enquired.

"Yes, please," Hannah pleaded. "My band has just signed with ERCO and we're here to see Miss Conway."

There was a moment of silence as the lady looked at her screen and moved her mouse with her right hand. "I'm sorry but there's nothing booked. You'll have to come back later."

"HELLO HAMMERSMITH!"

"That's okay." Hannah replied, opening the door fully so that the others could come in. "We'll just wait here until she can fit us in."

"You don't understand. Miss Conway isn't actually here at the moment."

"That's quite okay," Hannah insisted. "We can wait here until she's available. We have plenty of time." And with that, she sat down on the floor under the window and motioned the others to do the same.

"But you can't. It's not allowed."

"We're going to," Rick assured her with a big smile, aware that they outnumbered her. "This is im-por-tant." The rest of them joined Hannah on the floor in the small room. And so they waited.

"If you refuse to move, then I'm going to have to call secur…." The lady's voice tailed off as the phone rang next to her. She listened before pausing and saying. "Yes, Miss Conway. I'm sorry to have disturbed you. That's right. Light Stone would like to see you. They say they won't leave." She stopped to listen. "Yes, I understand. I'll tell them that." She put the phone down.

"Miss Conway is on her way back to London but she won't be here for another couple of hours. She suggests that in the meantime you go back to the room downstairs as instructed and work on the song choices that Ben left with you. She'll find time to see you once it's completed."

The band looked at each other. "I suppose we'd better go back down and start then," Dan shrugged. "Better than sitting around here doing nothing."

With murmured agreement, they headed out towards the room downstairs. Jack quickly looked closer at a framed magazine cutting on the wall that he'd noticed while they were waiting. It featured the Top 50 most influential people in the UK music business from a weekly Music Industry paper from a few years before. It listed Ernie Conway at number 13, Eric at number 20 and lower at number 49, Erica.

Get You Into My Heart (January 2016)

The room downstairs was as they had left it. The open laptop seemed to have been waiting for them at the meeting table. Liam tapped on the pad and the screen livened. With a sigh, they sat down around it. Dan started playing the clips. Most of them were greeted with a "next" as soon as they started and just a few made it to more than a minute. They boiled the choice down to a couple and settled on a simple four-chord loop in E minor/B minor/A minor/B minor. Liam was sniffy about it. "This is just a *Get Lucky* copy. We would never write something as simple as this anymore. Should be easy to come up with something quickly so that we are done with this and can move on."

There were about three minutes of the chords on a loop. With little enthusiasm, they set about coming up with basic lyrics, which they then recorded over the loop using the software associated with the file. They started with what they thought could be the main hook.

> *Gotta get - you into my heart*
>
> *Gotta get - you into my heart*
>
> *Oh I need to – get you in my heart*
>
I was just a lonely man
Couldn't make a start
Why won't you just understand?
Oh I need to – get you in my heart
> *Chorus*

Every day the sun comes up
It hurts when we're apart
Why won't you wake up with me?
Oh! I need to – get you in my heart

"HELLO HAMMERSMITH!"

With a final chorus, the song came in at just less than three minutes. They added some rough vocal harmonies, saved the file and left it at that.

When they opened the door to leave, it was blocked by the bodyguard who they had first seen at the college escorting Erica and Vicky. "Stay there," he commanded. "Have you finished the track?"

They nodded meekly.

"Good, then you can go back upstairs. Miss Conway is ready now."

Erica Conway sat behind her mahogany desk at the end of the room and her bodyguard followed them up and squeezed into a chair in the outer room with the secretary. Erica's perfume hit them as soon as they stepped in. They wondered why it was necessary for the desk to be on a plinth, which meant that even when she was seated, she was at eye level with anyone who was standing in front of her. Involuntarily, they lined up in front of her desk. She wasn't looking her usual manicured self. The designer suit was still immaculate, but her hair appeared to have been hastily tidied up. She immediately launched into a tirade.

"*Right*! What's all this *rubbish* I've been hearing? You've only been here *five minut*es and I'm getting fed up with the lot of you already."

"Well, you are looking slightly rough today, to be fair," Rick started and smiled, before realising that he probably hadn't started well.

"We don't want any trouble, Miss Conway," Liam intervened, keen to diffuse any problems. "There just seems to have been a few misunderstandings about how this is going to work."

"Yes," an indignant Hannah continued. "We came here to record the songs that we've written and rehearsed over the past year and they're just getting ignored. Instead, you've given us a load of clicks and beats to work with. That just isn't who we are as a band."

"Do you want to be in the Top 40 or not?" Erica questioned with a dismissive shrug. "Didn't you *read* the contract that you signed?" she enquired, pointing at nobody in particular. "If not, you had better read it and look at it closely. It will make clear to you that ERCO are in control and you're going to work to *our* rules. Look, you people clearly don't listen to the charts at the moment. Your juvenile bolshie political protest songs aren't what people want. Clicks and beats is what it's all about now. We've done the research and we know."

"And what if we don't want to?" Liam hesitantly asked.

"Check the contract," she cut in, finger now moving to point at him instead of Hannah. "You do as we say. There is no get-out clause."

"But we didn't actually receive independent legal advice, did we?" Rick questioned. "It was ERCO's legal team that went through it with us."

"You waived your right to independent legal advice," stated Erica.

"Did we?" asked Hannah.

"And what about the cooling-off period? That would be standard in any contract like this?" Rick insisted.

Erica looked at her calendar and sneered. "You think you're *clever*, don't you Mr Sterling? I shall need to watch you closely. Indeed, there was. A 14-day cooling-off period is standard in all our contracts and – oh look! It expired yesterday. I've no idea how you all missed that! Right, I think we have everything straightened out now and everyone should be clear where they stand. I understand you've done the demo recording for the song now, so we'll see you all in the studio tomorrow to record it. Am I making myself *crystal* clear?"

"Wow, you're a right Boadeceiver," Rick mumbled through his teeth. A dumbfounded Erica frowned at the barely heard sound while his friends struggled to stifle giggles. She stared at them impatiently with an inquisitive look. The band knew they had little choice but to go along with it and mumbled assent. Erica rose from the chair, answered her buzzing mobile phone and wafted past them out of the door, her face still thunderous. As she walked down the stairs, followed by her bodyguard, they could hear her sternly saying, "All sorted and under control – there won't be any more trouble. I'm on my way." Out of the large picture window that overlooked the street, they could see her getting straight into the back of a waiting limousine.

They started discussing what had just happened, but Rick stopped them. "Let's go back to the flat. This place could be bugged. On second thoughts let's go to a café. The flat could be bugged as well."

Over a drink around the corner, they went over the events of the last few hours. Rick and Dan weren't too worried. Rick confessed that he had expected something of that nature and believed that ERCO would be the first rung on the music ladder. The others weren't so sure.

"Let's see what happens tomorrow," was Rick's opinion. "We should be careful though. I really think she's a real-life Boadeceiver," he said with a wry smile.

Jack also smiled. "Think you've made up another new word, Rick?"

"Maybe... possibly. She's a formidable woman who you just can't trust. I think I quite like her though!"

Some smiled and some nodded. Jack wrote Rick's new word down in his notebook, next to the note about Erica being 49th on the Most Influential list.

In the back of the limousine, Erica was on the phone to Vicky and the message was blunt. "Can't you keep the numpties under some sort of control, Tucker? They're beginning to treat the building as their own, just going into any old room when they feel like it. It's a good job they didn't venture into the room where we were working on the algorithms with the in-house team; otherwise the game could have been up.

Luckily, my secretary could stall them while I showered and put my makeup on again. Make sure it doesn't happen again!"

And with that, she hung up and continued to seethe.

When a subdued band arrived back at the flat, a Special Delivery letter was waiting for Jack. He recognised the Barton and Co name on the franking stamp as the solicitors' firm in which Paul Eagle was a partner, so he made sure that he opened it carefully before reading the letter inside.

Dear Jack,

I hope this letter finds you well. I have been trying to catch up with you for some time and I understand from the Michaels that you are up in London with ERCO. Please don't sign any contract with them until you have allowed me to review it with you. I need to warn you I have experience with ERCO and their contracts with your parents. Whenever I have come into contact with them, I have found them to be one-sided and quite ruthless in their execution.

In the meantime, I write to inform you I was contacted by a local law firm as the co-executor of your parents' estates. As the surviving child of Gerald and Bernadette Stanford, you have been left a substantial sum in the will of a local man. Should you not have been alive at his time of death, the sum would have instead gone to two road safety charities, Brake and Road Peace. The donor's name rang a faint bell and it soon dawned on me it matched the sole witness to your parents' accident. The man could never give much detail of the two people in the car that caused the accident and left the scene. But he mentioned they were a young lady and an older man in a white Range Rover.

The whole thing is suspicious because, as you know, they never identified the driver that the coroner held responsible for the accident. I have alerted the police and they are now investigating and interrogating the man's family. Those closest to him have apparently said that he was a changed person after the accident and withdrew into himself. I will let you know as soon as I have more details.

In the meantime, I still need to see you to explain the details of your parents' estate. As the Michaels would have told you, a trust was set up which reverts to you on your 18th birthday, which passed some time ago. I need your instructions about how you would now like to proceed.

Kind regards,

Paul Eagle

Having skim read it the first time, Jack now scrutinised it more carefully but skipped the first paragraph with its reference to the ERCO contract. He then folded it up again, neatly placing it back in the envelope and tucked it into his rucksack.

This had all come as a surprise. Mabel and Jim had only said that the accident was a hit and run and that as so much time had passed, no one was expected to be held responsible for it. So why was he being left some money?

Get You Into My Heart (January 2016)

Chapter 22 - Good Morning Judge (1 July 1993)

Gerry and Bernie were up early. They would have preferred a lie in and would have gladly taken the day as it came. But today was their first day in court. They would be defending the ownership of their biggest song, the one that broke them in the US and stayed near the top of the charts for four consecutive weeks. This second single from their third album on the Multiplier label brought them to a new audience around the world and turned the album into a multi-platinum seller. The icing on the cake had been that the most successful version that caused the bulk of the royalties to pour in was under their deal with Good Record Co. The first version with Multiplier was only on the old 7.5% rate and the Good deal was way better.

The hearing was scheduled to run for two days at the London court. They hurried in early to meet their barrister and avoid the crowds. The case had received a fair amount of publicity even before it started. The speculation questioned the point of defending such a claim when, on the face of it, Stanford didn't stand a chance of success. It looked like a standard case of 'successful songwriter steals song from struggling songwriter'. The Stanfords had been adamant in the run up to the case that the claim was baseless and couldn't be taken seriously.

The judge listened to the opening statements from both barristers and summarised them for those present. "It is my task to decide whether the accused, Mr and Mrs Stanford, have consciously or unconsciously appropriated the compositional work of Joe Johnson. There are two questions that I must consider and we will devote a day to each. First, is there evidence to corroborate the similarity of the two songs and so determine if one has been copied from the other? Second, we need to determine which one has been copied. I must judge this carefully, as there is much at stake." He took a brief sip of water from the glass in front of him before continuing. "Would the plaintiff's legal team please call their first witness?"

"HELLO HAMMERSMITH!"

Joe Johnson's barrister stood up. "Thank you, Your Honour. The plaintiff has instructed an expert witness to consider his claim and that witness will open the proceedings here. Can the clerk please call Thomas Cronin to the witness box?"

A young, dark-haired and bespectacled man made his way to the lectern and duly took his oath.

Joe Johnson's barrister stood up and addressed the witness. "Mr Cronin, for the benefit of the court, could you please state your name, profession and your experience in works related to this court's interest?"

"Certainly. My name is Thomas Cronin. I am currently a Senior University Lecturer and I am a professional songwriter and musicologist. I specialise in the extensive analysis of all forms of music. As a result, I have developed the objectivity to listen to music without bias on its quality, simply to determine the extent of similarity between two pieces. Music publishers, advertising agencies, composers, songwriters, lawyers and the courts have commissioned my services to advise on matters. Although I cannot give details about my previous clients, I am considered in the music industry as one of the top forensic musicologists in the country."

"Thank you, Mr Cronin. Can you please clarify your role for the court today?"

"Of course. The plaintiff has asked me to listen to both songs, establish their level of similarity and to give evidence of whether one of these songs has copied the other. I'm looking for what is termed 'commonplace elements' or 'substantial similarity'. There is then the question about whether the second artist had access to the work that they are said to have copied and I cannot comment at all on that."

"And what are the conclusions of your extensive analysis, Mr Cronin?" the barrister encouraged.

Good Morning Judge (1 July 1993)

"Well, I should start by defining music plagiarism. The law defines this as the use of material subject to copyright that has been used without the express written permission of the owner of the rights. If an artist then presents the song as their own, they can be found guilty of plagiarism.

"Artists can commonly commit plagiarism by sampling audio from another song, which would be a breach of sound recording copyright. There is no accusation of that nature in this case, and I have found no evidence of such plagiarism either.

"The second type of plagiarism occurs when a composition has been copied in a breach of musical work copyright. To establish whether this is the case, I analyse a piece of music, pull it apart and work out its notes, progressions and other more technical aspects, such as its waveform, the sounds used and how these might contribute to similarity."

He paused, and after sipping on his glass of water, continued. "The main question everybody wants answered is *has copying taken place?*"

The barrister took over, almost helping to keep the audience in suspense.

"Thank you, Mr Cronin. Before you give us your opinion, could you maybe first explain to us how likely it is that one song can copy another? My knowledge of music tells me that there are just twelve notes and so it must be easy to think that two songs sound similar."

"Well, you could be forgiven for thinking that. But in practice, it's not nearly so straightforward. If you look at it mathematically, the chances of one note following another is 1 in 12, the chances of another one following those two to make a sequence of three is 1 in 144; add one more and you're up to 1 in 1,728. Now I have exaggerated that a bit because it's more likely that a sequence of notes in a popular song will be close together rather than jump around all over the place, but you see the point. Then you have to look at more than just the sequence of notes. Once you think about aspects like the length of each note and the underlying rhythm, then you're into some huge odds in just one line of a verse. Add another line and the odds can be incalculable."

"Thank you for setting the scene so well for us, Mr Cronin. And now could you please refer to the matter at hand and tell us the conclusions of your expert analysis?"

"Certainly. I will first look for similarities in chord structure, lyrical content and melody. Many songs have used the same I-V-IV-vi chord structure. This structure is the most common chord progression and features in a huge number of songs such as *Let It Be* by The Beatles, *No Woman, No Cry* by Bob Marley and *Take on Me* by a-ha. It's not possible to copyright a chord sequence. It has a bearing when considered with other evidence, however. Here, both songs share the same unusual chord sequence of I-IV-V-vi, which is looped. Both songs are mid-tempo at exactly 120 beats per minute. They both have a similar rhythmic feel – straight 8s 4/4 time, in 8-bar sections. This similarity is not remarkable, given that it applies to a huge number of songs. Both songs are simple minor pentatonic riffs, so anyone composing this type of riff would use the same 5-note palette from which to choose pitches.

"The songs are in different keys, which isn't unusual, as keys are selected to suit the singer. When you transcribe the pieces into the same key and look at the melody, they are similar. In fact, one chorus could be said to be a direct copy of the other and the key payoff line is identical. I have presented to the court a comparison which shows that with only a few differences, the notes line up perfectly. The lyrics are similar also, especially as the titles match so closely, *Let's Do It* and *Let's Do It Now*. They are in different music styles. Mr Johnson's is definitely guitar-based and Mr Stanford's, while sounding keyboard-based, has probably been written on a guitar as well. I say this because the chords in Mr Stanford's song suggest that. Interestingly, they both end with an emphasis on the word 'now' which has some roots in the Sweet song

Good Morning Judge (1 July 1993)

Teenage Rampage and others. There's a slight pause on the Joe Johnson song before 'now'."

"And what then do these findings suggest, Mr Cronin?"

"There is no doubt in my mind that there are 'commonplace elements', so I believe one song is a direct copy of the other. You would have needed to hear one to write the other that closely. The close match of the chord progression and lyrics could not have been achieved without some copying being involved."

"Thank you, Mr Cronin. Now, as you will be aware, our client could open themselves up to the need to defend their own claim of plagiarism if another songwriter believes that their song was in fact plagiarised by Mr Johnson. Such a claim could negate your client's claim in this case. Have you researched that aspect?"

"Yes, I have indeed conducted what is termed 'prior art research' to see if the melodies are, in fact, so common that other examples exist already. There are plenty of common elements with other songs in existence, but in terms of the actual melody I could find no other examples of relevance to this case."

"Thank you, Mr Cronin. So you are telling me that Mr Johnson is protectable by copyright. And in your expert opinion, was that copying accidental or intentional?"

"Are you asking me if this was a case of cryptomnesia, where someone mistakes a buried memory for an original idea?"

The barrister looked serious and inquisitive but there was no doubt he was smiling at his game inside. "Yes, Mr Cronin, is it possible that this was just an accidental copy and has the industry ever faced such a dilemma before?"

"The best example of this could be George Harrison, who was successfully sued for subconsciously plagiarising The Chiffons' *He's So*

Fine when writing his big hit *My Sweet Lord*. I have no doubt this is not a factor here. Whichever song was copied, the act was definitely intentional."

"No further questions, Your Honour," the barrister smiled as he sat back down.

Stanford's barrister stood up. "Thank you for that explicit statement, Mr Cronin. I have just one question for you. Is it possible to establish whether one song was written before the other?"

"I'm afraid there is no way of knowing which of these songs was written first."

"So, it would be absolutely possible for the Stanford song to have been written first and played on the radio before Joe Johnson wrote a similar song and try to pass it off as an original by foul means?"

"Yes, it would. Either could have been written first."

"I have no further questions." The barrister sat down.

"Thank you, Mr Cronin," the judge followed. "You may stand down. This hearing is adjourned until tomorrow."

"All rise," the clerk called.

Good Morning Judge (1 July 1993)

Chapter 23 - Going Forwards In Reverse (January/February 2016)

Light Stone reluctantly went to the studio the next day. They weren't looking forward to a whole session with Ben after the brief experience they'd had with him.

Hannah tried to be reassuring. "It might not take long. He probably has a party that he's missing." She then puffed on an imaginary spliff as though it was something she had done before.

Liam seconded her words with a further suggestion. "Let's at least give this a chance. You never know, this could go well." Whilst nobody really believed him, they started the trudge through the London streets all the same.

An extremely unhappy Vicky Tucker greeted them on arrival, her arms folded and her face frowned in a hard stare.

"Crumbs Vicky!" Rick exclaimed. "That's a few wasps you're chewing there! Still looking quite sexy though."

"I'll be chewing you in a minute, sonny. What on earth are you doing demanding to see Miss Conway at short notice? If you're unhappy about anything, you come and talk to *me*. Miss Conway has quite enough to worry about without having to deal with your pathetic minor issues. Next time just tell her that everything is fine and we'll deal with it, alright?"

As Hannah was about to take Vicky on, Liam physically restrained her. She struggled for a bit and then stopped, realising that Liam was much stronger. The rest of the band simply nodded in agreement and Rick diffused the situation with a smile and a joke. They were afraid of Vicky's temper but realised that complaining was pointless.

"HELLO HAMMERSMITH!"

They were surprised to find Ben in the studio, ready for them, and apparently so for some time. "Right, let's create this hit, guys. Let me play you what I've got." He played his version, which had a fresh drum and bass sample and washes of keyboards over their original vocals. "Don't worry about your vocals – we're going to re-record them today."

"What about all the instrumentation?" Hannah asked. "It needs to be done by us otherwise it's not a Light Stone record. There are none of Liam's guitars in there."

"And there aren't proper drums," Rick added. "It's not real if there aren't proper drums on it."

"Or bass," Dan echoed.

Ben held his hands up. "Don't panic, don't worry. This is just a starter track. Make yourselves at home in the vocal booths and we'll record something while there's still daylight."

He had them do two versions of the song. In the first version, Hannah sang the lead. Her nerves soon defeated her again and she hit a few notes flat. She pleaded to redo the part.

"Oh, don't worry about a few bum notes," Ben quickly reassured her. "We can fix that later. Right, I hear you can sing a bit, Jack. Jump in and give it your best shot." Hannah stamped her feet in frustration while Liam put a comforting arm around her.

Although he didn't feel that motivated to give a virtuoso performance and he had never worked like this before, Jack gave it his best effort. Overall, everyone agreed that, on the day, he had done the better version.

"OK, that's great guys! We'll go through the recordings later and see whether one of you gets to lead or we do this as a duet. Leave it to us. Right – time to capture some backing vocals. Everyone in the booth!"

Half-heartedly, they all crammed into the vocal booth and with headphones to one ear, as they had seen in documentaries, listened to the backing track they hated and shouted into the one microphone. They knew it sounded terrible. It took a few takes for them not to keep putting each other off, but finally Ben was happy with what he had.

Liam was hesitant about his singing part. "Can we do one without me? I've never been able to sing."

"Sure, one more go. But then that's it."

Once the vocals were done, Ben conceded they could record their different parts.

Rick struggled with the studio drum kit as it was set up differently compared to what he was used to. He tried to move the kit around but was told that it had to stay in that format for ERCO's house drummer. "That guy must have twisted limbs to play that," he muttered before he still produced a solid backing track that impressed Ben, raising his eyebrows.

Dan struggled to hear the backing track on his headphones and missed a few cues. Only Liam nailed his part without a problem.

By the end, they wondered whether any of their recordings were going to be used. Whenever they asked to do it again, the response was always, "It's fine, don't worry about it. We can fix a few bum notes."

As they finished, they asked Ben for a copy of the different versions so they could pick the best one.

"Don't panic, don't worry!" Ben sang with no particular melody, with his hands up again. "We have a separate team who listen to everything once I've finished and then we go with the best one. Believe me; they know what they're doing. They've never been wrong yet. We've done the research, you know."

"HELLO HAMMERSMITH!"

"So, we don't even get to voice an opinion on which version is used?" Hannah asked.

"Not since we had a disaster many years ago with someone. Can't remember her name."

"Was that Gillian Fox?" asked Hannah pointedly. "We heard that ERCO really screwed her up."

"Never mind that. Check the contract, young lady. I think you'll find that ERCO has the first and final say on anything that happens in this studio and it's the only studio you're able to use. Don't worry. We've wasted enough time on you lot as it is. This baby is getting released digitally just as soon as we've finished mixing and mastering it."

"That's bollocks!" Hannah shouted as they shut the front door and started walking back to the flat.

"It was worse than bollocks," suggested Rick, who for once wasn't happy. "I think I'm going to have to work harder on charming Vicky." The others agreed how disappointing it had been and none of them held high hopes for the result.

As they came up from the basement studio, their phones came to life as the signal returned and Jack found a message from Colin. He was up in town and could pop round to the flat. When they arrived back at the flat, they found him waiting for them on the doorstep.

"Hey guys, you're here! That's lucky. I've just been having a discussion about a small TV project with a producer and thought that I could swing by on the off chance that you were here. How's it all going?"

He asked even though their faces said it all. It was Rick who summed it up best.

"We're going forwards in reverse."

Going Forwards In Reverse (January/February 2016)

They all looked at each other at the same time and agreed that was a great title for a song. Not wanting to spend too much time in the flat that could be bugged, they piled into a small cafe and started playing with some lyrics. Every instrument that they had to hand with them was then taken out to pin the basic chords down, much to the bemusement of the other customers.

Before long, they had something that worked. Colin suggested they did it in the style of Bruce Springsteen. He also inspired them further with Michael Jackson's Moonwalk on YouTube. The video showed the King of Pop appearing to walk forwards whilst actually moving backwards. Soon, lyrics were formed:

The way I live my life, it don't make no sense

I plan the future, but it's all in the past tense

You'll think my life's mixed up, of that I'm sure

If you could see me coming in through the out door

And I can't work out if it's a blessing or a curse

    I'm going forwards in reverse

It seems so natural; let me tell you how it feels

I press the loud pedal but I'm just spinning wheels

I take one step back, but I'm better than before

I get demoted but the Boss he pays me more

I go back to go forward, it's so perverse

    I'm going forwards in reverse

"HELLO HAMMERSMITH!"

There was room here for a solo from Liam who attacked it with gusto and smiled for the first time that day. They went onto the Middle 8, which was much slower:

> *This crazy messed up life has some advantage sure*
> *I'm older now but looking younger than before*
>
> *Don't be surprised if you see me moonwalk past you*
> *If I'm to get somewhere, it's what I have to do*
> *If I look happy, it's because I'm feeling sad*
> *You see me smile, then that means my life is bad*
> *I must feel negative to end up the converse*
> > *I'm going forwards in reverse*

They agreed to keep this one to themselves and then talked seriously about what their next move would be. They were due to go back into the offices the next day to put some more lyrics to some of Ben's ideas. Although there had been a vague offer of some studio time to do some of their own songs, that plan was better put on hold for the time being. Hannah suggested she feign illness to avoid the recording. They recognised that this would cost them money but also knew that wasn't a priority at the moment. They felt bad making excuses, but it seemed like the only sensible thing to do.

♪ ♪ ♪ ♪ ♪ ♪ ♪ ♪ ♪ ♪ ♪ ♪ ♪ ♪

Ben was at least good to his word. Before long, the single was ready for digital release. The band spent the release day in Canterbury. The usual ERCO release campaign was in full swing. They had arranged an arty video to be teased a few days beforehand and then released in full on the day. The band mimed to it in some trendy new clothes that had been chosen for them. Their discomfort and lack of enthusiasm were obvious and for good reasons beyond the aforementioned. The released version had the original backing instrumentation Ben had played to them when they arrived at the studio. The listening group, which included Erica, judged the band's recorded instruments to be "too rough" by some distance. They chose the version in which Hannah sang. Her flat notes were clearly pushed to fit the key. While an untrained ear would miss this pitch change, Colin had taught them to recognise these at the college studio. The result just wasn't a fair reflection of them. Was it their plan to push Hannah to the front all along? After all, it was Hannah who won the ERCO competition and refused the contract without her band. Had they been used to ensnare her?

There had also been some interviews arranged with "young and hip" radio stations and the group spent weeks being on the receiving end of inane questions that they tried hard to answer honestly. Although the ERCO marketing team had told them what to say and how to present themselves, there was no stopping the leakage of their true feelings. This meant another scolding from Vicky and a warning that they had "better watch their step or bear the consequences."

Jack had gone round to the Chapel with Macy and played an advance copy to Colin, who sat impassively through it at first and then harboured a questioning look across his face. He scurried over to his computer and tapped some words into the search box of his music library. "Have a listen to this and tell me what you think," he said, hiding the track information.

As Jack listened, he realised what was on Colin's mind. Ben appeared to have taken samples from the original song and looped them for their single. He also had no problem recognising the singers, although he had never heard the song before.

"That's mum and dad?"

"Exactly. And which company released this song as a single in 1983?"

"HELLO HAMMERSMITH!"

"Guess that was ERCO."

"Exactly. They were known as Stanford-Williams in those early days. This was one of their first singles, *Haunted by the Pain,* and would have been on Top of the Pops during its chart run. That's a bit of a coincidence. Do you think ERCO know you're their son and have done this on purpose?"

"Can't imagine how they could have worked that out. Come to think of it, the backing was just one option they gave us, so actually we chose it."

"Hmm. That could be intuition on your part. It's cheeky that ERCO once accused Stanford of copying other ERCO songs and yet they are now doing it themselves! Maybe this is what their mysterious research project is all about – recycling old hits. You could have a case against them, but I wouldn't worry too much. If I know anything about the pop world, it is that this song will soon disappear without a trace."

Jack was thoughtful. "Don't think I can ignore it. Might come in useful sometime."

When the reviews came in, they were mixed in the extreme. Some of them were glowing in their praise, which surprised Colin and the band, while others were suitably damning. They watched their social media platforms and were not surprised when their die-hard local fans were not at all impressed. Their supporters even questioned what on earth had happened to the authentic live sound that they had spent so long honing at gigs?

The preparations didn't require the band's presence in London at the ERCO offices, which, in the circumstances, was just as well. Stories reached them that since they had done the recording in January, the atmosphere in the offices had darkened considerably. Erica Conway was rarely there and when the chauffeur-driven car brought her in, she could be heard shouting, even screaming, at anyone with whom she came into contact. A steady stream of men in dark suits arrived at the offices and left much later. About the only person who was not reduced to tears was Vicky, who took the brunt of the anger and replied with her characteristic firmness. Erica's appearance reportedly became more haggard over the weeks and months so that even her makeup lady could not disguise the strain she was under.

The reason for Erica's mood had become obvious earlier in the month. One of the world's biggest offshore law firms had been the victim of a leak of 11½ million files to a German newspaper. A rumour quickly circulated that ERCO had been a hidden owner of some offshore companies and related bank accounts for many years and this was now visible to investigators. Rick was also worried. It seemed his own father had an offshore account, which he was now going to need to declare and pay some tax on. This meant that comments such as "serves them right" and "about time too" that the rest of the band felt strongly about, couldn't be made in Rick's presence.

In the meantime, Jack had been doing more research into his parents and their lives. He had never bothered with this until now. Soon enough, he came across the 1993 court case that his parents had lost. The event was featured in various lists of "Most famous cases of alleged plagiarism in music." He listened to the two songs back to back and had to admit that there were marked similarities, even to his young and still minimally trained ears.

A few days later, Jack had a call from Paul Eagle, who jumped straight to the point, as always.

"Hello Jack. I hope you don't mind me calling. I need to give you some important information as soon as possible. Mabel gave me your mobile number, but I haven't shared with her what I'm about to tell you. Do you understand?"

"Sure."

"HELLO HAMMERSMITH!"

"Do you remember my letter to you a few months ago, the one about the substantial amount of money left to you in the will of a witness to your parents' accident?"

"Yes, remember that."

"Good. The solicitors have now confirmed the amount." Paul communicated the sum and paused before he continued. There was no audible response from Jack, although his mind was turning cartwheels.

"The police continued their investigation into the witness's affairs. His bank account showed that this exact sum was deposited into his account just a few months after the accident. This was suspicious and the police agreed it was too much of a coincidence. They believed that the money was likely paid by someone trying to hide the identity of the white Range Rover car driver. Their trail went dead after that since they couldn't identify the source of the funds from the description on the account. That was until the Panama Papers leak hit the papers at the beginning of the month. A bit of digging swiftly found that the money had come from an offshore account in the British Virgin Islands controlled by ERCO!"

Jack was shocked, intrigued and more. "What …. does that mean?"

"It almost certainly means that Ernie Conway, who seems to have been the sole signatory on the account, was involved directly in the crash or at least knew who was involved and wanted to protect them by keeping their identity quiet. He's been interviewed by the police, but he is suffering from a touch of dementia. He's denied all knowledge of the transfer and can't explain how it happened. The police also found that he owned a white Range Rover at the time of the crash and that the vehicle was scrapped soon afterwards. With no better proof than this circumstantial evidence, the police can't take any action, but they wanted to let me know how far they had dug. The witness must have felt guilty having accepted the money and has eased his conscience by passing it on in his will. If he at least had given a deathbed confession, they would have had some evidence to use in court, but as it is, there isn't a trail that can be investigated further."

"OK, understand."

"There's just one other thing that you should know. The witness had only said that the driver of the Range Rover was a smartly dressed youngish lady and there was an older man with her. It's pure speculation at the moment, but Erica Conway was aged 16 at the time of the accident and would not have been legally able to drive. I'm just putting a couple of strands together here, but it's conceivable that she was the driver of the car that was in the accident with your parents. I'd repeat that this is still speculation though and best not repeated."

"So Erica Conway could have been responsible for my parents' death?"

"That is mere speculation. Another thing while I remember. Mabel told me that your band had released a single on the ERCO label. I hope an experienced lawyer reviewed it before you all signed?"

"Sure. Some lawyers talked us through it."

"OK – I hope they did a proper job for your sake."

Once Jack put the phone down, he took some time to process this new information.

Going Forwards in Reverse can be streamed free here:

https://soundcloud.com/the-colour-spectrum/going-forwards-in-reverse

Chapter 24 - Scandalous (June 1993)

On 8 June 1993, Prince's publicist announced the artist would henceforth be known not by the name on his contract with Warner Brothers, but as a symbol. He would not tell people how this symbol was to be pronounced. Prince hoped that this would help him release the music that his record company didn't want elsewhere. When that didn't work, he wrote the word 'Slave' on his face.

This didn't unduly trouble Gerry and Bernie, who were recording some songs for their next, as yet untitled, album. But then they received a visit from Harvey D'Angelo, who looked more than a little concerned.

"I have a lot of bad news for you," he announced in one breath. He paused and swallowed. "I've heard that Multiplier Records are in financial trouble."

"What!" Bernie exclaimed. "How the hell did that happen?"

"It seems they had a run of flops after you left them for Oscar's label. David Black's A&R team seem to have lost the plot somewhere along the way and they've been caught out overpaying for what initially looked like some good signings but all turned out to be poor."

"I noticed that all of their releases have been panned by the press as soon as they came out," noted Gerry. "They couldn't seem to feature on any radio playlists, and very few people bought them."

"That's right. The royalty cheques have dried up as well, but they always came up with a plausible story when I called. They claimed they were the target of some malicious practices by unnamed rivals, but they couldn't work out who was behind it."

"I think we can guess," observed Bernie. "What does that mean for the royalties that we're owed and from future sales?"

"HELLO HAMMERSMITH!"

"Well, that's the next bit of bad news for you. It seems that ERCO found out and made an offer to the directors to take over the catalogue and the assets, but leave the contracts behind. The deal means all contracts are worthless and there won't be any more royalties until they've recouped what they paid."

"What a surprise. We can kiss goodbye to anything else from that," Gerry concluded. "It's a good job we moved to Oscar when we did, I guess."

"Yes, you're right. Unfortunately, I've yet more bad news for you. I've received another letter suggesting that you didn't write one of your songs."

"Oh, not again!" Bernie exclaimed. "Aren't people bored with wasting their flipping time and ours with nuisance value claims like this? None of the previous accusations have had any substance and most of them are just laughable. Which song are they saying this time?"

"I'm afraid they're going for the big one this time, Bernie."

Bernie's temperature visibly soared. "Not *Let's Do It Now*? But that's outrageous. We've already defended that song in court. There's never been a song quite like it before, which is why it sold so well and won so many awards. Who's having a laugh this time?"

"That's the thing. It's not an established artist this time. It's an unknown singer-songwriter who says that he had a co-writing session with Gerry before *Blindside* was released. He alleges he played Gerry the song, which was then used without crediting him," and specifically turning to Gerry, "Joe Johnson. Does that ring any bell?"

"That's crazy!" a visibly annoyed Gerry retorted. "I remember Joe Johnson. We didn't hit it off at all and he was on his way pretty quickly. It was a waste of time and nothing of any value came out of it. Surely he can't afford to bring a case?"

Scandalous (June 1993)

"Well… it seems he can. I have a letter from a big law firm, who seem to be happy to take a bit of a chance if you're flying a kite of a claim."

"What are they asking for?" Bernie wondered.

"They're asking for lead credit on the song and a substantial settlement as compensation for loss of royalties."

"Can I see?"

Bernie took the letter from Harvey's hand and read the long letter in silence. "This is total rubbish from start to finish." She handed the letter to Gerry. "It says that they have sent a CD that includes the version of the song they say was stolen."

"Yes, I have the copy here. Shall I play it?"

"Why not? Give us all a laugh to see how unlike ours it is." Gerry smiled with confidence.

Harvey popped the CD into the tray and pressed play. They listened in silence as they realised that the song was indeed similar to their biggest hit.

"I don't understand," Gerry almost whispered as the song concluded. "I've certainly never heard this before and I can only think that he's heard our song, copied it and is now trying to extract a chunk of change out of us."

"You would think this guy would have realised that we haven't given in to any of those claims in the past, out of principle," Bernie added. "Once you give in to one of them, you're flooded with claims just like that. We'll probably have to defend again then… won't we?"

"Absolutely," Gerry affirmed. "Can't give in to something as blatant as this. Right Harvey, can you tell Paul Eagle about this? He's dealt with a few of these before and hopefully he can make this one go away as well."

"Do you think we should stop recording while we deal with this?" Bernie asked. "If it's successful, then we're going to need all the money that we have to pay them off."

"No way!" Gerry insisted. "They'll think that we're doing that out of guilt. Everything carries on as usual."

A few weeks later, it was Paul Eagle who sat in the front room with Harvey next to him. "I'm afraid the other side isn't giving an inch on this one. In fact, they're giving us a choice between settling out of court now, going to court in the UK, or going to court in the US. They say that they have a credible witness who is happy to testify that the song was played to you during that songwriting session. I pushed them to make a disclosure and they've identified him as Bruce Dean."

"Bruce?" Gerry exclaimed. "Well, we know he was pretty upset about how he was sacked from the band during the world tour. Surely nobody can believe evidence from him?"

"Apparently, they think he's credible. Mr Johnson seems to have some heavyweight backers to have made it this far and to be suggesting a hearing in the US as an option. I've been asking around, but nobody says or maybe even knows who they are. I'm afraid the only way that you're going to fight this one is in court."

Bernie felt aggrieved. "Fine! Let's see them in court. Let the law decide. It must be mainly Gerry's word against his and hopefully our barrister will convince the judge that both this Johnson character and Bruce are unreliable and can't be believed."

"If you're sure, I'll push the wheels in motion. We should go for a hearing in the UK as your costs are going to be much greater in the United States. Plus, the case here will be decided by a judge. In the US, you would probably be in front of a jury who are more easily convinced

Scandalous (June 1993)

of similarities where none exist. Hopefully, when they see that we're not going to back down, they'll drop the case and go away as others have done in the past. I'm not convinced it's going to happen this time though. There is clearly more at play in the background."

"I know what you mean, Paul. Unfortunately, I feel the same. It's almost as if Ernie Conway's finger is pressing buttons, but what's in it for him? He surely can't bear a grudge against us from so long ago?"

"Stranger things have happened," observed a sanguine Gerry. "Let's carry on down this road and see what comes out. Can you secure the best barrister that there is in this area, Paul?"

"Well, I would, but the barrister that I've always used before has been nabbed by the other side. I'll see who the next best-rated one is and see if they are available."

"Wow! There really is something going on! Well, that will have to do. Let's hope that they see this as an opportunity to beat the guy in the number one spot."

♪ ♪ ♪ ♪ ♪ ♪ ♪ ♪ ♪ ♪ ♪ ♪ ♪ ♪

Eventually, Gerry and Bernie were on their own. They continued to mull over the implications of the turn of events.

"This doesn't look good, pet. Are you absolutely sure that you never heard this guy play that song to you?"

"Of course I am Bernie. It's scandalous. And Prince would agree with me!" He forced a wry smile.

"How can the truth be so twisted? It feels like that old legend about Lie stealing Truth's clothes and wearing them to fool people," he thought aloud and absent-mindedly.

"HELLO HAMMERSMITH!"

His wife felt the inspiration. "Definitely sounds like it should be a song to me."

"Yes, I guess." His mind could grasp that it was a great idea but the news was far too distracting. He meant at least to acknowledge it and Bernie's comments.

"I might have a crack at that sometime... Maybe when this is all over..."

Scandalous (June 1993)

Chapter 25 - The Wisdom Of Crowds (23 June 2016)

It was the end of June and Light Stone were back in Canterbury for the summer to do some gigs. The recording of their first album, which the band had reluctantly contributed to, had stalled amid heated arguments between the band and ERCO. They had vacated their flat and handed the keys back to the receptionist at the office. They quickly retreated before they could feel the reaction. Jack had the room in the flat to himself lately as Liam had quietly moved into Hannah's room. This became obvious when Hannah's voice was raised during the night.

Get You In My Heart was popular on the streaming sites in the first week and threatened to graze the bottom reaches of the singles chart before disappearing, just as Colin had predicted. The band thought this was strange as ERCO had an outstanding record of getting new acts to chart quite high and then hang around for a while – but not this time. What was going on? It had been a minor hit, which was good for a new act, but in the past others in a similar position had more success.

The ERCO offices were quiet, largely because Erica had not been visiting at all. Apparently, she was too ill to travel in, but the band could feel there was a lot more to it than the reported sickness. Everyone spoke in hushed tones and even the arrangements for the annual Summer Ball were held up. There was so much confusion that Light Stone took advantage of the circumstances to refuse to play at the Ball. It went down like a lead balloon with Vicky but otherwise slipped by.

Hannah reminded Vicky that she had already refused the year before, which did not help Vicky's blood pressure. Those that went reported that the Summer Ball was a subdued affair. Neither Ernie nor Erica made their usual grand entrance, as they had done without fail in the past.

Vicky was the only person in the ERCO office who still raised their voice. She constantly nagged the band by text, email and phone to stop complaining and finish recording the songs that had been prepared by Ben and the team.

Hannah enraged her in a phone call they took at the Chapel when she suggested they would stay in Kent and build a stronger profile by doing some gigs.

"That's strictly forbidden under your contract. Any concert has to be arranged and promoted by ERCO."

Hannah confronted her. "Well, that's kind of you but we're perfectly capable of booking our own gigs and getting paid for them. We don't need your crappy company to take care of us."

Vicky was on the verge of exploding. "You kids just don't understand, do you? ERCO owns you. If you disagree, then we'll let the law decide."

Jack decided it was about time that he started asserting himself. "Fine. See you in court."

Vicky was taken aback. "And how are you going to manage that, young man?"

"Have to find a way." Jack looked directly at the speakerphone.

Rick tried to diffuse the situation, but only made things worse. "Come on Vicky, give us a laugh...," which resulted in the call being swiftly ended.

Even Hannah was quiet for once and Liam, like the rest of the band, did not utter a word until they were on their own. "Jack, are you sure about this? I'm normally with you and I know we don't have much to lose, but there's no point in us being pulled through the courts when most of us don't have any money."

"Don't worry," Jack smiled. "It seems I've come into some money. Would cover court fees. Can get us out of this hole if we play our cards right."

Jack was back home when he finally confessed to Mabel and Jim that things had not been going well in London. The band was unhappy with the ERCO deal and wanted out. His guardians sat him down and reminded him that Gerry's previous band had got clear of ERCO only thanks to Paul Eagle and it didn't cost them too much. So it was lucky that Jack had allowed Paul to see the contract before he signed it. When he admitted that Paul Eagle hadn't seen the contract and he had been talked through it by ERCO's legal team, his former guardians hit the roof. They also reminded him he still needed to see Paul regarding his parent's estate. Finally, Jack agreed they set up an appointment to replace the one that he missed on his 18th birthday.

Chastised, Jack went upstairs. He could hear that Mabel and Jim were continuing to argue downstairs. Jim was in full "I told you so" mode while Mabel kept reminding her husband that now Jack was 18 he could make his own decisions.

As he half-listened to the arguments as they played out, he opened the suitcase that he had taken from the Stanford warehouse. In there he found a cuttings file Bernie had kept. It filled in more of the backstory. There were magazine articles from 1983 written about the band, from how Gerry and Bernie became a team, to Stanford's last concert at Wembley Arena. He also found out why the case was so heavy.

Covered in bubble wrap was an award with the inscription:

Stanford

Special Ivor Novello Award

Let's Do It Now

Jack already knew much of the history, but opened up his laptop and put the song title in the search box. It didn't take him long to find the full story of the song. The lyrics could be interpreted in various ways and there were possible sexual innuendos, which were subtle and harmless enough. It triggered massive album sales and Stanford's biggest world tour. Then an unknown singer-songwriter appeared out of the blue and claimed that the song was a copy of one that he had pitched to Gerry while he was writing the album.

He also found some handwritten pages torn out of an exercise book and dated just after the case concluded. The verse was based on a 19th century legend which told the tale of how Lie stole and wore Truth's clothes and ended up wearing them.

> *Truth and Lie went walking - it was a beautiful day*
>
> *Lie stole Truth's clothes and put them on, wears them to this day*
>
> *And so, you find confusion - with Lie now dressed as the Truth*
>
> *You find the crowds believe them - the naked Truth has no use*

Jack couldn't trace that Stanford had ever released the song. In his mind, he immediately drew parallels with the politics of the day and particularly the recent vote for the UK to leave the European Union. Another protest song emerged. Like others in their generation, the band had thought about what the UK leaving Europe would mean to their prospects. They had realised that as a band, the European market was nearby and would be easier to conquer than the US. The freedom to move with their equipment was the foremost thing on their mind.

The song that he started building was borne out of the deep frustration caused by the narrow margin between the choices in the vote to leave the European Union. He had added to the core lyrics and started *The Wisdom of Crowds*.

When they next met up at his house, he invited Liam and Hannah to hear it. The pair agreed it was a good basis for a song. The three of them worked on the lyrics and music. They took the first verse and went straight to the chorus up an octave:

The Wisdom Of Crowds (23 June 2016)

And the wisdom of crowds will get its way

And Lie dressed as Truth fools us today

And still, we go on believing Lies

Ignoring Truth, laid naked before our eyes

For the bridge:

Truth has hidden from the world of charlatans and thieves

It's time that we stood up against the leaders who deceive

And a last verse:

The legend's true today – and sinks its claws in us

The promise of independence – on the side of a big red bus

The crowd accept the lies – that we'll be better off

In truth, the rich get richer - the poor can just ………

It went onto the promising 'let's keep this away from ERCO' pile of songs. The credit read 'Duncan/Michaels/Ross/G Stanford/B Stanford' with the added names recognising the source of the song. Hannah and Liam then hurried off together.

Jack packed the award back into the suitcase, put the Hofner guitar into its gig bag and called Colin on his mobile.

"Are you at the Chapel?"

"Sure, just tinkering around in the studio. You can pop around if you like. Actually, I was going to call you as you probably haven't heard today's hot ERCO news. I'll tell you when I see you."

"Great. Coming around now. Think we've got a good song."

The teenager popped his head into the living room to let his auntie and uncle know where he was going. They were still clearly far from happy. He then rushed to the Chapel, eager to hear Colin's 'hot ERCO news'.

"HELLO HAMMERSMITH!"

Once he settled down, Colin filled him in. "Oh, you definitely haven't heard then. It's all over the music press. It's incredible. Remember when you told me about the payment made to the witness of the accident? Well, the Fraud Squad had become involved by then. While they were looking through the account transactions, they also found payments to a Bruce Dean."

Jack thought for a few seconds. "Stanford's ex-bass guitarist. Testified against mum and dad in the big plagiarism trial."

"That's right. Bruce Dean has been charged with perjury and he's then suggested that ERCO put him up to it but there's no concrete proof to support that except for the payments. And that's not all. They also found payments before then to Joe Johnson. It seems that ERCO acquired the rights to his songs before the case came to court. That's how they could fund the case and they received all the royalties, not him. Apparently, Johnson then blew what little money ERCO allowed him and died of a drug overdose some years ago. So, we might never know the truth, but there's a strong suggestion that he wrote his song after *Let's Do It Now* had been released, not before as he then claimed. It's possible that ERCO put him up to it."

"Must be more to come out," Jack thought out loud. "Can't see how ERCO are going to survive this."

Colin agreed. "We need a band meeting - soon."

Later that afternoon, the band gathered at the Chapel. They fist bumped each other as per usual and waited quietly while everyone arrived. Rick tried to liven things up as he acted his normal animated self. He eventually quietened down after getting little to no response from any of them. For a change, it was Jack who arrived last. He had his gig bag across his shoulders and was out of breath from running up the lane with Macy.

The Wisdom Of Crowds (23 June 2016)

"Thank you for coming," he exhaled, as he took his bobble hat and hoodie off and sat on the floor with them while Macy went to the kitchen to get water from her bowl . "Guess you've all heard about ERCO's dodgy dealings."

"Sure, it's been all over the business press," Rick replied. "How do you think that will affect us? Will they have enough money to finish our recording and release the album?"

"Well, sounds like they have plenty of money stashed offshore," Jack revealed. "Don't think that's the problem for us. The thing is, do we want to be associated with them?"

"It's a good point," Rick said. "Can we trust Boadeceiver?"

"Surely we should stick to the contract and do what they ask us to do," Liam suggested. "Why poke the bear?"

"Personally, I'm never going to be happy recording for them," Hannah exclaimed. "The process of getting the single done was the final straw for me. I'm so disillusioned with the whole thing and I'm having trouble getting motivated to go back in there and waste time with some wide boy producer who takes the money and doesn't give us any credit."

"I feel the same way," Dan agreed. "They're just using us to keep Hannah under contract."

Hannah agreed. "I just don't think I'm ever going to be confident enough to do this solo."

"To be honest, I don't mind either way," Rick offered. "I'm here for the ride. It's been kind of rubbish so far but I just don't see how you tear up a record company contract without having a bucket load of cash to waste. There's loads of chilling tales from the past of even big stars who couldn't break free. George Michael… Bruce Springsteen… Prince… Queen… Come to think of it, maybe it's something that you have to do on the journey, but surely this is too early?"

"I think we are better off lying low and getting on with it for now," Liam resolved. "In a few months, this will all have blown over and things will carry on as normal. We'll probably find that all these record companies have offshore accounts – they seem to be as bad as each other. They can't all disappear, can they?"

They all looked at Colin, who had left them to discuss their future without commenting so far. "All I can tell you is that record labels have deep pockets and aggressive lawyers. They sue first and ask questions later. I'm not sure that you have the resources to go head-to-head with them. Two of you seem to want to go, one wants to stay and one doesn't mind, that just leaves you, Jack. It's time to say what you think?" He turned to look at Jack as he finished, all the while knowing pretty much what Jack was going to say.

"Think we've all learned a lot in the last few months. If we're truthful, it's been a miserable time all round. Maybe accept that we've been foolish to think that we could see things done our way while working inside the corporate machine when their business is being seriously threatened. They've a formula which they'll keep spinning until there's no spin left and they don't mind who they destroy in the process if it means protecting themselves. Reckon that with the latest revelations, I can't work with ERCO anymore and if we stay, we're just going to dig ourselves a deeper hole. Think we need to move out now."

Rick hesitated. "That's fine Jack, but how are we going to manage that? As Colin said, they have loads of cash and the best lawyers. They'll make mincemeat out of us and spit out the remains. We'll be finished."

"Well, maybe we don't need to start a fight with them," Liam suggested. "Maybe they'll see that they're not getting the best out of us and let us go."

Just then, all of their mobile phones beeped. They would normally have ignored the odd notification, but as they all had one, their curiosity took over.

The Wisdom Of Crowds (23 June 2016)

The text messages were the same and simple:

"Time is up people. Party time is over. Come back to London and be in the studio tomorrow. Flat will be ready. Need to finish the album ASAP. Vicky."

"Well, that's pretty clear," Rick started.

"Who's in favour of doing what they ask?" Colin asked.

Only Rick's hand went up.

"And who's in favour of standing up to them?" Jack asked with his hand in the air. Liam and Hannah followed him straight away and after some hesitation, Dan smiled weakly at Rick and put his hand up as well. "Right. That's fairly clear cut. I think I'll message back now and see what happens."

Jack opened his message and replied to all,

"Sorry Vicky. Won't be entering the studio again until a lot of sorting out is done. Band input top of the list. Meet up?"

He pressed SEND and Colin went to put the kettle on as they braced themselves for an explosive reply.

They didn't have to wait long. Before the kettle had time to boil, all their mobiles pinged again.

Nothing to discuss. Read the contract. See you all at 9 tomorrow. If you're not here, then I'll be sending a minibus round to collect you. There could be a few fingers broken. Vicky.

They then all received an email with an attachment of a massive pdf document. They opened it and started reading but their screens were too small. Colin had a better option. "Forward it to me. I'll print it out."

"HELLO HAMMERSMITH!"

"Are you sure?" asked Rick. "It's 80 pages long! Anyway, I don't fancy my fingers getting broken. I'll be finished as a drummer."

"80 pages is about average," Colin explained. "If you had argued about it upfront, the lawyers could have stretched it up to 100 pages…"

He printed out one copy and they went through it page by page, but much of the language meant nothing to them. Colin explained some terms to them as he read through it, having seen a few of these before on his own projects. "I think this is the clause that they're going to use. *'The band (Light Stone) shall all attend meetings whenever and wherever requested by ERCO with 24 hours' notice'.* Let me see what happens if you don't do that." Colin went quiet while he concentrated. "Here we go, *'Failure to perform any part of this contract entitles ERCO to retain all future royalty payments and such a breach will give rise to a claim for damages as calculated in Schedule 8.'* Let's have a look at Schedule 8." After a time, he pulled a face. "I didn't think that this would be good news. I think you're going to need a lawyer to go through this with you. You can use the London lawyer that I know, if you like. He'll be expensive though."

"My dad has a good local lawyer," Rick proposed. "I think his name is Peter Eagles."

"Paul Eagle," Jack corrected. "Auntie and uncle know him. Leave this to me."

"Ok, if you're sure. Best not to hang around though. Don't let the grass grow too long and all that."

Jack went into the kitchen and shut the door behind him. He opened his phone to view previous callers and selected a recent one. "Is Paul Eagle there please?"

"Speaking," said Paul. "Ah hello Jack, I understand you're coming in to sort out the estate. Is that what you're calling about?"

"Not really. Something else came up."

"Ok – tell me what that's about and maybe we can deal with it together."

"Doubt it, but we'll see. I know Mabel told you I'm in a record contract with some others and we've hit a few problems. One thing in particular we need you to have a look at. Is that something that you could do?"

"I rather feared that you were going to make this call. It's come sooner than I thought. Are you trying to get out of it?"

"Yes," Jack said sheepishly. He then recounted the details that Colin had been through.

"I think they have to give you longer than 24 hours to deal with an instruction from them like that. That just sounds unreasonable. Email it over and leave it with me. I'll come back to you this afternoon. Is it alright to call you on this number?"

"Sure… and thank you." Jack went back into the living room and forwarded the contract over to Paul before telling the others what Paul had said.

"That's a bit of hope," Hannah sighed.

"Not sure there's any point in hanging around," Rick thought out loud. "I think I'll pop into town and see who's there. Are you coming Dan?"

"Sure."

Once they had left, Hannah turned to Jack as if to comfort him. "Are you OK? Me and Liam have noticed that you've been rather distracted the last few days."

"Just some personal stuff," Jack confessed. "Nothing to worry about."

"HELLO HAMMERSMITH!"

They tried kicking some song ideas around, but weren't really in the right frame of mind.

Jack's phone rang. Having seen who it was, he held his breath as he answered. "I wish you had let me have a look at this before you signed it," Paul Eagle scolded. "It's made it hard to fight back but I think there are a few possibilities. We need to act quickly though. Can you come in tomorrow?"

"Sure. Should the band come?"

"No, I don't think that's necessary. If I can make something stick for you, then they'll all benefit. If you can come in with Mabel and Jim, then that would be handy. We can tackle the trust fund at the same time?"

"The trust fund? Oh yes, that…"

The Wisdom of Crowds can be streamed free here:

https://soundcloud.com/the-colour-spectrum/the-wisdom-of-crowds

The Wisdom Of Crowds (23 June 2016)

Chapter 26 - Everything But The Kitchen Sink (September 1992)

It had been a week since the *Everything but The Kitchen Sink* live album had been released. Gerry and Bernie waited for the chart announcement on Sunday afternoon with trepidation.

"We shouldn't be going head-to-head with Abba," Gerry joked. "They'll wipe the floor with us and wring us into a bucket."

"Well, what can we expect after *Album 5*?" questioned Bernie. "We'll be lucky to make the Top 50."

They were at their Islington house and listening to the singles countdown on Radio 1 with Bruno Brookes. The Sunday afternoon 4pm to 7pm countdown was the only thing that they ever listened to on Radio 1. *Let's Do It Now* had been the lead single but had now dropped out of the charts.

They agreed it was a shame that Annie Lennox was slipping down to 29 with *Walking on Broken Glass*; enjoyed *Goodbye* by The Sundays which was new in at 27; duetted along with Luther Vandross and Janet Jackson on *The Best Things in Life are Free* at 12; danced around the kitchen to Bob Marley's *Iron Lion Zion* at 5 and laughed when The Shamen still held on to number 1 with *Ebeneezer Goode*. "I think our time at the top is running out, old girl," Gerry commented.

Their album chart placing just inside the Top 30 was respectable given that it was a double album and as Gerry had expected, *Abba's Greatest Hits* had knocked Belinda Carlisle's hopefully titled *The Best of Belinda Volume 1* down to 3, while Mike Oldfield's *Tubular Bells II* was up again to 2. "Maybe there's hope for us after all," Gerry smirked. "Fancy doing another tour, dear?"

"You are joking, aren't you?"

"HELLO HAMMERSMITH!"

The last tour had left some indelible marks on the duo. When the offer was made to them, Bernie already had a constant ringing in her left ear and made it clear she was now tired of touring. "Look pet, I never wanted to be in a mega successful band. I wanted to see the world, but not from the inside of a tour bus. All I wanted was to be in a band for a few years and then settle down, get married and have kids. It hasn't worked out like that."

Gerry had accepted, but pushed for one last blast and Bernie reluctantly agreed on a world tour of the USA, South America, Asia and Europe. However, if this was maybe their last tour, then it would have to be big, really huge. That involved a lavish production with 70 people involved in getting trucks and planes between the locations. In each territory, a full orchestra was commissioned, plus a gospel choir for the big numbers. It was estimated that it took 250,000 watts to power the elaborate stage setup and running costs were £30,000 per day.

As was now becoming common practice, they stayed out of the UK for a year so that they wouldn't need to pay tax on the royalties and tour income earned. It was to be a greatest hits tour covering the songs from their old albums. They made the mistake of deciding to put the band on a percentage of the ticket sales rather than a wage. The shows all looked like they would sell out so surely there would be enough money to reward the team for spending so much time away from their families? Even though Harvey had looked forensically at the costs compared with the ticket sales, unexpected costs of the undertaking ate into all the benefits that they gained by being away from home.

Being away for so long, and with some gaps in the schedule to give people a rest, the road crew had grown bored and the level of practical jokes rose out of all control. Particularly memorable was the evening where a small water fight ended up flooding two floors of the hotel so thoroughly that everyone had to be evacuated.

Once they arrived home and looked at the results, Gerry and Bernie couldn't believe how little they'd made, but the figures didn't lie.

Everything But The Kitchen Sink (September 1992)

Normally, a tour would help to increase the sales of the back catalogue, but that didn't happen this time either. It seemed everyone who wanted to see Stanford had already bought the albums on CD and there were enough floating around second-hand stores to mean that the new CDs didn't fly out of the shops.

To make matters worse, while they were in South America, Bernie's auntie died, which left her distraught and brought back terrible memories of a previous tour.

As the tour drew to a close in the UK, the idea of recording a live show for CD and video floated around. Everyone agreed that only one venue would make sense for this, and it fulfilled their 6-year-old stated ambition to play Wembley Arena. It wasn't suited to a full orchestra, but that issue was put to one side once they all agreed that this goal deserved to be achieved while they had the chance.

In Harvey's view, it would recoup a lot of the costs that they had spent. But it cost them more than expected, as they needed so many manned cameras to cover all the angles of the performers and the whole arena needed to be prepared with cables. They were going to record both nights so that they could pick the best performances from each. That was just as well as on the first night the sound was distorted just enough to make it unusable and there were also issues with the visuals. This meant that the pressure was on for the second night and nerves had to be held tight. There were still some glitches that had to be sorted out later, but that was the only night that could be used at all and they had to make the best of it. It meant that Gerry spent a month in the editing suite making sure that things were right. Over that period, he lost a stone in weight. Problems included poor microphone placement, which meant that some parts were lost. The only solution was to re-record some tracks in the studio later, which just added to the costs. Some songs weren't included as there wasn't room on the double album.

"HELLO HAMMERSMITH!"

The second encore was always their most famous song, *Let's Do It Now*, which Gerry had rearranged to incorporate both the orchestra and at the climax, the gospel choir.

In keeping with the title, the CD packaging was lavish and included a booklet full of photos from the tour, costing a fortune to produce.

The album title came from a saying by Gerry's father whenever they loaded up the family car to go on holiday somewhere in England. He would joke that Gerry's mother had packed 'everything but the kitchen sink', suggesting that the entire contents of the house were coming in the car with them. As the idea of the tour was to do the best of everything that they had ever done, with money being no object, the title stuck. It was also a riff on Everything But The Girl. Ben Watt and Tracey Thorn had been friendly rivals with Stanford throughout the Eighties and Stanford didn't think that they would mind it being recycled.

"Well, thank goodness that's finally out," Gerry sighed. "Maybe now we can move onto other things. We have some wonderful songs in the bank. I think it's time to plan *Album 6*, you know… maybe go back to our roots. We could do what The Beatles did and just spend time in the studio messing around and jamming until something comes out."

Bernie agreed. "That sounds like an idea. We should certainly hold back some money this time and not spend everything on recording and promotion. We always seem to be broke when we release a new album and then have to wait for some royalties to come in before we can do anything else."

"Maybe we should do what bands did in the '70s and go off to a remote part of Scotland with a little 4 track recorder and go back to basics?"

"It's a delightful idea, but after the all-singing and all-dancing productions that we've done before? Hmmm… We're not quite starting from scratch here are we?"

Everything But The Kitchen Sink (September 1992)

"Well, maybe we are. I think the live album has brought this cycle to a close. We're not going to do any touring for the foreseeable future so maybe we should go back to square one," and seeing Bernie's screwed-up face, "but you're not convinced, are you?"

In fact, the cycle hadn't quite been brought to a close. They thought that their days of awards might be behind them for a while but a thick embossed card had arrived at their home, with an invitation from BASCA, the British Academy of Songwriters, Composers and Authors to the 38th Ivor Novello awards at Grosvenor House in London. Bernie suggested that might be because they were previous winners. Gerry was unsure.

"Yeah, that's possible. Doesn't explain why we've missed a few years though."

Nearer the date, they had been contacted again by the organisers, asking if they would be prepared to do an acoustic version of their song *Let's Do It Now* for the event. This was the single that broke them in the US after it appeared on the *Blindside* album, and again after they re-recorded it for *Album 5* on the Good Record Co label. They were a long time out of their ERCO contract by then, which had apparently infuriated the record company since they would not benefit at all from the record's success.

They had intended not to release it again as a second single, but *Let's Do It Now* ended up getting so much radio airplay that a rush release made sense – hence the request for a stripped back live version. As a band, they had rehearsed with their drummer Leon Manford a few days beforehand and decided just to do it with Gerry on his Hofner acoustic guitar rather than keyboards.

As they mingled self-consciously at the welcome drinks, they heard a familiar voice behind them. "Good to see they're letting a few more previous winners back in then."

"HELLO HAMMERSMITH!"

"Colin Garrett!" Gerry exclaimed as he turned around to see the smiling, spectacled face of his old adversary. They hugged and Gerry reminded Bernie that they had last seen Colin in the studio next to theirs when they were putting the finishing touches to the *Here We Go Again* album.

"So Colin, I don't think I've ever seen you wear anything but blue check shirts and jeans. Where did the tuxedo come from? And are you up for yet another award?" Gerry asked.

"No, not this time, mate. I'm happy with the two that I have, to be honest. Let others have a turn I say. They did work wonders for my career though. Put me in the top league and enabled me to go for the jobs that I wanted to do and charge more for them. What are the two of you up to then?"

"Oh, we're working on *Album 6* at the moment."

"I seem to remember you had writer's block a while back. Did that go away entirely?"

"It seems to pop up and haunt me every now and again, usually after a long, exhausting tour. At the moment, it's behind me and the juices are flowing."

Bernie smirked at Gerry's side and Colin smiled as well. Gerry wondered what was going on.

"Yeah, I saw you had a tough time with that." Colin touched his head as he continued. "Touch wood it hasn't happened to me yet, but you never know. Anyway, I won't take up any more of your time. I see that you're performing tonight – best of luck with it and let's keep in touch mate."

"Oh, sure we will."

"What a nice bloke," Bernie remarked as Colin moved away. "It's refreshing to see someone so humble about their achievements."

Everything But The Kitchen Sink (September 1992)

"Sure. I still hated him when he sat down at that college piano before me though."

Seated at their table that evening, they laughed as Right Said Fred won the award for the Most Performed Song, clapped as Charles & Eddie won the Best Selling Song award, cheered as Annie Lennox won the award for Best Song Lyrically and Musically with *Why* and applauded as The Hollies won the Outstanding Contribution award.

At the end, it was their turn with Leon. There were cheers as they took to the stage. Gerry and Bernie came up to the microphone and it was Gerry who spoke first.

"Thank you everyone and a special thank you to BASCA for inviting us up here tonight. It was a genuine surprise. And I'm guessing that most of you are also surprised when you see us up here without a keyboard in sight. Well, I think I can trust you with a secret. Pretty much all our songs were composed not on keyboards but on this battered old Hofner guitar. So when I played this on Top of the Pops, it wasn't as silly as people thought. This guitar has a special place in my heart. It was the first guitar that I owned. My parents bought it for me when I was a teenager. Although I was also playing piano from an early age, I could never write many songs from playing the piano. For a reason that I still can't explain, whenever there is a tune in my head, I just find it easier to pick it out on six strings than on 88 keys and make sense of it. And the song we're going to play for you is a case in point. As you know, I suffered a period of writer's block, which I wouldn't wish on anyone, after we thought we had finished recording Stanford's famous *Blindside* album.

"The Multiplier label told us we needed another single. You've all heard the story, I'm sure. Bernie suggested we should crack on with things and I remembered we had this old song that we had written when we were on the verge of leaving ERCO. We didn't want them to release it and make money from it! I played the basic version of it to Bernie while she was making breakfast for herself. A bit like Paul McCartney and *Yesterday*, I was never convinced that I hadn't heard it somewhere before and had copied it, but I played it to a few people who all said that it was an original. And I know that a certain label is still miffed that they didn't get hold of it. [Laughter] So here we go. Over to you Bernie."

"This song is so special to us. People have come up and told us that this was the song that made them decide to go for it and ask someone out. That someone then said 'yes' and later they would be married. Others have told us that their children have been conceived while this song was playing. I tell them it was only three minutes long so I hope it was on repeat. (Laughter) You heard the original single, which was a hit all around the world and made it to the top 10 in the US. You've heard the re-recorded reggae version; you've heard the orchestral version that we did for a compilation album and you've heard the recent live version, which was a hit all over again. Now here is the stripped back version, which would have been how it started life, just for you."

And with that, the three of them ran through a slowed down and sparse version of Stanford's most popular song to a hushed hall. Before the first chorus, everybody stood up and joined in. They stayed standing and singing, with Bernie leading them in the swaying arms section at the end. As always, the song ended with everyone's hands in the air and clapping.

They made a move to leave the stage but were stopped by the host who came back onto the stage holding one of the famous statuettes.

"Wait there just a moment. BASCA have a final award for the night. They have agreed that the song that you have just played was one of those rare occasions where they felt wrong-footed. *Let's Do It Now* has become such an anthem since it was first released that they have taken the step of recognising a song that was written outside the usual time requirement. As the song has a new lease of life again because of the live version being released, we can give it a special award that we missed before. Congratulations Stanford and we look forward to seeing you here again in the future."

Everything But The Kitchen Sink (September 1992)

Gerry and Bernie were speechless. Bernie took the award as she was nearest, gave it straight to Gerry and burst into tears while Gerry hugged her and Leon.

But backstage they were greeted by grim faces as they were taken aside and escorted away from the area where the press were waiting to interview the winners.

A person who Gerry recognised as the head of the BASCA approached them. "I'm dreadfully sorry guys, but there's been a mistake. That last award should never have been made. It's been pointed out that the judges didn't have the authority to make such a special award."

"You're joking, right?" Bernie asked, perplexed, tears of joy still running down her cheeks. "How can that happen?"

"I can't explain it at the moment. I'll tell you what though. Keep the award. It would be churlish of us to take that away from you when it has your name engraved on it. All that will happen is that it won't appear on the final awards list."

As they sat down, gobsmacked, a grinning Ernie Conway moved away from behind a curtain where he had been listening to the conversation.

"That will teach them to make fun of ERCO Records!" He pulled his Motorola phone from his inside pocket and pressed a preset key.

"Have you fixed it?" asked the voice that picked up.

"Of course."

"So I don't need to send anyone around to sort things out, then?"

"Not this time."

"Shame. I don't feel that I've inflicted pain on any of my enemies for some time. I have withdrawal symptoms. Speaking of which, I have another idea to share with you. That song belongs to ERCO you know."

Chapter 27 - Baby, What A Big Surprise (24 June 2016)

Jim Michaels apologised to his current clients so that he could drive Mabel and Jack into town to meet Paul Eagle. They left the car in the town centre's multi-storey car park and made their way through the quaint streets. The lawyer's office was positioned on a quiet road that came to life after office hours as it was opposite two bars popular with students looking for entertainment.

After a brief wait in the reception area, during which they were offered drinks, Paul's PA escorted them up to the office. Paul sat at his desk, looking at the papers in front of him with his oval-shaped reading glasses on the ridge of his nose.

"Ah. Come in, come in. Good to see you again, Jim and Mabel. And hello Jack, it's been a long time since I've seen you in the flesh. You've grown a little since then. I'm glad you have come in at last. We have a lot to catch up on. Have a seat everyone. Ah, here come the hot drinks.

"Right. I think we should start with the most urgent matter at hand, this ERCO contract. A pretty gruesome document, if I'm honest. Why on earth did you sign it without seeking my advice?" Paul peered over his glasses in the stern way that lawyers do.

"We suggested he should bring it in to you," Jim said, "but off he went on his own without telling us anything. And now here we are."

"Took advice. Thought it would be ok," Jack mumbled. "Haven't got much to lose."

"Not that you knew of," Paul said. "Now, from the email stream that you sent me the first message came at just before 3pm, so the clock is still ticking. I've drafted a reply, which I'm going to send to them just as soon as you approve its content." He had a copy for each of them, which they read in silence. Jack would have confessed that he didn't understand much of it, but at the end of it were bullet points that firmly told Vicky that the time limits in the contract were unreasonable and were unlikely to be upheld by a court. A court would also take a dim view of the absence of any arbitration clauses in the event of a disagreement. He proposed the parties meet in London at a convenient date and time. In the meantime, he wanted confirmation that no action was taken otherwise he would immediately apply for an injunction.

Mabel spoke first. "I'm afraid I can't say that I understand much of it… but it's a good and firm response and we'll see how serious they are. OK to send it Jack?"

Jack nodded.

"Great, then give me a minute while I send that," Paul said. He picked up the phone and spoke to his assistant. "That email is ready to send from the general account. Could you make sure that you forward me any reply that comes in? Great, thank you." He put the phone down.

"I should explain that I'm not being lazy. I'm only getting my assistant to send this as I have crossed swords with ERCO before and I don't want anyone getting spooked just at the moment. We might need to play that card later.

"Now, we'll see how long it takes for them to answer that. In the meantime, let's look at the other matters at hand. First, let's deal with the bequest from the witness to your parents' car accident. The police say that they can't investigate further. If there were a case to be answered, then the money would have been subject to a Proceeds of Crime action. As it is, the bequest can be released to you and it should appear in our client account in the next few days."

"So, they can't prove that Erica Conway was driving or that her dad paid the witness off?" asked Jack.

"Well, all they can say for certain is that the witness was paid £250,000 from a bank account controlled by Ernie Conway. He says he couldn't remember what it was for and blamed his accountant for transferring the money incorrectly. His accountant, of course, is nowhere to be found."

"Typical!" Jim snorted.

"So that's all we need to say about that at the moment. I'll let you know when the money arrives."

Meanwhile, in her office at ERCO HQ, a stressed Erica was disturbed by a knock on the door. "Come in, but make it good."

Vicky strode through the door. "Sorry to disturb you Miss Conway, but I thought you should see this immediately. As you know, I've been putting pressure on Light Stone to come back into the studio and finish the album ready for release. I invoked the 24 hour meeting request clause in the contract and this email has just come in." She laid out the email in front of Erica.

"Barton & Co? Who on earth are they?"

"A provincial firm down in Kent."

"Hmm. That name rings a bell. Where have I heard that before? I'm not surprised that they can't even seek advice from a decent London firm who know the music industry. We should wipe the floor with them." She thought briefly. "Send them a strongly worded reply quoting breach of contract, breach of trust and insist on a meeting up here ASAP so that I can take this guy down a peg or two. It will give me some satisfaction."

"Yes, Miss Conway. I'll send that reply immediately."

"Then maybe we can record and release that album and create a bidding war for Hannah Ross."

"HELLO HAMMERSMITH!"

Back in the solicitor's office, Paul Eagle was moving on.

"That then brings us to the other matter, the trust fund that your parents set up for you as part of their wills." And turning to Jim and Mabel, "Have you shared anything with Jack about this?"

"No, we thought it best not to say anything until the time was right," Mabel replied. "There didn't seem to be much point in telling Jack while he was growing up."

"Fine, I'll start from square one then. Well Jack, on your first birthday, your parents signed their wills which made provision for your guardianship and support. These made Jim and Mabel your legal carers until your 18th birthday last August and preserved all your parents' assets in a trust fund. When they passed, the only real asset they had was the Chapel and the rights to the songs, which weren't producing much income. The contents of the store didn't have much value but we wanted to keep that for you. We had to sell the Chapel to pay off some debts and provide some liquid funds. In fact, another musician, who it seems knew your father well, bought it."

"Yes," Jack said. "My music tutor at college. Bit of a manager to us now."

"OK, well he could have helped with the contract if you ask me, but never mind about that. Your aunt and uncle thought it best to move you from your original primary school and I agreed to that as there weren't the funds to send you to a private school. Anyway, your father's old band before Stanford arranged a benefit concert at the Carling Apollo in Hammersmith, which quickly sold out. That prompted the *Stanford's Greatest Hits* album to be released in 2004. Royalties started coming in and there weren't any actual costs apart from the small allowance that Jim and Mabel drew out with my approval for your upbringing. Plus, royalties from the previous bands that your parents were involved with finally trickled in as well, although there has never been very much.

Baby, What A Big Surprise (24 June 2016)

When I questioned this, it seemed all the money was still going to an old manager called Morris Philpott, who's disappeared. He managed both bands it seems. I couldn't find out much about him but he seems like quite a rogue and we hit lots of dead ends."

"He was a nasty little piece of work," commented Mabel. "He went to college with Gerry."

"Did ERCO pay up?" Jack asked.

"Yes, eventually. They had to be threatened with being sued, mind. They weren't too keen on releasing any royalties from the first two Stanford albums, either. We all received some threatening phone calls. It all ended up very messy.

"Anyway, it's probably about time that I cut to the chase. You're a rich lad and you didn't know it. At the end of May, when we reconciled everything, the fund stood at £2.2 million. It's been invested in safe shares and bonds but there's some readily accessible cash in there. Quite a tidy sum. Don't spend it all at once, will you?"

"Hardly!" Jack confirmed as his mind processed the colossal figure that he hadn't been expecting. "Could come in handy though." His mind was already racing as he started planning.

Paul moved back to his computer. "Let's see if they've replied. Yes, here we are. What are they saying? Very unhappy…. breach of contract… breach of trust… liable for damages if no agreement is reached. All standard stuff. The upshot is that they're not going to take any action until we have met to see if we can sensibly move this forward. That's a result then. Shall we meet separately about that? Sorry to rush you but I have another client due in soon. Jenny can see you out."

Mabel looked relieved. "Thank you, Paul. Gerry always said that he could count on you."

"HELLO HAMMERSMITH!"

Jack reflected on the way home. Jim watched him in the rear-view mirror. "Are you going to tell the rest of the band about the money?"

"No, don't think so. Might tell Colin though; he knows about the legacy."

"And they still don't know what your real name is and who your parents were?"

"No, they don't. It's not time yet."

"That's wise. As Paul said, you won't do anything reckless with the cash, will you, Jack?"

"Course not," Jack smiled as he turned and looked out of the window as the Kent countryside wafted by. He knew he had to seek justice for his parents and a plan was coming together. As well as that, the structure of a new song titled *Boadeceiver* continued to form in his head.

Baby, What A Big Surprise (24 June 2016)

Chapter 28 - Album 5 (December 1991)

It had been four weeks since *Album 5* was released, and they had never been sure that the plan would work. They were exhausted after their last mammoth tour, promoting the reimagined ERCO songs plus the batch of new ones. The whole thing had been more traumatic than either had let on. Afterwards, Bernie found she could only write songs of grief and loss, which had never been Stanford's style. Try as he might to write songs either on his own, with Bernie, or with someone completely different, Gerry's blockage remained.

The title itself had been an issue. This was actually the seventh album that they had released. However, they wanted to make a point to the record buying public that they didn't count the first two albums because a contractual issue forced the pair to release them on the ERCO label.

The only good news was that they were in a good shape financially and were no longer struggling to keep head above water as they had been in the early days. They were still getting some royalties from their previous bands and they were debt-free, given the unusual nature of the deal with Oscar Good. The first album on his new label had been their best seller to date and even the high touring costs didn't put much of a dent in the finances. But tired out from touring, the writer's block had returned and coming up with new songs was a slow process. The plan had been to record an even better album than *Blindside* and spend a lot on the production.

Stanford had vaguely considered getting the more usual type of record contract with someone other than Good Record Co, but that just didn't make sense to them. The options were simple: edit the vast amount of footage that they had from the last concert and release it on CD and video or 're-imagine' songs from their Multiplier albums and issue these as *Album 5*. The first option made more sense. The footage was already shot. It just needed some time for editing and releasing. But as usual,

"HELLO HAMMERSMITH!"

Gerry wanted to go for maximum risk. He had been quite happy with the Multiplier albums and the fans had loved them. But he wanted to explore the outer limits of his creativity. Could the songs be given a different angle but re-recording them in a different style than the original? The Multiplier contract didn't restrict them in that respect. With more royalties coming in soon, they planned their approach. The most 'sensible' way was to go with random choices; it would certainly make a good story if nothing else.

They picked what they thought were the best 12 songs from the Multiplier albums, wrote them down on fresh pieces of paper and put all the bits in one of Bernie's stage hats. They then brainstormed 12 different styles of music and did the same in another hat. One piece of paper was then drawn from each hat with the promise that they would stick to the choices they'd made. And that was how they landed up with *Snake Oil* in a bossa nova style and *I'd Sing Along* as heavy metal. For luck, they added the first song that they had written together and which, as yet, hadn't been released. *Today's the Day* was a remnant from the ERCO days which had been missed from the *Re-Recorded Hits Plus* album – it was given the ska treatment. Their biggest hit, *Let's Do It Now*, became a slowed down reggae song.

This all looked good until Gerry realised that the current band couldn't perform all the different styles. He needed to bring in an army of guests to help. Various stars popped down to the studio for a few days to contribute their part to each song.

Gerry was then inspired to video the recording process and make a special edition out of it. The special editions had the CD and a VHS tape in a box. The video actually revealed how exhausted the pair of them became during the process. Pretty soon, the cash reserves dwindled as the project neared completion.

One positive thing came out of all this. Just as the recording was being completed, Gerry's writer's block was lifted. That allowed a handful of songs to replace some of the rehashed ones, although secretly both

Album 5 (December 1991)

Gerry and Bernie wondered whether the new ones were up to their old standards.

During the recording, Bernie's sister gave birth to a baby daughter. Bernie went to visit and stayed for two weeks to help. She was besotted and started dropping hints to her husband. Gerry, of course, was engrossed in the recording process and side-stepped any other discussion. One morning, however, Bernie decided not to take 'no' for an answer and sat Gerry down for a long heart-to-heart.

"My biological clock is not so much ticking as thumping."

"What are you suggesting?"

"You know what I always say. 'Let's do it now, before it's too late'."

This led to a long conversation about what they were doing, with Gerry promising, not for the first time, that they could soon take a break and start a family. Bernie wasn't convinced.

The duo chose the new version of *I'd Sing Along* to be the first single, which set the tone. The track featured a big bass drum sound and visitors to the studio had complained that it was too loud. Gerry ignored them only to realise later that during radio airplay, the BBC compressor kicked in and the song just vanished. He'd put so much into the song that he was distraught by the results. But in hindsight, he had been too tired to make a good job of it.

Oscar had listened to some of the early recordings and spoke his mind. "Look, it was alright to redo the old ERCO recordings as you gave them a new life, but you're just going down the same track this time. The public wants more new Stanford songs than the three that you've squeezed in at the last minute."

"Yes, I know that," answered Gerry, "but it's the best that we can do just at the moment."

"HELLO HAMMERSMITH!"

The album came out in November, timed ready for Christmas. However, it spent only one week on the charts before falling like a stone. Critics laid into it without mercy.

"This rehash has no substance";

"How to ruin a reputation";

"They can't keep rehashing old songs and expecting people to keep buying them";

"Too few new songs of indifferent quality"; and

"Goodbye Stanford."

Try as they might to divert attention by releasing two of the new songs as singles, they didn't dent the Top 40 and had no chance of being featured on the newly revamped Top of the Pops.

The genuine fans of the band who had stuck with them since Day 1 were equally harsh. The only award that the album won was for the "Worst Pop Album of the Year" in Smash Hits. Stanford stayed away from that ceremony.

Album 5 (December 1991)

Chapter 29 - Rotten To The Core (to 5 July 2016)

For the following week, Light Stone were all bombarded with messages from Vicky, wondering when their solicitor would be in touch to set up a meeting. Paul Eagle had been busy with other clients and stonewalled any requests. He and Jack were planning how they would tackle the meetings. Paul put Jack in the picture about the contract that his parents had with ERCO when they started up as Stanford.

Paul informed him that Gerry's old band Splatt had been signed to ERCO. When they broke up, ERCO argued that Gerry was still tied, under the old contract, to produce three more albums for them. That meant that Gerry and Bernie felt forced to release their first two albums on ERCO. They had used ERCO's rehearsal space and it was these recordings that Ernie and Eric Conway had subsequently used to make the *Lost and Found* album. Paul had freed them from the contract because Splatt had formally split, but that would not help Light Stone.

In the meantime, Paul had researched other cases where ERCO contracts had been challenged. The costs went into the tens of thousands of pounds and often resulted in the contract standing and the band never being heard of again. There were also a few cases where the young band, excited about the chance to make it big time, had not bothered checking the terms of the contract too closely. Some stayed and went through the motions until they were dropped. Others were held for years. Paul reckoned that their only chance was to force Erica and Vicky to agree to a contract release. It was around that possibility that their plan formed.

In the meantime, reports from the Fraud Squad investigation into the offshore bank account suggested that ERCO had syphoned record sales out of their UK bank account and into the offshore account based in the British Virgin Islands, so defrauding both the taxman and the artists, who received fewer royalties on their sales. Some funds had then been used to fix the chart by getting a series of individuals to buy records around the country and push ERCO records higher up the charts. This then explained why many of the new ERCO acts achieved higher chart positions than they might have expected. With all the publicity, it looked as though the practice had stopped just before the Light Stone single came out. There were also confessions from shop owners that they had accepted payments for putting fictitious sales figures through the chart machines in the shops a few times an hour. If they didn't agree, threats had been made to their families. Some former record shop owners came forward to give evidence that when they refused to inflate the sales, their shops were ransacked and firebombed. Ernie Conway could also be traced as a beneficiary of drawings from the account on which no tax had been declared.

While this was all going on in the background, the band stayed in Kent and met up at the Chapel to write and rehearse. Jack noticed he became more content when he was at the Chapel. Playing the Danemann piano or the Hofner guitar at home was one thing, but at the Chapel the inspiration just seemed to flow better. Liam and Hannah also noted that Jack seemed different at the Chapel, all at once less uptight and more creative.

Colin wasn't always at the Chapel as he needed to rehearse his students for the upcoming college end of term concert. He kept quiet whenever Vicky came along to sit in classes but he could see that she would often leave when a call came in. Her raised voice outside the room confirmed that all was not well on the ERCO ship.

That didn't stop him from setting 'homework' for the band and some extra pieces for Jack. He had previously seen that the band was stuck in the keys of D or G when writing so he had given Jack and Hannah a task to go beyond this and into the key of A Aeolian. This meant that they had to include a G sharp and an E7 chord in the melody.

Jack had picked up on a saying in passing, *Rotten to the Core,* and was exploring various angles. Colin was still of the opinion that there was space out there for a young band who wrote songs about more than love and heartbreak. Just to see what all the options were, he asked all of them what upset them most about the world and their lives.

They struggled for a bit before Hannah came out with "Global warming."

Colin smiled and encouraging, let out, "That's more like it!"

Jack was next. "Idiots who are gonna harm everyone having voted out of the EU."

"Controversial," Colin remarked. "But a good one if it's people your age you're after as fans."

"They're mainly the ones who have come to the gigs," Liam remarked. "Well, at least they were when we could do our own gigs."

There was silence before Hannah said "ERCO" through gritted teeth and they all nodded in unison.

Colin had challenged them further by asking them to incorporate key changes of 1 tone and 2 tones, but that proved to be a step too far. When he came back home at the end of each day, he would ask how they were getting on and record them live. He would then suggest things they should explore the next day.

After Colin left for college one evening, the others were galvanised and in no mood to go home. Jack could tell that Liam and Hannah just wanted to occupy the same space and guessed that Liam wasn't welcome at Hannah's house.

"Come on. Let's write another Duncan/Michaels/Ross banger," suggested Liam. They had long since agreed that all of their songs would be co-credited in alphabetical order, just as Lennon and McCartney or Jagger and Richards had done before them.

"HELLO HAMMERSMITH!"

The first verse questioned the influence of the media. Once again, it was a not-so-subtle comment on the recent 'Leave the EU' vote.

The papers report lies. We know they realise the game

The truth is theirs to bend, a right they still defend – such a shame

The smart money can buy, the space that they require

To feed their need to plant the seeds and add flames to the fire

CHORUS

It's rotten to the core

Won't take it anymore

What are they lying for?

It's rotten to the core

The second verse was clearly directed at major record companies who took advantage of their artists.

The music industry – traps you and me with their bait

They hold keys to the gate, decide who's in and who can wait

The contracts that they make are unclear and opaque

They draw us in and bleed us dry. The truth they then deny.

The last verse commented on the big businesses, including some global names, who were judged to be squeezing High Street stores out of existence.

In fruit and jungle hell – they tune the marketplace where they sell

Exploit the weak and poor and tax money they keep for more

Destroy the old High Street; it's losing its heartbeat

The biggest thrive, the small crash dive, be lucky to survive

"Another Duncan/Michaels/Ross smash. Chords aren't I-V-IV-vi either," Jack announced, almost triumphantly, when they played it back to Colin as a finished piece. "Loads of songs seem to have that chord structure and luckily we've steered well clear of it. Makes it less likely that we accidentally copy someone."

"That's wise," Colin commented, with a wink at Jack that the others didn't understand. "But there's a reason that the I-V-IV-vi progression is so popular – studies prove it resonates with people. Search YouTube for Axis of Awesome and watch them run through over 70 different songs in around 5 minutes."

They all stopped and watched as the band ran through songs seemingly as diverse as *Don't Stop Believing* by Journey, *With or Without You* by U2 and *Let It Be* by The Beatles.

While they then continued working on the song, Jack looked distracted. The two other songwriters deduced he was planning for the upcoming meeting in London with ERCO. They were right. Their careers in music depended on a good outcome, but they couldn't see how on earth Paul and Jack could pull it off.

Chapter 30 - All Around The World (January 1990 to March 1991)

In January 1990, Stanford's manager, Harvey, had come to the Islington house with an idea.

"Look, the *Re-Recorded Hits Plus* album is selling well. You have a UK tour booked for March and a small US tour booked for June. Why don't you take the entire tax year out of the country and tour the world? If we can make you both non-resident anywhere in the world next year, there'll be no tax on any of your earnings. How about it?"

"Really?" Bernie challenged. "Surely, we have to be resident somewhere?"

"No, not necessarily. It's just a step on from being a tax exile, which The Rolling Stones started. They were probably first, decamping to France in 1971, and then David Bowie went to Switzerland in 1976. Every country has its own rules of residence. In England, for example, you haven't been resident if you spend 92 days or fewer here. There's a US withholding tax, of course, but we'll deal with that. All we need to do is look at all the countries in the world where you're popular and plan to spend a couple of months in each country."

"But we have studio time planned for the summer," Gerry interjected. "We need to make a new album to keep momentum going."

"I think that can wait. With the better deal that you have with Oscar, the royalties are going to keep pouring in so long as you keep promoting the new versions."

"So we'll leave it up to other people to pay for the health service and police force," muttered Gerry.

"I think we've contributed enough over the years," retorted Bernie. "I suppose it will upset ERCO even more that the new versions are selling well. Mind you, hasn't Madonna announced a Blond Ambition world tour this year?"

"Yes, she has. But don't worry about that. I've planned things out so that you guys are never in the same country. Plus, she'll be finished by August."

"Clearly not so worried about tax when you ascend to her level then."

Harvey smiled at Bernie's comment before continuing. "Oh, I think she'll find a house somewhere in the world to rest up in. Look, you can have breaks in places around the world in between. Lead the proper rock star lifestyle," he smiled. "I've mapped it all out here."

He spread a map of the world out on the table.

"From the UK, you add some European dates in all the countries where sales are strong: Ireland, France, Spain, Belgium, The Netherlands, Denmark, Germany and Italy. You then have a break before you go to the US. Do that brief tour that's in the plan before doing these other cities that I've marked where you're selling well already. Some tour dates should bring in publicity and more sales which then fund the rest of the tour. Onto South America where you can cover the big cities: Cordoba, Rosario, Porto Alegro, Rio de Janeiro and Sao Paolo. Then onto Australia and New Zealand. Then head back via Japan where you're huge. I can book Tokyo, Yokohama, Nagoya, Osaka and Fukuoka. That will give you a good spread. Finish with some big shows back in the UK in March next year and then have a long break before the new album gets recorded. What can go wrong?"

"What can go wrong," started Bernie, "is that we've always done quick tours until now, so that we have had time to recuperate and return to normality before the craziness starts again."

"I know," agreed Harvey. "Which is why I'll build in breaks in between each country."

All Around The World (January 1990 to March 1991)

"But isn't it going to be hideously expensive to transit all the gear around these different countries? Shouldn't we find a transit company to sponsor us?"

"Yes, I've looked at that," Harvey said. "Sadly, because this is your first time doing this, the major ones see it as something of a gamble, which it is, by the way."

"I guess other sponsors are going to see it the same way?"

Gerry put his hand up. "Can I stop you there, love? We're having no sponsors on a tour like this. They just end up messing around with you and getting you to plug them in weird ways on stage. I've seen it happen and it makes me cringe. No sponsorship!"

There was silence while Bernie and Harvey took that in.

"My issue is that we're going to play the same songs every night for 12 months," Gerry sighed.

"Oh, come on Gerry!" Bernie pleaded. "It's not going to be every night. And remember, we've seen famous acts over the years who refused to play any of their hits. We both felt cheated and promised that we'd never do that to our fans."

"Um, I guess you're right. We can always change it around over the course of the tour."

Gerry and Bernie thought long and hard about the benefits and drawbacks and talked to the rest of the band about it at length. They all had young families to think of but the thought of earning so much tax-free money to send home meant that they were all persuaded by Harvey's idea.

The tour started out alright, but they hadn't cleared Europe before their drummer, Leon, was homesick and it was a struggle for him to perform some nights. The only solution was for him to go home during the breaks and rejoin later when they had arrived in a new country. "There's more to life than a bit of tax money," he defended.

A bigger issue came with their bass guitarist, Bruce. Because the US leg covered a lot of miles in a short space of time, he started having trouble resting and sleeping while they were travelling. At first, he was honest with Gerry who sent him straight to a local doctor to ask for a prescription for sleeping tablets. However, when the tablets didn't work, Bruce found some higher strength tablets. Those were so strong that Bruce then had trouble keeping awake at all. When he stopped taking them, the insomnia came back with a vengeance. He then got a collection of uppers to counteract the sleeping tablets and so oscillated between the two. Gerry was oblivious to this, but Bernie could sense that something wasn't right with their colleague. She kept asking him if he was ok, never getting a straight answer. She alerted her husband, who then started watching Bruce more closely. It was only when Bruce asked the tour manager to retrieve something from his bag backstage that the truth came out. In the bag was the selection of tablets, pipes and other paraphernalia associated with drug use. It was clear Bruce had a serious problem. They were in Chicago by the time they sat the drugged musician down and coaxed a confession out of him.

"Look pet," Bernie started, "for your own good, you can't carry on like this."

"Don't worry guys," Bruce tried to reassure them. "Give me a few days and I'll be back under control. You can throw all that stuff away. I'm sure I can manage without it."

"No, I'm sorry. We can't take the risk. You need to go home and get yourself straight."

"But you have a gig tomorrow night. Who's going to cover it? Give me a chance, please? I'll be ok."

All Around The World (January 1990 to March 1991)

Gerry firmly took over. "Bruce! We'll cover it. We'll book a flight for you."

Bruce flipped. "Send me home and you'll be sorry."

"But if you stay here, then it'll be worse," Bernie replied.

An unhappy Bruce was dispatched off home while they lined up a local session musician to listen to some of the live tapes. When he came to a rehearsal, it was clear he was going to pick up the parts with little trouble. Bernie had never spent a lot of time making the bass parts too intricate, so Bruce was probably the most replaceable member of the band.

They had a selection of support acts while in the US. One in particular, Heavy Weather, bemoaned the fact that their new deal had left them on 5% of sales. They were amazed when Gerry quietly told them of their 50:50 deal with the Good Record Co, but that they then had to bear a great deal of cost, starting with the recording. "I wish we could get a deal like that," the lead singer said, "but they've told us we're in debt for over $1 million. We just can't break away until we make it big."

"I know that feeling," Gerry revealed. "You'll have to stick with it and be careful about saying 'yes' to spending lots of money on marketing that feels nice to have but is unnecessary. Some companies will do that just to keep you on the line until they decide that they've had enough and want to move you on. Unfortunately, Oscar doesn't touch anyone with a load of old debt attached to them."

"I wish we could start all over again. It would be so different."

On the positive side, Harvey was right about taking a year out. The constant touring of new countries meant people kept buying the records and sometimes they had three or four albums in the local charts. Good Record Co's local distributors were happy to see the band and made a big fuss of them when they arrived in each country. In the meantime, the royalties kept coming in for that year, tax-free.

"HELLO HAMMERSMITH!"

One thing that specifically disappointed Gerry was the local orchestras that they hired for the high-profile gigs in some countries. First, they were expensive. Second, they didn't know who Stanford were and didn't care for them when they were given the music to play. Where the conductor was weak on discipline, conversations could be heard, particularly from the brass section, asking which bar they were drinking in afterwards and some of them behaved like children. In Chicago, they unwittingly linked up with an orchestra where the conductor needed an intake of Columbian marching powder to conquer his nerves before a performance. The rehearsal had been fine, but come the performance, a wired conductor meant everything speeded up. Gerry and Bernie looked at each other helplessly as the orchestra ruined one song after the next. It just confirmed to them that drugs and live music did not mix.

The low point came while they were touring South America and their tour manager sat them both down at breakfast after a triumphant concert in Buenos Aires. He didn't beat around the bush. "Bernie, I'm afraid to tell you that your mother has died."

Bernie's face dropped as she heard the news and Gerry immediately put his arm around her as she sobbed on his shoulder. "Oh no! I've got to go home to look after dad."

"Well, let's not be too hasty," he continued. "They've set the funeral date for 3 weeks' time when you've got a break in the schedule before we start the Brazil leg. I reckon you can finish up the last few nights here and I've booked you both on the next plane back that next morning. I think you can then get back in time for the first Brazil date."

Bernie was quiet while she got over the initial shock but Gerry's brain was whirring. "Hang on. If you've got all that organised, how long have you known about this?"

"Erm, just a few days ago. I didn't want to disturb your preparations for last night."

All Around The World (January 1990 to March 1991)

"So you knew about this and didn't tell us until now? Why?"

"Well, I guess I didn't want to upset you before you went on stage and there wouldn't have been time to cancel."

It was Bernie's turn to get to the point. "So you didn't want the aggravation of claiming on the insurance? A bit of paperwork is more of a problem than life and death is it?"

"I'm sorry – I've acted in what I consider to be the best way in the circumstances."

"Get out of my sight," exploded Bernie, as she ran back to the room in tears.

Harvey had to make a swift change of tour manager, and Bernie had trouble keeping a smile on her face for the rest of the tour.

Stanford knew they were big in Japan, just not how big, until they were mobbed at the airport. Their audience, made up of young professionals, clapped in unison, which Gerry particularly found disconcerting.

The ultimate show closed their second European tour. It was a free concert set in London for 80,000 people. It was a triumph but in the build-up they had announced that they had no further plans to tour. When they were asked why in interviews, Bernie flippantly replied that she was tired of standing in front of fans every night and the washing and ironing had been piling up at home. In fact, her hearing had deteriorated to the stage where it was becoming hard to hear the onstage monitors.

Unfortunately, Bernie's remarks were taken literally by certain groups, so while Madonna was getting in trouble in Catholic circles for her raunchy routines, feminists burned Stanford albums on a ceremonial bonfire.

Chapter 31 - Do You Want To Know A Secret? (19 July 2016)

A few weeks later, Jack and Colin made their way to ERCO's London HQ. They were escorted up to Erica's office and left to wait alone in the outer office. It was the secretary's day off, apparently. Jack pointed out the 'Number 49' cutting to Colin and they had a quiet laugh about it. They stopped talking when they heard a cough outside the room. Colin put his finger to his lips, as he suspected that someone was listening at the door.

The first person to walk in was Vicky Tucker. Her PA followed. "Come through," Vicky said as she led them into the main office. "Thank you for coming over to clear this mess, Jack. I'm a bit surprised to see Colin with you though. Is your solicitor on his way?"

"No, I'm the band's appointed representative and I'm here to support Jack and the band."

"That's strange. I would have thought that you would want someone from Barton & Co here to represent you. We've had correspondence from them."

"That's right," Jack said. "Dispute team told us their hourly rates. Since the band doesn't have that kind of money, we'll be representing ourselves with Colin here."

"Whatever!" Vicky interjected dismissively. "And the two of you can speak for the entire band?"

"That's right," Jack smiled.

"OK, where shall we start then? As far as ERCO are concerned, this is all straightforward. We gave you access to a legal team and they explained the contract to you before you all signed it. The evidence is all here." Vicky dropped the contract on the table with a thud.

"HELLO HAMMERSMITH!"

Colin spoke first, remembering his briefing from Paul. "Well, first, I'd like to question the fact that it was your own internal legal team that advised the band. Surely, since they drafted this, they couldn't advise Light Stone, as they were conflicted?"

Vicky was calm. "Quite so. I take it you haven't looked closely at this extra document that they all signed. They clearly waived the right to independent legal advice and understood they were being advised by the ERCO legal team."

Colin and Jack looked at the piece of paper in silence. "Never seen this before," Jack said. "Remember signing some blank documents which would be completed later though. Was this amongst those?"

"How dare you make such an inference!" Vicky exploded. "That's an outrageous allegation. Make a note of that!" she said to her PA. "If you repeat that, there will be a writ winging your way."

"Let's calm down," Colin said. "There was no accusation there. All Jack is saying is that he can't remember signing this actual document, but he can remember them all signing some blank pages. Isn't that right, Jack?"

"Quite right."

"Good. Then perhaps your PA should make a note of that too," said Colin calmly. There was silence.

"Look, Miss Tucker," Jack continued formally. "As you know, there was some legal advice and clearly this is a bad contract."

He waited and watched Vicky's face darken, then continued.

"That's alright. Easily solved if the contract gets torn up. Can then start again with a new agreement that gives the band more say in what is going on and more control over the decisions that affect our career. Views on the band's YouTube channel are now approaching one million and there's an enormous fan base out there who follow the live shows.

Just need to recreate that in the studio and everyone is going to be happy."

"Absolutely not," Vicky retorted. "What you're suggesting is ridiculous. ERCO has always been successful in managing the artists' activities and everybody comes out a winner."

"That's not quite true," Colin interjected.

"I challenge you to name one artist who didn't come out of a contract with us far better off than when they started."

"Gillian Fox?" Colin retorted without hesitation.

"That was her own stupid fault. She was doing fine while she followed our advice and did as we suggested. She wanted to do things her own way and paid the price," Vicky sneered.

"Having done a bit of research, I could name plenty more," Colin continued. "But that won't achieve anything. Are you refusing to tear up this contract and start again with a more even agreement?"

"Yes, I am. That contract was signed in good faith and all artists are bound by its terms."

Jack took a different tack. "Look Miss Tucker. You're frustrated that the studio's not being used. Costs being incurred. Just out of interest, how much to buy out this contract?"

"I thought you didn't even have enough money to pay your solicitor to come along here and represent you. You can't possibly buy yourselves out of this. It's never been done before, anyway."

"Sure," Jack smiled. "But the band wants to know. It's sure to be a big number which might convince everyone that the best plan is to come back to the studio after all. Just out of interest, you know."

"HELLO HAMMERSMITH!"

"It will be a waste of time, but I'll ask the finance team to calculate the number for you as soon as I can. The formula for release is all set out in the contract. And then if you can't afford the buyout, as we're sure you can't, you'll accept the contract and return to work?"

"I think we'll agree to that," Colin answered. "Thank you so much for sparing the time to meet with us. Why don't we meet again next week? If you email me the details of the amount needed to exit the contract, then we can clear this up quickly." He wrote out his email address and mobile phone number on the pad in front of him and passed it to the PA with a smile. Colin and Jack rose to shake hands with Vicky and walked out of the room.

Vicky and her PA waited in the room after they had gone. A few minutes later, Erica Conway wafted in. She took off her dark glasses and sat down at her desk. They could see the rings around her eyes caused by the recent stresses. "Bloody amateurs," she snorted. "Can you see to it the recording of that conversation is filed away in the correct place," she barked at Vicky's PA.

"Absolutely out of their depth!" Vicky agreed. "That guy Colin couldn't even reserve some seats for us at a Christmas concert. We can have this tied up next week. No problem."

"You'd better, Vicky. The one correct thing they said was that the YouTube views of their live gigs keep going up, as is the number of subscribers. I've no idea how they've managed that. Which means we need to haul them back to finish the album and release the wretched thing while everyone thinks they're good."

"They'll be back by the end of the month, and we'll have that album out ready for Christmas," Vicky assured.

"Good, but Hannah Ross is going to have to be out front. Apart from her and the drummer guy they're all ugly as sin. We need a big seller to move some of the press attention elsewhere. And in the meantime, you'd better do some digging into this Colin Garrett character. I want to know everything about him, especially his weaknesses," Erica concluded as her mobile phone rang. She looked at the display and answered it. "It's ok. All sorted – they'll be back soon enough." She listened to what was said at the other end of the phone and rolled her eyes. "Yes, I know it's all a bloody mess, but we're not dealing with intelligent people here. They're a bunch of imbeciles. Luckily, they're imbeciles without two pennies to rub together. Don't worry, if this negotiation doesn't work then you can send some of your people round. I know you'll enjoy that."

"I wish that man would get off my case," she muttered as she ended the call and threw the phone back on the table.

In a café around the corner, Colin treated Jack to a coffee. He phoned Paul Eagle to report in.

"Hi Paul. We're all set. I'll let you know when they email the amount in. Oh, and you were right, Paul. That room was bugged alright. And Erica was there as well. We spotted her car at the corner when we walked around the block afterwards. She will have heard everything. It's a good job you didn't come. It keeps the suspense going. We know Vicky Tucker is a right Jekyll and Hyde character. Nearly blew her top a few times."

Jack sat quietly and scribbled something in his notebook. "Look Colin. Been thinking. What would it take for you to be our manager full-time? You're doing all these things in the background. Maybe it's time to make things official?"

Colin became thoughtful. "Hmm. I'm not sure that's a good idea. Leave it with me."

On the train that took them back, Jack continued to scribble lyrics in his notebook. Indignant at the pompous attitude of ERCO, he started with the title *Leave Me Alone*. After a few minutes, the wailing chorus came to him. He then went onto the first verse:

> *Oh, I don't understand it; you got what you want*
>
> *Gave you what you demanded*
>
> *But you won't leave me alone. No, you won't leave me alone.*

Jack screwed up his nose. It wasn't great. Colin had looked at the pad as he wrote. "It's simple but it could be sung with some venom."

Jack carried on the verses:

> *I guess you're not giving up, but you're wasting your time*
>
> *It's the truth that I'm digging up. You can't cover up your crime.*
>
> *But you're not taking back what's mine*

"That's better. I know what you're referring to but plenty of people won't."

As he read through the lyrics, Jack had a matching melody in his head. He quietly sang it to himself and annotated the page with notes.

A middle 8 was next:

> *It's not how I planned it, but it's time I moved on*
>
> *You no longer command it, and you know you ain't won*
>
> *And you don't fool no one, no you don't fool no one*

Then a last verse:

> *Endless rivers await us. Right can never be wrong.*
>
> *If I can never forgive you, then it's time to move on*
>
> *Accept what's done is done*

Jack was resolved that with what they now knew, they had to escape from ERCO. He just had to figure out exactly how they were going to manage it.

While they were still on the train back, Colin saw on his phone that ERCO had emailed him a letter of offer with the eye-watering figure that would release Light Stone from their contract with ERCO. It was roughly what he expected.

In the meantime, more news had leaked out about the Fraud Squad's investigations into ERCO's offshore account. It was now alleged that record shops had been incentivised to promote and sell more ERCO records with the promise of pay-outs in cash for the best sales performers each year. The cash payments could be traced back to the offshore account where payments for sales had been syphoned. In effect, some of the money went around in a circle while the bulk stayed offshore. There was a trail that suggested that some funds had been transferred elsewhere so that it effectively disappeared without a trace.

Later that afternoon, a second email arrived. Colin had a quick look at it and then forwarded it to Paul Eagle and Jack. The message made it clear there was no expectation that the band had the funds with which to have the contract set aside, so they looked forward to seeing the band report back by the end of the next week to carry on recording.

After a consultation with Paul, Jack called the band together at the Chapel and showed them the emails from ERCO and Vicky.

"I'm not surprised," Rick said when he saw the amount requested. "It's a big number. My dad reckoned it would be in that region."

"Oh well, that's it then," Liam sighed. "We might as well go back in there and make the best of it. I wondered whether we'd be better off not wasting time or making them angry."

"HELLO HAMMERSMITH!"

Hannah voiced a different opinion. "I'm sorry, but I don't think I can do this. I'd rather drop out of the band and apply for a Performing Arts college place for September."

Liam jumped in straight away. "Oh Hannah, you can't do that. You're such a big part of the band's sound that it just won't be the same."

But Hannah wasn't budging. "I'm so sorry. You're all in this mess because of me and I can't forgive myself. I should have just told ERCO to go away when they made me the offer to sign the whole band. What do you think, Jack?"

Jack paused, then breathed out audibly. "Think it's time for me to come clean and 'fess up about my real background. Been keeping secrets from you all." The room fell silent except for a gentle breeze whistling through a window upstairs. All eyes were on him.

"Sorry for keeping this from you for so long. Needed to get my head around some things that have been going on recently. I think I'm just about there now. First, I think you're all aware that Mabel and Jim aren't my actual parents."

Liam and Hannah nodded, while Rick and Dan shrugged their shoulders as though it wasn't important.

"They became my legal guardians when I was five, after my parents were killed in a car crash. The driver of the car that caused the crash was never identified: it was a hit and run. Mabel and Jim adopted me and I took their surname before I went to secondary school. My actual parents were Gerry and Bernie Stanford." There were blank looks, as he expected, except for Hannah who looked as though there was some recognition.

"Back in the '80s they were signed to ERCO as Stanford-Williams. After they extracted themselves from there, they had some successful albums and did huge world tours as Stanford until it all became too much for them. They then lost a big plagiarism case and retreated to this area.

Bizarrely, this is the Chapel that I lived in with my parents for the first five years of my life – they're buried out there in the graveyard." He paused and could see that he had their full attention. "That battered old guitar over there was my dad's and it's been useful for writing songs. Think part of him is still in it," he smiled.

Liam and Hannah nodded and smiled at each other. They knew that there was something going on and now it was all making sense.

Colin then took up the story. "I went to college with Gerry Stanford. It was him I used to race to what was the only piano that they had back then. It's the one in the basement studio against the wall. We'd gone on our separate music careers, but I'd met Gerry and Bernie, including once when they picked up an Ivor Novello award for the song that was later the subject of the plagiarism case. I visited this place when Gerry was figuring out how he could recover from losing the case and rescue their music career. When they died I was abroad but picked up that the executors were selling the Chapel. I offered them the full asking price straight away. Then I met Jack down in the rehearsal rooms soon after I started at the college. It's spooky that he was playing the old piano. When he said he was Jack Michaels, I knew immediately who he was. I knew his auntie from way back and we had bumped into each other. When she told me she was guardian to the son of the Stanfords, then the jigsaw slipped into place. Then I heard some songs that Jack was coming up with. I didn't want to put him under too much pressure though, so I kept quiet about what I knew. So maybe I need to apologise to you all, too."

Jack then took up the story again. "When Paul Eagle said that he had experience with ERCO record contracts and getting out of them, he meant his experience with my parents."

Jack paused before he moved on. "A few months ago, Paul was contacted by another local solicitor. Apparently, the only witness to the crash that killed my parents left me a large sum of money. Seems he was paid to keep quiet about the driver's identity and thought that the right thing to do was to pass the money onto me when he died. It would be enough to cover this...," he waved the ERCO letter in the air. "And it would mean that we would be free to start again and do this our way, from the ground up."

"Strewth," Rick let out. "You're a proper dark horse with bells on."

"We knew that there was something going on," Hannah confessed, looking over at Liam, who nodded. "But that's a fantastic story there. How are we going to play this?"

Colin answered. "We're thinking that we all go up to ERCO next week as they have asked, but request a meeting with them first to make everything clear. We've made some arrangements in the background to smooth things through."

Jack continued. "There are still some loose ends to tie up and we need an element of surprise to make sure that we break out of this clean. Dealing with some pretty ruthless people. Agreed that we're going to keep this to ourselves just at the moment?"

They all nodded and agreed to meet at the West station on Monday at 10.20am.

Liam wasn't in any rush, so he stayed behind as the others left to prepare. Jack played him a recording of *Don't Tell Me What To Do*, an old Stanford song, which had caused some trouble when it was released and somehow seemed to resonate at the moment. It didn't take Liam long to set out the chords to the tune but he scratched his head a bit.

"Woah! That's weird," commented Liam. "When did you come across this song?"

"Only a few weeks ago when I was listening to their old albums online."

"OK, so what's the first line of *Rock the Cuban*?"

Jack didn't have to think for long. "Well, listen here – don't tell me what to do. Crumbs. Cryptomnesia in action."

"Absolutely right," said Colin, who was listening in.

"Anyway. So that's one thing. The other is that your dad's melodies are crazy, dude!" Liam laughed. "The first chord in the verse and chorus is clearly a D major, but the chords are all in the key of G. If I'm writing a chord progression from scratch, I'd never start with the fifth chord in the key. I guess that's why he caught people's attention. Maybe we should do some of that as well."

"Better be careful not to copy them too much!" Colin advised with a smile. "Jack might have to sue you on behalf of his parents!"

They quickly recorded what they had before having a few listens through. Liam had a motif to go at the start, on the bridge and at the end. Colin pulled some electric guitar effects out to make it sound rougher and more in keeping with the feel.

Another one for the pile labelled 'let's keep this away from ERCO' they agreed. It would be a good one to perform live.

The emphasis had changed. Were things finally looking up?

Chapter 32 - Re-Recorded Hits Plus… (December 1989)

The album that Gerry and Bernie thought would move Stanford into the next league was ready, as planned, in time for Christmas 1989. It was their first record on the Good Record Co label and therefore the first one that they were going to receive a decent return on under their new deal.

Paul Eagle had been over the new contract with a fine-tooth comb and admitted, "Well, it didn't take me long to be honest. It's one of the shortest and most concise recording contracts that I've ever seen, way better than the one that I first saw from another recording company that I could mention; I seem to remember that one running to over 70 pages. This one is less than 10 pages and it's clear and written in plain English so there's no ambiguity that could lead to the parties falling out in the future. It's clear that the net revenue to the label will be split 50:50 with the band. That is because the band will pay for the recording costs and the marketing. They can choose their own marketing campaign from the various options, with those costs being taken from net revenue."

"I'm happy with that," Bernie said, clearly relieved. "This leaves us much more in control of the process and aware of what is being spent on our behalf. So, you reckon we're going to be OK to sign this?"

"To be honest, Bernie, this is one of the few occasions where I'm not sending it back to the solicitors on the other side with it covered in red ink. I've suggested a few minor changes, but otherwise it's good to go."

The idea of re-recording the hits had come about when Gerry was discussing the next album with Oscar Good.

"I'll tell you what annoys me, Oscar. I think the old ERCO albums are still selling in reasonable quantities, but I've never been happy with the quality of the recording or the mixing. Digital recording has taken a huge step forward since then. I visited a local studio recently and I'm convinced that the original ideas for the fuller sound in my head could now be realised. There are boxes of tracks coming out all the time. Studios have become temples of art and science."

"That's an interesting thought, Gerry," Oscar mused. "I wouldn't see the point of releasing a greatest hits package, taking the best from the first two albums. Those versions belong to ERCO and I can't see them granting a licence to me, especially given our history. But supposing you re-recorded them? Using the new technology? I'm sure they would sound better."

"They would sound immense!" Gerry was already getting excited about the possibility of getting the sound that he had always wanted. "They sent us to a lot of cheap studios in the early days just to avoid too much cost and we knew we would end up paying for it somehow…"

"Well, while I was there I know they insisted on having re-record restrictions included in contracts, but I remember that the original Splatt contract they held you and Bernie to didn't have those clauses. I heard their lawyer got fired when the omission was spotted. They're your songs. And I guess you own the publishing? If so, why don't you go for that? You'd royally upset them, of course." Oscar paused in thought. "Actually, I have an even better idea. Why don't you do a double album with your new songs mixed up with the old hits? I don't think that many bands have had the nerve to do that."

"I like the sound of that."

It didn't take much time for Gerry to collect the band together and book a state-of-the-art studio on the outskirts of London. They all knew the songs and Gerry had a clear idea of the sound that he was looking for this time. The process did, however, take longer than anyone conceived.

Of course, there would be some drama before and after the release date. It was an open secret in the business that Stanford were going to

Re-Recorded Hits Plus... (December 1989)

"reclaim their legacy" and there had been plenty of reports of tempers flaring at ERCO. They shouldn't have been surprised that, with no pre-warning, ERCO decided to release their own greatest hits from the first two albums a fortnight before the re-recorded versions were due to come out. They clearly had a spy somewhere in the Stanford camp as the tracks were identical to the ones that Stanford had re-recorded. The band watched helplessly as some of their fans bought that CD only to realise that an improved greatest hits album was on its way as well.

Despite that setback, *Re-Recorded Hits Plus* was released to great acclaim. Reviews included:

"I thought that the original songs were good, but these re-recorded versions have lifted the songs to yet another level. I've stopped listening to the old albums and can only listen to this one in the future."

"This is brilliant. Stanford should re-record all of their songs in this style."

In response to these reviews, ERCO then ran full page adverts for their version in the music papers, but watched in horror as the new Stanford version continued to climb the charts while theirs dropped like a stone.

A factor of the interest in the new versions laid in the first video that was released. Many years ago, when MTV was in its infancy, Gerry had the idea of doing a video which exposed all the tricks of the trade, showing things in the background as they were in contrast with how they would appear on the screen. He had floated the idea when they were still with ERCO. Gerry wasn't surprised when it was squashed before it even made it to the drawing board. Now the duo had more control over the process. There was no stopping them.

The main song was called *Moving On* and so travel became its theme. Scenes constructed included the couple driving down what looked like an LA highway, then pulling back to show that the car was in a blank studio in front of a scene and not moving at all. Then the two of them were apparently walking a dog through the countryside but pulling back showed them to be on treadmills.

As nobody either had the courage or the control to do this before, fans greeted the reveals with joy. So, although MTV tried to show it as little as possible, people kept requesting and voting for it.

Things were going well. The last chart before the Christmas break was always an important one in the industry. If a record was doing well on the chart on Christmas Day, then money given to teenagers could be spent on records that week. They were looking forward to having a good showing on the charts when Oscar phoned them.

"Hi Bernie – is Gerry there with you?"

"No pet, he isn't. Is there a problem?"

"Well, there seems to be, but I can't explain it. I'm hearing complaints that people can't find the *Re-Recorded Hits Plus* album as it isn't available in most shops. That doesn't make sense. If all the ones we've shipped had been sold, you'd be Top 10, but the midweek charts are suggesting this isn't the case. The album has dropped out of the Top 40. In fact, I'm being told that lots of shops sent stock back to us and asked for refunds, but very few have arrived here. There's something going on, but I can't find any confirmation about it. Rumour has it that ERCO has bullied all the local shops to remove it from the shelves and hold it before sending it back. That has left their old version bubbling under the charts again. It's a nightmare."

"There must be something we can do, surely Oscar?"

"I don't think that there is anything we can do."

"Well, these ERCO guys need to be taught a lesson somehow. I've a good mind to dress up as Angie Pogo, go round to their offices and give them a piece of my angry mind."

Re-Recorded Hits Plus… (December 1989)

"A delightful idea, but probably won't solve anything."

"No, but it would make me feel a lot better."

Bernie told Gerry about the call as soon as he came in. He just put his head in his hands. "I can't believe this is happening."

"No, nor can I. It's as though there are evil forces trying to make sure that we never move ahead."

"We can't give up. We have to press on and make *Album 5*."

Phil Collins with *…But Seriously* ended up at the top spot that year, followed by Jive Bunny. Greatest hits albums were represented by Rod Stewart, Chris de Burgh and Level 42, with Stanford nowhere in evidence that week. In the weeks that followed, it gradually returned to the lower reaches of the charts and recommenced its steady climb up the charts, so there was an increasing flow of sales which kept royalties coming in for many years to come.

But crucial momentum had been lost.

Chapter 33 - Showdown (29 July 2016)

It was on a hot day that Light Stone and Colin met at the West station and rushed to reserve two tables with four seats on each side of the aisle for the trip up to London. The jolly mood masked the anxiety that they all felt. This was a big day for them all.

They arrived at the ERCO offices around midday. Security made them wait at the desk for a while before they were shown upstairs. The door of the reception room was open, and a secretary tapped away on a computer. "Ah, Light Stone and Mr Garrett," she greeted. "Miss Tucker is ready to see you in Miss Conway's room."

"That's a first," Hannah muttered under her breath. "I feel like I'm going to see the headmistress."

Inside the room, they were met by an unusually smiley Vicky who had her PA sitting next to her. Erica's mahogany desk at the end of the room stood empty on its plinth.

"Hello Vicky darling. You're looking unusually pleased with yourself," Rick teased, before getting a hard stare back and deciding that he had better keep quiet.

"Welcome, welcome!" Vicky said, turning away from Rick. "Sorry if it's stutty in here. We've only just opened the windows to let some air in. Anyway, I'm glad that you've all seen sense and have come back to start work. Now, you said that you have a few questions before we start. Let's clear those up now. What are they?"

"Well first," Colin started, as the nominated speaker for the band, "we have a few questions about the emails you sent us late last week."

"Sure, but is that relevant? You've seen the amount that would be needed to release you and I'm sure it's a higher figure than the pittance that you can offer, so you're coming back to the studio, surely? Why waste more time?"

"Not yet," Colin insisted. He paused while he cleaned his glasses. "We just wanted to clarify what the release would mean in the unlikely event that the band could gather that amount of money together. They need these things set out for them clearly. Otherwise, this misunderstanding might happen again and we certainly don't want that. We all want them to put these distractions aside and concentrate on getting the album ready for a Christmas release?"

"Yes, of course," Vicky said impatiently. "What were these questions, then?

"Would they keep all the publishing rights of the songs that they have written to date?"

"Well, as you know, they signed a publishing deal as part of the contract with ERCO. The figure that we gave you covered the ending of that for the future, but the existing songs that have been recorded stay under our control."

"Ok, we thought that might be the case. So, they would not be getting a clean break from ERCO to start again then? And do they keep all the recordings that were made in these studios when they were rehearsing, before and after they signed the contract?"

"Well, no! Those still belong to ERCO," Vicky responded, now shuffling uncomfortably in her chair. "I'm not seeing the point of these questions."

"And is ERCO prevented from releasing any Light Stone records in the future?"

"No, if we have some things that were originally recorded while they were under contract here then we retain the right to use them in the future as we see fit. That's standard industry practice."

Showdown (29 July 2016)

"I see. And will the band be able to keep using the Light Stone name once they are free of the contract?"

"Well no – we've protected the band name and logo at the Patent Office. Look, if you want to buy the rights to all these things, it will cost you more than the number that we've put in the letter. That was just the basic amount to help the guys move on and start again. So, you can see how unrealistic it is to pursue this conversation any further, right?"

"Then give them the correct monetary figure Miss Tucker, the one where you give up all rights to the band, its recordings, its name, its images – in fact, everything." Colin stopped and was silent, as was the room.

"Well, I wouldn't be able to find that exact number for you just now!" Vicky sputtered. "That would take time to calculate."

"But those extra things aren't worth a lot, Ms Tucker. Especially when I tell you that the band aren't interested in continuing with the Light Stone name and want a clean break. So, let me suggest a figure to you so that we can all move on. How about £250,000?"

There was silence again as Vicky tried to process what was happening.

"£250,000 will do nicely but are you sure that you want to do this?" came a voice from the door and they looked round to see Erica Conway standing under the frame with hands on hips. "I'm assuming that you're putting up the money Mr Garrett. I understand you are quite a wealthy individual."

"Ah... Miss Conway," Colin greeted the newcomer. "I'd hoped that you were listening in so that this could be resolved quickly."

"Yes," Erica drawled. "I've had enough of all these shenanigans. We have more important things to deal with at the moment, much more important than some going-nowhere-slowly, little group of cretins who think that music stopped developing in the 1980s." Erica moved to sit at

"HELLO HAMMERSMITH!"

her desk at the end of the room, carefully taking the step up and leaving a trail of perfume behind her. "You see, ERCO have been working on a research project, the results of which will guarantee that all future ERCO releases go viral. I guess you don't want to be part of that success? Well, to be honest I'm bored with these games and I'm calling your bluff. The offer of £250,000 stands until the end of the day. I'm guessing that you have the money after all, Mr Garrett, and it seems you're willing to waste it on these no-hopers. I thought you were smarter than that, so let's agree before you come to your senses, shall we?"

"Well, absolutely!" Colin paused before continuing. "At midday, the band's solicitor sent your lawyers a draft agreement covering all the extra elements that we want included in the contract release. That includes securing the rights to any songs from rehearsals by the way. It was quite short, so your solicitors should have checked it by now."

"Yes, they have," Erica sneered. "What I can't understand is what you're achieving with this stupid game."

Colin pulled a copy of the agreement out of his bag and took it over to the desk. "So you'll be happy to sign this and give us until the end of the day to have the money transferred, otherwise the agreement is void?"

"Of course," Erica replied, picking up a fountain pen on her desk and signing the contract with a dismissive flourish.

"Which account do you want the £250,000 paid into?" Jack inquired.

"Well, the lawyers' client account of course. I've asked my lawyers to give your solicitor the details, so as not to waste any more time."

"Are you sure that you don't want the money paid back into the account it originally came from? The British Virgin Islands offshore account? The account with the reference EC131313?"

Erica's eyes narrowed. "How can you possibly know the reference of that account? Only a handful of people know about that account."

Showdown (29 July 2016)

"Apart from those people who received money from it?"

"Don't be ridiculous. We've paid you your allowance from the ERCO UK account. What's going on here?"

"Let me explain," Jack calmly uttered, as the rest of them held their breaths. "It seems some years ago, there was a car crash in a Kent country lane in which two people were killed. The driver of the car responsible left the scene and the only witness then received a payment of £250,000 from the British Virgin Islands account EC131313. In return, he declared he could not identify the driver of the hit and run car and the passenger – a white Range Rover was all he could recall. The driver was a young smartly dressed young lady, with an older man as the passenger."

"I don't know what you're talking about," Erica said, looking slightly flustered. "An interesting story but clearly fanciful. What have you been smoking?"

"The witness felt such guilt that he left £250,000 in his will to any descendant of the victims of the crash." He paused for effect. "But you know the truth, don't you, Miss Conway? There's a suggestion that you were the driver that day and you would have been underage. That driver should have been arrested and faced a court case. And better yet, wasn't your father the passenger who then paid off the witness to protect you?"

"Utter rubbish. Where is your proof of that?" Erica blustered.

"Well, we're clear now," Jack carried on unaffected by her reaction. He moved towards the desk, took the contract, turned it around to face him and scribbled 'J Michaels' in the space marked, before passing it onto the others to sign their names.

"You're wrong, you see. Colin isn't putting up the cash for us. It will actually be your dirty blood money coming back to you. And please don't worry. We're making a new start. You can keep the Light Stone name. And as of now, I'm reverting to my real name… Jackson Stanford."

The room fell completely silent as Jackson pressed the preset number on his phone and waited for Paul to answer. "Please transfer the money, Mr Eagle," he said and then listened. "Yes, we've all signed the agreement," and then he disconnected.

Vicky and her PA both sat with open mouths. Erica's mobile phone rang. She answered it and listened before saying. "No, there have been a few developments on this end. It seems I have the Stanford child in front of me. I'll have to deal with this and call you back." She hung up.

"Oh, now I see," she chuckled slowly. "I knew I recognised the name Paul Eagle from the dim and distant past. You're looking for revenge. Well, you ought to thank that driver, shouldn't you? I bet you came into some money when you turned 18? Well, how much? A couple of million I'd guess."

"None of your business," Jackson replied. It was now the turn of the rest of the band to be open-mouthed.

"Well, if your parents hadn't died that day they would never have sold so many greatest hits albums, would they?"

"So, you're admitting that you were the driver of the white Range Rover?"

"Don't be stupid. Do you think I'm going to confess to you?"

"That would be foolish when all these rooms are bugged," interjected Colin, looking round and pointing at various tiny microphones and cameras. "Somebody could leak a confession like that."

"You're making a *huge* mistake here," Erica declared, standing up so that she towered over them, her temper visibly rising. "One which I'm going to make sure you regret. If the band doesn't stay signed to ERCO, I'll make sure that you're all ru…"

"Right," Colin interrupted. "I think we're done here, guys. We'll see ourselves out."

As they hurried out, Jack was the last one through the door. He turned around and smiled at Erica, who grimaced in return.

"One other thing, Miss Conway. Seems that our single featured a sample from an old Stanford single. You should check that out. If you don't own up to this, then I'll ask a forensic musicologist to have a listen to that and other recent songs. We'll be looking for you to correct the song credits and include Gerry and Bernie Stanford. Heard that Thomas Cronin is still around."

"Get out of my sight, you wretched boy!"

"*Don't Tell Me What To Do*!" Jackson replied and winked as he left. It took Erica some time to work out the significance of his last words.

They stood in the street below and fist bumped each other. Through the open window, they heard Vicky shouting, "*GET BEN UP HERE NOW*!"

The next thing they knew, Ben was scuttling out of the front door being chased by two security guards who rugby tackled him to the pavement before dragging him back inside to meet his fate. Fascinated, they waited a few moments more to see If they could hear what was going to happen next, but the open window was slammed shut and locked.

Colin and the band sat quietly on the train going back. They weren't able to secure the seats with the tables this time. Jackson ended up next to Colin and separate from the rest of the group. His lyric book was open in front of him and he jotted down some words that summed up the day for him.

"HELLO HAMMERSMITH!"

We've fought the darkness that we thought would never end

We've battled evil as a random group of friends

They called us misfits from the sticks; I guess that's true.

They didn't understand the strength that we carry through

They can't tell us what to do

    We face the light

    And trust that everything will work out right

    We all stand tall,

    Send a message to dark forces with our backs against the wall

The chorus fitted in with a simple riff that Liam had played him recently. He paused.

"There's something troubling me," Colin whispered.

"Oh. What's that?"

"Erica didn't seem quite as surprised as she should have been. I think I should check the Chapel for bugs."

"Yeah, I noticed that too. Mind you, she suggested it was you coming up with the cash. If the Chapel had been bugged, then she would have known that I had the legacy coming."

"Good point. She was pretty confident that the money was coming from me wasn't she? Mind you, I still think I should check for bugs. Can't take any chances."

"You're right. We're going to have to be careful given the problems that my parents experienced once they were free of ERCO. They seem to carry grudges for a long time."

Showdown (29 July 2016)

A thoughtful Jack turned back to the lyrics. He had in mind that there should be some lengthy guitar solos after each chorus which would give Liam free rein, so there was just a second verse:

> *The battle's over but the war carries on*
>
> *We got our freedom so I guess that means we've won*
>
> *Luck came our way and hit them hard out of the blue*
>
> *I guess it seemed unfair, from their point of view*
>
> *They can't tell us what to do*

Jack put the pen and notebook to one side, satisfied with how the verse tied things together.

When they arrived back at the station, they agreed to meet up again the next day at the Chapel to plan their next moves.

Chapter 34 - Come Up And See Me (25 June 1989)

The invitation came through the post to their London home. Gerry showed it to Bernie as soon as he opened the envelope. He read the contents and immediately grabbed the telephone.

"Ah Harvey! I thought I'd just call and let you know about the invite that I've had this morning."

"No need to give me the details. I think I've received a similar one. I was just about to call you to see if you knew what on earth was going on?"

"You must be joking. I've never been able to work out what goes through that guy's mind and what crazy thing he might do next. We never saw this one coming, that's for sure."

The card read:

Ernest Conway, MD of ERCO Records,

requests the pleasure of the company of

Gerald and Bernadette Stanford at his offices in London

on Thursday 25th June 1989 for lunch at 1pm.

"He must know that today's your birthday, pet. He's too calculating not to miss that!" Bernie offered.

"There are plenty of other places where I'd rather have lunch today. And plenty of *other* people that I'd like to share it with. Mind you, Ernie knows full well that I like mystery. Are you free for that, Harvey?"

"Yes, nothing that I can't move around. Perhaps I should pop around now so we can catch up properly. You know how I like to be prepared before we go in and see what he's up to."

"HELLO HAMMERSMITH!"

"Good idea. Bernie and I are here all morning. Come around when you can."

He put the phone back in its cradle and started thinking through the reasons for the invitation.

A bit later, Harvey arrived. Once he had confirmed that he was indeed 'alright' to Bernie, he gave the couple an update on all the calls that had been coming in over the last few weeks and the status on the tours that were being lined up.

The couple then began telling Harvey where they were at. "Well, the *Re-Recorded Hits Plus* project is coming along quickly," Gerry started. "We thought that we might have bitten off more than we could chew, but apparently not."

"We just have to wait until cheques come in from the Performing Rights Society before finishing things off," Bernie added. "There's one due next month so that should help. There are so many tracks with different instruments and sounds that it was always going to be a slow process. All the songs differ vastly from each other and they'll each need a fresh approach. It's been a challenge but hopefully, it will be worth it."

"It's either going to be massive or it will be a monumental sodding flop," Gerry echoed.

"No doing things by halves then," Harvey remarked. "And with the country in recession for the foreseeable future and interest base rates staying above 10%, you don't want to throw caution to the wind and seek a loan to speed it up?"

"Absolutely not!" Bernie asserted. "Based on the last interest rates the bank offered, it would be madness even for a short period. We're better

Come Up And See Me (25 June 1989)

off sitting tight and doing it all from available funds. Is there any news about ERCO?"

"Not a lot," Harvey revealed. "They're still doing well with breaking new acts but they must be suffering in the recession as well. They're not getting many artists transferring to them at the moment. I'll tell you what. I think Conway wants you to sign up with ERCO again. That's my bet. The fact you are re-recording hits from your ERCO days will make him keener to snap you up and limit the damage to his catalogue."

"Oh, I'd never thought of that," Bernie said. "But surely he's not going to try that after what's gone on in the past?"

"There's only one way to find out," Harvey maintained, downing his cooling coffee in one. "Let's not be too early arriving there. I guess he'll make us wait."

"He loves his power games," Gerry agreed.

"OK," said Harvey. "I have a bit of time to investigate what's going on. Oh, and one other thing that's relevant, while I remember. I don't know if he's told you, but I don't think it's a big secret. Oscar too had a call from Ernie Conway. He made an offer to buy his company even before his label has released an album! He promised to give him a reasonable price, for old times' sake."

"Really?" Bernie exclaimed. "What is he playing at?"

"Well, it just adds to my theory that he wants to bring you under the ERCO umbrella once more. Apparently, Oscar laughed out loud when Conway gave him the offer figure and he lost interest when Oscar explained you are just on a one-album deal and could leave anytime. Conway clearly hadn't been paying attention to Oscar's model."

"So Oscar wasn't tempted?" Bernie asked, curious and leaning towards Harvey as if she was expecting some confession.

"HELLO HAMMERSMITH!"

"Not at all."

"And do we agree that there's nothing he can tempt us with – that we're going to stay loyal to Oscar who is standing by us and has given us full creative control, which Ernie always refused to do?"

"I think that's a given," her husband assured her.

"These are the actions of a desperate man who is running out of options and will do anything and everything to get his own way. I worry about what he might do when we flat out refuse to his face. Maybe we should thank him but refuse the invitations?" Bernie suggested.

"Or maybe we should listen to whatever he has for us, thank him for his offer and promise to call him back – which is still a firm 'no' by the way. I hope we are clear on that?" Gerry proposed.

"Well, I guess we have nothing to lose," Bernie replied. "And I'd quite like to say 'no' to his face, actually. He's asking for it, isn't he?"

♪ ♪ ♪ ♪ ♪ ♪ ♪ ♪ ♪ ♪ ♪ ♪ ♪ ♪

At 1 o'clock precisely, Gerry, Bernie and Harvey arrived at ERCO's offices. The security guard led them up to the top floor where they knew Ernie had his office. The reception door was open and a secretary tapped away on a typewriter. "Ah, Mr and Mrs Stanford and Mr D'Angelo!" she greeted them. "Mr Conway is ready for you now."

"That's a first," Bernie muttered under her breath. "He's always kept us waiting before. Must be up to something."

"Welcome, welcome…" Ernie bellowed as he stood up from behind his massive mahogany desk covered with green leather. Bernie noticed that the desk now sat on a wooden riser so that in a negotiating situation, he would always be higher than anyone else in the room. His hand was outstretched as he came down the step and greeted each of them with a crushing handshake, which he twisted to ensure his hand stayed on top.

Come Up And See Me (25 June 1989)

He did, however, grimace slightly as Bernie questioned whether he was "alright or what" in her inimitable style.

"So glad you could make it and Happy birthday to you Gerry. I appreciate you finding the time today when you could have been enjoying your time elsewhere in town. Starters are here already. Let's tuck in while you tell me how you are."

"Thank you, Ernie," Gerry answered, sitting down and eyeing the prawn cocktail in front of him. "We're slowly getting there with re-recording all the hits from our days with ERCO. They're sounding great – just as I imagined them. We'll be able to start the mixing soon and we're hoping to release it through Good Record Co in time for Christmas."

"Oh, well done! I've been hearing about that. Full marks for bravery, by the way. But then you are at the top of your game at the moment. I always think that there are two times to take a massive gamble, when you're at the bottom and have nothing to lose and when you're at the top so punters will buy any old thing that you put out," Ernie commented with a guffaw.

"I don't think we see it quite like that," Bernie said indignantly. "We've more respect for our fans than to put out something sub-standard."

"Quite so," Ernie interposed, brushing the comment aside. "And are you planning any live dates to promote the record?"

"Oh absolutely," Harvey interjected. "The reports of the recording are bringing in offers from promoters in some far-flung places around the world. Some big shows are being mooted as well. We'll do a lot of promotional work just before it's released and will host some listening parties."

"I think that we've just about recovered from the last tour," Bernie added.

"HELLO HAMMERSMITH!"

There was a pause while they ate the starter, which was Harvey's opportunity to press things forward. "Well Ernie. Thank you so much for inviting us all here today, especially to celebrate Gerry's birthday. As you might imagine, we've been speculating as to the reason for this curious invitation. You must know it was unexpected."

"Yes, quite right, Harvey." Ernie pushed back in his chair while a waitress scooped up the plates and closed the door behind her. "I didn't think that I would make it to the main course without having to tell you what was on my mind. As you might imagine, I've kept a keen eye on your career despite our little fallout. But that was some years ago and I always think that the future is more interesting than the past could ever be." He paused for effect. "I'd like you to think about coming back to ERCO for your next few records. I was thinking of a five-album deal to give you more security than Good is offering you." He looked at three open mouths. Just at that moment, the door opened, and the main course arrived.

"You can't be serious?" Bernie attempted after the door had closed and they were alone again.

"I quite understand your surprise. But I've thought long and hard and understand that you were absolutely right. The old contract we had with you was one-sided and unfair. You were correct to fight against it and the success that you've had since has proven your point. Since then, as you know, our worldwide distribution channels have become far stronger. Sure, you could stay with Oscar and his new label in the established markets, but there are new markets opening up in Russia and Eastern Europe that I think he has been slow to take advantage of. The Korean market is one that is exploding at the moment. We're already active there and selling huge amounts of CDs. You're big in Japan and the Korean market seems to even be more fanatical." He paused again before continuing. "I've no doubt that the re-recordings are going to be a worldwide hit, so I'm prepared to bust the bank over this one and offer you 12% of the gross with ERCO covering all the marketing costs involved. My plan is to release a special version with the original

Come Up And See Me (25 June 1989)

recordings back to back with the new ones. You've done all the recording, but we can release money for the mixing now to make sure that we do the best job on this one. Releasing it just before Christmas suits us just fine. We have a ready-made gap in the schedule all ready for you. What do you say?"

"Well, you're going to have to give us some time to think about it," Harvey mused, before Gerry and Bernie could say anything. "How quickly will you need an answer from us?"

"The sooner, the better. We have big plans for this one."

"I see," Gerry reflected. "You haven't secured a new signing to perform at the ERCO Summer Ball, have you?"

Ernie shifted uncomfortably in his chair, suggesting that Gerry was quite right in his summation, before saying "Well, of course, if you signed, we would want to announce it at the ball and of course you would be the surprise reveal at the end. That just makes so much sense, no?"

Bernie looked at Gerry, who knew exactly what was on her mind. "I'm sorry, Ernie, but there's absolutely no way that Stanford is going to be considering going back to ERCO. Our memories are still raw from the past and there will be no going back for us."

"But at least look at the terms," Ernie suggested. "I forgot to mention that there would be some ERCO shares included as a sweetener to the deal. You would receive them for free and as you know, the price on the stock market is flying high at the moment."

"Ernie," Gerry started. "Let's not forget that you tried to sue us on a laughable pretext. There's absolutely nothing that you could offer that would make any difference to our decision. It has to be a 'no'."

"Yes, I apologise for that writ," Ernie insisted. "Unfortunately, our legal team were rather overzealous at the time and the solicitor's letter had been sent before I heard about it. Fired the lot of them, I can assure you.

"HELLO HAMMERSMITH!"

There's still dessert to come, you know. A black forest gateau plus a birthday cake for you."

Now it was Bernie's turn to make matters clear. "Nice try Ernie. I must confess that I didn't think you would be foolish or desperate enough to try getting us back after all we've been through with you. Can I remind you that the idea of re-recording the old hits came about so that we could take back control of those songs? That would then mean that every time we played them live afterwards, the royalties would come to us and not ERCO. In the meantime, I have to inform you that Good Record Co are going to be giving us way more than the 12% royalty and some shares that you're offering."

"Really? What nonsense figure has he offered you?"

"I can't possibly comment," said Bernie with a knowing smile.

"You're making a huge mistake here...," Ernie cautioned, his temper visibly rising. "One which I'm going to make sure that you regret. If you don't sign for ERCO, then I'll make sure that you're ru..."

"Are you threatening my clients?" Harvey suggested with a noticeable frown.

"Come on you two, this has gone far enough," Bernie announced as she stood up from the table and threw her napkin down.

"Ernie, I thought that by now you would have realised that you *Don't Tell Me What To Do*," Gerry let out as he left.

"Ouch, that was brutal," Bernie whispered.

There were no handshakes as they left the room.

♪ ♪ ♪ ♪ ♪ ♪ ♪ ♪ ♪ ♪ ♪ ♪ ♪ ♪

Later that afternoon, in Ernie's office, the door was flung open without

Come Up And See Me (25 June 1989)

warning. A man in a grey suit entered and stubbed out the remnants of a cigarette in an ashtray. "I'm guessing that they didn't take the bait?"

"I'm afraid not," Ernie answered. "But I'm not giving up just yet."

"And did you tell them about the research that ERCO has been doing to identify what makes records infectious and irresistible?"

"No, I didn't think that would be wise with the way things were going."

"I'm not concerned. We knew it was a long shot. They made a mistake with their re-recording lark. I don't like being made to look a fool. I have plenty of time to get even with Mr and Mrs Stanford."

Chapter 35 - The Colour Spectrum (30 July 2016)

The band formerly known as Light Stone arrived at the Chapel on the Saturday morning; Hannah was first at 10 o'clock and she paced the main room impatiently until everyone had arrived. Liam was last as usual and caused much laughter by removing his bobble hat to reveal a closely shaved head.

"Woah! What happened there? Have you had some kind of accident at the barbers?" Rick exclaimed, unable to help himself.

"Felt like a change," was all Liam said as Hannah stroked his head before he brushed her away with a look.

Colin made them all drinks and they sat in the front room and looked to the lad now known as Jackson to start the proceedings.

"Thought I should apologise to you all again," Jackson started. "To be fair, it wasn't until recently that I found out about the trust fund and the legacy. I'd been brought up to think that my parents had died with nothing to their name, no legacy and certainly no fortune."

"Yes, that would be a start," Hannah admonished. "I understand it will have taken you some time to get your head around this, but you could have saved us all an awful lot of aggro by coming clean a good deal earlier."

"And in my defence," Colin added, "although I reckoned that the fund would have built up with the CD sales and royalties over the years, I didn't think that it was fair of me to share that with Jackson. He needed to find out the truth in his own time."

"And do we have to call you Jackson now?" asked Rick.

"I quite like Jackson actually," Hannah hesitated. "I think it always felt weird, like something was missing with Jack… not just because you always acted a bit like you were not your complete self."

Jackson smiled. "You guys can call me Jack if it's easier," and looking at Hannah and Liam, "but from now on, our songwriting credits will be Duncan/Ross/Stanford."

"I don't understand," Hannah replied. "You shouldn't be last at all!"

"Agreed that it was going to be alphabetical and why should that change now?"

Everyone nodded as though they understood.

"I think you all have a lot to talk about," Colin noted. "I've made a list. There's no particular order except that some of these things are more important than others. First, are you all happy to stay together as a band? I know Jackson is in. We all know there isn't much of a career stacking supermarket shelves, but if any of you have had enough of this business and want to go off and do something else with someone else, then this is the time to do it." There was silence. Colin turned to Hannah. "What about you, Hannah? You can easily be accepted into an advanced music and drama school in September and develop. I'm sure that you could do well."

"To be honest, I think there might be an interesting future developing here at the moment. I can go to drama school later if needs be," she declared firmly.

"Ok, and Liam, you said that you were thinking about going back to your college course. Has that changed?"

"I think I'll wait and see what comes out of today."

Dan felt he was in the same place. "I was happy to stay where we were and give ERCO a chance to push us forward, but I'll see what we agree on today."

Rick gave his best goofy smile to everyone. "And I've nothing better to do than hang around with you guys - and girl."

"OK, that's good for now, but not terribly clear and conclusive," Colin said. "The next thing I guess is if you stayed as a band, do you want to look for another record deal or do you want to go more DIY and independent?"

"DIY and independent," everyone let out in unison.

"Actually, I think you've little choice on that one," Colin pointed out. "ERCO issued a press release yesterday, hinting that they had a difficult relationship with the band. Normally, the word 'amicable' would be featured and when it isn't, the industry guesses why. Paul Eagle had put a clause in the agreement saying that both sides would keep the details of the ending of the contract confidential but there are always coded words that can be used or are avoided."

"I think that the funds that I've got mean that we don't have to be beholden to anyone but ourselves," Jackson added.

"But that's not fair to you if we use all your funds to release us from ERCO and start recording again," Hannah commented. The others nodded.

"OK, let's see if there's a way we can fix that," Jackson suggested. "Going to go to see Paul Eagle again soon to have the funds transferred over to me. He might have a way to deal with that."

"I think access to funds like that gives you a tremendous advantage," Colin explained. "Young bands rarely have ready money for a start and record companies have always been able to use that fact to hold them to ransom and force them to do their bidding. You've seen it with ERCO.

Good, that's one thing decided. Next is an exciting bit. You need a new band name!"

For the next half hour, the band kicked various alternatives around but agreed to nothing. Then Colin reminded them about one of his lessons where they looked at Newton's Colour Circle from 1704 – The Colour Spectrum, where colours were associated with musical notes. This transported Jackson to when he lived at the Chapel a long time ago. He remembered the spectrum of colours reflected by the platinum, gold and silver albums when the sun was shining through the stained-glass windows.

Hannah started drawing diagrams in her notebook as soon as Colin mentioned The Colour Spectrum and once there was a lull in the conversation, she pitched in. "One of the O Levels that I did was psychology and we studied Carl Jung's different personality profiles. I think between the five of us we have most of them covered." They all looked at her in a puzzled way, including Colin.

"So, there are four different quadrants depending on whether you're an extrovert or introvert and whether you're more task-orientated or into relationships. Let's start with Rick. You're an extrovert and into relationships, right?"

"Can't dispute that darlin'!"

"That makes you Sunny Yellow – always joking and positive. But please don't call me darlin' again. So that's one. Then there's Dan. Definitely introvert and task-orientated?"

Dan thought about this as if to prove Hannah right before agreeing.

"That makes Dan a Calming Blue. He thinks a lot. Incidentally, I don't know how you and Rick are such good buddies. You ought to get on each other's nerves. Sunny Yellow and Calming Blue are opposites."

"We do get on each other's nerves," Dan confessed to Rick's amusement.

"You have to watch the quiet ones," Rick joked.

"Liam is pretty calm about most things, so could be Blue again, but actually he's more about relationships, so I think he's different from Dan. Also, he's quite relaxed about stuff, so I reckon he's Earthy Green."

Liam shrugged his shoulders as he normally would to suggest that he wasn't going to argue.

"My case is proven. The only problem that we have is that we don't have anyone who is Stormy Red," she continued.

There was silence in the room as they all looked at her.

"What are you guys staring at? It's obvious that I'm a Yellow, like Rick."

Nobody could contain their laughter. "Stop laughing, I'm serious."

Rick regained his composure first. "Who agrees with Hannah that she's as Yellow as me?" The laughter continued but otherwise there was no reaction.

"Then let's see everybody's hand up. Who thinks that she's Stormy Red and this problem is solved?"

"Alright, alright. I think that you're all wrong and you're going to see how Yellow I am once you know me better, but I'll take the Red for now to help you guys out," she glowered.

"I think this shows that the best judge of your colour is usually other people," Colin commented. "That just leaves Jackson."

Hannah had regained her composure. "Well, he's definitely been introverted and task-driven hasn't he? So he's been Blue up 'til now, but coming into that money and the episode with ERCO has shown a different side of him. Plus, he can be lively on stage. So Jack's a puzzle and I think he might move into Red and like me into Yellow, but we'll see. The teacher said that your colour can be quite fluid when you're young."

They all nodded in agreement – were they the perfect team?

Colin had been drawing his own diagrams. "You've just reminded me of something. Who would you all say was the most successful group of all time?"

"Abba?" Hannah suggested, to more laughter. "I'm serious. I love ABBA."

"Steps?" Rick offered with a laugh. "Ok, Led Zeppelin."

"Maybe. What about The Beatles?" asked Colin, to murmured agreement. "They only produced music over a seven-year period, and over that time you had John as the Red leader, driving them forwards with Paul, who was Yellow and tried to get on with everyone." Colin put his thumbs up in McCartney style. "Then you had George who was the quiet one and Blue, with Ringo who was Green and pretty much along for the wild ride. I reckon they only broke up because John hooked up with Yoko and wasn't leading anymore. He probably went Green and started caring about things outside the band, like world peace. So Paul took over, much to the disgust of George, who by this time had a stack of songs that weren't being heard. They broke up as it had all got too messy and they were no longer in the roles that made them so successful."

"Wow." Hannah was impressed, as was everyone else. "That makes so much sense." Everyone agreed. "I'm not sure you should blame Yoko though." She pulled her laptop towards her and started searching for any other well-known groups using that name. The closest band she found was Colours of Spectrum.

The Colour Spectrum (30 July 2016)

Everyone liked the fact that they could use the name to cover different styles and move from one to another. When Hannah pointed out it was the title of a short song on Coldplay's last album, which they all liked, it was decided. 'The Colour Spectrum' it was.

They reckoned they didn't need to spend much more time writing new songs. They had enough to use now that they had retrieved the rights of their existing ones from ERCO, so it was time to have them recorded the way they wanted.

"Can you produce them for us?" Jackson asked Colin.

"That's kind of you to ask me, but there's a new term starting soon and I'm expected back there. I can find a few people who you can have a try-out with, to see who you like. Leave that with me." He made a note. "I'll tell you what though, term doesn't start for another month. I'm sure Sue McLeod will let you use the college studio. I can say that I'm just putting it through its paces before the new year comes in. Record as many songs as you can and we can take things from there. I can help produce those for you at least."

They all agreed to that plan. "But what happens after that?" Liam worried.

"Well, I was going to suggest that if you wanted to, I could finally fix this analogue gear up. It's been fine for me doing some rough demos over the last few years. Really, I need it stripped down and refurbished, or rip it all out and put a new studio in. I've never made proper use of it while I've been here, so now's the chance."

"How about we start off seeing what we can make out of what's here?" Liam suggested. "How do you feel about digging up the past, Jackson?"

"That would be interesting. Let's record the college songs first, then spend some time getting the studio together as we're working out what to do with them."

"HELLO HAMMERSMITH!"

"Right, I think the next thing that you need to agree on is how you are going to build up your profile again," Colin continued. "You're going to need to surround yourselves with a team of people now that you don't have ERCO. You need a proper manager to replace me, someone to post you on the streaming sites, a booking agent to push you for the bigger festivals next year, someone to do the PR and marketing like managing the new website and social media accounts and someone to do videos for YouTube."

"A few people from college were doing videos and sticking them up on YouTube when we played live," Liam reminded everyone. "I'll see if I can track them down."

"Do you mean Angie Elkins and Sarah Hage?" Hannah offered. "I kept in touch with them. They've set themselves up as a PR agency. They thought the local ones around here were a bit too zany and trying too hard to be colourful and wacky. I'll look them up. In the meantime, I can set up the social media accounts with the new band name and link all of us to them so that whatever fans we have left can jump in."

"That's cool," Jackson said. "So, are you all in? If any of you are out, then we're going to have to hit the pause button and regroup before we do anything else."

They all nodded to suggest that they were in, but some did not seem as positive as others.

"Right, then we'll give Colin a chance to talk to the principal and then we'll be straight in to record some songs. All agreed?"

They did. Nobody was in a particular rush to be somewhere, so they picked through some of the song ideas that Hannah, Liam and Jackson had been kicking around. One which sounded promising was a simple piano riff in the key of C that Jackson said had come to him as he woke up that morning. They used the riff as a loop and added guitar, bass and drum loops over it. A change of key up to D once everyone had their parts was the signal for Liam to solo over the top before they phased the loops out again. They agreed it worked well as a jaunty instrumental and the title of *The Colour Spectrum* stuck.

Chapter 36 - Abbey Road (2 June 1989)

This was a big day for Gerry. The Beatles had been his favourite childhood band and he was well aware of their residency at the Abbey Road Studios in West London during what he considered to be their most creative later period, culminating in the Abbey Road album of October 1969. "One day," he would tell himself, "I'll record at Abbey Road and it will have to be in Studio 2."

With their Multiplier contract at an end, his opportunity came when another label asked if Stanford would contribute a song to an orchestral compilation album that they planned to release. Current bands were invited to re-record an old hit using an orchestra at Abbey Road. Gerry immediately thought of *Let's Do It Now*, which was their most recent hit and still in the lower reaches of the chart. He had always thought that the song would lend itself to having a full orchestra and this presented him with the perfect excuse to fulfil his dream.

Coming from the next generation, Bernie didn't live through The Beatles, but appreciated their ground-breaking studio work. To her, a studio was a studio and she didn't think that Abbey Road would feel different from any other one. Yet, there was something about the steps up to the front door and being greeted by the receptionist behind the large wooden desk. When they were asked to sign in, Bernie was suddenly star-struck. "Oh my goodness, Elkie Brooks was here yesterday," she babbled. "I bloody love Elkie Brooks."

"That's right," the receptionist smiled. "Her new album is going to be a mixture of covers and originals and she wanted to record *Maybe I'm Amazed* and some others here."

The duo were met by the manager of the orchestra that was involved in all the recordings. Not everyone had arrived yet. They walked down the wood panelled corridors to the café at the back of the property to have a drink while preparations were being made. They both sat outside on the terrace in silence, drinking coffee while they took in the feel of the building.

Eventually, the couple were called in through the main doors of Studio 2. The manager greeted them once more and ushered them up the wooden stairs in the corner, which led to the control room above.

Everything seemed calm up there. Some engineers were sitting on a sofa at the back of the control room having spent the last few hours placing microphones at strategic points around the room to pick up the sound as cleanly as possible. The producer sat in the chair in front of the control desk. He was speaking into a microphone that carried into the studio below and echoed around, asking various parts of the orchestra to play random parts so he could check the sound levels. He then nodded to the manager to suggest that they were ready to start.

"Right, we're all set. Come down and meet everyone."

Gerry walked down the stairs with Bernie to shake hands with the conductor and lead violinist. "Have you rehearsed much?" he asked.

"Shouldn't need to," the violinist replied. "We normally just look at what's in front of us and follow the conductor."

Gerry was impressed. He scratched his head in amazement, thinking back to the days of rehearsals that the Stanford band needed before a live performance. He walked around some sections and had a look at the sheet music that had been laid out in front of them. This was quite beyond his limited musical knowledge, and he had no problem with commissioning an arranger to add these parts to the original songs.

"You might be interested in this Gerry," the studio manager said, pointing to an upright piano against the wall at the far end of the studio.

Gerry looked at it quizzically. "It doesn't look like much."

Abbey Road (2 June 1989)

"No, it doesn't," his guide agreed, "but it's the piano on which Paul McCartney wrote and recorded *Lady Madonna*." Gerry's mouth fell open. His mind a blur, he immediately sat down on the stool and gently opened the lid. He played the opening bars of Lady Madonna and closed his eyes to think back to his days as a young teenager listening to the song, then realised that the entire orchestra were looking at him while the conductor pointed at his watch. Muttering an apology, he closed the lid and stood up to follow his guide.

"And this is the instrument that you will play today." The guide motioned to the grand piano to the left of the conductor. "We think it was certainly one of the three pianos used to play the final E major chord on *A Day in the Life*."

"Oh, wow!" Gerry mouthed as he quietly sat down and played some scales to get a feel for the keys. He was the only musician not to have sheets of music in front of him. He couldn't read music but he knew the songs and arrangements better than anyone. Bernie went back upstairs to listen to the recording take place.

From the control room, complete with the basic track that was playing through the headphones of the orchestra members, it sounded great. When she tiptoed down to listen on the floor of the studio, it sounded even better.

Later in the day, the conductor approached Gerry while they were re-recording the last section of the song. "We're just about done, Gerry; did you want to conduct the orchestra on this last bit?"

Once again, Gerry's mouth fell open. "I… I don't think that I'm qualified," he stuttered.

"Nonsense," the manager exclaimed. "No harm in giving it a go. If it doesn't work, we won't use it."

"HELLO HAMMERSMITH!"

"Go on Gerry," Bernie prodded. "You know very well you've always wanted to have an orchestra under your control. You can't afford to miss this opportunity, can you?"

"I suppose not," Gerry surrendered as he nervously ventured to the podium at the front. He picked up the spare headphones that the conductor offered him. He heard the producer's voice.

"Right, everyone, we're going to have another run through of the finale of *Let's Do It Now*, just for Gerry. I'll start the playback now and Gerry will start you off at the end of the last chorus."

As Gerry heard the outro start, he raised the baton and swung it down in an amateur fashion. He had to concentrate as he then heard the strings come in on the beat before swinging away again. He shut his eyes and felt the music in his mind and, at one with the music, continued to move his baton in time. The forgiving orchestra stayed with him until the last crescendo.

With tears now visible in his eyes, Gerry took off the headphones and motioned to everyone else to do the same. "I just want to thank you all for being here on this incredible day. It's one that I'll remember for as long as I live." The orchestra stood up and applauded both Gerry and each other.

"How was that?" Gerry asked as he returned to the control room. "For a first-timer, that was good," the producer nodded, impressed "But I think we'll go with the earlier one and keep the other version just for you."

"You're probably right. Thank you."

The last item to be ticked off their bucket list for the day was for them both to use the famous crossing. A borrowed photographer captured them assuming different poses. The photo that was used on the inside sleeve of the compilation album featured an irate taxi driver shouting at them to clear out of his way while Bernie blew him a kiss.

Abbey Road (2 June 1989)

They both agreed: this was definitely a day to remember. The experience had also made Gerry think about the possibility of re-recording more of the Stanford back catalogue.

Chapter 37 - Come Together (August 2016)

It wasn't so easy to get permission from the college to use the recording facilities. ERCO had somehow heard of the band's plans and Vicky Tucker was straight on the phone to Sue McLeod.

"Look Sue, as sponsors of the college, any permission to use the recording facility during holiday time should come to us for approval."

"Oh, really?" replied a surprised principal. "I don't think that's ever come up in all the years that you've been sponsors and I don't remember seeing any reference to that in the huge sponsorship contract that your lawyers insisted on."

"That might not be specifically referred to, but it's a bit of a red line for us now."

Sue's brow furrowed as she thought through the implications of the suggestion. "Yes, I understand that you could have a problem with it now, Vicky, but the fact remains that I'm the principal here and I have the authority to decide how the facilities get used. That's something of a red line for me. And one other thing, maybe you should bring your sponsorship payments up to date before you go making demands."

"Yes, as you are fully aware, we have had a few funding issues at this end which we are striving to resolve."

"And in the meantime, you are in breach of your contractual obligations."

Following the call, Sue swiftly called an EGM of the governors and proposed that ERCO be removed as sponsors with immediate effect. Erica Conway attended the meeting, but failed to impress anyone. Her fellow governors were fed up with her bullying techniques and threats and stood up to her. For the first time, she could not change their minds. Everyone, in fact, was glad to see the back of her.

In the background, Colin had quietly revealed Jackson's true identity to Sue McLeod and it took her a while to comprehend. Like everyone else, she had no idea. She bristled with pride to think that a Stanford had attended the college on her watch.

Colin duly secured her permission and the band were free to use the familiar college facilities for a few days after the builders moved out with their usual holiday maintenance work completed. The band pulled together, with Colin in charge of the recording and engineering side of the project.

Hannah had tracked down Angie and Sarah to see if they would cover the PR activities. The girls set up a new YouTube channel for The Colour Spectrum. They also came to see them and talk through the PR possibilities. Everyone recognised the girls from the earliest Light Stone gigs. Jackson vaguely remembered that Angie had tried to chat him up after a gig. He had made a lame excuse and backed away.

The band discussed going full on with the PR but then delayed their decision until after the start of the term. That way, they could concentrate on recording while they had the facilities immediately available.

Hannah had spent the last evening getting The Colour Spectrum set up on social media. She had also secured 'www.the-colour-spectrum.com' as a domain name for future use. In her search, she stumbled on a collection of songs that had been released by the band The Dear Hunter. Luckily, the collection used the American spelling as 'The Color Spectrum' so it wasn't long before they broke free from that potential confusion in online searches.

Come Together (August 2016)

The band all messaged their online friends to let them know that the Light Stone accounts, which had been controlled by ERCO for some time, were no more and that they should follow The Colour Spectrum instead.

In the college studio, they first tried to save time and record everything live, but they spent an entire morning trying to place the microphones correctly for the drums. After that, they went with Colin's advice to go back to basics and build the recording up on separate tracks.

As a fan favourite with a good tempo, *Going Forwards in Reverse* was chosen as a good one to start with. Rick and Dan laid down the backing tracks first before Hannah and Jackson added rhythm guitar and keyboards and Liam put his guitar down. Finally, Jackson and Hannah swapped vocals, as they usually did. This was one they thought would work best with the two of them alternating and then joining in the chorus. Colin got them to face each other around one microphone so that they could watch each other's actions. He had recently seen a TV programme showing that ABBA had recorded their biggest hits this way. The complete song was done in an afternoon and they agreed to break and come back early tomorrow to start on the next one.

The following morning, they started on *It's Time To Take Action*. Rick put down the drum track first but this time Liam recorded his guitar riff before Jackson added some keyboards. Dan had gone missing so the bass had to wait until he came back later. This was a sparser track, so Hannah's rhythm guitar wasn't required. It was a personal song for Jackson, who had written it alone. They agreed he should be the lead singer and that Hannah would provide backing vocals. A similar process was adopted with *The Wisdom of Crowds* so that, by the end of the second day, they had three songs completed.

They started the third day listening back to the three songs they'd recorded. Clearly, they needed a few overdubs.

They then tried out a new song. Colin had encouraged them to write about things around them, so *How Can a City Ever Sleep* had been a

"HELLO HAMMERSMITH!"

group effort while they were living in the London flat and continually finding it hard to go to sleep as the nightlife thrived in the streets below them. It was another one of Rick's innocent quotes that ended up as the basis for a song title. Colin had also been suggesting that they write in unusual keys and demonstrated the E Aeolian key to them.

Rick, whose family had treated him to a trip to New York during a red moon display, suggested the first verse.

> *Underneath the blood-red moon*
>
> *New York city screams its discordant tune*
>
> *Yellow taxis refill traffic, nose to tail*
>
> *Clogging 59th Street, outside Bloomingdale's.*

Hannah had added a pre-chorus:

> *The homeless walk the streets in cast-off clothes that are now rags*
>
> *Or lie in empty doorways, inside their damp sleeping bags*

Jackson and Liam had constructed most of the chorus:

> *In these city streets, most stories don't get told*
>
> *They'd disappoint the ones who thought that they were paved with gold*
>
> *Many secrets get cleaned up by the road sweeps*
>
> *It can make a grown man weep. How can a city ever sleep?*

Rather than continue the New York theme, they moved the second verse to London:

> *Underneath the blood-red moon*
>
> *The streets of London shout their - discordant tunes*
>
> *Black cabs sit in static traffic nose to tail*
>
> *Police car blues and twos holler whoop and wail*

Come Together (August 2016)

Jackson added a middle eight while the others had been doing their parts:

Penthouse dwellers drink champagne from crystal flutes

Look down at men in suits and those with holes in shoes

And they finished with a nod to their home city:

Underneath the blood-red moon

Chaucer's city hums its - discordant tune

Foreign tourists mill and fill the quaint old streets

Pass fake beggars who say they can't afford to eat

They had purposely not practised this while they were in ERCO's studios, so they were not so sure about the way it was going to sound. For that reason, they took longer to record it. They tried different styles before settling on something anthemic. It was always going to be a later track on a release, but the format was something that was still up for discussion.

They only had one more day available before the new students were due to come in to be introduced to the facilities.

"Should we record another song tomorrow or stick with the four for the time being?"

"I think stick with what we've got and get Angie and Sarah in here with the video team," suggested Rick. The rest agreed with him.

Getting in early, they listened to the city song and made a few more changes to it before preparing for the shoot. They tried a mime run through. The exercise didn't work and reminded them how false their experience with the ERCO single was. So they ended up recording a live version. As expected, this had a lot more life to it and it was easier to make it look dramatic. It didn't matter if a few notes were missed; the passion was there for all to see. Near the end of the day, they viewed some unedited cuts. The producer that Sarah had called in a favour from explained which bits he thought he would use and how he would cut them together.

Satisfied, the group piled into the closest pub and discussed plans until closing time.

They were tired but happy. Near the end of the evening, they turned their thoughts to how they were going to get the music out there.

"We could always go back to the Good Record Co foundation," Liam suggested. "Remember, they gave us a £1,000 grant when we were getting going? They send me emails every so often to see how we're doing. I'm pretty certain that Oscar Good himself will probably be interested when he realises that Gerry and Bernie Stanford's son has benefitted from his foundation. Stanford released some albums on his label?"

"Yes, that's right. It's coming back to me now. I think he visited the Chapel one time. If he helped my parents, then maybe he could help us as well."

How Can a City Ever Sleep can be streamed free here:

https://soundcloud.com/the-colour-spectrum/how-can-a-city-ever-sleep

Come Together (August 2016)

Chapter 38 - You're My Best Friend (January 1989)

Gerry took the call at his home out of the blue. "Hi Gerry. It's Oscar Good here."

"Oh, hi Oscar. This is a surprise. I haven't heard from you in a long time."

"That's true. I hope you don't mind me calling you at home… Harvey was kind enough to give me your number."

"No, that's fine. I trust Harvey to give the number out to the right people only."

"Absolutely. Ok, you remember I left ERCO because I was fed up with all their politics and double-dealings?"

"Yes. You were always a fish out of water there, Oscar. You're far too honest to have stayed there. I'm eternally grateful to you for warning us we needed to get the hell out of there as soon as we could."

Oscar chuckled before continuing. "I told you I was going to disappear to hatch a plan which I hoped would disrupt the music industry for the better, remember?"

"You did. And you've been gone a long time. We thought you might never come back, to be honest."

"There was no rush. I had plenty of money saved up so there was a silver lining to that ERCO cloud. Thankfully, I only tried cocaine once and it did nothing for me, so I didn't feel the urge to shove all my earnings up my nose. That gave me the time I needed to plan how this was all going to work." He sighed the way one does when they have finally reached the end of a long journey. "I think that I'm just about there now!" He paused as if for dramatic effect. "Since I promised I would check how you were fixed before I went looking for artists elsewhere, here I am!"

"HELLO HAMMERSMITH!"

"Wow! Yes, yes... I remember Oscar. Well, the situation at the moment is that, as you probably know, the last three albums have been released by Multiplier Records. They've been fine but their rules are much the same as ERCO's, just without the underhandedness. Why don't we meet up to talk more?"

"That would be great Gerry. I know it's cheeky but how are you fixed right now? I'm just around the corner from you."

"Hang on, Bernie's just walked in. I'll check with her." Gerry covered the mouthpiece of the phone. "Oscar's on the phone. Wants to come round and talk to us about a new model for the music business. Interested?"

"Oh right. Well, why not listen to him? He's always been a lovely bloke."

Gerry uncovered the mouthpiece. "We're all set, Oscar. Come round as soon as you'd like."

Within the hour, they were all sitting down in the lounge of Gerry and Bernie's London home. Oscar was leaning back on the sofa and every so often brushed his brown fringe away from his eyes. His face was tanned from many months on different exotic beaches around the world. Bernie, keen to hear what Oscar had to say, leaned forward. Oscar sipped his hot coffee before making a start.

"Well, can we start by saying that if the music industry isn't actually broken, then it soon will be?"

"All agreed on that one," Bernie affirmed. "I think it's only a matter of time before something comes along to wipe away all of this excess, greed and corruption that the big boys have been getting away with."

"That's an interesting point of view," Oscar continued. "And whilst I was on the beach one of the first things that I had to do was to go back to the reason I came into this business. Actually, it wasn't to make a lot of money and lie on a beach thinking about the inequities of the music business. I realised I had always wanted to help young bands to navigate the sharks and choppy waters of the music business. That was the reason I was keen to work with the young bands that ERCO signed. I realised that after many years with ERCO, I wasn't allowed to talk to the young bands anymore and that's why I became jaded and disenchanted with everything." He paused to allow it all to sink in. "The most important thing was to establish the new company as a supporter of new and young artists. Now let me make something clear. At the moment, the label itself isn't targeted at those starting out in the business. I thought long and hard about the possibility of rescuing new artists who are trying to crack the market, but it just doesn't work for them as yet. I can only help established artists to break free and take control of their own destiny. Does that make sense?"

"Keep going," Gerry encouraged him. "We're with you, aren't we love?" Bernie nodded before Oscar continued.

"So, what I'm doing instead is pledging that 20% of the profits from the label go into a foundation which will support young bands before they think about getting a record deal. It will give grants that will allow them to buy better gear. There'll also be mentors by their side as they develop. Just me initially."

"That all sounds interesting, Oscar!" Bernie interrupted. "But where exactly might we fit in?"

"Well, as I remember it, you extracted yourselves from ERCO with a fairly clean sheet. And the royalties that Multiplier have paid you since have made you less reliant on record company funding. Am I still on the right line?"

"That's right, up to a point," Bernie explained further. "Multiplier are still happy to have us on a standard contract with a 10% royalty rate whereby they pay all the costs upfront and then claw it back from us from royalties later. You probably noticed that *Blindside* is still selling really well. The royalties have been pouring in. It was just a three-album deal. We've learnt to avoid tying ourselves up for too long."

"HELLO HAMMERSMITH!"

"Good, that's important just at the moment. You know roughly how the numbers work out right now. There's probably 30% each to the record company and the retailer, 22% to the distributor, 5% for manufacturing the CDs, 3% for the producer, leaving the songwriter and artists with 10%. I reckon that the ratio of artists who have made it like you, to the rest who are signed to major labels, is around 20 to one. You must realise a load of the profits that the company makes on Stanford are being wasted on other bands. So, my first question to you is this. Would you be prepared to reinvest the money that you've saved in the recording process, so that you have more freedom from the record company that you are signed to?"

Gerry and Bernie thought for a minute. "Well, I don't see why not," Bernie started. "At the end of the day, it *is* our money anyway, isn't it? Why wouldn't we want to spend it as we see fit and be in control of it? We know from our own experience that having an open cheque book from ERCO just tempted us to overspend on unnecessary extras."

Oscar smiled. "So far, so good. Good Record Co would then handle the production of the CDs and distribution. I've been spending the last few years doing deals around the world so that I have the coverage that artists need to be represented in all the markets where they are likely to be popular. Between you and me, all I've needed to do is contact the distributors around the world that ERCO tried to beat down on price to the stage where they refused to deal with them. If the research doesn't suggest that you are going to do well in a certain market, then we don't push too hard on it. When the product sales income arrives from the distributors, what do you think would be a fair split between the artist and the label? I'll give you a clue. You'll be paid more than the normal 10%."

"I'd hope so!" Gerry interjected. "But I don't really know. I've never thought about it in that way before. What do you think, dear? You have the better business head on you."

You're My Best Friend (January 1989)

"Um. If those costs are being deducted first, then it would certainly have to be more than 30:70, maybe one-third to two-thirds?"

Oscar looked quite pleased as he announced, "I think I can do better than that. Remember, I'm not going to have an army behind me managing your career and booking video shoots and tours." He held them in a few more seconds of suspense before uttering the words, "How does a 50:50 split sound?"

The couple looked at each other, jaws figuratively dropped. Bernie turned to Oscar. "That sounds like we should talk further."

Gerry concurred. "It's compelling. What I can't understand is why no one has thought about or done it before. It could have saved us a complete load of grief."

"To be fair, I don't think I'm breaking much new ground here," Oscar admitted. "There are small independent labels that have been doing something similar and it seems fairer all around. The difference is that they tend not to do it with big established artists like you guys."

"Oscar, your timing is good," Gerry admitted. "We were just in the process of gathering up songs to take to Multiplier and talk about negotiating a new contract and recording a new album. We've some great new songs lined up."

"That sounds perfect. Why don't I come back so you can show me what you have? I'm going to be picky though, certainly for the first album, anyway. I'll tell you if I don't think that what you have is going to be worth my investment in the distribution. But I think I know the two of you well enough to believe that you'll only want to record solid hits."

"At least, that's the aim," Bernie smiled. "And you know we used Paul Eagle to look after all our contracts after he wriggled us out of the ERCO deal. Would you be happy to deal with him?"

"Oh absolutely! Always happy to deal with a straightforward solicitor who isn't going to make a meal of these things. I think he'll find that the contract is pretty simple. If not, then he must tell me, and we'll look to change it."

Gerry stood up. "Thank you very much for coming around. I think we're all going to be happy moving forward with this arrangement."

Once Oscar was gone, the couple had a long discussion. "The only thing that worries me," Gerry confessed, "is that it all seems too good to be true. My parents always warned me to be wary of too good a thing."

"Sure, but look at it this way. We only receive £1 per CD sale at the moment and Oscar's deal means we would cut the pie after the manufacturing and retailers' costs have been taken out. I reckon we could end up with £2 per CD sale after deducting the recording costs. We could sell less CDs and make more money! Plus, we'll be helping new bands if Oscar's going to put 20% of his profits into a foundation. This could be the start of something great if we get this right."

You're My Best Friend (January 1989)

Chapter 39 - A Whole New World (15 August 2016)

The Colour Spectrum arrived at the Chapel well before the 10am visit from Paul Eagle and Oscar Good. They rehearsed various songs ready for recording. It was some time before they realised that the two men had been quietly standing in the corridor to the lounge, listening to them play. "Don't let us interrupt you," the visitor who had yet to be introduced said. "Keep rehearsing and let me see what you sound like live." The band ran through a few more songs before deciding to have a break.

As Oscar crossed the threshold into the lounge, he swept the now grey hair from his temples before he shook hands with each band member. Gerry and Bernie would still easily have recognised him all these years later. He took longer than the maximum safe three seconds to shake Jackson's hand. "It's so good to meet you again!" he confessed in the sincerest manner. "I saw you many years ago in this very building when I came to discuss the release of a greatest hits CD with your parents. I don't suppose you remember it."

Jackson avoided eye contact but said, "I vaguely remember something, but most of my memories from around that time have faded."

"I understand. Anyway, thank you very much for getting in touch. I did quietly come to see you at one of your concerts after we sent the grant. I do like to see evidence that the funds have been used as intended and not disappeared up someone's nose," he winked at Colin.

Rick confidently pitched in. "What did you think of us? Were we great?"

"Oh, you were very rough and ready, but then it was early days," Oscar replied honestly. "That's why I wanted to hear you rehearsing just now. You've improved, no doubt about it, but there's a long way to go before you'll be ready to follow in Stanford's footsteps and tread the boards at the likes of the Apollo in Hammersmith."

"HELLO HAMMERSMITH!"

There was silence as the criticism sunk in.

"I was going to contact you when Jackson's real identity came to light, but the foundation administrator told me that the band were now looking for advice anyway. That is why I took this one myself. And by the way, thank you for paying back the £1,000. It was a grant, not a loan, but it's always useful to replenish the funds and help another band that might have missed out.

"While I'm here, I can tell you, Jackson, that there's been renewed interest in the Stanford catalogue since your true identity came to light. There's a whole new world of fans out there to add to the existing ones who have gotten older. I'd even go as far as saying that the average age of a Stanford fan has come crashing down in the last few months! If your mum and dad were still alive, they would easily have an audience on the reunion circuit, although knowing your dad, he wouldn't want to do it without new material. He was bored with the old hits."

They all crammed around the kitchen table. Paul Eagle spoke first. "Thank you all for coming. Since you are now free from that ERCO contract, I thought you might like to hear what the options are from an expert in the recording business and someone who your parents came to trust, Jack… sorry Jackson. Apologies, it's going to take me some time to get used to the change of name."

"That's quite OK, Mr Eagle. I understand."

"And you can call me Paul," he laughed. "Over to you, Oscar."

"First, let me dispel any myth that I'm bang up to date with what is going on in the music industry at the moment. I keep vaguely in touch with what's going on and I'm amazed that the dinosaur labels have stayed alive as long as they have. What I know is that ERCO have certainly been spreading dirt on you and threatening any label that takes you on with what they term 'disruption'. I've been on the receiving end of some of their dirty tricks over the years and it's not to be taken lightly.

"Anyway, back to the subject. I can tell you that the old model of: record an album's worth of songs; release the best ones as singles and do a bit of touring to promote it; then start all over again, is dying out. For much of the 20th century, this release cycle was driven by time. Because everything was analogue, it often took a long time to record, mix and master the songs. It then took more time to press the vinyl or latterly the CD. And it took time to print the album artwork — then add on the time to ship all these physical products to far-flung destinations. These limitations made it virtually impossible to do anything quickly. Then digital came along and time was no longer a constraint. Now, tracks can be recorded, mixed and mastered in the same place. Physical items no longer need to be made so there's no copying, printing or shipping time to add on. You just load it onto the Internet and the only problem is getting heard above everything else that is fighting for the limited attention of the public.

"In the last century, albums were an artistic endeavour that musicians used to share their perspective, make a statement, or share their grand view of the world. For labels, an album was a way to make more money; a larger collection of songs meant a higher price. But with so much content being created, how does a musician break through the noise? You'll still find artists who see the album as a statement, but they will release singles and EPs many months before the album comes out. Each release is a chance to build traction and get on the playlists while building expectations with the fans. That means that each release gets its own PR, pitching and promotion strategy to keep you on the scene. With some tweaks, the old album strategy still works. This took a twist last year when Drake released both his semi-mixtape album *If You're Reading This It's Too Late* and *What a Time to Be Alive* as an example of the fresh approach to releasing. This was successful, but for most artists it ignored the one important change in listening behaviour."

"We're not buying albums or even individual songs these days – we're streaming individual tracks," Hannah offered.

"HELLO HAMMERSMITH!"

"You're absolutely right, Hannah. Your generation is streaming from the web, but there's still a demand for a physical product in some quarters and you can't ignore that. We now have Spotify on the block, with Apple and Amazon also in the mix. Its track-focused playlist approach might make it harder for bands to stand out, but once you've fought your way onto their playlists, you can then find yourself featured based on the target market's listening habits and preferences. There are a couple of stumbling blocks. First, the three major labels seem to get on the playlists easier than others. Second, only one track can be submitted for consideration to Spotify editors for every given release. That means that whether you put out a single or a nine track album, you only have one chance, one track, to impress in the whole release**.** This then also drives bands to release singles to build fans and grow their following before releasing an album or EP. That's not to say that the artistic value of the album is compromised. Rather, the way it's released has changed. Instead of an album being dropped all at once, it comes out in pieces.

"To make the most of these opportunities, releasing two singles plus an EP has become the standard for new bands in the industry. It gives you three opportunities to pitch your new songs to playlists and media. It also allows you to focus on a few tracks that have the potential to be real hits. Also, remember that most magazines have a three-month lead time. That means you need to send your larger releases like EPs and albums three months before the release. So, the plan could now be to send your EP, artwork, and press release to print publications in month one. Then release the first single digitally. In month two, follow up with the print publications, include any playlists or press you received off the first single and released the second single. In the third month, release the EP and see what happens next." Oscar paused to drink some coffee.

"I think we're set to go with that plan," Liam said. "We've four songs recorded. Can you help us release them?"

Oscar laughed. "I'd love to, I really would. But the move to streaming has pushed me out of my comfort zone. I see what's happening but I'm a bit too old to do something about it. There's a huge amount of free music available on the Internet and it's tougher than ever for new stars to cut through. It seems it's all been done before. Hip hop has become an international language, as it's easy to rap into a phone and reach modern youth. Who needs a band? But I still think that you should research a new breed of online businesses like AWAL."

They all looked puzzled.

"Oh sorry, AWAL stands for 'Artists Without A Label'. There are new organisations like this that feed on new artists' disillusion with the big labels. They're distribution outlets so you upload your music to them, and they sort out all the paths to the streaming sites. Typically, they take around 15% of the revenue. That leaves you with 85%, significantly more than a normal label would. The key thing for me is that you keep all the rights to your music. I know a few people in that line of work with whom I can put you in touch. They're trying to shift the industry as I did in the late 1980s."

"We'd appreciate that, right guys?" Liam asked, looking around him and seeking his mates' approval. They all nodded enthusiastically.

"I should mention a well-known problem with Spotify," Oscar continued. "Depending on who you ask, Spotify pays royalties of between 0.004p and 0.009p per play. Yes, those figures are accurate. The big artists will be fine with that but the vast majority of indie artists don't make any money. The Pareto principle suggests that 80% of the money goes to 20% of the players. In Spotify's case, about 80% is all going to the top 1%. So you can't rely on it as a money spinner – the best it will do for a new band is build awareness.

"I'll tell you what I would do in your position now though. With the funds available to you, you can push on past a lot of others. I think you should keep control of everything. That means publishing, live events, social media, merchandising, the lot. You'll find that most people in the business are interested only in their own short-term results and that will work against you. The best platform out there for an indie band like you

"HELLO HAMMERSMITH!"

is Bandcamp. You set your own minimum price and I hear that 40% of buyers pay more than that, and they only take 15% of the retail, whereas Amazon and iTunes will charge 30%. You can still release individual songs to match the Spotify release and you can sell physical products and merchandise through it as well."

"That makes sense," Hannah thought out loud.

"And there's another thing. Take a long view. The worst thing you can do is to light a flame with a single followed by an EP and then silence. You need to have other songs ready to follow on from the EP in the early days, otherwise you lose momentum. I'd advise you to write a load of songs and record them ready. How many songs have you prepared at the moment?"

"About 40," Jackson worked out.

"Well, I think you need double that number so you can select the strongest songs to record and cover the first couple of albums. I always tell artists that to write a great song, they must write lots of naff ones first. Also, once you raise some interest, you'll be out touring. Your parents found songwriting can be hard on the road, Jackson. A pipeline of new stuff takes the pressure off."

Everyone nodded to signify they understood.

With that, Oscar said his goodbyes, which was an opportunity for others to go home as well.

After everyone else had left, Paul sat down with Jackson alone while Colin tidied up.

"Right Jackson, I have everything in place to transfer the trust fund to you entirely. I've talked things through with Mabel and Jim already and they've signed all the paperwork, but only on condition that you sit down with a financial adviser first, who will help you invest some of this for the longer term. I've someone at my firm who can talk to you about that, but there's no obligation to go with us if you don't get on with them."

Jackson nodded in agreement but didn't really understand why he needed a financial adviser when he had a bank account with a savings account attached to it.

"And are you certain that you want to use at least some of that money in kick-starting the band's music career?"

"Yeah. To be honest, I haven't got great qualifications and I don't want to go back to stacking shelves. If Oscar thinks that the cash behind us will make a difference, then it makes sense to use it."

"Well, in that case," Paul resolved, peering over his spectacles, "I'm going to insist that the band sets up a limited company, with you all as equal shareholders. The company will hold all of your intellectual property rights. Then any money that you put in is subject to a formal loan document so that any surplus money that collects up can be returned to you first."

"If you think we need to do that."

"I'm absolutely certain it's the right thing to do."

Chapter 40 - I Owe You Nothing (25 June 1988)

Gerry woke up on the morning of his 38th birthday feeling happy with life. He came down and found an enormous pile of letters on the doormat along with the morning papers. Flipping through the envelopes, he recognised the handwriting of relations, which suggested that there would be birthday cards inside. There were also some bills and one envelope in particular, addressed to both him and Bernie, which they had been expecting.

The letter bore a frank marked "D'Angelo Management." He opened it first. Inside was a cheque in the sum of £124,697 made out to 'Stanford'. Attached to it was a breakdown showing the sums earned in various regions around the world and Harvey's agreed deduction. It was mainly from the UK, which had always been their biggest market, but Gerry noted decent sums coming from Europe, the US and Japan. The bulk of the royalties had been derived from *Blindside*, their latest album on the Multiplier label.

Bernie came down the stairs wiping sleep from her eyes. "Happy birthday, pet!" She threw her arms around him. "I've left your card and present on the kitchen table. What do you want for breakfast, Birthday Boy?"

Gerry waved the cheque in Bernie's face. "Oh, I think we're eating out!"

"Let me see." She peered at the cheque and cooed. "That's nice. It will be sad to lose bits of it but I suppose we cut some deals to pay the producer and the band. As for the balance, we can reinvest it in the next record. Anyway, give the cheque to me. You know you can't be trusted with money."

She snatched the cheque away and tucked it into her dressing gown pocket, before going into the kitchen to fill up the kettle and turning on the radio. She was greeted with Bros's number 1 single; *I Owe You*

Nothing. Pulling a face, she changed station only to hear the latest Wet Wet Wet single. "Hey Gerry, with this lot on the charts, are you sure that Stanford are still going to be relevant by the time we release the next album?"

"At some point we're going to fall out of fashion, and then we'll either reinvent the sound again or retire to the country."

When they returned from breakfast, a message was on the answerphone. "Hi guys – Harvey here. Hope the cheque has arrived with you this morning. We should celebrate. I have more great news. An agent for Coca-Cola has just been on to say that they'd like to use *I'd Sing Along* in their next advert. They said they want to hark back to the *I'd Like to Teach the World to Sing* vibe for a big advertising campaign ready for Christmas. You'll just need to change a few words to mention the great taste of Coke and re-record it for them. I nearly said 'yes' there and then but thought that I'd better check it with the two of you first. There's another offer that I need to talk to you about as well. Oh, and happy birthday Gerry."

"The cheek of it," Gerry exclaimed. "Not a chance!"

Bernie knew what was coming and pulled a face. "What do you mean? That would be a great deal for us, especially if we secure repeat fees every time they show it. I know you hate the taste of Coke, but surely it would be worth it?"

"I'd feel as though I was selling my soul to the devil. They represent the worst type of commercialism. The cash would stick in my throat."

Bernie's voice betrayed her annoyance. "Oh well, if you're sure. I'll give Harvey a call and thank him for passing on the message. He'll probably be as surprised as I am."

"Sorry to be so grumpy."

I Owe You Nothing (25 June 1988)

Bernie pressed the preset number on the phone. "Hi Harvey. Thanks so much for the call…. Yes, he's having a great birthday. We've just had the Multiplier cheque. Just about to open his cards that came through the post. Listen Harvey, I'm afraid Gerry won't stand for Coca-Cola using any of our songs in their adverts. It's not something that he's interested in." Bernie was quiet while she listened. "Oh really? Well, I don't know just at the moment Harvey. I'll check with Gerry and call you back. That's great. Bye."

"Don't tell me," Gerry interjected before Bernie could open her mouth, "they've offered a stupid amount of money. We still won't do it."

"Well, the fee was somewhere near the six-figure mark, but no, it's nothing like that. Multiplier have been onto Harvey this morning. Someone contacted them asking for permission to remix *Blindside*." Bernie shrugged. "Apparently, they think it will go down well in the clubs."

"What a cheek! Why can't they mess around with someone else's songs? They'll just reduce everything to its lowest common denominator and destroy what we've created."

"I guess it's a 'no' then?" Bernie asked even as Gerry's words and face answered her question.

"We're creating a legacy for our kids here. We don't want it being destroyed, do we?"

"I suppose not," Bernie agreed half-heartedly. "I'll call Harvey tomorrow. He probably thought this was going to be a great day for him…"

They sat upstairs in the music room, surrounded by various instruments they kept at home. They tried to come up with some lyrics on to which to put melodies and music. It soon became clear that Gerry wasn't at all in the right frame of mind for the exercise. The day that had started off so well had disintegrated as they found out about others wanting to earn money off the back of Stanford's music. All the words that came out were bitter and twisted and the songs all seemed too sad. If they had to choose between a rush of dopamine and an infusion of prolactin, they always opted for the happy songs.

The couple packed it in for the day and went to the cinema instead. Looking down the list of what was on offer, they opted for *Three Men and a Baby* before treating themselves to another meal out.

It had been an interesting birthday.

I Owe You Nothing (25 June 1988)

Chapter 41 - Post-Truth Society (September to December 2016)

A flurry of activity followed the meeting with Oscar Good as the band all committed to pursue success in the music business.

Paul Eagle set up a new limited company incorporated in England and Wales. The Colour Spectrum and Colin all signed the Shareholders' Agreement that Paul had drawn up. He explained what it all meant until everyone understood the terms. Separate classes of shares were issued to Jackson, Liam, Hannah, Dan, Rick and Colin. Colin was included, as he had reluctantly agreed to continue to manage the business side. They all paid £100 into the company bank account and anyone who left the band for whatever reason would need to return their shares for cancellation and have their money returned. There would be a review every three months to assess whether a dividend could be voted and everyone in the band would receive an equal amount unless the majority decided otherwise. Jackson's loan sat separately, accruing a modest rate of interest. Everyone agreed to take a nominal salary only to cover basic living costs, while they tried to become established.

They couldn't use the college recording facilities now that term had started. The obvious solution was to record in the Chapel. Colin had only been using parts of the recording equipment, so a lot of it was still under dust sheets. Unperturbed, he agreed to remove the sheets and see if the equipment could be brought to life. Some blown fuses later and he finally looked for a specialist to help. Luckily, while he was underneath the desk, he noticed the gouge marks stating "Les Evenson Woz Ere."

"I think I remember Les Evenson," he mused as he prised himself out of the tight space. After a fruitless Internet search and a few more helpful calls, he located Les himself on the other end of the phone.

"HELLO HAMMERSMITH!"

It was clear Les remembered the work that he did at the Chapel. "One of the strangest jobs I've ever done," he confided, "but I had a lot of time for Gerry and Bernie and I'd be delighted to help."

When Les came down for a look, he did indeed suck in his cheeks as he completed a quick test of the circuits. And what a lot of cheeks he had to suck in, given the substantial amount of weight he had accumulated with time. It seemed his stomach could not digest the quantities of junk food that his metabolism could have easily handled when he was younger.

"Are you sure you want to spend more money on this old girl?" he questioned, pulling his jeans up over his white Jockey underpants, the sight of which had made Hannah feel quite ill. "This was only just up to date when we put it in over 20 years ago. There's probably not much that's going to be usable given that it was a cast off from another studio when we started."

To Colin and Jackson, it was worth the trouble. They both wanted an old-fashioned and raw recording. So, Colin agreed to incur the estimated cost of renewing all the electrical circuits and wiring in the old analogue desk. This was on the understanding that the band would pay to use the studio, so that Colin would claim some money back. Colin suspected that the resident Chapel mice had been nibbling away unseen for some time.

The band stopped their live performances for a few months to concentrate on the album. Colin refused to be considered both as producer and interim manager. Les scratched his head to think of an alternative to fill the producer's role. "To be honest, you're going to struggle to find anyone who's prepared to work with this old gear. I'm happy to be the engineer. Actually, I think the guy who produced the first two Stanford albums for ERCO is semi-retired now. I'll look him up. There's word out that Erica Conway is going to be very unhappy with anyone that offers to help you, but he won't care as he hates her guts after he refused to toe the line and she didn't pay him for his last work with them."

Post-Truth Society (September to December 2016)

The Chapel was clearly going to be the hub of activity for a lengthy period. This gave Jackson the courage to do something that had been on his mind for some time. He asked Colin if it was alright to move into the Chapel as he had already been spending the odd night in his old room. He slept much better there. Colin readily agreed; he had been on the verge of suggesting it himself just for the pleasure of having someone else around the house.

A tearful Mabel waved goodbye to Jackson. She extracted a promise that she could visit whenever she was worried about them. Deep down, she knew Colin could look after himself and Jackson was one of the tidiest boys in the county.

The band set about holding some intensive writing sessions at the Chapel and moved next door to the Old School House each time the noise of the electrical work became too much. Before long, Colin had offered that they stay in the rooms next door to make the most of the time available.

A white board was brought into the Chapel to keep track of all the songs that were written and planned for recording. The aim was to write a song a day as a minimum. With the concerted effort of band members coming in at various times to check on progress, over 40 new songs were written in a short space of time. As soon as the studio started functioning again, the handwritten notes and voice recordings were transferred to the updated hard drive recording facility installed by the electrician.

The electrical rewiring work was finally completed just before Christmas. As the mixing desk flickered back to life, crates arrived from the store. They contained the Stanford keyboards and other gear. They fitted in where Jackson remembered them and Les was a great help. The last piece in the jigsaw arrived in the afternoon just before the New Year with the old Danemann piano in the back of Jim's van. It was manhandled back into the main room against the wall where it had been previously.

"HELLO HAMMERSMITH!"

"That's going to need some tuning after that trip," mused Colin. He played a few scales with a puzzled look on his face. It was still fine. Over the next few months, it was only Mabel who noticed that it still repelled any collection of dust on its surfaces.

The band had several discussions about who would look after the multitude of things that needed to be progressed. They took Colin's advice and concentrated on songwriting and recording and not on things in which they had no expertise. Although she had done a sterling job getting the band up to over two thousand followers, Hannah could no longer look after their social media activity. Angie and Sarah were brought back in and, enthused by the plans, took on the promotion for a monthly fee with a one-month notice period on either side.

There had been constant requests from magazines for interviews following the revelation that Gerry and Bernie Stanford's son was now venturing into the business that had made and then broken his parents. For the time being, all requests were politely postponed until later when there would be something to talk about. It was a gamble, since people could easily lose interest.

Oscar's contacts duly called and agreed to take on the posting of any singles, EPs or albums to Digital Service Providers. Some of them could also organise the manufacture of physical copies for the market and for sale at gigs. It also made sense to go with them on the live show ticketing.

Jackson had been writing out lyrics to a new song of frustration. He could not seem to progress further than the first verse and a chorus.

They say the truth is out there; it seems it's buried deep

Under a mountain of opinions, that we all seem to keep

So, tell me where the truth is, how I can be sure

Something I can put my faith in, the rest I can ignore

CHORUS

Don't know where the truth is anymore

Hidden it so well takes too long to find the core

Can't believe what you read, can't believe what you hear

Maybe the truth has disappeared,

Maybe the truth now can't be feared

One afternoon, Jackson's writing and pondering was interrupted by a phone call from his bank. The voice on the phone informed him that the bank had just prevented the fraudulent transfer of a large amount of his funds. They kept him on the line for half an hour. To prevent a second attempt, they had set up a new bank account for him. They'd be grateful if he would go onto his online system and transfer the money to the new account so it would thereafter be safe. Jackson asked why they couldn't move the money to safety themselves. Although the answer was convincing, something just didn't seem right. Putting his caller on hold, he asked Colin if he could borrow his mobile to call his bank.

"You're lucky you called us," the bank said. "There's been no suspicious activity on your account. If you had transferred that money, you would surely have lost it." He had just received a rude awakening as to the perils of his new-found wealth.

Jackson thanked them before hanging up the scammers on his own mobile. The second verse just flew from the experience:

"HELLO HAMMERSMITH!"

My bank is on the phone, they stopped a fraud for me

I should transfer my funds elsewhere, to keep them in safety

My new account is ready, and transfer in I must

Suspicions raised I smell a rat is there no one you can trust

He was pleased with the way the middle 8 and third verse then formed:

My Facebook feed is full of fakes

Murdoch's media a mockery makes

Trump tweets, he taunts, he tricks, he takes

Spin satisfies Satan's slippery snakes

So now we're living in a post-truth society

Where we lap it up and listen, accept it silently

But your opinion will not change the truth of who I am

I'll make my mind up, thank you, I have my own plans

A final chorus had a few changes:

There's still a truth, of that I'm sure

Let's all keep digging, 'til we find the core

Don't believe what you read, don't believe what you hear

Oh no the truth ain't disappeared,

Let's prove the truth can still be feared

Let's prove the truth can still be feared

Satisfied, he handed the lyrics to Hannah and Liam to help him add the music. That meant that they had to stop cuddling up on the sofa.

Post-Truth Society (September to December 2016)

Chapter 42 - Blindside (September to November 1987)

Let's Do It Now was just another song that Gerry and Bernie thought might do well as a single. The recording of the *Blindside* album was finished as far as they were concerned and the unmixed recordings were sent to Multiplier for comments. The head of A&R, David Black, had called them with the statement that artists dread.

"There are some excellent songs on here but I'm not hearing a second single. Can you keep writing and see if you can come up with something short and punchy that people can sing along to?"

"But we've already written *Everything You Want, Everything You Need* and spent a load of studio time on it," Bernie muttered under her breath when she took the call. Anyway, they tried to write a 'hit' and found that writing and recording *Blindside* had left Gerry's songwriting tank empty. He would stare at a blank page for hours before giving up. Trying to speed-write and brain dump anything in order to come up with something of interest didn't help either. The classic image of a waste basket full of discarded bits of paper and further balls of paper that missed their target stared back at his disgusted face. For once, sitting down with Bernie and seeing what ideas came through didn't help either. Desperate, Gerry decided on something he had done once before. He advertised for new co-writers, an action he would come to regret bitterly.

The day after his fateful meeting with Joe Johnson, Bernie gave Gerry his guitar with a pad of paper and exhorted Gerry to 'stop messing about and let's do it now'. The lights came on in Gerry's mind and he remembered they had a song called *Let's Do It Now* that they had written many years ago. They had worked on it while they were trying to extricate themselves from the contract with ERCO and agreed that it should be held back until they were clear.

"HELLO HAMMERSMITH!"

"Hey Bernie. Where's the 'let's keep this away from ERCO' pile of songs?"

"Oh those. I think I know where I filed them away."

After some searching, Bernie presented Gerry with a small lever arch file. Gerry went to the 'L' divider and found the solitary page of A4 paper he was thinking about. It had been folded and was torn in places. Gently placing the paper on his knees, he played it through on the guitar, while Bernie, remembering the melody, joined in.

Ooooh there's somethin' troublin' me

Alarms are sounding in my head

I think that I have found a recipe

A way to live my life instead

Oooh, let's do it now, before life gets in the way

Oooh, let's do it now, and make it happen today

CHORUS

    Let's do it - NOW   Let's do it - NOW

    Let's do it - NOW   Let's do it - NOW

Ooooh that sense of urgency

A call to action comes my way

I think it's an emergency

Blue and red lights both in play

Oooh, let's do it now, before life gets in the way

Oooh, let's do it now, and make it happen today

CHORUS

    Let's do it - NOW   Let's do it - NOW

    Let's do it - NOW   Let's do it - NOW

Blindside (September to November 1987)

Bernie agreed it was a good one, short and sweet and a singalong, just as David Black had requested and a good bridge between the verse and chorus. The piece of paper was showing its age, so Gerry wrote it out on a fresh piece of paper and triumphantly threw the original into the full waste basket.

"Don't throw that away, pet. You know we always keep every scrap of paper so that we can see the song trail."

"Don't worry. This one is identical," said a dismissive Gerry.

They called the rest of the band straight away and met them in the studio the next day. After just a couple of run throughs, they tried it live and in three takes the basic song was in the can. The only overdubs needed were on the NOWs in the chorus, with the whole band crowded around the microphones in the studio.

"That's what I'm talking about!" David Black yelled down the phone before shouting "NOWWWWW. It's cheeky but let's get this album released and the show on the road."

"What do you mean cheeky?" Bernie questioned innocently. "It's about getting things done while you can."

"Really?" David sounded surprised. "I thought it was about you and the Gerry man getting it on!"

"Err, no," Bernie retorted indignantly, knowing full well that was partly their thinking all along.

Unfortunately, or maybe fortunately, David wasn't the only one to misconstrue the meaning of the lyrics. As much as the Stanfords insisted, it was a song about not procrastinating and getting things done, many people misinterpreted the lyrics and some radio stations banned the song without closely listening to it. Smelling a story, David Black did nothing to dampen the flames. To him, any publicity was indeed good publicity. He even had the nerve to suggest that Bernie sensually spoke the lyrics rather than singing them in a remixed and slowed-down version of the song. He was lucky that the suggestion was made on the phone. Bernie's inner punk rocker surfaced and David's ears took the brunt of the assault. He took the hint and apologised profusely at their next meeting.

The drama didn't end there though. As the single kept on climbing the charts, it looked as though this was going to be their biggest hit by a long way. But a solicitor's letter winged its way from ERCO. It accused Gerry of plagiarising a song he had written as part of the boy band Splatt. It was a piece called *This is the Time*. The songs apparently had a 'similar sound' and a direct link between them. This was outside Paul Eagle's area of expertise so he called on a specialist colleague to advise.

"There is a direct link between the two songs," Gerry later admitted in court. "I wrote both of them," he added, unable to keep a straight face. The judge admonished him and threatened to find him in contempt of court. The musician then asked if he could show the court that he was the only connection between the two songs.

It was an unusual request, but intrigued at the suggestion, the judge allowed Gerry to bring in his Hofner guitar and show that the two songs had different chord progressions, melodies and lyrics and the only thing that they had in common was that he had written and performed on both. Shortly afterwards, the judge called ERCO's barrister to his chambers and asked what on earth they were doing, bringing this pointless and frivolous case to court. The case was swiftly dropped, and Stanford were awarded their costs.

To Multiplier's delight, the case merely drew more attention to the song and many DJs started playing both it and the Splatt song to confirm that they had little in common.

"I wonder if this is what ERCO planned all along...," Bernie thought out loud. "Another vain attempt to garner some publicity for themselves and the Splatt back catalogue. How bizarre."

Blindside (September to November 1987)

"You might just be right," her husband echoed. "It wouldn't surprise me one bit."

The aim was that *Blindside* would be their best-selling album to date and the one that would properly break them into America. Multiplier's US distributor wasn't of the same opinion after listening to an early version. They stated that there were no hits, called it a 'commercial suicide'. They didn't want to release it and certainly not with any fanfare. This puzzled the band and Multiplier, given the reasonable success of their albums on the label. As usual, Stanford had tried to move the sound forwards following Gerry's treasured mantra "If you don't progress, you're in a mess." So *Blindside* didn't sound like any of their previous albums.

A few months later, the entire A&R team at Multiplier's US distributor had been replaced. Stanford learned that the new team had heard the current version and were raving about it. "We love it! There must be at least three hits here!" The new verdict left everyone all at once relieved and confused.

The first weeks following the release were promising and the album charted well all over Europe. A UK tour helped, especially as the first dates announced quickly sold out. The promoter suggested appending extra dates in Europe to the schedule, which prompted more album sales in the new countries and kept *Blindside* in the charts. The album easily sold over 100,000 copies just in the UK. As a result, Gerry and Bernie were presented with their first gold disc by Multiplier and pictures duly appeared in the music press.

Looking at the disc more closely, Bernie noticed and pointed out that there were six tracks on the disc whilst both sides of *Blindside* only had five songs… Intrigued, she investigated the numbers scratched into the run-out groove which, like an ISBN number on a book, were individual to each album and found that the record underneath was one of Cliff Richard's.

"HELLO HAMMERSMITH!"

Gerry reckoned it could be worse but later asked David Black about it. "Oh yes," he said. "You've rumbled us. The records that sell well are too valuable to be sprayed in gold. I tell the team to go out to a second-hand record shop and find some cheap records in good condition. There could have been anyone on that disc." The couple looked at each other with a silent 'This industry is mad' reaction.

Soon after the album had been released, the team behind the *Now That's What I Call Music* (NTWICM) series of compilation albums contacted Harvey.

"Would Stanford be interested in having one of their songs considered for inclusion on NTWICM 10?"

"Oh, this could be massive for us!" Bernie exclaimed, excited. "We'll be reaching lots of people who might not have thought about buying the album. Plus, if it sells as well as the previous ones, there'll be a pile of royalties coming our way."

"I like your positive thinking, but Multiplier is a minor label," Gerry observed. "It's more likely that the slots will go to EMI, Virgin and Polygram artists first and nothing will be left for us. Also, I've always thought of us as outsiders and taking the Now shilling won't do that image much good."

Unfortunately, they thought about the pluses and minuses a little too long and, assuming that they wouldn't make the cut, missed the boat anyway. Released in November of that year, the NTWICM 10 album went straight to number one and eventually achieved quadruple platinum status.

"Another missed opportunity," opined Bernie ruefully. "I thought we agreed I was in charge of the business decisions? You keep over-ruling me!" A frosty evening followed.

Blindside (September to November 1987)

As the UK tour wound down, Harvey received a call from a US promoter looking for a support band for a tour of America. It turned out that the record was continuing to gain traction as a decent seller.

"Oh, America!" Gerry exclaimed. His eyes twinkled with the opportunity to fulfil a dream. His wife knew there was no way to talk any sense into him and that, if it were at all possible, they would be off to the US for the autumn. They had done a few support tours in the US in the early days, but that couldn't prepare them for the journey ahead.

Their every move was bound to an itinerary covering the next four weeks. It stipulated the exact time that they should be on the bus, leave the hotel for the venue and soundcheck, as well as the precise times they needed to be on and off stage. Nothing was left to chance. They incorporated a focused timetable into their own future tours, not least to avoid past scheduling issues.

Only the five members of the band needed to travel. The main act, a rock band from Detroit, took care of everything else. Bernie felt vulnerable as the only female in the touring party. During their own tours, she had always made sure that there was at least one other female on the crew to provide an alternative to Gerry for company. Thankfully, her hard Welsh accent and hard stare seemed to scare the Americans and she was always treated respectfully.

In other ways, the headliners were not so respectful. They took a long time to soundcheck and left little to no time for Stanford to set up their gear at the front of the stage and do their own soundcheck. If they were lucky, the band had 20 minutes before the call to open doors. This also made them more deferential to their own support acts later on, something that they kept even when they were so big that they didn't strictly need them.

They also had to relearn how to deal with being the support act rather than the headliner. When they took to the stage, the arena would typically be half empty and those in their seats would talk to each other, oblivious to the band on stage. Warming up for a US act was very much trial and error. At first, they tried to open with a soft acoustic song, hoping that the audience would quieten down to listen. More often than not, this had no impact. Going to the other extreme, they tried starting with their loudest song. That meant that the audience paid attention, but Bernie would end up straining her voice after five minutes. She then had to take care during the rest of the set not to do any more damage to her vocal cords.

The plan that worked best was to start with their best-known song, which they knew had received some airtime in areas of the US. The strains of *Let's Do It Now*, which was something vaguely familiar, did the trick for the first song and Bernie could then charm the audience. Her cup of English tea, which tasted horrible as the milk was never that great, was by her side all the time and helped to break the ice with tough audiences.

In Chicago, where they had some spare time, Gerry and Bernie toured the city. They had the pop star look about them. Before long, they were chased by a small crowd. It wasn't until the crowd moved closer and they heard what was being said that they realised they were being mistaken for Dave Stewart and Annie Lennox of Eurythmics. Turning round and saying "We're not Eurythmics" didn't work, so they gave up and signed whatever was thrust in front of them anyway as 'Dave' and 'Annie'.

"I think I'm going to have to stop with the blond hair dye!" huffed Bernie. "This is getting ridiculous."

The tour did the trick of pushing *Blindside* into the lower reaches of the Billboard Hot 100 and making sure that their next tour in the US would be as headliners.

Blindside (September to November 1987)

Chapter 43 - It's Time To Take Action (November 2016)

The band finally agreed that they had enough powerful material to start some momentum going. They stuck to the plan of releasing the four songs that they'd recorded at the college first. The next phase of the plan then swung into action. Recording of the new songs continued while different teams were now coming in to pick up the marketing and promotion. Their declared purpose was to 'wake up our generation to take action on things they care about'. This fed into the design of the multi coloured band logo, based on some designs Jackson had created during breaks. The pace of the recording and mixing process was relentless, with Les, Colin and Jackson getting little sleep and tweaking everything many times until they were happy with the sound.

The social media campaign started. Angie and Sarah posted teaser sound snippets on Facebook and Twitter, plus similar snippets and counterparts from the end of the college filming session onto the new YouTube account. Many people had migrated from the Light Stone account following regular posts, reminding everyone that there was a new destination. General opinion of those leaving comments was, "that's more like it!" Angie took the promotional photos for the EP cover. Some of the band felt self-conscious posing, except Rick, who was used to it from all his own selfie snapshots. Angie did the best she could but knew she had to prepare them for the next photo session.

It's Time To Take Action was selected as the lead single. Following Oscar's advice, it was released ahead of the full EP. They hoped this plan would give them two quick shots at getting on the Spotify playlists. As a new band, they weren't surprised when the release didn't exactly set the world alight. They understood they were going to have to reconnect with their old audience, many of whom they had lost with the ERCO debacle. It would take time to coax them back.

"HELLO HAMMERSMITH!"

The following single, *Going Forwards in Reverse*, received a lot more streams and downloads. With that, the marketing team received some calls from the magazines that had been put on hold. There was a strange spike in the streaming activity and Bandcamp downloads. It was traced back to a link posted on a Stanford Facebook fan page.

Some small local gigs were booked to coincide with the EP launch, and they sold out quickly. That then prompted the band to spend some money manufacturing some physical CDs and vinyl copies to be sold at the gigs. Angie asked a local printing company to make some branded T-shirts and took control of the merchandise.

Everything was geared up ready for the launch of the EP on Friday 4 November, with *The Wisdom of Crowds* being the lead track.

The Wednesday beforehand had been set aside for rehearsals. It was Liam who came in with the bad news. They huddled around his laptop as he typed 'The Colour Spectrum EP' into his browser. They all looked aghast at the screen. The first page was full of 'free' download offers from various foreign sites.

"Well, that's going to kill our download revenue," Hannah stormed, thumping the table with her fist so hard that it hurt her.

"Looks like we've been properly taken to the cleaners and rinsed," Rick echoed.

"How could that have happened?" Liam exclaimed. "And more to the point, why would these sites be interested in little ol' us?"

"Two good questions," Colin noted. "The leak is probably from someone who had an advance copy. Let's think through all the people who have had access to the CD files since they were recorded."

The list was quite long.

It's Time To Take Action (November 2016)

Jackson knew who he should call first. "Hey, Oscar, it's Jackson here. Sorry to trouble you. Just found out that our EP was leaked online before its release. How sure are you that the distributors that you put us on to are on the level?"

Oscar was quiet as he thought through the issues. "Oh, that's a shame! I'm afraid that pirating like this is a fact of life these days. We've been a victim as much as everyone else and it's one reason I scaled down. There are so many people in the chain that you can't be sure that none of them are going to do this. I reckon my distributors are as good as they can be though. They go as far as keeping the files on their own servers rather than entrusting them to the cloud. No guarantees though."

"Who do you think might be the most likely to have done this?" Jackson insisted.

"Well, in my experience, the reviewers are the weak link. They are paid on a piece rate per article and it's quite small. Some of them will do it for love rather than money, but there are bound to be some who would flog an advance copy to a download site for some cash. It could take you months, even years, to track them down."

"OK, that's helpful to know," Jackson replied thoughtfully. "Thank you for taking the call, Oscar."

"Not at all. I'm not sure I have been that helpful. This might be a bit late, but good luck with the EP."

The group discussed it further but before long they agreed that there was probably not much to be gained from a witch hunt. Who would admit to it? They agreed to put this behind them and focus on the launch, although it obviously preyed on their minds. What sort of people were they dealing with? Was there anyone they could trust?

Jackson wrote an impassioned message on the Facebook page:

"HELLO HAMMERSMITH!"

Hi guys. It has come to the band's attention that even before our EP was officially released, some foreign websites started offering free downloads. Don't have to tell you that the band earns no money from unofficial sites like these that are sucking the life out of the music business. When Friday comes, we'll be delighted for you to stream it for free from Spotify or check out our Bandcamp page where you can listen to it before deciding whether to buy. If you want to download your own copy, then please look for it at one of the official retailers so the band can earn some money and please use official retailers. There are links on our website. Bandcamp is our preferred option, as they pay us a larger percentage of the revenue. You can find physical CDs there as well, with some extras. This is the best way for new bands to earn a living from music.

He was greeted with some sympathy but there were also plenty of replies from what turned out to be fake accounts with a handful of followers telling him to quit moaning and accept that this was a feature of the current music business.

On the positive side, they had numerous pre-orders for physical copies of the EP. So much so that they had more orders than they had copies in stock. Nobody had thought to limit the sales to the number that they actually had! Emails were hurriedly sent to many people, advising them that their order would be fulfilled as soon as extra stock was delivered. It wasn't a huge number in the scheme of things, but it suggested that there was a growing audience out there following the band.

The Wisdom of Crowds didn't trouble the Top 100 singles chart. In the week of release, the top spot was again taken by Little Mix with *Shout Out To My Ex*. It seemed they were still in an age where manufactured groups that Oscar and Gerry had discussed many years ago could achieve prominence. How were they going to emulate them?

They returned to mixing the new songs and planning the full album release. Jackson, Hannah and Liam were normally in attendance to direct proceedings, with Hannah and Liam using the excuse to move into

It's Time To Take Action (November 2016)

the Old School House next to the Chapel. Another room was used by Les who was a great help while the bulk of the recording was being done on the ageing equipment. It was his suggestion to seek some 'bog echo' as The Beatles had done at Abbey Road on some recordings that he reckoned he was present at. They rigged up a microphone in the downstairs toilet and the three of them squeezed in and closed the door behind them as best they could before recording the backing vocals. Les would take the tapes and discs away at the weekend to work on them further. Rick and Dan came in and out as needed and in the meantime always seemed to have a party to go to. There were some arguments about the recordings and the direction but it was focused time. As the recording went on, everyone became more excited about the future.

Clean Bandit took up residence at the top of the singles charts, the band received a letter at the Chapel. It was a bit out of the ordinary for them, as Paul Eagle's office was the registered office for the company and most of the post would go there. Jackson opened it as soon as he saw it on the doormat and stared at the content for a few minutes. He still had a shocked expression on his face when Colin came out of the kitchen, wondering why he was taking so long.

The key extract read:

Please be advised that ERCO intends to sue Liam Duncan, Hannah Ross and Jackson Stanford, the listed writers of the song 'It's Time To Take Action'. We believe it to be a plagiarised version of a song by Splatt entitled 'Action Time', written by Gerald Stanford and part of the ERCO catalogue. We further believe that Jackson Stanford, the main singer on the song, has copied the singing style of Gerald Stanford, who was under contract with ERCO while he was part of Splatt. We seek material damages and if we do not receive a substantial offer of settlement within 14 days, we will instruct our legal team to issue court proceedings.

Colin scanned a copy over to Paul Eagle who quickly phoned Jackson back to put them all at ease. "I don't think you should worry about this at all. I think it's quite comical. Nearly 30 years ago, I saw a similar letter written to your dad also accusing him of the same two things. That one went to court before a smart judge stopped the case in its tracks on the first morning. A year later, there was a case in the US regarding John Fogerty and Creedence Clearwater Revival. I don't suppose either of those names mean anything to you?"

"I've heard of Creedence Clearwater Revival."

"Well, John Fogerty was the main songwriter in Creedence Clearwater Revival and, like your dad, he was bizarrely accused of self-plagiarism. He also won the case and received $400,000 of costs back. This is slightly different as you're Gerry's son and therefore, it would be expected and forgiven for you to sound like your dad. I reckon there will be plenty of other examples that can be used in your defence – John Lennon and Julian Lennon, for example. Leave it to me; I'll draft a reply for you."

"OK, thank you, Paul." Jackson put the phone down and exhaled in relief.

When he relayed the tale to the rest of the band, their amazement was obvious. They called Angie and Sarah to talk it through. Once they had had time to think about it, they suggested a high-risk plan with which Paul Eagle wasn't happy. A music website had wanted an interview so they went ahead with it and during the interview dropped into the conversation the circumstances behind the band being sued. This had the desired effect. Most of the interview was overshadowed by the headline "JACKSON STANFORD SUED FOR SOUNDING LIKE HIS FATHER!" Before long, other music websites had picked up on it and it quickly made its way into the weekend national papers, which then featured The Colour Spectrum as 'one-to-watch' and gave details of the EP. Sales of downloads and streams spiked, as did the number of followers on Facebook and Twitter. This meant that ERCO made further threats to sue based on the band's attempts to subvert the course of justice. They were greeted with a polite letter from Paul saying that they were perfectly at liberty to draw attention to the legal action which was in the public domain and that the band would welcome the opportunity to fan

It's Time To Take Action (November 2016)

the flames of intrigue and popularity created so far. The legal action was quietly dropped the next day.

One of the completed songs now incorporated the rap that Jackson had first started in class two years previously. The verses were in the key of D:

> *I look at us and I feel ashamed*
>
> *We harm this world, but no one takes the blame*
>
> *When will we recognise that nothing comes for free?*
>
> *A broken planet might well be our legacy*
>
> CHORUS
>
>> *Heal the world, take its pain*
>>
>> *Release the pressure so that it can breathe again*
>>
>> *Allow the wind and waves to give us energy*
>>
>> *Remove the rubbish from the sea. A better world for you and me*

He thought the rap would slot in nicely:

Our planet Earth screams pain unheard. Again, it seems our fragile world tells us in truth the ozone roof gets thinner still, don't blame the youth. Forgive us, Lord, when will we see the errors implied in our ways that fill the waves with rubbish tipped from bins that we dump in the skip?

The second verse followed:

> *There are people with something to answer for*
>
> *Ignoring warnings that the Earth can take no more*
>
> *They put us on the edge of catastrophe*
>
> *Risking lives and worldwide calamity*

"HELLO HAMMERSMITH!"

The chorus moved to the key of E, before the second part of the rap:

> *The world we have can't be replaced. No chemicals can fix this place. The mix is set; the die is cast, if we don't change things pretty fast. Each breath we take could be our last. The smoke inhaled will make us choke. Whole nations sink beneath the waves 'cos people just will not behave*

The third verse continued in E:

> *We know it's time, we should now unite*
>
> *And make a start to put the world to right*
>
> *Those little things we do make all the difference*
>
> *Just look around you and apply some common sense*

The next chorus moved to D sharp, although with the jumping around, this was going to be hard for them to perform live. There was then a final rap section:

> *Why do we kill the mammals who swim in the sea, seeming carefree? They're choking on a plastic spree delivered there by you and me. Let's heal the world restore its life, pull back from the edge of the knife. We sit upon a ticking bomb that'll blow us to oblivion*

Many of the songs had different mixes with lots of hidden tracks and instruments that were not used at first but blended in later on. The white board in the studio had to be wiped and rewritten many times until everyone felt that the final mix was achieved.

They re-recorded the four songs on the first EP as they were all felt to be strong and benefitted from being recorded on the same equipment as the others. The originals recorded at the college had been rushed and they felt that the second versions were much better since they could take more time at the Chapel.

Finally, they were happy that the best versions were captured. While Colin and Les sent the finished mixes off to be mastered in London, the band started planning the album launch events. Their Facebook page suggested the fan base was far-flung across the UK, with many asking when there was going to be a tour. Those plans started coming together.

Angie came to update their promo photos for the new release. She'd been quietly encouraging Jackson, Liam and Hannah to brighten up the clothes they wore. To relax their expected resistance, she pointed out that their band name, The Colour Spectrum, needed to flow through their image. They could see her point and let themselves be dragged into clothes stores. The girls would sit outside the changing rooms and comment on the outfits they tried on. Liam was happy with green so long as it was reasonably dark, while Jackson was less comfortable with the variety of bright colours pulled off the rack for him. "Go on, give it a go. Trust me, you'll look great!" Angie cajoled him. The new colours slowly brought out more confidence in him, but it would be some time before they would completely replace his original black clothes.

Getting away from the local area for a photo shoot was another one of Angie's ideas. Dungeness beach hosted lots of evocative windswept images. The band was increasingly getting used to being photographed now, both as a group and as individuals. Angie advised them to "be as natural as possible" and encouraged them to spend the first hour being relaxed and "just mess around; don't mind me." Everyone loosened up, which made for several natural photos and a great atmosphere.

Near the end of the session, they came across a metal tower with a sign that clearly read "No Climbing – Anti-Climb Paint." Carried away in the moment and despite the sign, Rick impulsively climbed up as far as he could. He hadn't gone far before he realised his hands were now covered in the paint. A warden suddenly appeared out of nowhere in a pickup truck.

"What on earth do you think you are doing?" the man stormed. Rick lowered his head apologetically, trying to wipe his hands on his jumper.

"I'm so sorry," he mumbled. The entire scene diverted attention away from Angie hiding her camera as she suddenly noticed a sign reading

"HELLO HAMMERSMITH!"

"Filming by Permission of the Dungeness Estate Only." They ended the shoot.

An embarrassed Angie contacted the owners later. Thankfully, they were only concerned about video filming, and agreed to a few photos being. On balance, they reckoned it was safer not to use any of the photos and do another shoot. Another false start and another lesson learnt.

Worse was to come when Jackson arrived back at the Chapel and found a grim-faced Colin in the kitchen. "This is getting out of hand," Colin said as he hit the play button on the answerphone and a synthesised voice was heard.

"You must be wondering who leaked your band's EP to the world, Jackson. Well, if you don't want the full album to face the same fate, then be ready to withdraw £10,000 in used notes and leave it where you'll be instructed."

Colin and Jackson looked thoughtfully at each other.

It's Time To Take Action can be streamed free here:

https://soundcloud.com/the-colour-spectrum/its-time-to-take-action

It's Time To Take Action (November 2016)

Chapter 44 - Sweet Dreams Are Made Of This (April 1987)

Gerry and Bernie had been hard at work writing and rehearsing songs for the next album. They had not rushed to start recording too soon after the last tour, as they were determined that their next album for Multiplier would be the one that broke them into the big time. They wanted to put the sorry episodes with ERCO behind them, finally.

Having taken a tour of studios that were available in London, news that Stanford would record their next album at Church Studios in Crouch End surprised everyone. Eurythmics had made the place their own, recording *Sweet Dreams are Made of This* and many other hits there. The band was Stanford's closest match in the era. To carve out their own identity, Stanford would need to distance themselves from the competition and this move did not seem to follow that logic. But the moment Gerry and Bernie set foot inside the Church, they realised that this was the right place to record what they hoped would be their best work to date. Of the many places they had investigated, this one just had the best feel to it.

It was here that a germ of an idea lodged at the back of Gerry's mind. At some point, when this was all over, he would like to buy a church or chapel and convert it into a home and recording facility. Unlike the Chapel studio that they would build for themselves in the future, this conversion was strictly studio-focused, so that the main part of the church was left as it had been when it was built nearly 150 years before. Recordings could be made in many areas. The main studio particularly, with its vaulted ceilings, would allow the sound to reverb of its own accord. The centrepiece of the church was the Victorian harmonium that belonged to Annie Lennox herself. It stood in the middle of the oak-panelled primary facility, Studio A, one of the largest remaining recording spaces in London. Gerry was tempted to use the harmonium on some new songs, but the irony was a step too far for him.

"HELLO HAMMERSMITH!"

One thing that had initially put Gerry off was the size of the mixing desk. Realising immediately that he was going to struggle to produce their songs as had been his preference in the past, he made sure that included in the hire was Mal, a local recording engineer who knew his way around the music-capturing beast.

Before the recording started, they took their time to browse through the many song choices to pick out what were their perceived hit singles. Bernie bought a chalkboard, which was used to write out the different options and could be easily wiped when they needed to start all over again. They planned extra time to spend on the likely singles. For the first time, there was to be no compromising on an album. The fundamental problem rested with Gerry who had a sound in his head and wanted it recreated as closely as possible. This meant that they spent the first few days trying just to find the right drum sound in the echoey church. Everyone got fed up of hearing Leon doing nothing but "Dum Dum Dum Dum. Dem Dem Dem Dem. Dim Dim Dim Dim."

Gerry struggled to explain to Mal exactly what he was after. All suggestions to go with the best sound they had and move onto another song were rebuffed.

In desperation, Gerry called the only person from his past who he knew would understand what he was seeking to achieve.

"Is Forsyth there please? It's Gerry Stanford and I need his sonic help," he pleaded on the phone.

"Forsyth is busy recording at the moment, but tell me how you think he can help and I'll have a word with him."

Gerry spent the next five minutes explaining the issue, and when he put the phone down, he hoped that he had done enough.

To his relief, the next day the serene figure of Forsyth glided into Church Studios, accompanied by an assistant and surrounded by an air of expectancy. He quietly observed the process and Gerry's frustration.

Sweet Dreams Are Made Of This (April 1987)

"Would you mind if I try a few things?" he proposed.

"Sure," said a bemused Gerry, who knew how Forsyth worked and sat back to wait for the magic to happen.

Forsyth went out in the studio and instructed his able assistant to twist the drum mics from pointing at the drums to instead be 90 degrees to the heads.

"Try it like that." He said as he returned, folded his arms and listened. Leon, their drummer, played it through again and a more relaxed Gerry let out, "Much better, but not quite."

"Thought so," Forsyth mumbled deep in his thoughts as he headed out again. This time, he instructed that the mics be turned to point away at 45/135 degrees. "And again." Gerry's face lit up when he heard the result. "That's amazing. I would never have thought of that."

"If the directional mic hadn't worked, then I would have had to get desperate and suggest some 'bog echo'."

"Bog echo? What on earth is that?" asked a dumbfounded Gerry.

"Something I picked up at Abbey Road back in the day," confessed Forsyth.

"But what on earth would we do out on tour?"

"You wouldn't. So it's just as well that these 45/135 mic positions worked for me. Anyway, I'm sure you'll have things under control now, Gerry. Just call Forsyth if you need help," he uttered as he made a triumphant exit.

"What on earth happened there?" questioned Mal.

"A genius at work," mused Gerry. "A genius at work."

"HELLO HAMMERSMITH!"

It felt only fair that, as a joke, Forsyth was credited with 'bog echo' on the sleeve notes.

Having sorted that out, what nobody foresaw was that they would then spend another four weeks on *Everything You Want, Everything You Need*, the first single they picked.

Their guitarist, Eddie, was fed up with hearing that same song time after time. When backing vocals came to be recorded, instead of singing *"I can give you everything you want, I can give you everything you need"* he would replace it with *"I am really fed up with this song, it is making both my poor ears bleed."*

Everyone laughed the first time, then scowled at Eddie when he kept repeating it.

This meant that they had less time for the remaining tracks.

To avoid boring the other members, Gerry only asked the others to come as required, through a phone request. Bruce Dean took advantage of this to grab a few days away in Scotland. His absence was soon felt and his session delayed.

The missing bass guitarist, the time spent on the first single, the insistence on making things sound perfect and the expectations for the album all upped the tension in the studio. U2 had just released *The Joshua Tree,* which not only went straight to the top of the charts, but would remain there for weeks to come. Gerry and Bernie knew the stakes had been raised.

Of course, even after the sound issues had been resolved, it was not all plain sailing. Fuses were blown regularly, apparently caused by spikes in the supply of electricity to the church, which were never explained. The staff arrived one morning to find water pouring into the church after thieves had stolen the lead from the roof. All of which led Mal to complain afterwards that they were the most technically disrupted

Sweet Dreams Are Made Of This (April 1987)

sessions he had ever experienced. He commented it was "as if dark forces didn't want them to succeed".

They spent most of their waking days at the Church. They took full advantage of the facilities, including the kitchen and a New World stove, which saved them from takeaways. The Islington house wasn't a great distance away. This encouraged Gerry to stay later and later to complete work while becoming a hindrance for the engineer who had recently become a father.

While Gerry rushed around the studio, organising everything, Bernie sat on one of the large benches in an adjoining room. Her eyes were shut in meditation as she centred herself before her vocals were required. Much later, they would see that Annie Lennox had exactly the same habit when they watched a Border TV programme that followed her on a tour of the then newly acquired church and studio.

"That's spooky," observed Gerry.

"Not really. One of the studio team told me that Annie did this and I thought I'd give it a go. I know that we've tried our best not to copy what they do, but they're a smart team. If we shift half as many albums as they do, then we'll have done well."

Finally, the band sat back and listened to the final mix. Gerry smiled. He had finally quenched his desire to record the sound as played in his head. It had been hard work and he was now drained. One verdict from the record company would now change their lives forever. But for now, he had fulfilled his ambitions.

Chapter 45 - It's Over (January 2017)

The tension was high as the band prepared for the release of the full The Colour Spectrum album on 23 January 2017. They knew they would go 'head-to-head with Ed'. This did not bother them even though some artists might choose to put back a release to avoid getting lost.

Two weeks before that, they met at the Chapel to review the release of the EP. Liam arrived last as usual and this time it was Angie who told him the bad news. "We've done the search on 'The Colour Spectrum album' just now and it's already available for free download on the same load of illegal sites. They look Russian to me. I can't believe this is happening again."

"We shouldn't be surprised," Colin calmly pondered as he came in with mugs of coffee. "We never found out who leaked the EP so there was always a good chance that it was going to happen again. How much damage do you think was done?"

Angie was already tapping away on her laptop. "Colin is right. The first two search pages are full of download versions of the full album." There was a pause while she continued searching. "And the Facebook page is full of comments from people saying that they have seen it. Some have downloaded it, but others are refusing to until they receive a proper copy from us… aww, that's nice. I hope that those who downloaded it find a nice extra special virus as a bonus!"

Rick put his head in his hands. "I don't believe it. After all that effort. It's over. I especially feel sorry for you guys," he said, looking at Jackson, Liam and Hannah. "You three have put so much into this and then this happens. It just isn't fair."

"You're quiet, Jackson," Hannah noted. "What's going on in that head of yours? Are you not surprised this happened?"

"Well, as Colin said, this was likely to happen again, but let's wait and see how it develops."

"You're joking, right?" Hannah exclaimed, barely suppressing her anger. "What else can happen apart from a couple more pages of Google getting filled up with free downloads rather than adverts for the proper album? Do we just sit and wait while we get screwed over?"

"Not much else we can do at the moment," Angie muttered as she continued to scroll through the search engines. "There are no clues coming up here."

"I guess we should delay the album release on the streaming platforms? Hold back until the fuss dies down?" Dan proposed.

"No point I think," Liam replied calmly, as he looked at the screen over Angie's shoulder. "It would all have been set up a few days ago. Might as well leave it to run and see what happens."

"I think that's the best course of action," Colin interjected. "Let's carry on as normal and monitor things. You were going to discuss a proper tour after the launch dates, weren't you?"

"I suppose we might as well," Liam concurred. "Wasn't the booking agent going to call us this morning?"

"Yes, actually he was," Hannah mused. "Maybe he's decided not to bother. Can't say I'd blame him. Too much crap floating around."

"No, he's going to call," insisted Jackson. "He used to set up tours for Stanford, so I knew we could trust him."

Just then, the Chapel phone rang. Colin suspected it was the promoter calling in, so he put it on the loudspeaker.

"Heh!" Monty greeted at the other end. "What's happening to you guys? I'm getting a load of emails into my spam filter warning me not to

It's Over (January 2017)

touch you with the proverbial barge pole. I don't know what you've been up to, but you've awoken some pretty dark forces."

Jackson looked at Liam and they both smiled. "Yes, that's the first track on the album. It's called *Dark Forces Awaken*. So you still want to fix up this tour for us, Monty?"

"I'm not going to be put off by a few nasty emails. I believe in you guys and the energy that you bring to your live performances. So, where shall we start?"

"How about one of the Scottish islands?" Rick teased, ever the comedian.

"That's not a bad idea in principle," Monty consented without a hint of irony. "Start at the top of the country and work your way down. I know a few venues where they have separate rooms. You can book the smallest one for starters and then if tickets sell well, they can move you to a bigger one. It works the other way as well, of course," he laughed. "I'll see what I can do about trying to arrange this so that you're not crossing backwards and forwards all the time – save the planet and all that, eh?"

"Monty, that would be great if you could!" Jackson said. "It's one thing for us to sing about global warming and then someone being able to point at what we're doing and suggesting that we're responsible for part of it. One other thing, Monty... Would it be possible for us to end the tour in Hammersmith?"

"What, the Eventim Apollo? Are you kidding? I think I know what's on your mind Jackson but I'll be honest with you. That's a long shot at the moment but I'll bear it in mind. It's a popular venue and a big place to fill. I could see if there's a smaller venue near Hammersmith though. I'll have to see how things go elsewhere. Leave it to me. I'll be in touch." Monty rang off and the air of depression soon fell again.

Angie broke the silence. "That's strange; I wonder what's going on here?"

"HELLO HAMMERSMITH!"

"You can't just say that and leave it there," Hannah whistled, exasperated. "What can you see?"

"Well, people have downloaded the album and listened to it a few times. They're saying that the songs are OK but the sound isn't that great... which serves them right for getting an illegal download!... but then they are saying on the hidden song at the end they can hear what seems to be Morse code tapping away over it."

Liam was thoughtful. "Perhaps that was put there by the website. It's not possible to spread a virus by Morse code, is it?"

Everyone shrugged their shoulders. None of them were that technically minded. It didn't seem plausible, but with the pace of technology, who could be sure?

"Maybe we should download a copy for ourselves and see what it's all about?" Dan suggested.

"I wouldn't bother," Angie insisted. "First, I've only just bought this laptop and I'm not risking it getting infected. Second, I have a load of people online here who have listened to it a few times already and know a bit about Morse code. They reckon they can piece the message together for us once they have had a few more listens. Apparently, it's quite long, so I'd leave them to get on with it and we'll know what's going on soon enough."

Jackson and Colin stayed quiet throughout all of this, which made Liam more quizzical. "Do you two know what's going on here?"

"We might have an idea," Colin admitted. "Let's wait and see if we're right though. We don't want to prejudge anything."

Angie continued to look at the laptop until her mouth opened wide. "They've found it. Oh my God! Come and see."

It's Over (January 2017)

They all crowded around the laptop as Angie increased the view to 200% and sat back. The Morse code read:

DAN TRAITOR BOADECEIVER KILLER

They all sat in silence as the meaning of the words sank in. Jackson was the first one to speak. "Anything you want to tell us, Dan?"

"I don't know what stunt you are trying to pull here, but I'm not responsible for this!" Dan said hesitantly.

"OK, if that's the way you want to play it, let us lay our cards on the table." Jackson began. "Just after the EP was released there was a message left at the Chapel by whoever leaked it. They wanted £10,000 in cash, otherwise they threatened to leak the album in the same way."

"You didn't pay it did you?" asked Hannah. "If you did, then you've wasted your money."

"No, we reckoned that if we paid up, then they would either leak it anyway or ask for more," Jackson declared, looking at Colin.

Colin took up the story. "We decided we would be better off trying to work out who was responsible for the leak. I explained what had happened to the college's IT Department. They had the idea of putting a different message in Morse code on each publicity copy that we sent out. Each person's name would be the first name embedded in the code and the other three words stayed the same. The first marker on the hidden song triggers the Morse code part to become louder by five decibels each time it's played."

"That way we could work out exactly who was responsible for the leak," Jackson continued.

There was further silence in the room as they all turned to look at Dan, whose face started going red.

"HELLO HAMMERSMITH!"

Hannah, who was still watching the messages coming in, gasped. "Oh, what's going on now? The websites are taking the album down."

Jackson smiled. "I expect someone has warned them. Did you pass your test copy to ERCO so that they could blackmail us, Dan?"

"So what if I did?" Dan snapped defiantly. "Look, I didn't know that they were going to hold you to ransom. But you're a bunch of losers! At least with ERCO, I'm going to carve a career out of this."

"Then I guess you're agreeing to leave the band immediately?" Colin asked.

"Sure, you can pay me my share of the royalties later," Dan snarled.

"Mmm, I don't think so," Jackson mused. "Paul Eagle inserted 'bad leaver' clauses in the company's shareholder agreement. Remember, he explained the meaning of that to us all? If you break the agreement and do anything to harm the band, then the most that you get back is the £100 after handing your shares back. Contest it if you like but you're not getting a penny more. The better quality version of the album that's going up in a few weeks will have all of your bass lines replaced by me or Colin. We changed the sleeve notes to credit the bass to Alan Towns, a name that we've made up, so there wouldn't even be performer royalties for you. We overdubbed them while you were asleep next door. Goodbye Dan, and don't forget to take your stuff with you."

Jackson turned back to Angie. "How many of them are still up there?"

"It's down to three now. I think I'll give Sarah a call. There must be a story here."

"Yes, I rather think there is. All jolly handy with two weeks to go before the release of the real final version of the album."

Dan looked over at Rick, who shrugged and nodded his head towards the door. "You know the way out, mate."

It's Over (January 2017)

"You've not heard the last of *me*," Dan bellowed as he slammed the door behind him.

Colin looked around the room and sensed the discomfort of the others with the confrontation. "For Dan, it's over. You have to watch the quiet ones."

"If Rick had said that it would be a song title," joked Liam.

"Actually, I think I did," commented Rick.

Chapter 46 - The Whole Story (21 July 1986)

The following article by Rebecca Marsden appeared in a leading weekend magazine:

Stanford, one of the most unlikely combinations in the current pop sphere, is making serious progress towards being a stadium band of the future. Gerry and Bernie Stanford have explained to me that the much trumpeted masterplan is still intact, despite a few bumps along the road. I'm meeting them to get the whole story.

Just a year after Live Aid, there are lots of acts who were involved that day who want to emulate the success of the event on their own. There are also acts that missed out on the day itself who have plans to make the jump to the top of the pop tree.

I met the Stanfords a few days after the victorious last concert of the 1986 tour. Unfortunately, in his joy at reaching one of the band's initial objectives, Gerry had shouted and sung so loudly that today his voice is reduced to a croak. The concert itself was on Bernie's birthday. Luckily her practice of inhaling steam and eucalyptus every afternoon, in order to preserve her vocal cords while on tour, means that she was still in fine voice and any thoughts of cancelling were given short shrift. "You must be joking!" was Bernie's response to my suggestion. "We can't cancel you, of all people, Rebecca. It was you who introduced us all those years ago. If we hadn't met, then I might have ignored Gerry's advert for the audition later on. Plus, this is the first time that a weekend magazine has asked us for an interview. If we cancel you, it doesn't look good."

Bernie had placed a blank notebook and pen in Gerry's lap with a smile. "Keep this next to you, pet. If you can't whisper an answer to me, you can write it down and I'll call it out for you."

"You're enjoying this, aren't you?" Gerry had whispered.

"I might be," she smirked before kissing him on the forehead.

"HELLO HAMMERSMITH!"

It was lovely to meet them again. I'm often telling people I was the one who first introduced the two of them at the Glastonbury festival of 1981. So far as I'm concerned, I'm their biggest fan and I've been really looking forward to this interview. I thought they were great at their most recent gig in Hammersmith. One of the best concerts I've ever been to.

"We'd been looking forward to it too," Bernie agrees. "What with it being the last date of the tour and everything, I'm afraid Gerry was carried away with the emotion and now he's paying the price. I haven't known him to be speechless since we were introduced to Karen Carpenter – and before that Olivia Newton-John."

"And Dusty Springfield?" Gerry croaked with a smile. "I love their voices!"

I scan through my prepared questions as the photographer started taking photos. This had been Stanford's biggest tour to date and I'm wondering how they're feeling now that it's wrapped up.

"Well," Bernie started, "This tour has been huge for us. We only had a few dates booked for starters in April, but the reaction was so incredible that we thought we'd better extend it and play some more venues around the UK and Europe. It's obviously been a novel experience for us at this level. We've done a few shows outdoors for the first time and on stage it's either boiling hot or freezing cold. We've felt ill backstage or in some kind of pain, but you walk on stage and the adrenalin just kicks in, takes over and sweeps you onwards."

I comment that the constant touring has meant that *More, More, More*, Stanford's second album on their new Multiplier label, has stayed in the charts all year as well.

"Yes, it's been floating up and down and each new single brings more sales to the back of it. It has sold a lot more than we could have imagined."

The Whole Story (21 July 1986)

We brush over the torrid time that the band endured with ERCO. As far as they are concerned, the past is gone and they need to look ahead to a brighter future. There's still a feeling that they're a bit of an underground band that haven't broken through to achieve their full potential. They also dismiss the statements made by ERCO that they would never succeed on another label and also the industry rumour that ERCO tried to remove them from the Radio 1 playlist permanently.

As for the next year, the plan is to keep working on the new songs that they wrote while on tour. They think that they have some great new ones.

"We have a song called *Blindside,* which sounds like a single. We've learned over the years that you need to keep writing even though you might have just finished recording an album. The momentum has to keep going, you see? But actually we're both tired and I think we need a break for a good few months, maybe even a year, before we start work on the next album."

There have been some illustrious relationships in pop music. Others, like Graham Nash and Joni Mitchell, Annie Lennox and Dave Stewart, or Carly Simon and James Taylor, have broken up along the way. I've often wondered about the secret behind them staying together.

Gerry started writing, but Bernie answered first. "Well, I think it's been an advantage in our case to be in the same band. Carly and James had different careers to nurture and that would have been difficult for anyone. What have you there, Gerry? Oh – he says that he just does everything that I ask him to do. That's not the truth at all. Is it Gerry love? Together, we're a great team and we have a great structure around us. We each concentrate on different things. Gerry is the main songwriter and I'm the one who can be honest with him about what's good and what could be better. Plus, I look after the business side." Gerry nods at that.

"HELLO HAMMERSMITH!"

My next question is tricky as Stanford have been accused of being dragged along in the wake of Eurythmics, who could be said to have blazed a trail for them?

"Well, it's not quite The Beatles vs The Stones. And those two did actually get on really well and tried to keep their releases apart. We aren't that close to Dave and Annie, but we respect each other and do our own thing."

Gerry and Bernie have been married a few years now and questions about the chances of them having children bring the slightly embarrassed response.

"Who knows? We have plenty of time to think about that. At the moment, we're concentrating on the next album and we're going to make it as good as it can be… maybe doing our first US tour if there is any interest there. The pop world is changing around us and it's a transient existence. Just one wrong step and nobody wants to know you anymore. We'll have to make the most of the opportunity while we have people's attention." Gerry nods sagely.

I think that if they had children, there would be some serious musical genes bouncing around and I have to contain my excitement at the thought, but this seems like a great place to end. I leave them to continue Bernie's birthday celebrations.

The article was published a few days later. For once, there was nothing at which Gerry or Bernie raised their eyebrows. Nothing was fabricated. "I think we should ask Rebecca to do all our interviews," Bernie commented. "And maybe I should just be given a pen and paper and told to shut up," Gerry whispered jokingly.

The Whole Story (21 July 1986)

Chapter 47 - I Can't Tell You Why (17 July 2017)

Six months had passed since the release of The Colour Spectrum's self-titled debut album. The band felt that they were stuck in a whirlwind. The news surrounding the failed attempt to leak the album and the reasons for the departure of Dan Lailey had been more than enough publicity to push it forward. For an independent album, it was selling well and it featured in many of the half-year 'best of' lists.

The track *It's Time To Take Action* from their first EP had been adopted by a minor political party as a call to the younger voters to come out and vote, although in fairness the promise of the abolition of university fees played a big part in the increased turnout of the 18 to 24 year-old group.

Now at the end of a long campaign during which they had toured the UK fairly non-stop, they longed to pause and take stock before their biggest show to date at the Eventim Apollo in Hammersmith. Album sales had risen as they toured and with it the possibility of getting a decent-sized audience in London. Monty had been persuaded to gamble on them breaking even. The band was in London preparing for the concert of their dreams and agreed to do a magazine interview during their downtime. The PR team had arranged for the band to meet a journalist who had been looking forward to this meeting since Jackson's identity became public. Angie and Sarah had booked a suite in a hotel in Central London for the occasion. They shepherded the magazine representatives through the corridors.

Rebecca Marsden was now 57 years old, but her love of pop music had not withered. She held more authority at the weekend magazine where she still worked and had insisted on pitching for a meeting with The Colour Spectrum. This meeting, she insisted, could then be put back-to-back with some of the many interviews that she had enjoyed with Stanford. Jackson had been advised of the angle that she proposed to take with the interview and remembered seeing her name against some press cuttings that his mother had kept. The band were happy to make the most of the association with Stanford, which had done them no harm at all and had broken them into a whole new audience of nostalgic fans who wanted to relive the 1980s' glory days.

In a strange twist of fate, it was Jackson's turn to nearly lose his voice. The constant touring and the lack of proper preparation for such a long tour, which kept getting extended as the album continued to sell, meant that he had been plagued by vocal issues throughout the tour. Some dates had needed to be rescheduled as a result, but the last date of the tour had always been set in stone. Aware of the interview and mindful that Jackson should avoid jeopardising his performance, he was under instructions not to comment and be available for photos only.

Rebecca came in carrying a copy of an old magazine under her arm. She proudly gave it to Jackson so he would read one of her first big interviews with his parents many years ago. Jackson whispered a "Thank you so much! And thank you for introducing my parents to each other at Glastonbury in 1981," before quietly reading the article with fascination.

Rebecca started by questioning the other members of the band. With Jackson's lost voice making him no longer the centre of questions, Liam, Hannah and Rick could hold court and answer more questions than usual. They agreed their messages seemed to have cut through, not only to their peers in the younger generation but also to their parents and some grandparents.

"Have you been surprised by the level of success that your first record has had?"

"Absolutely!" Hannah replied. "Most people have trouble with their first album, and we thought it was going to be harder for us given that we don't have any major label support. To have this much success straight away was a genuine surprise. After all, Jackson is still a teenager until next month and the rest of us have only recently had our 20th birthdays."

I Can't Tell You Why (17 July 2017)

"I am guessing the labels are now knocking on your door?"

"More like hammering!" Hannah smiled. "There's no actual need for them at the moment, although we might have to reconsider if we decide to go global. We've also had calls in from established artists who want to mentor us. We'll sit down soon and see if that is a goal that we're set on."

"Exciting times. And your following has built up steadily since the album was released?" Rebecca pushed.

"We only had a few dates in the diary when the album was released," Rick conceded. "The promoter planned for us to start in Scotland and then move down the country to finish in London, but that plan was soon left by the side of the motorway. We sold so many so quickly that it made sense to add more dates and make the most of it while the momentum was there. Sadly, that meant that we ended up travelling all over the place. It hasn't done our green warrior credentials much good, but the fans seem to understand. And we became a lot tighter while on the road."

"But it's still charmingly ramshackle?" Rebecca joked.

"Yes, of course, we're young and still getting the hang of things," Liam added. "In the meantime, we've still found time to write and record some new songs in between breaks during the tour. They will be ready to go soon."

"I see that Gillian Fox is supporting you at Hammersmith," Rebecca noted. "That surprised some. Many people didn't know what had happened to her. How did that come about?"

Hannah took up the answer. "Well, Gillian was scheduled to support Stanford 14 years ago. Plus, Jackson found some old recordings that his dad had done with Gillian while she was in college and reached out to her. Even Gillian had forgotten about them but hearing them rekindled her flame. She's turned some of them into a great little EP, which is out now. She's still quite reclusive but it fitted in to have her as support while she thinks about making another full comeback."

"And you're still recording at the now-famous Chapel?"

"Yes, of course," Hannah replied. "We all still live in the area and we all stay in the Old School House there when we're recording."

"Oh, that's great. I was due to interview Gerry and Bernie before their reunion concert, but didn't get the chance. I hear that it's a peaceful place. And now a tricky question…" Rebecca shot a sideways glance at Jackson, who was still reading. "Have you forgiven Jackson and Colin for not letting you in on the famous Morse code incident with Dan Lailey?"

"Maybe just about," Hannah laughed. "We gave them a hard time about it and I felt like hitting Jackson for not telling us, but we felt better about it when we found out that the copies of the CDs that the rest of us were given didn't have the Morse code on them as Colin and Jackson were pretty sure that it was Dan leaking the stuff online. All forgiven now."

"Was Dan the only one to be given the Morse code version?"

"No, some others were sent out to reviewers that they didn't quite trust. We think the reviewers got wise and didn't pass them on as they might normally have done, although they might be collector's items at some point."

"And have you heard any more from Dan?"

"No, not since he walked out having realised that the game was up. We think he is doing something with ERCO – they've been quiet as well. They still have plenty of issues to resolve."

"And you have a new bass guitarist for the tour?"

"Yes, Bryan Taylor has joined us on the tour and we're seeing how well we all rub along," Rick said.

I Can't Tell You Why (17 July 2017)

"No room for the mysterious Alan Towns who was credited on the album then?"

"No, he wasn't available," Rick continued with as straight a face as he could muster.

"And was Bryan chosen as he has the Calming Blue profile you were after?"

"Yes, that helped the decision, but then you don't see many Red or Yellow bass guitarists!" Rick added with a smile.

"Your fans really seem to have adopted the four-colour thing?"

Hannah took over again. "Yes, with the easy profiling tool on the website, they diagnose themselves and can then come along to gigs wearing their chosen colour if they wish. And plenty of them do. You'll see when you come to Hammersmith that it makes for a more colourful evening."

"To think our favourite colour used to be black!" Liam joked.

Jackson had finished reading and was now listening more intently to the questions being asked.

"And to what do you attribute your success?"

"Oh, to a number of things," Rick answered. "Foremost, we should be honest and recognise the impact of Jackson's inheritance. It made things much easier knowing that we didn't have to lose our identity to a big label and could do things our way. Also, we're all devilishly good-looking." He winked at Rebecca who tried hard to ignore him.

"One thing in our favour is the team that we have around us," Liam continued. "Everyone does what they are good at and they're trusted to get on with it."

"HELLO HAMMERSMITH!"

Ignoring the frown from Angie, Jackson decided to quietly comment. "If we stay independent, then we might sign some other artists to our own label in a few years. Probably young artists like us who need a helping hand."

"That's a great idea," Rebecca concurred. "And Jackson, what do you think about the people who have said that your story is almost a real-life version of Star Wars or Harry Potter, with an orphan taking on the forces of darkness with a mentor, some new friends and winning?"

There was a pause while Jackson thought through his answer. "I think that they have overactive imaginations and are reading too much into it. Unlike Obi-Wan and Dumbledore, my mentor is very much alive and well," he said, grinning at Colin, who sat in the corner looking on. "And they weren't able to go back to their original homes as I've been able to do."

"OK, I see the point," Rebecca almost interrupted. "Still, you can't deny that there is a hint of magic in your story? You've spoken before about the special feeling that you experience whenever you touch an instrument that your dad has played in the past."

"Yes, that's true. They all joke that I'm feeling the force whenever I have something of mum or dad's at hand. Music is the strongest form of magic though, isn't it? It just appears from nowhere like a rabbit from a hat."

"You're not following the musical style of your parents at all, are you? They had lots of love-related songs, for example?"

"Yes, they wrote a lot of love songs and I've found more that were only recorded on some old tapes. Might do something with them at some point. To be honest, we've written some love songs but they're not very good. Plus, there are a lot of more important things going on in the world at the moment. Love's going to be worthless unless some of those issues are tackled quickly."

I Can't Tell You Why (17 July 2017)

"Maybe the fact that they had found each other made it easier to write great love songs... Jackson, there doesn't seem to be anyone special in your life at the moment or...?" Rebecca was certainly trying her luck there, maybe hoping she could be a matchmaker once again.

"No," Jackson quietly affirmed. "These are my best friends and we have a job to do."

She swiftly moved on. "Going back to the band itself, one of your successes has been the number of physical sales as opposed to streams. The packaging was great and the multi-coloured vinyl set you apart from anything else out there. Including the *Secret Song* at the end must also have helped. Speculation about who the subject was hasn't gone far past the fractious relationship with your former record label but you've never confirmed that – are you ready to do so now?"

"We couldn't possibly comment," Liam butted in. "There are plenty of Boadeceivers out there. People can keep guessing about that one."

Jackson whispered his reply. "As far as we're concerned, the past is gone and we need to look ahead to a brighter future. In this article that you brought, you commented that my parents still felt they were a bit of an underground band who hadn't broken through and achieved their full potential yet. That's the way we feel at the moment."

"The next album is nearly ready to go," Liam added. "We just need a few days after this to agree on the artwork and then prepare it ready for release."

"That's great. Much of a progression from the first album?"

"Well," said Hannah, "to be honest it sounds quite like the second part of the first album. We wrote so many great songs in the initial rush it seemed a shame to do nothing with them. The first album was very much themed with the Darker and Lighter sides and there were a lot of songs that didn't fit in either. Plus, we've been so busy in the last year on the tour; there are loads of songs that we haven't had any time to record."

"I seem to remember that's another thing that your parents kept doing while they were on the road, Jackson? So, *Album 3* is coming soon then?"

"Sure."

The article was published a few days later. For once, nothing was fabricated.

"I think we should ask Rebecca to do all our interviews!" Hannah commented.

"And maybe I should just be told to shut up," Jackson added jokingly. His voice had returned after he had followed his mum's advice in the article and was inhaling steam and eucalyptus every afternoon.

I Can't Tell You Why (17 July 2017)

Chapter 48 - Don't Tell Me What To Do (19 July 1986)

Gerry had specifically chosen this day as it was Bernie's birthday. The stage was dark at the Hammersmith Odeon. There was a wave of expectancy in the audience. Some were old enough to boast about having seen Queen deliver their 1975 concert here on Christmas Eve.

Earlier that day, Gerry and Bernie stood outside and looked up at the sign that read 'STANFORD CHARITY CONCERT – SOLD OUT'. "We set this as an ambition and we've done it," Gerry recounted. Bernie let herself be hugged. "Do you remember when we were first rehearsing and writing together and agreeing on all our goals for the band? Didn't we have a birthday concert at the Hammersmith Odeon on that list?"

"We did!" Bernie smiled. "You also said that you wanted to be as big as Queen though and we've a long way to go on that one."

"How's this for a birthday present?"

"Well, it's certainly daunting! A quiet drive in the country and an enjoyable meal out would have been fine." She screwed up her nose.

"Our time has finally come, old girl!"

"Don't 'old girl' me, pet; I'll always be 11 years younger than you…"

"Hang on. We need a photo. Stay there. I'll gather the band and a cameraman. We need to capture this image for posterity. Maybe we can show it to our children."

"Hmmm… you're presumptuous, aren't you?" But Gerry was already walking away.

Bernie turned around and watched the traffic as it moved round the venue, with pedestrian lights halting vehicles to allow people to cross

"HELLO HAMMERSMITH!"

the busy road between the venue and The Broadway shopping centre. It was 3 o'clock in the afternoon so the crossing wasn't that busy. None of the people who passed recognised her. The story would be different in a few hours when the audience started arriving. A few minutes later, Gerry arrived back with the rest of the band, including a grumpy Bruce Dean who had been woken up from an afternoon nap.

"Right, it must be soundcheck time!" Gerry exclaimed as soon as the photographer was happy with what he had captured. "Same set list as the last few nights with the covers that we rehearsed added in. Should run like clockwork. Oh, hang on a minute. We said we were going to do that old one tonight. Do you all remember it?" They all nodded.

Bernie was hesitant. "Is that wise? It doesn't take a genius to work out who it's about and they're going to find out aren't they?"

"I doubt they really care," Gerry shrugged. "What can they do, anyway?"

♪ ♪ ♪ ♪ ♪ ♪ ♪ ♪ ♪ ♪ ♪ ♪ ♪ ♪

After the soundcheck, a few people visited the dressing rooms backstage. One who came uninvited was an old bandmate of Bernie's from her days in the punk band. Angie Pogo, as she was known then, had been the guitarist and songwriter with Bernie. "Hi Bernie! Congratulations on making it to Hammersmith. I know it was one of your ambitions," she smiled sweetly.

"Yes, it was...," Bernie replied coldly. "Frankly Angie, I don't know how you've the barefaced cheek to come backstage. What the hell were you playing at with Gerry?"

"Oh, he's blown that out of proportion," Angie replied dismissively. "You all need to calm down a bit. Anyway, if I'm not welcome, I'd better find my seat then – break a leg, old stick!"

Don't Tell Me What To Do (19 July 1986)

Before Bernie could report the visit to Gerry, the altogether more friendly face of Oscar Good appeared. "Hi Oscar," Gerry greeted. "Wasn't expecting to see you here!"

"To be honest, I shouldn't be here, but the security guy recognised me and turned a blind eye while I popped in. I just came to let you know that I've left ERCO."

"Oh wow, really?" Gerry exclaimed. "I'm definitely happy for you. Have you joined someone else? Not that we can do much about it at the moment, we have another album with Multiplier to deliver before we can look at options."

"No, I'm taking a bit of time out. All those years at ERCO have left me burnt out. I need a complete break. Anyway, ERCO has a restrictive covenant over me that isn't worth challenging. Plus, I have an idea in my mind for a new style of a record label that is fair to everyone. It'll need some thought though. I just popped in to let you know that I'll be in touch to see what you think of it once the time is right. I value your opinion, so it's fine if you think it's not for you."

"We'd be happy to listen to what you have planned. This business needs a bit of a shake-up."

Before Oscar could say anymore, a call came up from below. "ON STAGE IN FIVE MINUTES."

♪ ♪ ♪ ♪ ♪ ♪ ♪ ♪ ♪ ♪ ♪ ♪ ♪ ♪

As the first set approached the end, Gerry moved from behind his keyboards to the front of the stage. "Right!" he shouted. He waited as the echo subsided. "Here's an old song for you... It caused some issues when it was released but it's about standing up to bullies. Nobody likes bullies, do they?" He then nodded to Eddie who launched into the riff of the song before Gerry started the first verse:

"HELLO HAMMERSMITH!"

I've got to know the real you, the one you try to hide

But when you let your guard down, I can see what's deep inside

But you don't fool me anymore

Bernie came in for the chorus:

Don't tell me what to do, I ain't listening to you

With all the things I've been through, don't tell me what to do

Don't tell me what to say, I ain't listening, anyway

So please just go away. Don't tell me what to say.

Straight into the second verse:

You lie and you do anything to control what you can

But when you get found out your temper tantrums hit the fan

But you don't fool me anymore

Another run through of the chorus and a solo from Eddie and the song was over in less than three minutes. Although Gerry had never confirmed it, many in the audience suspected who the inspiration of the song had been, including a small group sitting at the back of the circle, trying to go unnoticed.

During the interval, the man in a grey suit turned to Ernie Conway. "I hope you're not going to let them get away with that?"

"Don't worry. We have plenty of scores to settle with the Stanfords and time is on our side."

"I do hope I can trust you. There *ARE* scores that need to be settled and I'm relying on you." He turned and put his arm around Angie who was by now sitting next to him. "And did you find any dirt on them backstage, my dear?"

Don't Tell Me What To Do (19 July 1986)

"No. Well, they clearly didn't want me to stay long. Clearly, the minor episode a few months ago rattled them. Oh, and that weasel Good was backstage as well."

"Probably telling them he's off and going to shift the industry," Ernie laughed. "Poor deluded boy. He'll never be one of the big boys. Really not worth worrying about him. Oh, look. They're coming back."

At the start of the encores, Gerry moved to the front and asked for a bit of quiet. "I'd like to thank you all for coming and giving to the Live Aid charity tonight. We missed out on the big gig last year. We just weren't on the radar then, so it's great to contribute. This is the first time that we've played here at the Hammersmith Odeon, and it's said you play this venue twice in your career. Once on the way up and again on the way down."

He left it to Bernie to deliver the punchline. "And we hope that it's going to be a long time before we come back!"

Gerry continued after the laughter had died down. "I would just like to mention that we meant to play a few songs from our old bands, but I'm sad to say that certain people wouldn't agree to donating the royalties they would have received from tonight's performance." A chorus of boos greeted this and Angie turned in her seat to look with a questioning expression at the man in the grey suit. He did not flinch and instead pulled out another Marlboro cigarette.

"But never mind," Gerry went on. "We have three songs from artists who played at Wembley who are more generous." With that, he rushed behind his keyboards as Eddie started the riff of Status Quo's *Caroline* and the crowd went wild. While Gerry had been introducing the next songs, Bernie had slipped backstage and now bounced out wearing double denim and a long-haired wig.

Chapter 49 - "HELLO HAMMERSMITH!" (19 July 2017)

Jackson had suggested this specific date to Monty as it was the anniversary of the day that Stanford had been due to make their return to the stage and play this venue for the second time. The crash had put paid to that. It was also his mother's birthday and the anniversary of their triumphant concert in aid of Live Aid.

Again, the stage was dark at what was now known as the Eventim Apollo in Hammersmith. Once more, there was a wave of expectancy in the audience. A few times, a version of the comment "I preferred the name being the Hammersmith Odeon" could be heard.

Jackson had arrived early at the venue. He had spent a few moments standing outside under the flyover. It was 3 o'clock in the afternoon so the crossing wasn't that busy. None of the people who passed recognised him. The story would be different a few hours later when the audience would be arriving. He looked up at the old cinema-style hoarding which from back in history had advertised the name of the film or latterly the artist who was scheduled to play that evening. He wondered if his parents had stood in the same place. Tonight, the big red letters read "THE COLOUR SPECTRUM – SOLD OUT with Gillian Fox." He took a selfie on his phone and posted it to his connected social media accounts with the comment "Made It." Before long, thousands of people had liked and commented on the post. Many reported that they were on their way to the venue now and looking forward to the evening. He had learnt early on not to reply to any comments that were made, but there was a curious one from someone who said that he was the paramedic who took his mother to the hospital where he was born. Along with the comment was a photo of a scrap of paper which read:

To Dave, the best paramedic ever. Love Bernie (Stanford) xx

"HELLO HAMMERSMITH!"

It certainly looked like his mum's handwriting from notes that he had seen, but you can never be sure what you read online or anywhere else.

Jackson walked through the double doors into the main auditorium to witness the normal frantic loading in of the equipment. Colin had put together a competent crew at short notice and they were hard at it. The seats had all been removed in the stalls area as the band thought it was 'more rock'n'roll'. This had been a gamble as while it increased the capacity by 1,400 to over 5,000, it wouldn't look good if the sales were not great and there was too much space downstairs. They had nothing to worry about. The continued publicity of the new band that had taken on the big bullies of the music industry and won through had continued to breathe oxygen into their online publicity machine. Streaming figures had continued to climb, as had all the social media figures, swiftly followed by CD and download sales. The real success had been the multi-coloured vinyl special editions, which all sold out in a few days and were re-pressed . Each one featured a different band member on the front cover, with the vinyl coloured to match their personality profile. Jackson's had been multi-coloured.

Once it was confirmed the show was a sell-out, lots of fans were disappointed and in danger of throwing themselves at the mercy of the touts. The band announced they would stream the show free on their social media channels. It was going to cost some money and there was a risk that the link would fail, but there was good publicity in it and it meant that they could reach an even wider audience.

Everyone was ready for the soundcheck. Previous set lists had been posted online, which meant that the band tried to switch things around as much as possible. Without a huge number of songs to draw from, this meant that they occasionally popped in some songs that didn't make the album. This included some old songs that they had only done on stage and that had become fan favourites online. This kept the audience on their toes and made every evening special. There was one song that had been called for every night and Jackson had always smiled and said – 'sorry, not tonight – we haven't rehearsed that one'. That didn't seem to

"HELLO HAMMERSMITH!" (19 July 2017)

matter to the audience, who in lulls while Liam was tuning his guitar would start singing it anyway. They were greeted with Jackson smiling and putting his index finger to his lips.

But tonight, it felt like the right time. It wasn't a complicated song, so the "we haven't rehearsed it" line didn't fool anyone. When Jackson said, "Let's go for it tonight," they all knew what he meant and after just one run through they were ready. The rest of the soundcheck went as planned. The sound echoed through the Art Déco interior of the famous venue.

There had been up-and-coming support acts from each local area but tonight would be different. After the soundcheck, while Gillian Fox was on stage, they relaxed in the dressing room. The room was one of the best that they had seen on the tour, complete with microwave, mini-bar, sofas and, unusually, a window to the outside world. Normally, dressing rooms were subterranean with no natural light.

A knock on the door announced Colin and a group of friends of a similar age – all with their "Guest" lanyards around their necks. "Crumbs, this is better than we remember, right lads?" he asked as he looked around. "Allow me to introduce this lot to you. Meet Jimmy, Tommy and Big Steve." The three guests were also looking around the room and talking about the last time they had been here, many years ago.

"Hi guys!" Jackson greeted Colin's pals. "Your names are familiar. Where do I know them from?"

"Well spotted mate!" Colin smirked. "I should have introduced them as the original members of Disassociation."

"Of course. I thought you had lost touch with them all?"

"Ah, the Internet is a wonderful thing, after all. While you've been busying yourself away on tour, I decided to see if I could track anyone down. It turns out there was quite a large forum on Facebook. Once the administrator had calmed down from the shock of me wanting to join, he sent me in the right direction. They knew I had been at the college for a few years but reckoned that it would be fairer to leave me alone. The rest of the band had been getting on with their lives and doing their own things, but we've now all reached an age where they're saddled with jobs they don't like but with decent pensions and grown-up kids who can look after themselves. We met up in town last week and agreed it was time to put the old band back together and see if we could come up with anything in the studio while nobody else was using it."

"And?"

"And it's been just like old times. We're having a break today, but we've lots of ideas for a new concept album. One of the longer songs is about someone who takes the wrong mixture of drugs and lies in a coma for 30 years. Of course, when he wakes up, he doesn't recognise much of the world around him. The song is about the things that he has to learn to survive in the new world. And of course, this is prog rock, so there's plenty of room for shifting time signatures and solos. What helped was that once the word was out, the forum started getting lots more members and before we knew it, we had people saying that they'll travel from all over the world to see a show in London. It's unbelievable."

"That's brilliant," Jackson exclaimed. By this time, the whole band were clustered around Colin.

"Hang on, there's one more person here that you should meet. I found him at the stage door, arguing with security. I'd recognise him anywhere, but most people wouldn't, including you, I guess. Jackson. Let me introduce you to Leon Manford – he played the drums for Stanford."

Leon stepped forward to shake Jackson's hand. "Pleased to meet you, young fella. I just wanted to come here to say that your mum and dad would have been so proud of you. They were looking forward to playing

"HELLO HAMMERSMITH!" (19 July 2017)

here all those years ago, before the accident happened... I've brought something that you might like to see."

Leon handed over an old photograph, which was faded at the edges. It showed Gerry and Bernie, with Eddie, Bruce and Leon, outside the Hammersmith Odeon on that day 31 years ago. Before Leon could say anymore, a call came up from below. "ON STAGE IN FIVE MINUTES." Jackson looked at the photo quietly.

♫ ♫ ♫ ♫ ♫ ♫ ♫ ♫ ♫ ♫ ♫ ♫ ♫ ♫

The stage curtain had been lit from above by the band's own rig, which shone four primary colours downwards as *The Colour Spectrum* instrumental built to its crescendo. The curtain rose, revealing a darkened stage, and the music slowly disappeared into silence. All that could be seen on the stage was the luminous form of an acoustic guitar. It appeared to float. The spotlight fell on Jackson. Eyes closed and head up, he was dressed in a multi-coloured jacket and trousers. His dad's glowing Hofner guitar was slung round his neck. The crowd whooped and cheered, but Jackson stood motionless, a little way back from the front of the stage. Throughout the tour, the first song had been the first track from the album, *Dark Forces Awaken*. Tonight would be different.

When the noise finally subsided, Jackson put the microphone to his mouth. A second microphone on the stand was at waist height and picked up the simple G chord that he played on the battered guitar.

"*Boadeceiver*" was all he needed to sing as he stood back slightly to strum the guitar chords while the crowd took over.

> *You didn't win this war...*
>
> *Our spirit was too strong, and you found the out door.*
>
> *Boadeceiver, you'd always lose this game*
>
> *You paid the price of little fame...*

"HELLO HAMMERSMITH!"

Jackson then joined back in.

"*And you only have yourself to BLAME,*" at which point the lights come on in full.

Rick, dressed in a bright yellow vest and shorts, bashed the drums while Bryan in a bright blue suit, kicked in on the bass with a sustained G. Both Liam and Hannah started jumping up and down in unison. They wore green and red stage clothes respectively that matched the design of Jackson's as they also played the sustained G chord. The concert hall erupted as those standing downstairs found little option but to jump up and down as well.

With a nod to the band, Jackson launched into verse two.

> *You offered to come help us. What did you do?*
>
> *Brought an agenda in to split us up in two*
>
> *You had some history we now know to be true*
>
> *You drew the battles lines – we knew*
>
> *The one you looked out for was YOU*

The song hadn't been mentioned on the album cover, but was the hidden 'Morse Code' track that could either be found by waiting for five minutes after the last listed song had ended, or by digging into the folders on the CD. This had helped the CD sales, as it wasn't featured on the normal download versions.

> *It was quite obvious your luck just couldn't last*
>
> *And that's the reason why we stuck hard and held fast*
>
> *Oh Number 49 – your time has passed*
>
> *It's pretty much as I'd forecast*
>
> *You've run the white flag up your mast*
>
>   *BOADECEIVER.......*

"HELLO HAMMERSMITH!" (19 July 2017)

Everyone could guess who the song was about, but Jackson and the rest of the band, on strict advice from Paul Eagle, would neither confirm nor deny it. Many struggled with the Number 49. "It can't be about one person," Jackson said in interviews. "This is such a despicable person. They couldn't possibly exist. Surely a Boadeceiver can only be the fruit of someone's imagination?" Try as he might to keep a poker face while saying this, the truth leaked, but there was never an admission.

Onto the first bridge, when Hannah stepped forward,

> *You changed your mind, when the wind blowed*
>
> *Faithful to no one, that's what you showed*
>
> *You had our trust; you blew it all away*
>
> *You showed contempt for us, most every day.*

The band paused momentarily after the last word before Jackson launched into the next verse.

> *It was quite clear we could not reason with you*
>
> *'My way or no way' was your choice. What could we do?*
>
> *You always knew what's best – yes you were sure*
>
> *But now you're gone please close the door*
>
> *Don't want to deal with you no more*
>
>   *BOADECEIVER…..*

The basics of the song had come quickly to Jackson after he had left the ERCO offices in London for the last time. Rick's comment about Erica being like Boadeceiver had stuck with him for many months, but inside the ERCO machine there had been no point in doing anything with the idea. Once he was free, there was no stopping him.

Hannah went into the second middle eight on an A minor chord.

"HELLO HAMMERSMITH!"

We know it's black, you called it white

It seemed the object was start a fight

You sought to control most everything

Just had to argue 'bout anything

There was a version in the archives with all 10 parts included, but a few verses were cut out of the recording. The best parts remained.

Boadeceiver, it's goodbye, we won't miss you

You're on your way. Guess you've found someone else to chew.

Then spit them out just like a dummy on the floor

Your childish antics scare no more

You have a lot to answer for.

And onto the last verse, during which Jackson went around each of the band to sing parts directly at them.

Fear not, my friends, we kept the faith and we came through

We knew we'd win. It's something that we had to do.

Only the strong survive, of that I'm sure

She won't be troublin' us no more

And she don't seem so hot no more.

    BOADECEIVER…..

The ultimate word, up an octave, was again left to the crowd.

    "BOADECEIVER…."

Meanwhile, not a mile away in a dingy flat, a laptop flickered as the images from the Eventim Apollo streamed in. A sour-faced Erica Conway squirted some perfume behind her ears and planned her next move. "I wouldn't get carried away if I were you, Jackson Stanford. My father ruined your parents and I'm going to ruin you."

"HELLO HAMMERSMITH!" (19 July 2017)

In the darkness, a shadow was barely distinguishable behind her on the bed. "I hope you're not going to disappoint me again, my dear. If so, I think that the next move will be mine to take."

"That won't be necessary," she replied. "It's alright for you. Your reputation hasn't been trashed in a song has it?"

"I rather think that honour has been bestowed upon me in the past. Anyway, how is the research project coming along?"

"It's still a work in progress. The algorithms are hard to work out and there's been a few other things going on, obviously."

"Now Erica - you know I don't want reasons. I want *results*."

Back on stage, Jackson waited while the cheering subsided. But as that happened, there were exclamations and shrieks as people pointed either behind the bank of keyboards or just to Jackson's right. The noise subsided and was replaced by chattering.

Jackson had intended to start by welcoming everyone and thanking them for coming, but when he approached the microphone, the unexpected commotion meant that he forgot that. A feeling of calm came over him as he intuitively completed his dad's plan and at the top of his voice shouted the now-immortal words...

"HELLO HAMMERSMITH!"

Songs from The Colour Spectrum can be streamed free from:

https://soundcloud.com/the-colour-spectrum

"HELLO HAMMERSMITH!"

To be continued in book two in the trilogy:

"WHAT'SUP WEMBLEY?"

If you enjoyed this book, then that's great! I'm delighted!

Positive book reviews are an enormous help to independent writers, so please consider leaving a review on your local Amazon.

If you would like to be kept updated on the progress of book two, then you can sign up to the newsletter on the band's website; https://the-colour-spectrum.com

There is going to be a bonus short story available – *When Hannah Met Liam.*

The author would like to thank:

My daughter Rebecca for the original inspiration when we were 'driving home for Christmas' and proof reading the result.

My wife Theresa for giving me the space to write this and proof reading.

Rebecca Collins and Greg Evaristo who read early versions and both said that this was just book one of a trilogy...

Manuella Essaka of 3E Web Media for the editing.

Maria White and Shelly Sutton for proof reading.

Emma Colyer for cover and website design.

Dave Rogers, Parisa Shahmir and Jack Bowden for bringing the songs to life.

Some background about the author…

Many years ago, when ancestry records were on paper and microfiche, my dad was researching the family tree. He found some interesting characters, including the last person to be hung, drawn and quartered at Tyburn, but we won't dwell on that.

He found we had a very musical ancestor, who had been born Richard Michael O'Shaughnessy in Dublin in 1811. At a young age, he became the musical director of the city's Theatre Royal Orchestra. As an unusually gifted violinist, on his first visit to the Crystal Palace Handel Festival in London, an event would lead to a change of name. When asked his name by the official in charge of enrolment, he promptly replied "Richard Michael O'Shaughnessy".

"Richard Michael O'Whatnessy?" echoed the astonished official.

"O'Shaughnessy" repeated the bewildered violinist.

"My friend," volunteered his questioner. "You can never hope to make a success in professional life with an unpronounceable name like that. What was your mother's maiden name?"

When told that it was 'Leavy', he instead wrote 'Levey' and so announced, "Hereafter you will be known as RM Levey in this establishment". And so it's by that Hebraic surname that he is known in musical history.

He was later a professor of the violin at the Royal Irish Academy of Music in Dublin, which he co-founded in 1848 along with other individuals, included John Stanford and Samuel Pigott.

Fast forward to the current day and having been a published author of some non-fiction books and short business stories as part of my professional career, it felt natural to revert to the original family surname for the trilogy of musical books that tell the story of The Colour Spectrum.

Printed in Great Britain
by Amazon

00fb537c-0c13-4c56-80e3-ea35dff42eb3R02